Three powerful men…
Three beautiful women…
Three passionate affairs…

One Man's Mistress

Three intense and sexy romances from three
amazing Mills & Boon authors!

D1324605

One Man's Mistress

SARA CRAVEN

MAGGIE COX

LEE WILKINSON

All the characters in this book have no existence outside the imagination of the author, and have no relation whatsoever to anyone bearing the same name or names. They are not even distantly inspired by any individual known or unknown to the author, and all the incidents are pure invention.

First published in Great Britain 2011
by Mills & Boon, an imprint of Harlequin (UK) Limited,
Eton House, 18-24 Paradise Road, Richmond, Surrey TW9 1SR

ONE MAN'S MISTRESS © by Harlequin Enterprises II B.V./S.à.r.l 2011

One Night with His Virgin Mistress, Public Mistress, Private Affair and *Mistress Against Her Will* were first published in Great Britain by Harlequin (UK) Limited in separate, single volumes.

One Night with His Virgin Mistress © Sara Craven 2008
Public Mistress, Private Affair © Maggie Cox 2007
Mistress Against Her Will © Lee Wilkinson 2008

ISBN: 978 0 263 88440 1

05-0711

Printed and bound in Spain
by Blackprint CPI, Barcelona

ONE NIGHT WITH HIS VIRGIN MISTRESS

BY
SARA CRAVEN

Sara Craven was born in South Devon, and grew up surrounded by books in a house by the sea. After leaving grammar school she worked as a local journalist, covering everything from flower shows to murders. She started writing for Harlequin in 1975. Sara Craven has appeared as a contestant on the Channel Four game show *Fifteen to One*, and in 1997 won the title of Television Mastermind of Great Britain.

Sara shares her Somerset home with several thousand books and an amazing video and DVD collection. When she's not writing, she likes to travel in Europe, particularly in Greece and Italy. She loves music, theatre, cooking and eating in good restaurants, but reading will always be her greatest passion. Since the birth of her twin grandchildren in New York City, she has become a regular visitor to the Big Apple.

PROLOGUE

HE'D had, he decided, more than enough. First, there'd been that burning nightmare of a journey, wondering if each moment would be their last, then the flight in the Hercules, and now this damned farce of a press conference with its endless questions.

When all he really wanted was complete solitude, an opportunity to get out of clothes that stank and felt as if they were crawling, and a torrent of hot water to rid him of the dirt and the fear and make him human again. And God help anyone who got in his way.

But now the idiot female reporter in the front row was batting her eyelashes at him once more. She'd been behaving as if she knew him, he thought wearily. And what was that all about?

'So,' she said, 'can you describe for my readers how you felt?'

'I was running for my life,' he said tersely. 'What do you think?'

'But you were the leader,' she went on. 'You got everyone to safety. What's it like, finding you're a hero?'

'Madam,' he said curtly, 'I'm tired and filthy, and no one's bloody hero. Not now. Not ever. I simply did my job. And, if you've nothing more sensible to ask, I'm out of here.'

They'd laid on a car to take him home, and he was thankful, knowing he wouldn't have been fit to drive himself. He was also grateful that, by some miracle, he still had his wallet and his keys and that soon he'd be able to find sanctuary and the peace he craved.

Yet as soon as he walked into the flat and closed the door behind him, his senses, honed by the dangers of the past few days and nights, told him that something was wrong. That he was not alone.

He stood, listening intently for a moment, recognising that it was the sound of a shower he could hear, then went soft-footed down the hallway towards his bedroom.

If *he's* still here, invading my space, he thought, I may well kill him.

He strode into the bathroom and halted, his furious gaze fixed incredulously on the slender shape clearly visible behind the glass walls of the shower cabinet.

'God in heaven,' he spat under his breath, 'I don't believe this.'

And he stepped forward and wrenched open the doors of the shower to reveal a naked, beautiful and terrified girl.

CHAPTER ONE

A week earlier

'IT SEEMS almost too good to be true,' Tallie Paget said with a sigh.

'In which case, it probably is,' her friend Lorna cautioned dourly. 'You hardly know this guy. For heaven's sake, take care.'

Tallie gave her a reassuring smile. 'But that's exactly what I shall be doing, don't you see? Taking care of Kit Benedict's flat while he's in Australia. Living rent-free, with just the electricity and heating bills to pick up, which I shall naturally be keeping to an absolute minimum.

'That has to be better than starving in a garret while I get the book finished—even if I found a garret I could afford.'

She paused. 'There's a word for this kind of thing.'

'I know there is,' said Lorna. 'Insanity.'

'Serendipity, actually,' Tallie informed her. 'Making happy and accidental discoveries, according to the dictionary. Just think—if I hadn't had an evening job in one of the wine bars which Kit's company supplies, and he hadn't seen me scouring the evening paper for a shed in someone's garden at less than a thousand pounds a month, none of this would have happened.'

'And moving out of your present flat,' Lorna asked dryly. 'Is that another happy accident?'

'No, of course not.' Tallie looked down at her empty coffee cup. 'But I can't stay there, not under the circumstances. You must see that. And Josie made it quite clear she wasn't planning to move out and live…with him.'

'God, she's a charmer, your cousin,' said Lorna. 'It wouldn't surprise me if she asked you to be her bridesmaid.'

'Nor me.' Tallie bit her lip. 'I can hear her now. "But Natalie, Mother will be *mortified* if you refuse. And it isn't as if you and Gareth were ever *really* involved."'

'No,' said Lorna. 'And just as well, under the circumstances.'

Tallie sighed. 'I know. And I also know I'll come to see that myself one day.' Her voice wobbled slightly. 'But not quite yet.'

Lorna gave her a searching look. 'And this Kit Benedict—promise me you're not falling for him on the rebound.'

'Heavens, no,' Tallie said, aghast. 'I've told you. He's off to Australia touring vineyards to learn more about the business. Besides, he's not my type in the slightest.'

Her type, she thought with a pang, was tall, with blond hair falling across his forehead, blue eyes and a lazy smile. Kit Benedict, on the other hand, was medium height, dark, and rather too full of himself.

'He needs a house-sitter,' she went on. 'I need somewhere to live. Done deal.'

'So what's it like, this place of his? The usual bachelor pad, overflowing with empty bottles and take-away cartons?'

'The total opposite,' Tallie assured her more cheerfully. 'It's on the top floor of this Edwardian block, with an utterly fabulous living room—wonderful squashy sofas and chairs, mixed in with genuine antiques, plus views all over London. There's a kitchen to die for, and two massive bedrooms. Kit said I could use whichever I wanted, so I'm having his—the master with its own gorgeous bathroom.'

Her room at Josie's was like a shoe box, she thought. One narrow single bed, with a zip-up plastic storage container underneath it for her limited wardrobe. No cupboard, so the rest of her clothes were hanging from two hooks on the back of the door. One tiny table, fortunately just large enough for her laptop, and a stool.

But then her cousin had never really wanted her there in the first place. Her offer of accommodation had been grudgingly made after family pressure, but neither she nor her flatmate Amanda, who occupied the two decent-sized bedrooms, had ever made Tallie feel welcome.

But the rent was cheap, so she'd have put up and shut up for as long as it took—if it hadn't been for Gareth.

Wincing inwardly, she hurried on. 'In fact, the whole flat is absolutely immaculate because there's a cleaner, Mrs Medland, who comes in twice a week. Kit says she's a dragon with a heart of gold, and I don't even have to pay for her. Apparently, some legal firm sees to all that. And I send the mail on to them too.'

She took a deep breath. 'And, from tomorrow, it will be all mine.'

'Hmm,' said Lorna. 'What I can't figure altogether is how it can possibly be all his—unless he actually owns this wine importing concern he works for.'

Tallie shook her head. 'Far from it. Apparently the flat is part of some family inheritance.' She paused. 'There's even a room that Kit uses as an office, and he says I can work in there and use the printer. I'm spoiled for space.'

Lorna sighed. 'Well, I suppose I have to accept that the whole situation's above board and you've actually fallen on your feet at last. I just wish you could have moved into Hallmount Road with us but, since Nina's boyfriend arrived, we're practically hanging from the light fittings as it is.'

'Honestly,' Tallie told her, 'everything's going to be fine.'

And I only wish I felt as upbeat as I sound, she thought as she walked back to the advertising agency where she'd been temping for the past three weeks, filling in for a secretary who'd been laid low by a vicious bout of chickenpox. She'd soon adapted to the strenuous pace of life at the agency, proving, as she'd done in her other placements, that she was conscientious, efficient and highly computer-literate. At the same time she'd revelled in the stimulation of its creative atmosphere.

In fact, it had been one of the nicest jobs she'd had all year and she was sorry it had come to an end, especially when her immediate boss had hinted that it could become a permanency. That she might even become a copywriter in due course.

And maybe Lorna was right and she was insane to throw away that level of security for a dream. On the other hand, she knew that she'd been given a heaven-sent opportunity to be a writer and if she didn't grasp it she might regret it for the rest of her life.

Everything she'd done that year had been with that aim in mind. All her earnings from the wine bar, and as much as she could spare from her daytime salary, had gone into a savings account to support her while she wrote. She'd be living at subsistence level, but she was prepared for that.

And all because she'd entered a competition in a magazine to find new young writers under the age of twenty-five. Entrants had been required to produce the first ten thousand words of a novel and Tallie, eighteen years old and bored as she'd waited for her A level exam results, had embarked on a story about a spirited girl who'd disguised herself as a man and undertaken a dangerous, adventure-strewn odyssey across Europe to find the young army captain she loved and who was fighting in Wellington's Peninsular Army.

She hadn't won, or even been placed, but one of the judges was a literary agent who'd contacted her afterwards and asked her to lunch in London.

Tallie had accepted the invitation with slight trepidation, but Alice Morgan had turned out to be a brisk middle-aged woman with children of her own who'd been through the school and university system, and who seemed to understand why career choices were not always cut and dried.

'My brother Guy always knew he wanted to be a vet like Dad,' Tallie had confided over the wonders of sea bass followed by strawberry meringue at the most expensive restaurant she'd ever visited. 'And at school they think I should go on to university and read English or History, before training as a teacher. But I'm really not sure, especially when I'll have a student loan to pay off once I qualify. So I'm taking a gap year while I decide.'

'Have you never considered writing as a career?'

Tallie flushed a little. 'Oh, yes, for as long as I can remember, but at some time in the future. I always thought I'd have to get an ordinary job first.'

'And this gap year—how will you spend that?'

Tallie reflected. 'Well, Dad always needs help in the practice. And I've done a fairly intensive computer course, so I could find office work locally.'

Mrs Morgan leaned back in her chair. 'And what happens to Mariana, now in the hands of smugglers? Does she get consigned to a file marked "might have been"? Or are you going to finish her story?'

'I hadn't really thought about it,' Tallie confessed. 'To be honest, I only wrote that first bit for fun.'

'And it shows.' Alice Morgan smiled at her. 'It's not perfect, but it's a good rip-roaring adventure told with real exuberance by a fresh young voice, and from the female angle. If you can sustain the storyline and the excitement at the same level, I think I could find more than one publisher who might be interested.'

'Goodness,' Tallie said blankly. 'In that case, maybe I should give it some serious thought.'

'That's what I like to hear,' the older woman told her cheerfully. 'One aspect you might consider is your hero, the dashing William. Is he based on anyone in particular—a boyfriend, perhaps?'

Tallie flushed. 'Oh, no,' she denied hurriedly. 'Nothing like that. Just—someone I see around the village sometimes. His parents have a cottage they use at weekends, but I…I hardly know him at all.'

Although I know his name—Gareth Hampton.

Mrs Morgan nodded. 'I rather got that impression because, as a hero, I couldn't get a handle on him either. And if Mariana is going to risk so much for love of him, you must make him worth the trouble. And there are one or two other things…'

Tallie caught the train home two hours later in something of a daze, the back of her diary filled with notes about those 'other things', but by the end of the journey any indecision about the immediate future was over and she had A Plan.

Her parents were astounded and a little dubious when she outlined it.

'But why can't you write at home?' her mother queried.

Because I'd never get anything done, thought Tallie with rueful affection. Between helping Dad when one of his assistants is sick, walking the dogs, giving a hand in the house and getting stuck into loads of batch baking for the WI or some do at the village hall, I'd always be on call for something.

She said, 'Mrs Morgan emphasised that I need to get my research right, and living in the city is just so convenient for that. I'm going to spend my Christmas and birthday money on a subscription to the London Library. Then I'll do what Lorna's done and find a flat-share with two or three other girls. Live as cheaply as I can.'

Mrs Paget said nothing, but pursed her lips, and a few days later she announced she'd been talking to Uncle Freddie and he'd agreed that living with strangers was unthinkable, and insisted that Tallie move in with her cousin Josie.

'He says her flat has a spare room, and she'll be able to help you find your feet in London,' she added.

Tallie groaned. 'Push me off the Embankment more likely. Mum, Josie's three years older than me and we haven't a thought in common. Besides, she and Aunt Val have always looked on us as the poor relations, you know that.'

'Well, I suppose we are in material terms,' said her mother. 'But not in any other way. Anyway,' she continued with cheerful optimism, 'I expect working for a living has smoothed off some of Josie's edges.'

Not so you'd notice, Tallie thought now as she rode up in the lift to the agency floor. At least, not where I'm concerned. And waiting on tables in the evening as well as holding down a day job may have been tough, but at least it's kept me out of the flat and away from her.

And, more recently, by dint of working until closing time and beyond at the wine bar, and leaving very early each morning, buying coffee and a croissant en route to work, she'd managed to remain in comparative ignorance about whether or not Gareth was now spending all his nights in Josie's room. Although the nagging pain deep within her told her the probable truth.

Stupid—stupid, she berated herself, to have built so much on a few lunches and a couple of weekend walks. But Gareth had been her 'bright particular star' for almost as long as she could remember, and simply spending time with him had seemed like a promise of paradise.

Until the moment when she'd had to stand there numbly, watching her star go out and paradise disappear, she thought bracing herself against the inevitable pain.

However, it was her last day as a member of the employed, and she wasn't going to break her self-imposed rule of never taking her personal problems into the workplace. So she straightened her shoulders, nailed on a smile and marched through the double glass doors into the open plan office beyond.

In the event, it turned out to be a much shorter afternoon than she'd expected. Before it was half over, her boss called the other staff together, champagne was produced and the managing director made a brief speech about what a valuable team member she'd been and how much she'd be missed.

'And if the next job doesn't work out as planned, we're only a phone call away,' he added, and Tallie heard a wobble in her voice as she thanked him.

When she called at the temps bureau later to collect her money, the manageress there also made it clear she was loath to lose her services.

'You've always been so reliable, Natalie,' she mourned. 'Isn't there a number where I can reach you in case of emergency?'

'I'm afraid not,' Tallie said firmly. Apart from her family and Lorna, no one was having the contact number at Albion House. Kit had made it clear she was not to hand it out to all and sundry, and she was happy to go along with that.

Besides, she was going to need every ounce of concentration she possessed for her book, which completely ruled out being at the beck and call of The Relief Force, as the bureau titled itself. They would just have to manage without her, she thought, although she had to admit it was nice to be needed, if only in a work sense.

Meanwhile, finishing early today meant she would have the flat to herself when she got back, and she could do her packing before she set off for her final stint at the wine bar. So many doors closing, she thought, but another massive one about to open in front of her, and who knew what might lie beyond it.

At the flat, she made herself some coffee from what little was left in the jar. In theory, they all bought their own groceries. In practice, Josie and Amanda were always too busy for a regular supermarket shop, and they used whatever was available.

The prospect of living on her own for the first time was fairly daunting, but at least there would be fewer minor irritations to cope with, Tallie told herself as she unzipped the storage box. She didn't have many clothes—just the plain black skirts she wore for work with an assortment of blouses and a grey checked jacket, the three pairs of jeans that constituted leisurewear, a few T-shirts, a couple of sweaters and a handful of cheap and cheerful chain store undies.

And right at the bottom of the box, neatly folded, was the shirt. Almost, but not quite, forgotten. Slowly, she took it out, letting the ivory silk slide through her hands, watching the shimmer of the mother-of- pearl buttons. Allowing herself the pain of this one last memory.

She'd been working for a firm of City accountants, she recalled, and had been sent to fetch a tray of coffee for a clients' meeting from the machine in the reception area. As she'd been on her way back, going past the lift, the doors had opened and someone had emerged in a hurry, cannoning into her and spilling the coffee everywhere.

'Oh, God.' A man's voice, appalled. 'Are you all right—not scalded?'

'The drinks are never hot enough for that.' But there was a hideous mess on the carpet and her once-crisp white shirt was splashed and stained across the front and down one sleeve, plus damp patches on her skirt too, she realised ruefully.

She knelt swiftly, reaching for the scattered paper cups. Aware, as she did so, that her assailant had also gone down on one knee to help her, but that he'd paused and was staring at her rather than the job in hand.

Looking up in turn, she recognised him instantly, her lips parting in a shocked gasp. 'Gareth,' she said unsteadily. 'I mean— Mr Hampton.'

'Gareth will do.' His sudden smile dazzled her like the sun breaking through clouds. 'And you're Guy Paget's little sister. What on earth are you doing here, miles from Cranscombe? Apart from being drowned in coffee, that is?'

'I live in London now,' she said quickly. 'Mr Groves's assistant is on holiday. I'm the temp. Or the ex-temp unless I get this mess cleared up quickly,' she added, seeing Mr Groves himself approaching, his face a mask of disapproval.

'All my fault, I'm afraid.' Gareth rose to meet him, spreading his hands in charming apology. 'I wasn't looking where I was going and nearly knocked poor little Natalie for six.'

'Oh, please don't concern yourself, my dear boy.' The look he sent Tallie was rather less gracious. 'Bring another tray to the conference room, Miss Paget, then call maintenance. This carpet will need to be properly cleaned. And tidy yourself too, please.'

The last instruction proved the most difficult to follow. Tallie did her best in the cloakroom with a handful of damp tissues but felt she'd only made matters worse. And the most sickening thing of all was the knowledge that Susie Johnson was in the meeting in her place, taking notes and feasting her eyes on Gareth at the same time.

I had no idea he was a client, she thought wistfully, wishing that she'd put on eye make-up that morning and was now wearing something other than a coffee-stained rag. Something that would have made him see her as rather more than Guy's kid sister.

Yet that was hardly likely, she acknowledged with a soundless sigh, remembering some of the girls he'd brought down to the cottage over the years. Slender creatures with endless legs, designer tans and artfully tousled hair.

Tallie's hair was the same light mouse-brown she'd been born with and it hung, straight as rainwater, to her shoulders. And while her mother loyally told her she had 'a pretty figure', she knew she was an unfashionable version of thin. Her creamy skin and hazel eyes, with their fringe of long lashes, were probably her best features, she thought judiciously, but her nose and mouth hadn't come out of any box marked 'Alpha Female'.

In a way, it was astonishing that Gareth should have remembered her at all, particularly as natural shyness combined with inexplicable adolescent yearnings had invariably made her vanish into any convenient doorway at his approach. She wasn't aware that he'd ever favoured her with a first glance, let alone a second.

And she'd now blown any chance she had of appearing cool, composed and efficient. A pillar of young serenity in the staid adult world of accountancy.

'Oh, Miss Paget's wonderful,' she imagined Mr Groves saying. 'I don't know how we ever managed without her.'

And pigs might take flight, she told herself, turning away from the mirror with another sigh.

But if she'd hoped to catch another glimpse of Gareth, she was to be disappointed. Instead, she was immediately waylaid by Mrs Watson, the office manager, who looked her over, compressed her lips and sent her off to the cubby-hole where the photocopier was housed with a pile of paperwork to be replicated.

And, by the time she emerged, Gareth was long gone and Susie Johnson was smiling smugly and reporting that he hadn't been able to take his eyes off her legs during the meeting.

She was about to leave for her coffee and sandwich lunch, buttoning her jacket to conceal the worst of her stained shirt, when Sylvia, the receptionist, called her over. 'This was delivered for you a few minutes ago.'

'This' was a flat package wrapped in violet and gold paper. And, inside, enclosed in tissue, was a silk shirt—soft, fragile and quite the most expensive garment she'd ever had the chance to own.

The accompanying card said:

To make amends for the one I ruined. I'll be waiting to hear if it's the right size from one o'clock onwards in the Caffe Rosso. G.

As she fastened the small buttons, the silk seemed to shiver against her warm body, clinging to her slender curves as if it loved them. A perfect fit, she thought. As if it was some kind of omen.

Against the ivory tone, her skin looked almost translucent and even her hair had acquired an added sheen. While her eyes were enormous—luminous with astonished pleasure.

Lunch, she thought with disbelief. I'm having lunch with Gareth Hampton, which is almost—a date. Isn't it?

Well, the answer to that was—no, as she now knew. As it had been brought home to her with a stinging emphasis that had almost flayed the flesh from her bones.

Like the false bride in the fairy tale, she thought, who'd put on a wedding dress that didn't belong to her and been destroyed as a result.

And kneeling there in her tiny room with that lovely, betraying thing in her hands, she shivered.

She folded it over and over again, her hands almost feverish, until it was reduced to a tiny ball of fabric, then wrapped it tightly in a sheet from a discarded newspaper and buried it deep in the kitchen bin on her way out to the wine bar.

Wishing, as she did so, that her emotions could be so easily dealt with—could be rolled up and discarded without a trace. Only it didn't work like that, and she would have to wait patiently until the healing process was over—however long it might take.

It will be better, she told herself fiercely, when I'm away from here. Everything is going to be better. It—has to be…

And when, the following evening, she found herself in sole occupation of her new domain, her belongings unpacked and her laptop set up in the study, she began to feel her new-found optimism could be justified.

It hadn't all been plain sailing. There'd been a final confrontation with her cousin that she'd have preferred to avoid.

'Quite apart from the inconvenience of having to find someone else for your room, do you realise the stick I'm going to get from Dad when he finds you've moved out?' Josie demanded shrilly. 'And that I don't even know where you've gone?'

Tallie shrugged. 'You're not my babysitter,' she countered. 'Besides, I thought you'd be glad to see the back of me.'

'Oh, for God's sake.' Josie glared at her. 'You're not still obsessing about Gareth, surely? Isn't it time you started to grow up?'

'More than time,' Tallie returned crisply. 'Consider this the first step.'

As a consequence, she'd arrived at Albion House, bag and baggage, much earlier than arranged, only to find Kit Benedict clearly impatient to be off, as if she'd kept him waiting.

'Now, you do remember everything I've told you?' he said, hovering. 'The fuse-box, the alarm system, and how to work the television. And you won't forget to forward any post to Grayston and Windsor? That's pretty vital.'

'Of course,' she said. She smiled at him, trying to look confident. 'I am fairly efficient, you know. I could have supplied references.'

'Well, I didn't really have time for that. Besides, Andy at the wine bar reckoned you were all right, and he's a shrewd judge.' He paused. 'My friends all know I'm going to be away, so you shouldn't have to fend off many phone calls. But if anyone should ring, just say Mr Benedict is away for an indefinite period.' He paused. 'And if they ask, save yourself a lot of hassle and tell them you're the cleaner.'

Why not the truth? Tallie wondered, but decided it was not worth pursuing as the problem was unlikely to arise.

'There's stuff in the fridge to finish up,' he added over his shoulder as he headed into the hall where his designer luggage was stacked. 'Clean bedding in both the rooms, and the laundry calls each Wednesday. Also, move whatever you need to out of the closets and drawers to make room for your things. Any emergencies, talk to the lawyers. They'll sort everything out.'

And he departed in a waft of the rather heavy aftershave he affected, leaving Tallie staring after him in vague unease. What emergencies did he have in mind? she asked herself wryly. Fire, flood, bubonic plague?

Although he was probably just trying to cover all eventualities, assure her there was back-up in place if necessary, she thought as she began to look round in earnest. Starting with the kitchen.

The 'stuff in the fridge' he'd mentioned was already finished and then some, she thought, eyeing it with disfavour. There were a few wizened tomatoes, some eggs well past their sell-by date, a hard piece of cheese busily developing its own penicillin and a salad drawer that made her stomach squirm.

Cleaning out the refrigerator and then restocking it at the nearest supermarket would be her first priority.

And her next, lying down on one of those enormous sofas and relaxing completely. Listening to the peace of this lovely place and letting herself soak up its ambience.

It was, she thought with faint bewilderment, the last kind of environment she'd have expected Kit Benedict to inhabit. Where he was concerned, the contents of the fridge seemed to make far more sense than the elegant furniture and Persian rugs.

It was a background that would have suited Gareth perfectly, she mused, her face suddenly wistful, imagining him lounging on the opposite sofa, glass of wine in hand, his hair gleaming against the dark cushions. Smiling at her…

Stop torturing yourself, she ordered silently. There's no future in that kind of thinking and you know it.

She managed to distance any other might-have-beens by keeping determinedly busy for the rest of the day. Settling herself in so that the real work could start in the morning. And the blues remained at bay during the evening, thanks to the plasma screen television that only appeared when a button was pressed in a section of panelling, but seemed to have every channel known to the mind of man available at a flourish of the remote control.

How entirely different from the TV set at the other flat, which seemed permanently stuck on BBC One, she thought. Although not everything had changed for the better, of course. The news still seemed uniformly depressing, with no sign of peace in the Middle East, another rise in the price of petrol, which would cost her father dear with all the miles he had to travel to visit sick animals, and a breaking story about an attempted military coup in some remote African state.

Sighing, Tallie restored the screen to its hiding place and went to bed.

And what a bed, she thought, stretching luxuriously. Quite the biggest she'd ever occupied, with the most heavenly mattress and pure linen sheets and pillowcases. And great piles of towels in the bathroom too, and a snowy bathrobe hanging on the back of the door.

She was almost asleep when the phone rang. She rolled across the bed, reaching blearily for the receiver. The caller started speaking at once, a woman's voice, low-pitched and husky, saying a man's name, then, in a swift rush of words, 'Darling, you're there—what a relief. I've been so worried. Are you all right?'

Tallie swallowed, remembering Kit's suggested formula. 'I'm sorry,' she said politely. 'Mr Benedict is away for an indefinite period.'

She heard a sharp intake of breath at the other end and the voice changed—became clipped, imperious. 'And who precisely are you, may I ask?'

There was no point in saying she was the cleaner—not at this ridiculous time of night, thought Tallie. Besides, that rather hectoring tone—the phrasing of the question—sounded just like Josie, and it riled her.

'Just a friend,' she said brightly and rang off.

She was half-expecting the caller to ring back, but the phone remained silent.

And just as she was drifting off again, it occurred to her that the name the unknown woman had said at the start of the conversation had not sounded like Kit at all, but something completely different.

I must be wrong, she told herself drowsily. After all, I was half asleep. Anyway, it's too late to worry about that now—much too late.

And, turning over with a sigh, she closed her eyes.

CHAPTER TWO

TALLIE closed down her laptop and leaned back in the padded black leather chair with a sigh that contained more relief than satisfaction.

At last, she thought. At last I seem to be back on track.

She could acknowledge now how scared she'd been, gambling on her future in this way, especially as she'd made comparatively little progress with her story since that momentous lunch with Mrs Morgan.

But then conditions over the past months had hardly been conducive, she reminded herself ruefully. Her free time had been severely limited and when she had tried to work at the flat she'd had to compete with the constant noise of Josie's television and Amanda's stereo system blasting through the thin panels of her door.

And then, of course, there'd been Gareth's intervention…

She took a deep breath, damming back the instinctive pang. Well, at least she now had an insight into what it was like to fall in love, even a little. Could see why a girl like Mariana might give up so much to pursue this reckless adventure if it meant she'd be reunited with a man she wanted so desperately.

Up to then, she realised, she hadn't given much thought to her story's emotional input, concentrating instead on the fun of it all—her heroine's rollicking escape from her stern guardian and the threat of an arranged marriage.

Now, she realised that Mariana's decision would have far more impact if she was, instead, deserting a loving home with parents who were simply over-protective, who knew the uncertainties of a soldier's life and wished to spare her danger and heartache.

And this would naturally change the entire emphasis of the book.

Less of a light-hearted romp, she told herself, however enjoyable that had been to invent, and more of a story about passionate love and its eventual reward, which, in itself, was going to present her with all kinds of problems.

Because the events of the last few weeks had brought home to her how signally—ridiculously—unacquainted she was with any form of passion. Or even likely to be.

She swallowed past the sudden tightness in her throat. Oh, well, she told herself with false brightness, she'd cross that bridge when she came to it. After all, imagination was a wonderful thing.

And it would help that she wouldn't have to write too much about 'doing it' until the very end of the book because, no matter how precarious the situations she found herself enduring, Mariana was obviously saving herself for marriage to her gorgeous William, with his smiling blue eyes and his slanting smile.

And the way he talked to her as if he was really interested in what she had to say…

She stopped hastily. Oh, God—this wasn't the book at all. She was back to Gareth again and the endless, punishing reliving of every precious moment she'd spent with him. All that witless, pitiful self-deception over it being the start of something important—even valuable—which had begun with that lunch at the Caffe Rosso.

She'd been tongue-tied at first, trying to express her halting thanks for the beautiful shirt.

'Well,' he said, 'it seemed the least I could do. Henry Groves is a terrific accountant, but appearances matter to him.' He grinned. 'I bet that carpet in reception has been shampooed already.'

It was quite an ordinary lunch—lasagne and a couple of glasses of the house red—but for Tallie it was caviare and champagne, nectar and ambrosia all rolled into one.

Gareth wanted to know what she was doing in London. 'I had you down as a home bird—sticking close to Cranscombe.'

In other words, as dull as ditchwater.

She looked down at her plate. 'I'm having a kind of gap year—while I decide what I want to do.' She decided not to mention the novel. It seemed pretentious to do so while it was still in such an embryonic stage. 'And how's the world of law?'

'It has its moments.' He paused. 'I'm probably going to specialise in tax. That seems a reasonably lucrative field.'

'You don't want to defend master criminals?'

'That always sounds more glamorous than it really is.' He shrugged. 'And, on the whole, they deserve what they get.' He signalled for the dessert menu. 'Did you know my parents are deserting Cranscombe too? They've sold the cottage and are buying a place in Portugal—warmer climate and masses of golf.'

'Oh.' She looked at him, startled. 'So if you hadn't come to the office today, I might never have seen you again.'

The moment she said it, she could have bitten out her tongue. Oh, God, she thought despairingly, she couldn't have given herself away more blatantly if she'd taken all her clothes off in front of him.

She felt the mortified colour rising in her face and wanted nothing more than to get up and run out of the restaurant. Only to find her hand taken, her fingers caressed very gently by his.

'Even worse,' he said, 'I might not have seen you either. Shall we celebrate our fortunate escape from disaster with some tiramisu?'

Over coffee, he suggested that they should meet again on Saturday evening—go to the cinema, perhaps, or a club, forcing Tallie to explain, her voice husky with disappointment, that she had an extra job, which she couldn't afford to lose.

Yet he didn't seem offended at all. He suggested instead that they meet for lunch on the river and afterwards go walking.

'The best way to see London is on foot,' he told her. 'And I can't wait to show it to you.'

In a way, she was almost relieved, because she'd seen Josie and Amanda dressed—or undressed—to go out to dinner, or clubbing, and knew that her current wardrobe simply couldn't cope. That becoming Gareth's girlfriend could take some living up to and she might even have to raid her precious savings account.

She floated back to the office on a cloud of euphoria, almost unable to believe that she was going to see him again. That he wanted to spend time with her. So lost in bliss, in fact, that it never occurred to her to question why this should be.

And Saturday afternoon passed like a dream. Gareth was extremely knowledgeable about the capital—knew all kinds of interesting places and fascinating stories, and she listened, rapt.

He told her about his job too, and the other barristers in his chambers, and about his own flat-share with a couple of university friends, waxing almost lyrical about how terrific Notting Hill was—great ambience, great restaurants.

It was clear that city living appealed to him far more than the country ever would. That he didn't regret the cottage at Cranscombe one bit, and this saddened her a little.

However, the only really awkward moment came when they were about to part and she realised he was going to kiss her, and she was so nervous—so unpractised—that it turned into little more than an embarrassing bumping of noses and chins.

She spent the whole evening mentally kicking herself at the memory. Telling herself that she should have kept still as he'd bent towards her, closed her eyes, smiling, as she raised her mouth to meet his. That he couldn't possibly know she'd only been kissed three or four times before, and generally because it had seemed rude to refuse.

And that Gareth's had been the first kiss that should have—would have—meant something.

Well, next time—and he'd arranged to see her on the following Saturday too—she would be prepared, and she would make sure that she was much less inept.

She spent the whole week in such a state of anticipation that reality was almost bound to be an anticlimax. Yet it started well—a glorious spring afternoon—and this time it wasn't so much of a guided tour because Gareth suggested that they went strolling in

Hyde Park. It seemed full of couples. They were everywhere Tallie looked—young, happy people, walking hand in hand, sitting close on benches—always looking at each other, always touching—even lying on the grass wrapped in each others' arms, oblivious to all but themselves.

And she found herself moving nearer to Gareth as they walked, longing for him to take her hand or put his arm round her. That she wanted to be part of a couple too—half of him, with all that it would mean. Something she'd never contemplated before—or even desired…

But a sideways glance told her this seemed unlikely. He was gazing into space, not at her, seemingly lost in thought, even frowning a little.

She tried to keep her voice light, to recapture the almost intimacy of the previous week. 'A penny for them.'

'What? Oh, I see.' He hesitated. 'I was thinking about something we could do. That maybe we might…'

Her heart almost stopped. What was he going to say—to suggest? That the Park was too public and they should go back to—his place? Oh, please, she thought. Please, let it be that. Because even if nothing happened, and she knew it was far too soon—that she should be ashamed of herself for even thinking that, it went against every principle she'd ever had—at least it would show that he was beginning to consider her as part of his life. That she mattered to him.

It would prove, if nothing else, that he wanted her to meet his friends, maybe drink some wine, and, later, go out for a meal, even if she wasn't strictly dressed for it. She tried to think of an excuse she could give Andy at the wine bar for not working that evening—the first time she would ever have let him down.

He went on, 'I was going to say that tea at Fortnums would be nice.'

'Yes,' she said. 'Lovely.' And tried not to feel disappointed. Reminded herself that it was still early days and the fact that he didn't want to rush her into anything was a good sign. A sign that he respected her. And a warning that she must let things develop at their own pace.

She was still thinking that as they walked up Piccadilly. As they reached Fortnums and paused at the door because someone was coming out.

'Natalie,' Josie said, 'I didn't know you could afford places like this.' She turned, self-assured and smiling, to look at Gareth. Tallie watched her eyes widen, her gaze become fixed. There was a pause— a count of a few heartbeats—then she said, 'And who's this?'

'Gareth Hampton. A—a friend from Cranscombe.'

'Goodness,' Josie said lightly. 'And to think I used to go out of my way to avoid the place.' She smiled. 'Well, friend from Cranscombe, I'm Natalie's cousin, Josephine Lester, and I bet she hasn't told you about me either.'

'No.' Gareth's voice sounded odd, almost hoarse. 'No, as a matter of fact, she didn't.' He was staring at her too, his face set, almost stunned.

Tallie had the oddest impression that the pair of them were locked into some kind of exclusion zone—surrounded by a barrier like a force field which she would never be able to penetrate. It was such a strong impression that she almost took a step backwards.

She heard herself say in a small wooden voice she barely recognised, 'We were going to have tea.'

Was aware that they'd both turned and looked at her in surprise, as if they'd forgotten her very existence. Then realised that was exactly what they'd done.

Josie was smiling again. She said softly, 'What a lovely idea.'

Somehow, Tallie found she was pushing up her sleeve, glancing at her watch. 'Only I didn't realise how late it's getting, and I'm due at work pretty soon.' It was still only mid-afternoon, but she knew numbly that she could have said she was off bungee-jumping from the dome of St Paul's without it registering with either of them. She shared a swift meaningless smile between them. 'So, I'll leave you to it. Enjoy your tea.'

She went off, walking fast enough to convey an impression of haste—someone who needed to be somewhere else—but not so fast it would look as if she was running away.

Especially when there was nowhere to run to.

If the flat had seemed cramped before, it quickly became a living nightmare. It seemed that, no matter what time of the day or night she ventured out of her room, Gareth was there, and it was a minor consolation to know that Amanda was no more pleased with the situation than herself, or that she and Josie were constantly bickering about it.

'No live-in boyfriends,' she heard Amanda say stormily. 'That was the rule we made, yet here he is.'

'But he doesn't live here,' Josie returned. She gave a little throaty giggle. 'He just—stays over sometimes.'

'Seven nights a week is hardly "sometimes",' Amanda said coldly, going into her room and slamming the door.

Tallie did her best to be unobtrusive, speaking politely if it was required, her face expressionless, determined not to reveal the bewildered heartache that tore into her each time she saw Gareth or heard his voice.

Once, and only once, she came back from work and found him there alone. She halted in palpable dismay, then, muttering, 'Excuse me,' made for her room.

But he followed. 'Look, Natalie, can we lighten up a bit?' he asked almost irritably. 'It's bad enough getting filthy looks from Amanda, without you creeping about as if I'd delivered some kind of death blow. And now Josie says you're moving out altogether.'

He added defensively, 'For God's sake, it's not as if there was ever—anything going on between us. You were Guy's little sister, that was all.'

Not for me—never for me…

She swung round to face him. 'And you were just being kind—giving a child a day or two out. A few treats. Was that it? I—I didn't realise.'

'Well, it could never have been anything more than that.'

'Why not?' She was suddenly past caring. 'Am I so totally repulsive?'

'No, of course not.' He spoke reluctantly, clearly sorry he'd ever begun the confrontation.

'Then what? Because I'd really like to know.'

He sighed. 'Are you sure about that?' He hesitated, clearly embarrassed, then plunged in. 'Look, Natalie—it was perfectly obvious you've never been to the end of the street, let alone round the block. And I couldn't deal with that. In fact, I didn't even want to.'

She didn't pretend to misunderstand. 'I thought men liked that—knowing they were the first.'

'Not me.' He shook his head. 'I still have the scars from my one and only time with a virgin. My God, I had to spend hours pleading, a good time was not had by all, and afterwards she expected me to be eternally grateful.'

She stood, stricken, remembering low-voiced, rather giggly conversations at school between more worldly-wise friends, admitting that 'it' had hurt 'like hell' the first time—that, all in all, it had been messy, uncomfortable and incredibly disappointing. And then, the next time—miraculously—had begun to improve.

But it wouldn't have been like that with us—with me. I know it…

The thought came, aching, into her mind, and was instantly dismissed. Because the truth was she didn't know anything of the sort. And, anyway, the important thing now was to walk away, not crawl.

She lifted her chin. 'Well, whoever she was and, believe me, I don't want to know, my sympathies are entirely with her.' And she sauntered into her room, closing the door behind her.

It was, she thought, the last time she'd ever spoken to him. And maybe much of the pain she still felt about him was not so concerned with his preference for Josie—no one, she told herself, could help falling in love, and what she'd witnessed might have been a genuine *coup de foudre*—but the cruelly dismissive way he'd spoken about her sexual ignorance, as if it was some kind of blight. That it was her own fault that she hadn't been putting it about since she'd reached the age of consent.

However, it was impossible to erase him from her mind altogether, because he was still the image of William, her fictional hero, and too deeply entrenched in her imagination to change. Except that William was kind, loyal and tender, and Mariana would have the happy ending she deserved.

Unlike me, she thought, and sighed swiftly.

But she couldn't feel too dispirited for long—not in this lovely room. She loved the entire flat, especially the kitchen, and the wonderful *en suite* bathroom with its aquamarine tiles, huge power shower and enormous tub. But the office had to be her favourite of all—a big room filled with light and completely fitted out with pale oak furniture.

It was completely uncluttered, with not a stray scrap of paper in sight. Well, not until she'd arrived, anyway, she thought, wrinkling her nose. It was slightly more lived-in now.

Nor could she relate the Kit Benedict she'd encountered to all this orderly professionalism. Frankly, it had never occurred to her that working in the wine trade would require him to set up this kind of dedicated workplace at home.

Unless, like herself, he moonlighted, she thought, which in turn would explain how he could afford the array of suits with designer labels, the expensive shirts and handmade shoes she'd found in the master bedroom's fitted closets as she'd tried to make space for her own few things.

But, whatever Kit did in this room, he kept strictly to himself because everything was securely locked up—the desk drawers, the cupboards, the filing cabinets and the bookcases, which seemed, she noted with surprise, to be devoted to mathematics and scientific topics.

Not that it matters to me, Tallie told herself firmly. Unless it's illegal and the Metropolitan Police suddenly arrive.

But that was an unlikely scenario and, in the meantime, she had the use of the desk and the printer, and she provided her own stationery so she had no need or wish to pry any further.

She got up, stretching, then collected together the completed pages slipping them into the waiting folder before wandering off to the kitchen to put together some pasta carbonara.

She ate, as usual, from a tray on her lap in the sitting room. There was a dining room across the passage, but she never used it as it was clearly designed for smart dinner parties, not solitary suppers, and she found it a little daunting.

There was a drama series she wanted to watch on television and, while she was waiting for it to start, she took her plate and fork into the kitchen and loaded them into the dishwasher along with the utensils she'd used.

When she got back with her coffee, she found the start of her programme had been slightly delayed by an extended newscast. The situation in the African state of Buleza had deteriorated swiftly over the past few days. The initial coup had been defeated but the rebels had regrouped and a full-scale civil war had broken out. All British nationals had been evacuated from the capital, but there'd been concern over a group of engineers constructing a bridge across the Ubilisi in the north of the country who'd been cut off by the fighting.

According to the excited tones of the reporter covering the story, the men had now been traced and air-lifted to safety across the border. From there, they would be flown home, and the Foreign Office had a number for concerned relatives to call.

For once a happy ending, Tallie thought as the signature tune for her programme began and she curled up in her corner of the sofa to enjoy it. And that's what we all need—more happy endings.

The last of the groceries safely put away, Tallie straightened, moving her shoulders wearily. Thank goodness that's over for a while, she thought.

Shopping was never her favourite pastime at the best of times, and this afternoon the supermarket had been busy and the bus hot and crowded, forcing her to stand with her two heavy bags. To make matters worse, the journey had been held up by a collision between a car and a van. No one had been injured, but both vehicles had been damaged, tempers had been frayed and the police called as a result, so she'd got off and walked the last half mile back to the flat.

It was a humid, overcast day, as if a storm was threatening, and she felt grimy and frazzled, her hair sticking to her scalp. She'd have a shower before she prepared the salad for her evening meal, she decided with a sigh of anticipation.

In the bedroom, she chose clean underwear and a fresh pair of cotton trousers with a green scoop-neck top and left them on the bed. She undressed in the bathroom, thrusting her discarded clothing into the laundry basket, then stepped into the shower. She shampooed her hair vigorously and turned the water pressure to full as she rinsed the lather away, before beginning to apply her rose-scented body wash to her skin, smoothing away the remaining weariness and lingering aggravation of the day, then letting the water stream over her, lifting her face, smiling, to its power.

Then suddenly—shockingly—she became aware that she was no longer alone. Glimpsed a dark shadow, tall and menacing, outside the steamy glass of the cabinet. Felt the gush of cooler air as the sliding doors of the shower were wrenched open and someone—a total stranger—was standing there, staring in at her. A lean pillar of a man, wearing a shirt and trousers in stained and scruffy khaki drill.

Tallie had a horrified impression of black tousled hair, an unshaven chin, hands clenched aggressively at his sides and dark brows snapping together in furious astonishment as ice-cold green eyes swept over her.

She shrank back instinctively into the corner, cowering there, her voice cracking as she tried to scream and failed. As her own hands rose in a futile attempt to cover her body—to conceal her nakedness from this…predator, who was turning the worst—the ultimate nightmare into harsh reality. As fear warred with shame under his gaze.

Where had he come from? Had he been hiding somewhere in the flat, biding his time—choosing his moment? Her mind ran crazily like a rat trapped in a maze. Yet the door had been locked when she'd returned from shopping, and she'd re-locked it behind her. It was the most basic security precaution, and never neglected, so how could he have got in?

'Turn that bloody water off.' He spoke above its rush, his voice low-pitched and well-modulated, but grim as an Arctic wind. 'Then, sweetheart, you have precisely one minute to explain who you are and what the hell you're doing in my flat before I call the police.'

Ridiculously, the word 'police' brought a kind of fleeting reassurance. It wasn't the kind of threat a rapist or a psychopath would use—was it? she thought desperately, her fingers all thumbs as she forced herself to deal with the shower flow, shivering with panic and burning with embarrassment at the same time. And he'd said 'my flat', so what was going on—apart from her own imminent death through shame?

'I'm waiting.' He took a towel from the rail and threw it towards her and she snatched at it, huddling it almost gratefully round her body as she struggled to make her voice work.

'I'm looking after the flat while Mr Benedict is away.' It was hardly more than a shaken gasp.

'Is that a fact?' He looked her over again, standing with his hands on his hips, the firm lips twisting. 'Well, now Mr Benedict is back and I made no such arrangement, so I suggest you think up another story fast.'

'No, you don't understand.' She put up a hand to push the sodden tangle of hair back from her face and the towel slipped. She grabbed at it, blushing. 'My agreement's with Kit Benedict—who's in Australia. Are—are you a member of his family?'

'I'm the head of the damned family,' he returned icily. 'Kit, unfortunately, is my half-brother, and you, presumably, are one of his little jokes—or compensation for some misdemeanour I have yet to discover. Payment in kind rather than cash. My welcome home present.'

The green eyes narrowed, their expression becoming less hostile and more contemplative, bordering on amusement, and Tallie felt fresh stirrings of panic under his renewed scrutiny.

'Under normal circumstances, of course, I wouldn't touch Kit's leavings,' he went on, as if he was thinking aloud. 'But there's been nothing normal about the past few eternally bloody days, and maybe finding a naked, pretty girl in my shower is immaculate timing. A hint that a few hours of mindless enjoyment could be just what I most need.' He began to unbutton his shirt. 'So put the water on again, darling, and I'll join you.'

'Keep away from me.' Tallie pressed herself against the tiled wall as if she was trying to disappear through it. Her voice was hoarse and trembling. 'I'm not anyone's leavings, least of all your brother's. We had—we have a business agreement, that's all.'

'Fine.' He dropped his shirt to the floor and started to unzip his trousers. He slanted a smile at her. 'And now your business is with me, only the terms have changed a little.'

'You don't understand,' she insisted more fiercely. 'I'm just here as the caretaker. Nothing more.'

'Then take care of me,' he said equably. 'You can start by washing my back.'

'No,' she said, 'I won't.' She swallowed. 'And I warn you now that if you come near me—if you dare try and lay a hand on me, I'll have you charged with rape. I swear it.'

There was a taut silence, then he said softly, 'You actually sound as if you mean that.'

'I do.' She lifted her chin. 'And you'd better also believe that I'm not involved with Kit and I never was, and never would be either. I think, in his own way, he's almost as obnoxious as you are.'

'Thank you.' There was an odd note in his voice.

'I came here simply to do a job and, until a few minutes ago, I didn't know you even existed. I thought this was his flat.'

'I'm sure it pleased him to give that impression.' He shrugged a bare shoulder, setting off a ripple of muscle that she would have preferred not to see. 'It always has. But let me assure you that the flat is mine and so is everything in it, including that inadequate towel you're clutching, and the bed where you've apparently been sleeping,' he added silkily, watching the colour storm back into her face at the implication of his words.

'In reality, I'm Kit's occasional and very reluctant host. And currently, for some reason which I'm sure you're eager to share with me, I seem to be yours too.'

She made a desperate stab at dignity. 'Naturally, I do see that you're…owed an explanation.'

'Perhaps we should postpone any discussion on the extent of your indebtedness for a more convenient moment.'

His soft-voiced intervention had her biting her lip, but she pressed on doggedly, 'However, my reasons for being here are perfectly genuine. I—I have nothing to hide.'

'No?' he queried, the green eyes measuring her with dancing cynicism. 'You could have fooled me.'

He strode over to the door and took down the bathrobe that hung there. 'And now I intend to take my shower whether you remain there or not,' he said as he returned. 'So I suggest you put this on and make yourself scarce—if your maidenly reluctance to pleasure me is actually genuine.'

He paused, holding the robe. 'Is it—or could you still be persuaded to offer a weary traveller the comfort of that charming body?'

'No,' she said, teeth gritted, 'I could not.'

He shrugged again, tossing the bundle of towelling into her arms. 'Then go. However, I should warn you that I'm still considering having you charged with trespass.' He observed her lips parting in a silent gasp of alarm and went on, 'But some good coffee—black, hot and strong—might help your cause.'

'Is that an order?' She tried a defiant note.

'Merely a suggestion,' he said. 'Which you'd do well to heed.'

He watched with open amusement as Tallie turned her back to manoeuvre herself awkwardly out of the wet towel and into the robe.

'Your modesty is delightful, if a little belated,' he commented dryly as she sidled out of the shower cabinet, looking anywhere but at him, the robe thankfully drowning her from throat to ankle. 'I'll join you and the coffee presently.'

He paused. 'And don't even think of doing a runner, because I would not find that amusing.'

'You mean before you've counted the spoons?' She glared at him.

'Before any number of things.' He stripped off the khaki trousers and kicked them away. 'I suggest the sitting room as suitably neutral territory. Unless you have a more interesting idea?' he added, his hands going to the waistband of his shorts. 'No? Somehow I thought not.'

And, as he casually dropped his final covering and walked into the shower, Tallie turned and fled, hearing, to her chagrin, his shout of laughter following her.

CHAPTER THREE

DON'T even think of doing a runner...

If only I could, Tallie thought bitterly as she switched on the percolator and set a cup, a saucer, cream jug and sugar bowl on a tray. I'd be out of here so fast, my feet wouldn't touch the ground.

But, unfortunately, it wasn't as simple as that. For one thing, she had nowhere else to go. For another, nearly everything she owned was in the master bedroom—and so, now, was the master. In her haste to get away from him, she'd even left her change of clothing strewn across the bed. His bed, she reminded herself, groaning inwardly.

She'd steeled herself to creep back at one point to retrieve it, but the bathroom door had been wide open, the sound of the shower only too audible, and she dared not risk being seen—or seeing him again either, she thought shuddering, so it had seemed more sensible to turn away.

Which meant that when she did have to face him in a short while, she'd still be swamped in yards of towelling that also didn't belong to her. But at least she'd be covered this time, she thought, a wave of heat sweeping over her as she remembered that remorseless green-eyed gaze assessing every detail of her quivering body.

Not to mention the way he'd casually stripped in front of her, which had almost been more of an insult...

Tallie swallowed. People reckoned that there came a time when you could look back at moments of truly hideous embarrassment and laugh about them, but she couldn't imagine any moment, however far into the future, when she would be able to find the events of the last half hour even remotely amusing. When remembering them would not make her want to curl up and die of shame.

She was already cringing at the prospect of her next confrontation with him. It had already occurred to her that her agreement with Kit Benedict had been purely verbal, and that she hadn't a scrap of paper to back up her claim that she was flat-sitting on his behalf.

That the real owner, however vile, probably had every right to regard her presence as trespass. But not to assume she was involved in some sordid relationship with his brother, she told herself hotly. A discarded plaything that could be…handed on for his own use. Or who might even be willing for that to happen.

If she was being honest, she had to admit she'd had a lucky escape. That if he'd decided her protests were simply coy and not to be taken seriously, then her nightmare could have taken on a whole new dimension that she didn't want to contemplate. His hands—touching her. That mocking mouth…

Shivering, she hurriedly refocused her train of thought.

Too good to be true…

Her own words came back to haunt her. Well, she knew the truth of that now. Realised how stupid she'd been to ignore the obvious pitfalls in such a casual arrangement. To dismiss the clear anomalies between the Kit Benedict she'd met and this serene, luxurious background he'd apparently appropriated as his own.

He'd never really belonged here, she thought. And she'd always suspected as much. But then, for God's sake, neither did Real Owner—the sexist thug with his scruffy hair, filthy clothes and three-day growth. He was even more out of place—like the brutal invader of a peaceful foreign territory. Inexperienced as she was, she'd sensed the danger in him, the anger like a coiled spring threatening to erupt.

Shivering, she wandered restively out into the passage, noting that the door to the master bedroom was now firmly shut. There was no sound from beyond it, or anywhere else, but the stillness and quiet she'd cherished suddenly seemed to have turned into an oppressive silence beating down on her. As if she was waiting for some other dreadful thing to happen.

Don't think like that, she advised herself, swallowing, as she retreated to the kitchen. Put those ghastly minutes in the bathroom behind you and try to behave normally. Moving in here was obviously a mistake, but you're not a criminal and he must see that.

She set the coffee pot on the tray and carried it through to the sitting room, placing it on a charming walnut table in front of one of the sofas.

Television, she thought. Men liked television. The first thing her father and Guy seemed to do when they walked into the house was switch on the set in the living room, whether or not there was anything they wanted to watch. Real Owner might well think along similar lines.

She clicked on to one of the major channels and stood for a moment, adjusting the sound. The picture on the screen was coming from an airfield, showing a plane coming in to land, and a group of weary, dishevelled men disembarking from it. About to turn away, Tallie sent them a casual glance, then paused, her eyes widening as she realised that the tall figure leading the ramshackle party down the plane steps looked horribly familiar.

No, she thought, transfixed in spite of herself. No, surely not.

'Glad to be safely home are the British engineers, who found themselves stranded by the civil war in Buleza,' said an authoritative voice-over. 'At the press conference following their arrival, Mark Benedict, the chief consultant on the Ubilisi bridge project, said it had been a major target for the opposition forces and, as a result, completely destroyed.'

Mark Benedict, she thought with a swift intake of breath. *Mark Benedict...* Then it really was him. It had to be.

She heard a step behind her and turned. 'My God,' she said huskily. 'You were out there—in that African country where there's been all the terrible fighting.'

'Yes,' he said. 'And, believe me, I don't need any reminders.' He took the remote control from her hand and the screen went blank.

He was hardly recognisable, Tallie thought blankly, apart, of course, from those amazing eyes. He certainly hadn't the kind of looks she admired but, now that he was clean-shaven, she had to admit that he had a striking face, with high cheekbones, a strong beak of a nose and a chin that was firm to the point of arrogance.

Altogether, there was a toughness about him that Kit signally lacked, she decided without admiration, something emphasised by the line of an old scar along one cheekbone and the evidence of a more recent injury at the corner of his mouth, accentuating the cynical twist which was probably habitual with him.

The over-long dark hair had been combed into some kind of damp, curling order and the lean, tawny body was, thankfully, re-spectably clad in chinos and a black polo shirt.

He looked at the coffee tray. 'Firstly,' he said, 'you can take away the cream and sugar, because I never use them, and, at the same time, bring me a mug in place of the after-dinner china. And, while you're there, bring another for yourself.'

'Is that really necessary?' Tallie lifted her chin. 'After all, it's hardly a social occasion.'

'A fair amount of business can also be settled over coffee.' His tone was quiet but brooked no arguments. 'So why not just do as I ask, Miss—er…'

'Paget,' she supplied curtly. 'Natalie Paget.'

'And I'm Mark Benedict, as I expect you already know.' He paused. 'Please don't look so stricken, Miss Paget. I assure you that you're just as unpleasant a shock to me as I am to you. So let's sit down with our coffee in a civilised manner and discuss the situation.'

'Civilised,' Tallie brooded as she trailed back to the kitchen with the unwanted items, was not a word she would ever apply to her unwanted host. But 'discuss' was hopeful, because it didn't suggest that he was planning to bring charges immediately.

However, knowing that all she was wearing was his bathrobe still placed her at a serious disadvantage, no matter how businesslike the discussion. As he was probably well aware, she told herself bitterly.

On her return to the sitting room, she accepted the mug that he filled and handed to her and sat down on the sofa opposite, hiding her bare feet under the folds of the robe—a nervous movement that she knew was not lost on him.

'So,' he began, without further preliminaries, 'you say Kit's in Australia. When did that happen and why?'

She looked down at her coffee. 'He went at the end of last week,' she returned woodenly. 'I understand it's a business trip—visiting various vineyards on behalf of the company he works for.'

The hard mouth relaxed into genuine amusement. 'Well, well,' he said softly, 'I bet Veronica didn't consider that was an option when she wangled the job for her baby boy.' He paused. 'He didn't ask you to go with him?'

'Of course not.' Tallie stiffened indignantly. 'I hardly know him.'

'That's not always a consideration,' he murmured. 'And, where Kit's concerned, it could be a positive advantage.' He leaned back against the cushions, apparently relaxed, but Tallie wasn't fooled. She could feel the tension quivering in the air, like over-stretched wire. 'Anyway, if it was such a brief acquaintance, how did you get to find out about this place?'

'It was his own suggestion,' she said defensively. 'He knew I was looking for somewhere cheap to live for a few months.'

His brows lifted. 'You regard this as some kind of doss-house?' he asked coldly.

'No—on the contrary—truly.' Tallie flushed hotly. 'I suppose when I came here and saw what it was like, I should have realised there was something…not right about the arrangement. But I was desperate, and grateful enough not to ask too many questions. And, anyway, I thought I could repay him by being the world's greatest flat-sitter. Looking after it as if it was my own.' She swallowed. 'Even better than my own.'

'Or, knowing he was going away, you could have decided to squat here.' His eyes were hard.

'No, I swear I didn't.' She met his gaze bravely. 'If you don't believe me, ask my former boss at the wine bar. He was there when your brother made the offer.' She took a gulp of the hot coffee to hearten her. 'Besides, a squatter wouldn't know about forwarding the mail to the lawyers, or have a key, or been told the security code—any of it.'

'You've been working in a wine bar?' He frowned slightly.

'Why not?' she challenged. 'It's a perfectly respectable occupation.'

'Respectable—sure.' He studied her curiously. 'But as a career? I'd have thought you'd want better than that.'

'Well,' she said tautly, 'as we're total strangers, that's hardly for you to judge.' She paused, then added reluctantly, 'Besides, I also had a day job working as a secretary for a temps agency. The bar was…extra.'

'I notice you keep using the past tense,' Mark Benedict commented. 'Am I to take it that you're no longer gainfully employed?'

'I'm no longer wage-earning,' she admitted. 'But I am working.'

'At what? Your questionable duties as flat-sitter won't take up too many hours in the day.'

She bit her lip, unwilling to expose her precious plan to his undoubted ridicule. She said primly, 'I'm engaged on…on a private project.'

'As you've gate-crashed my home, Miss Paget, I don't think the usual privacy rules apply. How are you planning to earn a living?'

She glared at him. 'If you must know, I'm writing a novel.'

'Dear God,' he said blankly and paused. 'Presumably it's for children.'

'Why should you *presume* any such thing?' Tallie asked defiantly.

'Because you're hardly more than a child yourself.'

'I'm nineteen,' she informed him coldly.

'I rest my case,' he returned cynically. 'So what kind of a book is it?'

She lifted her chin. 'It's a love story.'

There was a silence and Tallie saw a gleam of hateful amusement dawn in the green eyes. 'I'm impressed, Miss Paget. It's a subject you've researched in depth, of course?'

'As much as I need,' she said shortly, furious to discover that she was blushing again.

'In other words—not very far at all.' He was grinning openly now. 'Unless I miss my guess—which I'm sure I don't, judging by your terrified nymph act when I walked in on you just now.'

Tallie's blush deepened hectically.

Oh, God, I might as well have 'Virgin—untouched by human hand' tattooed across my forehead, she thought, loathing him.

He was speaking again. 'And you've actually staked your economic future on this unlikely enterprise?'

She was almost tempted to tell him about Alice Morgan. Make him see that it wasn't all pie in the sky but a calculated and considered risk, except that it was none of his damned business. And, anyway, why should she explain a thing to someone who'd already mortified her beyond belief and was now going to ruin everything else for her?

'Yes,' she said, icily. 'Yes, I have.'

'Well,' he said, 'that pretty well explains why you snatched at the chance of living here when Kit dangled it in front of you.' He paused. 'Are you paying him rent?'

She shook her head. 'Just—my share of the utility bills.'

'Which can be pretty steep for a place this size. So how can you possibly afford them?'

'By working day and night for months and saving every possible penny,' she said huskily. 'In order to give myself some dedicated time—a window of opportunity.'

'You seem to have mastered the jargon anyway,' he commented dryly as he refilled his mug. 'Where were you living before this?'

'I was sharing a flat,' she said, 'with my...my cousin and a friend of hers.'

'Excellent,' he said. 'Then you have a place to go back to.'

Tallie stared into her mug. She said with difficulty, 'No—no— I don't. I—really can't do that.'

She was expecting him to demand another explanation, but instead he said with a kind of damning finality, 'Then you'll have to find somewhere else, and quickly. Because you certainly can't remain here.'

She'd known it would almost certainly come to that, but hearing it said aloud was still a blow. Not that she intended to meekly acquiesce, of course. This had been the perfect haven until *he'd* turned up, and she wasn't giving up without a fight.

She said, 'But there is nowhere else. Besides, I was invited by your brother. I was relying on him. Does that make no difference to you?'

'None at all,' he said brusquely. 'And if you'd known him better—or used a little common sense—you'd have saved yourself a lot of trouble. Because Kit had no right to make such an arrangement with you, or anyone else. And, in future, he certainly won't be staying here either,' he added grimly. 'So Veronica can go hang herself.'

He'd mentioned the name before. 'Is that Kit's mother?'

'Unfortunately, yes.' His tone was clipped.

'Then perhaps I could speak to her about all this. Ask her to contact Kit and get it sorted out. After all, she must know that the flat doesn't belong to him, and she might help.'

His mouth curled. 'I don't recommend it. For one thing, Kit is the apple of her eye, and therefore can do no wrong. She would simply blame you for misunderstanding one of the dear boy's misguided acts of kindness.' His voice was cynical. 'Besides, she's always regarded anything with the name Benedict attached to it as communal property and encouraged Kit to do the same.'

He paused. 'And she would almost certainly regard you as some female predator in pursuit of him, and decide that he'd gone to Australia simply to get away from you.'

Tallie stiffened. 'That's ridiculous.'

He shrugged. 'Undoubtedly, but that won't stop her, and I can promise you that a penniless would-be writer isn't at all what she has in mind for her only chick. So I'd steer well clear, if I were you.'

'If you were me,' she said, 'you wouldn't be in this mess.'

His smile was reluctant. 'No, I wouldn't.'

'So what happens now?' She tried for nonchalance, and missed. 'Do I get thrown—bag and baggage—into the street?'

He was silent for a moment, his mouth compressed into grimness. 'How long have you been living in London?'

'A year,' she returned defensively, guessing what was coming.

'Long enough to make friends who might put you up on a temporary basis?'

She didn't look at him as she shook her head. She must seem absolutely pathetic, she thought. A genuine Natalie No-mates. Yet several of the girls she'd worked with had invited her for a drink after work, which might have been a first step to friendship. But she'd always been obliged to refuse because she'd been working and she needed to keep every penny of her earnings for the future.

And, of course, there was Lorna, friend from her school days, who'd help if she could in spite of the inconvenience, especially if she discovered Tallie was in dire straits. Only it simply wasn't fair to impose that kind of pressure on her, she told herself. No, she had to find her own solution.

'And before London?' He sighed abruptly. 'No, don't tell me. You lived at home with your parents, probably in some nice village full of nice people.'

'And if I did?' she demanded, stung by the weary note in his voice. He looked tired too, she realised for the first time, with the scar deepening the strained lines beside his mouth and the shadows beneath those amazing eyes, reminding her of the ordeal he'd just returned from.

My God, she thought. In a moment I'll be feeling sorry for him—if I'm not careful.

She rallied herself. 'What's wrong with village life?'

'Nothing, in theory,' he said. 'In practice, it's not the ideal way to equip yourself for life in the big city. Too big a jump to reality. Which is why I can't simply get rid of you, right here and now, as I'd like to do, because it would be like throwing a puppy out on to the motorway.'

Tallie gasped indignantly. 'How bloody patronising is that? Kindly don't treat me like a child.'

'Well, you certainly didn't appreciate my willingness to treat

you like a woman,' he said softly. 'If you remember…' His voice
died into tantalising silence and the green eyes swept insolently
over her, as if the protection of the thick folds of towelling
suddenly no longer existed. Making it hideously, indelibly clear
that he hadn't forgotten a thing about their initial encounter, and
might even be relishing the memory.

'So while you're still under my roof,' he resumed more
briskly, 'patronage might be an altogether safer attitude for me
to adopt. Agreed?'

Her shocked gaze fell away from his. Her brave words were forgotten.

She said in a stifled voice, 'I suppose…'

He nodded. 'And I know…'

There was another silence—tingling—charged.

Tallie's heart was thundering. She said quietly, 'Believe me, if
I had anywhere—*anywhere*—to go at this moment, I'd already be
on my way…'

'In that case, why not spend some of your savings on a train fare
back to the village? Or don't you get on with any of your family?'

'Yes, of course I do. My parents are lovely.' She swallowed.
'But, even so, they wouldn't understand what I'm trying to do.
Why I so badly need to see if I can finish this book and get it pub-
lished. Actually make a career for myself as a writer.'

Mark Benedict frowned. 'Surely, if you explained to them…'

'It wouldn't work.' She spread her hands. 'They'd think I was
being silly—living in a dream world—and want me to slot right
back into the old life, treat the writing as a hobby—something I
do when I've finished the day job. And that I can also put down at
the drop of a hat when I'm needed for something else. Which I
would be—constantly.'

She paused. 'But it just isn't like that,' she added passionately.
'That's why I know I have to stick to my original plan and stay in
London. Although I promise I won't trouble you any longer than
I have to.' She lifted her chin. 'There must be somewhere af-
fordable I can live, and I'll find it, no matter how long it takes.'

'I wish you luck,' he said. 'I must also warn you that it had better not take longer than a week, my little intruder. Don't overestimate my capacity for philanthropy.'

She glared at him. 'Not,' she said, 'a mistake I'm likely to make.'

'Good,' he said, unmoved 'And, on that understanding, I want you and your belongings—all traces of you, in fact—out of my bedroom and bathroom within the hour. We'll discuss the other house rules later.'

Tallie bit her lip. 'I've been using your office to write in,' she said. 'Because there's a printer there.'

'Have you now?' His tone was cold. 'Egged on by Kit, no doubt?'

'Well, yes.' She looked down at her hands, clasped together in her lap. 'I have to admit a real work room was one of the flat's major attractions.' She sighed. 'I suppose he thought it was safe. That by the time you got back from Africa, I'd be gone.'

'No,' he said, 'he would have thought nothing of the kind. Even without the civil war, we'd have been on our way home within a few weeks. The project was nearly finished and he knew it. He also knew I wasn't expecting to find him here when I returned, because I'd already made it damned clear that I'd had more than enough of his freeloading and he could sling his hook.'

He shook his head. 'So I'd bet good money that he set the whole thing up quite deliberately. A serious piece of aggravation to await my arrival.'

'But I still don't understand,' she said. 'Why drag me into your private conflict? If that's what it is.'

'Oh, it wouldn't have been personal.' His tone was casual. 'I don't suppose he ever considered your feelings at all. You were just…a means to an end. A spiteful valediction to me before he removed himself out of harm's way.'

Tallie drew a breath. She said in a low voice, 'I've never been used like that before.'

'Well, don't worry about it.' He shrugged. 'Kit's just made you a member of a not very exclusive club.' He looked at his watch. 'And now I'd like to reclaim the more personal areas of my home, so perhaps you'd start moving your things. I'd like it all done before I go out tonight.'

'You're going out?'

'Yes.' He stretched indolently and got to his feet. 'As I mentioned before, I feel in urgent need of some rest and recreation.'

'But aren't you exhausted?' The words were uttered before she could stop them and she paused with a gasp of embarrassment as she encountered the glint of unholy amusement in his eyes.

'Not yet, sweetheart,' Mark Benedict drawled, 'but I certainly hope to be before the night is over. Any more questions?'

'No,' Tallie mumbled, her face on fire.

'Good,' he said. 'So maybe you'll shelve your gratifying concern for my well-being and do as you've been asked—please.'

Tallie rose too, her teeth gritted. There, she berated herself, that's what happens when you're stupid enough to feel sympathy for the bastard. So don't fall into that trap again.

She turned, heading for the door with an assumption of dignity completely spoiled by her unwary stumbling over the hem of the folds of towelling that shrouded her.

'Oh, and I'll have my robe back too.' Her tormentor's voice reached her softly. 'At some mutually convenient moment, of course.'

She found herself wishing with all her heart that she had the nerve to take it off right then and throw it at him, but such a gesture required far more chutzpah than she possessed, she realized, as she trailed, still flushed and furious, to the door.

Discovering, too, that some previously unsuspected female instinct was telling her without fear of contradiction that his mouth would already be curling in that nasty sardonic grin as he watched her departure.

Yet knowing at the same time that all hell would freeze over before she looked back over her shoulder to check.

CHAPTER FOUR

WITH her hair properly dried and severely confined with an elastic band at the nape of her neck, and safely back in her own clothing—jeans and a loose white overshirt—Tallie began to feel marginally better.

She could even be almost glad she hadn't slammed the sitting room door behind her as she'd been sorely tempted to do. But there wasn't any other cause for rejoicing.

She'd carefully collected all her clothes and personal possessions and transferred them to the spare room, before returning to the master bedroom to strip and remake the bed in its entirety, even down to the mattress cover, and choosing a dark blue satin spread as a replacement for the pale gold one she'd been using.

Then she'd gone over the room with a fine toothcomb to ensure that not so much as a tissue or a button had been left behind to remind him of her brief presence. She'd even dusted so there wasn't even a fingerprint of hers remaining on any of the surfaces, and she'd cleaned every inch of the bathroom.

He could do a forensic search and he wouldn't find me, she told herself grimly. I no longer exist in his space.

And at least he'd left her to it. She'd half expected him to stand over her, eagle-eyed, for any dereliction but, as far as she could gather, he was permanently on the phone in the sitting room.

No doubt telling a delighted world of his safe return, she thought, grinding her teeth. Or the female section of it anyway.

But she wouldn't think about that, she added with silent determination, turning her attention to the spare room.

Her new refuge wasn't as large as the one she'd just vacated, and the bed was much smaller—queen-size, she thought, instead of emperor, if there was such a thing—but it was furnished with the same careful, slightly old-fashioned elegance as the rest of the flat, and at least there was a table at the window she could use as a desk, she told herself as she retrieved her laptop and manuscript pages from the office.

And the wardrobes and drawers were empty, showing that Kit had taken his brother's eviction threat seriously enough to remove all his belongings.

Eviction...

The word lingered and stung, reminding her succinctly that her own tenure was strictly temporary and that she had just one week to find alternative accommodation. But could she do it?

Back to the evening paper, she thought with a sigh as she set about making up the bed, plus a serious trawl round very much cheaper areas—if there were such things in London—studying the cards in newsagents' windows. She'd probably end up paying a fortune for some boxroom where she'd be balancing her laptop on her knee.

However, even that would be bearable if it removed her from Mark Benedict's orbit, she told herself. Yet, in fairness, although it galled her to admit it, she could not altogether blame him for wanting her out of his home and his life. After all, he was entitled to his privacy.

And it was not his fault if she was left in an impossible and frightening position, but her own.

Oh, God, she thought, how could I have been so utterly gullible? But Kit was just so...plausible, insisting all along that it was a serious business transaction and that by accepting his offer I'd be doing him a real favour. Which was probably the only genuine remark he made in the whole affair. He just failed to explain the actual nature of the favour, she told herself ruefully. And he certainly never hinted that it could land me in any trouble—especially the kind of danger that a man like Mark Benedict could represent, she added, shivering.

But at least she hadn't been forced to spend the night in some seedy bed and breakfast, terrified to close her eyes in case she was robbed, although that comment about a puppy on a motorway still rankled.

But then almost everything about Mr Benedict grated on her, she thought, seething.

However—and here was the silver lining to this particular cloud—she needed a villain for her book. Someone rough, crude, dissolute, uncaring and generally without a redeeming feature, who'd make her hero's virtues shine even more brightly by contrast. And whose unwarranted interference in Mariana's life would involve her heroine in all kinds of misfortune and ultimately bring her to the edge of disaster.

But only to the edge, she thought, her heartbeat quickening. Because, in the end, it would be his own life that lay in ruins.

And Mark Benedict would provide the perfect template for such a man, his ultimate downfall and probable demise dwelt upon in painful Technicolor detail.

I'll make him so obnoxious that when he bites the dust the readers will be on their feet cheering, she resolved. And I shall gloat over every word.

It wouldn't be complete revenge, sadly, because her target would never know, but—hey—you couldn't have everything. And her own secret satisfaction would be all the compensation she needed.

And now, re-energised, she would see about her supper.

She marched cheerfully to the door, flung it open and stopped dead with a gasp, her face warming vividly as she confronted the villain himself, standing outside, his hand raised to knock.

He glanced past her, his brows lifting. 'I see you've settled in,' he commented acidly. 'Don't make yourself too comfortable, will you.'

Little chance of that with you around... Tallie thought it best to keep her instinctive retort to herself.

'And you look a little flushed, Miss Paget,' he added. 'Guilty conscience, perhaps?'

'On the contrary,' Tallie returned, her tone brisk. 'I thought I'd obeyed all your instructions to the letter.'

'Well, here's another,' he said coldly. 'From now on, you don't answer my phone. I've just had to spend a considerable amount of time trying to convince someone that I haven't moved another woman in here behind her back and that you're not "a friend", as you claimed, but a damned nuisance.'

'Oh,' she said airily, cursing under her breath, 'that. I...I'd forgotten.'

But she remembered now—particularly recalling the haughty voice of her interrogator and how it had needled her. Just like the harshness of his tone was flicking her on the raw now.

Two autocrats together, she thought. They're perfect for each other.

He was frowning. 'What the hell did you think you were doing?'

She sighed. 'Kit actually told me to say I was the cleaner if anyone rang, but it was incredibly late when your...your lady called, and it wasn't feasible that I'd be there doing a little light dusting in the middle of the night. So I said the first thing that occurred to me.'

'That,' he said grimly, 'is a habit you'd do well to break.'

'Consider it done,' she said. She paused. 'And I'm sorry if I injured your...real friend's feelings in any way, although I must say I didn't get the impression she'd be quite that sensitive.'

She took a deep breath. 'And I certainly hope she never finds out about your own little habit—sexually harassing complete strangers—because I'd say that leaves my own little *faux pas* in the shade—and might drive her into a total nervous breakdown.'

'Wow,' he said softly. 'The prim schoolgirl has quite a turn of phrase. But I think the lady in question would probably find it far more disturbing if I found a naked girl in my bathroom and wasn't tempted in any way—even if only for a moment.'

He added with cold emphasis, 'Also, sweetheart, one look at you would be more than enough to convince her that nothing happened between us.'

She stood staring at him, feeling as if she'd been punched in the stomach. First Gareth, she thought numbly, now this—bastard. Not only have I been totally humiliated by him, I now seem to be carrying the sexual equivalent of the mark of Cain.

Confirmation, as if I needed it, that no one could possibly want me.

Her throat tightened suddenly, uncontrollably as she fought to maintain her composure.

To hell with him, she thought shakily. Why should I give a damn what he thinks of me? If I've unfortunately failed to reach his required standard in female sensuality?

Besides, being regarded by him as undesirable has to be a positive advantage in the present situation, because at least I won't be spending the next few days and nights fighting him off.

That, she thought, is what I have to keep telling myself. And what I need, at all costs, to believe.

She swallowed. 'Thank you.' She added, 'That's—reassuring. Now, perhaps you'd go,' only to hear her voice suddenly crack in the middle and to realise that his tall, inimical figure had somehow become a blur.

Oh, no, she wailed silently, don't let this be happening to me. Don't let me cry in front of this uncaring swine of a man.

'Is something wrong?'

His voice seemed to reach her from the far distance. Tallie shook her head blindly and turned away, struggling to control the sobs that were choking her throat.

He said wearily, 'Oh, dear God,' and then his arm was round her, holding her firmly as he urged her across the room towards the bed.

She tried to pull away. 'Leave me alone.' Her shaking voice was thick with tears. 'Don't dare to touch me.'

'Now you're being absurd.' He pushed her down on to the edge of the mattress and sat beside her, handing her an immaculate white linen handkerchief before pulling her closer so that her head rested against his shoulder, and holding her there as deep, gusty sobs shook her slight body.

It was like leaning against a rock and Tallie knew, in some far corner of her mind, that, as soon as she'd stopped crying, she would want to die of shame for allowing it, because he was the last person in the world that she would ever want to see her like this, eyes blubbering, nose running, totally out of control.

Knew too that she should be pushing him away instead of blotting her wet face on his shirt. Telling him at the top of her voice that sleeping in a cardboard box would be preferable to spending even one more minute under his roof.

And he'd hear all that, and much more, if she could just… stop…crying…

She slumped against him, her tears fiercer and more scalding as she wept out her disappointment and hurt, her terrifying uncertainty about her immediate future, and her humiliated rage against the man whose arm encircled her like a ring of iron.

But, gradually, the tearing sobs began to diminish and the burning in her throat to subside, leaving a strange emptiness in place of the grief and anger. A vacuum that, slowly but surely, was being occupied by other, more insidious emotions. Feelings that she could not understand, let alone explain or justify.

She was suddenly, potently aware of the physical reality of the hard male warmth supporting her. Conscious that the comforting rhythm of his heartbeat under her cheek, the strength of his embrace and the clean, beguiling scent of his skin were all permeating her shaking senses in a manner as unfamiliar as it was disturbing. And that his other hand was stroking her hair back from her aching forehead with unexpected gentleness.

Like soothing a puppy abandoned on the motorway…

Tallie sat up abruptly and he released her at once, waiting in silence as she used his handkerchief to wipe her face and blow her nose. Mortified to notice, as she did so, that she'd left a damp patch on his shirt.

Eventually she said in a small brittle voice that still trembled a little, 'Please…excuse me. I don't usually embarrass myself like this—or anyone else, for that matter.'

'You didn't embarrass me,' he said. 'If anything, I feel guilty because it seems to be my comment on your obvious sexual innocence that acted as the trigger in all this.' He added quietly, 'However, what I don't understand is why that should be. Why you should feel insulted or troubled by my assumption that you're still a virgin, even if it could have been expressed more tactfully.

'After all, taking your time before you dash into some ultra-heavy relationship makes a lot of sense, especially these days.'

She kept her gaze fixed on the pale cord carpet. 'But not everyone sees it in quite the same way.' *And what on earth had prompted her into an admission like that?*

'Oh, dear,' he said, not unkindly. 'Has some callow youth been hassling you because you said no?'

'No,' she said. 'Not at all. It turned out that he…he preferred… girls with more experience.'

Oh, God, she thought, I can't be doing this. I can't be sitting on a bed telling Mark Benedict about my failed love life. And if he bursts out laughing, I shall only have myself to blame.

'Then he certainly won't have far to look,' he said caustically, the firm mouth surprisingly unsmiling. 'And you, sweetheart, have probably been saved a world of grief. Congratulations.'

'But I love him.' She hadn't intended to say that either, and her words fell with utter desolation into a silence that seemed to stretch into eternity.

She found herself stealing a glance at him, wondering, and saw that he was very still, gazing in front of him, the dark brows drawn together in a faint frown.

But, when he spoke, his tone was almost casual. 'Well, don't worry about it,' he said, getting to his feet. 'They say first love is like measles—lousy at the time, but conferring immunity afterwards. And one of these days you'll wake up and wonder what you ever saw in this crass Casanova.'

Tallie lifted her chin. 'Please don't call him that,' she said defensively. 'You know nothing at all about him—or me.'

'Agreed.' Mark Benedict nodded. 'And, where he's concerned, I'd find it hard to take an interest. But I'd bet there are a lot of girls out there who'll be waking up tomorrow in strange beds, feeling used up and disappointed, who'd like nothing better than to turn the clock back and find themselves in your shoes with life still waiting to happen.'

'Besides,' he added softly, 'think how much more you'd have to regret if he'd taken everything you had to give and still walked away.'

'I'm sure your logic is impeccable,' Tallie said coldly. 'But it doesn't actually make me feel any better about the situation.'

Nor did it justify this extraordinary conversation either, she thought, or explain how she was going to live with herself after this unforgivable piece of self-revelation.

She was bitterly aware that she'd allowed him to get too close—physically as well as mentally, as if the room had shrunk in some strange way—and knew that she needed to distance herself—and fast.

Swallowing, she rose too, folding her arms across her body in a defensive gesture she immediately regretted. She kept her voice level. 'I—I'm sorry to have involved you in all this. It certainly won't happen again. And I know you're…going out tonight,' she added primly. 'So please don't let me keep you.'

The grin he sent her had 'wicked' stamped right through it and she felt her stomach curl nervously in a response as involuntary as it was unexpected.

'Don't worry, sweetheart,' he said softly, 'you won't.' He paused, his glance flicking past her to the bed and the pile of white towelling draped across the coverlet. 'But, before I go, I'll have my robe back.'

Tallie bit her lip. 'Shouldn't I launder it first?'

'No need for that.' He held out a compelling hand, leaving her no choice but to fetch it. 'It's hardly contaminated after its brief acquaintance with you. Besides,' he added softly, 'it holds memories that I shall fully enjoy savouring each time I wear it myself.'

And he walked off, leaving Tallie staring after him, her heart beating like a kettle drum, furiously aware that she was blushing again.

This coming week is going to seem an eternity, Tallie thought as she picked her way without noticeable enthusiasm through her cheese salad that evening.

And I have no one to blame but myself, she acknowledged sombrely. Why couldn't I simply apologise for annoying his girl-friend and leave it at that? Why have a go, however justified I may have felt it was at the time? Especially when all I've achieved by it is to make a spectacular fool of myself?

Well, I'll know better next time—except that I'm going to make quite sure there is no next time. A policy of strict neutrality plus a swift and unobtrusive departure is what I must aim for now.

She'd already checked to make sure there was a bolt on the inside of the door in the bathroom she'd be using from now on, and she'd take care that it was securely fastened on every visit—and that she'd be wearing her own elderly dressing gown too, she thought, her skin burning again.

And, eventually, she'd be able to put the whole sorry interlude behind her, and send Mr Benedict to the dump bin in her memory. With luck, she might even stop feeling as if her skin had been scrubbed all over with steel wool.

However, she told herself as she washed up her supper things and put them away, the positive side to all this was having the flat to herself again, at least for the evening, if not all night. So she could get back to her writing undisturbed.

If 'undisturbed' was really the word she was looking for.

Because, try as she might, Tallie found concentration difficult. Long after she'd heard the front door slam, signalling his depar-ture, she discovered disagreeably, as she stared at her laptop screen, that her encounters with Mark Benedict were still occupying the forefront of her mind and lingering there to the detriment of the unfortunate Mariana, whose mule had somehow got free in the night and run off, forcing her to spend the day walking miles over rough terrain, until at last she came upon a stream that she could follow downhill.

Luxury—compared with the day I've had, Tallie muttered under her breath.

But eventually she became caught up in her story again, and when the sudden steep gradient of the track Mariana was descending turned the stream into a welcome cascade draining into a pool, Tallie allowed her hot, tired heroine to take off her boots and hide them behind a rock with the rest of her clothing and bathe her aching body in the cool water. A brief interlude amid the traumas of her journey when she could relax and dream about her eventual reunion with her husband-to-be.

Which might help make him more real—more desirable—as Alice Morgan had suggested, she reminded herself.

But as Mariana stood under the little waterfall, lifting her face to its fresh drops as if she was seeking the gentleness of William's lips, a man's harsh drawl invaded her paradise. 'A water nymph, by God. What an unexpected pleasure.' And, transfixed with horror, she realised she was no longer alone. That someone was watching from the other side of the pool, the sound of his horse's approaching hooves muffled by the rush of the water.

Hugo Cantrell, thought Tallie with immense satisfaction. That was what she'd call her villain. Major Hugo Cantrell—deserter, gambler, rapist and traitor. Maybe even murderer, although she'd have to think carefully about that. But dark, green-eyed, arrogant as a panther and twice as dangerous, with a soul as scarred as his face. Destined to be court-martialled and hanged. Slowly.

Her fingers were suddenly flying over the keyboard, the words pouring out of her, because this was Mariana's first traumatic encounter with him and she had to make it memorable—not difficult when she had all her own recent feelings of embarrassment and humiliation to draw on. And then she could slowly work up to the moment, building the tension, when Mariana would somehow manage to escape the threatened dishonour.

But how, with the evil Major Cantrell, now dismounting from his horse in a leisurely manner, his eyes appraising Mariana with an expression of lustful insolence that made her blood run cold?

Not that she'd be very warm anyway, standing stark naked under a waterfall, Tallie decided, doing a swift edit.

'Cool water and a pretty body.' His voice reached her, gloating. 'Just the kind of rest and recreation a man needs in the middle of a hot and dusty day.'

For a moment Mariana stood, paralysed with shock and growing fear, as she watched him tethering his horse to a tree, before stripping off his coat and sitting down on a convenient boulder to remove his boots.

Her glance slid to the rock where her own clothes were concealed.

Not all that far away, it was true, but certainly not near enough for her to reach them before he reached her. And how could she hope to outrun him—on foot and carrying her garments?

Somehow she had to devise a strategy, and quickly, because he'd stepped down into the pool and was wading purposefully towards her.

And then she remembered a piece of advice bestowed on her by her Aunt Amelia, her father's worldly younger sister. 'If you ever find yourself alone with a gentleman who is becoming altogether too pressing in his attentions, my dear, a severe blow with your knee in his tenderest parts will incapacitate him for sufficient time to allow you to rejoin the company in safety. And, naturally, having allowed his ardour to exceed his breeding, he can never complain.'

Not that the approaching brute showed any gentlemanly instincts, she thought with loathing as she forced herself to wait, eyelashes coyly lowered, as if suggesting that his presence, although unexpected, might not be entirely unwelcome to her. Because, if she was to achieve her purpose, she would have to allow him to come close, even within…touching distance. She had no choice, although the prospect made her stomach churn with disgust as well as terror.

As he got nearer, she saw that he was smiling triumphantly, totally sure of himself and his conquest. At the same time, she became all too aware of the power of his build, the width of his shoulders under the fine cambric shirt, and how the lean hips and long hard thighs were set off by the tight-fitting cream breeches, and felt a curious sensation stir deep within her that was entirely beyond her experience. Found herself wondering how all that total maleness would feel pressed against her when its covering was gone, and precisely how that hard mouth would taste on hers.

Realised, too, that a strange melting lethargy was overtaking her and that the drumming of the cascade was being inexplicably eclipsed by the sudden, wild throbbing of her heartbeat and the race of her breathing…

Hold on a minute, Tallie thought, startled, discovering she had to control her own flurried breathing as she dragged her hands from the keyboard. What the hell is all this? She's supposed to be about to do him serious physical damage, not melt into his arms. Have I just gone completely insane?

She read over, slowly, what she'd just written, eyes widening, lips parting in disbelief. Then, taking a deep, steadying breath, she put a shaking finger on the delete button and kept it there until the offending paragraphs were erased.

Mariana might be feisty and unpredictable, but she couldn't be stark raving mad. Because the entire plot of the book was her quest to be reunited with William, her one true love, and her body was intended for him and him alone. Which meant that even the merest contemplation of betrayal should be anathema to her.

Especially with someone like Hugo Cantrell, an utter bastard with no redeeming features whatsoever.

She does not fancy him, Tallie told herself grimly. She couldn't and she never will. Because I shan't allow it, any more than I'd let myself fancy that Benedict—creature.

Instead, she let herself elaborate pleasurably on the exact force of Mariana's knee meeting Hugo's groin, and the way he doubled up and turned away, groaning and retching in agony, exactly as Aunt Amelia had predicted.

Described vividly how Mariana made it to the bank and was already pulling on her clothing by the time he recovered and came after her, shouting she was a 'hell-born bitch', and, by the time he'd finished with her, he would make her sorry that her whore of a mother had ever given her life.

How he was far too angry and intent on his revenge to see the large stone in her hand until it was too late. How she hit him on the side of the head with all the force of her strong young arm, and saw him collapse first to his knees, before slowly measuring his unconscious length among the dirt and scrub at her feet.

Leaving Mariana to ascertain first that she hadn't actually killed him—because having the girl on the run for murder certainly wasn't part of the plot—then hastily complete her dressing and make her getaway on his horse, having discarded his heavy saddlebags because she was only a thief from necessity not inclination—and also because they might slow down her flight.

Her last action being to hurl his boots into the middle of the pool.

And that, Tallie thought with satisfaction, as she pressed 'Save' was altogether more like it.

And I only wish there'd been a handy rock in the shower earlier, she thought vengefully. Because there's not much damage you can do with a cake of soap, unless, of course, you can somehow get him to slip on it.

She dwelled for a moment on an enjoyable fantasy which dealt Mark Benedict a sprained knee, a broken arm and an even bigger lump on his forehead than Hugo's, leading hopefully to yet more scarring and a thumping headache lasting him for hours, if not days.

She sighed. She could get the better of him on the printed page, she thought wistfully, but grinding his face into the dust in real life was a different proposition, and so far he was way ahead of her on points.

And she mustn't forget that she'd come dangerously close to involving Mariana in a full-blooded love scene with his fictional counterpart.

Tallie bit her lip. That brief instant in the bathroom when she'd glimpsed him naked must have had a more profound effect on her than she'd imagined. And, disturbingly, it was still there, indelibly etched into her consciousness.

If only there was a delete button in the brain, she thought wearily, so that all my bad memories—all my mistakes—could be erased at a touch.

And then, with luck, completely forgotten.

CHAPTER FIVE

TALLIE emerged from the underground station and began the long trudge back to the flat, her feet whimpering in protest. She felt hot, sticky and dirtier than the pavement she was walking on, but she knew the sensation that her skin was crawling under her clothes was sheer imagination.

Nevertheless, the image of opening the cupboard under the sink in the bedsit she'd just been to look at, and seeing black shiny creatures scuttling for safety would lodge in her mind for a very long time.

It seemed to her that she'd spent most of the past week reviewing all the possible options. That she'd tramped endless streets, climbed endless stairs, and yet, in spite of her best efforts, she was still destined to be homeless in less than forty-eight hours.

Maybe I'm just too fussy, she thought wearily. After all, I can't exactly afford to pick and choose, not when time is running out on me. But everything remotely liveable is out of my price range, and in the places I might just be able to afford, I'd be afraid to close my eyes at night in case I woke up and heard hundreds of tiny feet marching towards me from the sink cupboard.

The only bright spot in her personal darkness was how little she'd seen of Mark Benedict since that first evening. In fact, he seemed to be spending the minimum time at the flat, which she suspected was a deliberate policy. That he was keeping his distance while he bided his time, waiting for eviction day when she would be out of his home and his life for good.

He was usually gone by the time she emerged from her room in the morning, which was her own deliberate policy, and he invariably returned late at night, if at all, so the rest and recreation season must still be in full swing.

Not that it was any concern of hers, she added hastily. And if Miss Acid Voice was the one to float his boat, then good luck to the pair of them.

Because the fewer awkward encounters she herself was forced to endure, the better.

Maybe, when the time came, she would simply be able to…slip away, leaving the amount she'd calculated she owed him for use of the electricity and the telephone on the kitchen table. A dignified retreat, with the added advantage that there'd be no difficult questions about forwarding addresses to deflect, and she wouldn't have to admit openly that she'd found nowhere else to live and that, as a consequence, she was going home.

In Mark Benedict's fortunate absence, Tallie had fielded two anxious phone calls from her mother that week, enquiring if she was all right and how the caretaking was progressing. She'd forced herself to admit there were a few teething troubles, adding brightly that she was sure they were nothing she couldn't handle.

Preparing the ground, she told herself wryly, for the moment when she turned up on the family doorstep confessing failure. And soon it would be as if she'd never been away, with the waters closing over her time in London as if it had not existed, and probably taking the book down with it too. Drowning it in loving routine and the domestic demands of a busy household.

Then there would be the rest of it. She could see her life stretching ahead of her like a straight, flat road. Finding a job locally, she thought. Running out of excuses not to go out with nice David Ackland, who'd joined his father's accountancy practice in the nearby market town, and who, her mother said, had been asking after her, wondering when she'd be back to visit.

And, hardest of all, trying to avoid all the places in the village that she would always associate with Gareth, even if he was never coming back.

The thought of him was simple misery—like a stone lodged in her chest.

But she had to get over it. Had to draw a line and prepare for her future, even if it wasn't the one she would have chosen.

Yet how many people are actually that lucky? she wondered drearily as she let herself into the flat, pausing to listen to the silence. Ensuring once again that she had the place to herself.

She dumped her bag in her room, kicked off her shoes and went straight to the bathroom for a long and recuperative shower, thoroughly scrubbing her skin and shampooing her hair until all lingering creepy-crawly memories were erased and she felt clean again.

She put on her cotton robe, bundled up her discarded clothing, and left the bathroom, only to walk straight into Mark Benedict in the passage outside, tall and dark in a business suit, his silk tie wrenched loose by an impatient hand.

'Oh, God.' Tallie recoiled with a gasp. 'It's you.'

He looked at her, brows raised. 'And why wouldn't it be? I do live here, in case you hadn't noticed.'

'Yes, of course,' she said shortly, annoyed at her overreaction, and wishing with all her heart that she too was fully dressed, with her hair dry, and definitely not clutching an armful of stuff that included her damned underwear. 'I was just…startled, that's all.'

'Well, not for much longer.' He paused. 'As I'm sure you're aware.'

'How could I forget?' Tallie tried a nonchalant shrug and found herself grabbing at her slipping bundle instead. Insouciance was never going to work for her with Mark Benedict around, she thought crossly. 'But please don't worry. I shan't exceed my deadline.'

'You've found another flat?'

'I have somewhere to go, yes.' She added with deliberate crispness, not wishing to be questioned further in case she let slip some hint that she was going home in defeat, 'If it's any business of yours.'

'You don't think I'm bound to be just a little concerned? Under the circumstances?'

'I think it's unnecessary.' Tallie lifted her chin. 'And please spare me any more references to abandoned puppies.'

'At the moment,' he said, his mouth twisting, 'a half-drowned kitten seems more appropriate.' He reached out and pushed a strand of wet hair away from her cheek with his fingertip. It was the lightest of touches, but Tallie felt it shiver all the way down to her bare feet. Found herself staring at him, suddenly mute with shock at her body's unwonted—and unwanted response.

'If you're still wondering why I'm home at this hour,' he went on casually, apparently unaware that she'd been turned to stone before his eyes, 'I have some friends coming to dinner tonight.'

'Oh.' She took a steadying breath, thankful that she hadn't been guilty of squeaking, jumping back in alarm or any other embarrassing giveaway. 'In that case, I'll eat early. Leave the kitchen free for you.'

'I shan't be slaving over a hot stove myself.' His voice held faint amusement. 'I use a firm of caterers—Dining In—but they'll probably be glad of some room to manoeuvre.'

'Naturally.' She managed a smile of sorts. 'Consider it done.'

'And when I have more time,' he said, his glance thoughtful, 'you can tell me all about your new place…Tallie.'

She was at her bedroom door, but she turned defensively. 'How did you know I was called that?'

'Because someone left a message for you on my answering machine earlier, and that's the name she used instead of Natalie.'

She flushed with vexation. 'Oh, heavens, my mother…'

'I don't think so. The name she gave was Morgan—Alice Morgan. She wants you to call her.' He looked at her curiously. 'You do know who she is?'

'Yes, she's the agent who's going to try and sell my book when it's finished.' Tallie took another deep breath. 'I'm sorry. I—I haven't mentioned to her yet that I'm moving, but I'll warn her…not to call here in future. You won't be bothered again.'

'For God's sake.' The amusement was tempered with exasperation. 'It's hardly a problem, if she needs to contact you. And why shouldn't I know that you're called Tallie? I've no objection to you addressing me as Mark.'

'Because Tallie's a private name,' she said coldly. 'Used only by my family and friends.'

Whereas, on your lips, it sounds as intimate as a touch, and I can't cope with that. Not again.

'From which I infer that I shall not find myself on your Christmas card list this year.' Back at a safe distance, he leaned a shoulder against the wall, folding his arms. 'Not very grateful when you've been granted a stay of execution.'

'But the sentence is still going to be carried out. Besides,' she went on hurriedly, 'I think it's much better if we remain on…formal terms.'

'However, even you must admit that formality's slightly tricky—under the circumstances.' His tone was sardonic and the green eyes held a glint that reminded her without equivocation that he knew exactly what her thin cotton robe was concealing.

She felt her face warm and cursed him under her breath. When she spoke, she kept her voice level. 'Circumstances that I did not choose, Mr Benedict. Now, if you'll excuse me, I'm sure we both have other things to do.'

Head high, she went back into her room, closing the door behind her with firm emphasis, then leaning back against its panels with a slight gasp as she tried to control the harsh thud of her heartbeat.

How did he do that? she wondered helplessly. How was it possible for someone she hardly knew to…wind her up with such ease? And why did he bother, anyway?

I'm still raw over Gareth, she told herself, which has made me more vulnerable than I should be. I ought to be able simply to shrug off Mark Benedict's crude, sexist jibes, instead of letting him see he can get to me.

But I can get back at him, and I will. While he's entertaining his friends this evening, I shall be busy with yet another encounter between Mariana and the revolting Hugo, and she'll be triumphing all over again.

She was smiling to herself as she dressed. In spite of her housing problems, she had to admit that the book seemed to be going really well, as she would be able to tell Mrs Morgan. And one of the reasons was clearly the introduction of Hugo the Bastard. In fact, she was enjoying Mark Benedict's character assassination by proxy so much that she might have to rein it in a little. Not allow him quite such a prominent role in case the gorgeous William appeared a little dull by contrast, which she could already see might be a danger, she thought regretfully.

But the battle of Salamanca was approaching, and he could play a starring role in that—leading a cavalry charge maybe, except that Hugo was probably the better horseman…

She bit her lip. Well, no need to mention that, and some judicious editing might be needed in other scenes. However, she thought more cheerfully, another couple of weeks and she'd have almost enough to show Alice Morgan as work in progress.

Or she would have done, if only the weeks in question remained at her disposal.

Come on, don't be negative, she adjured herself. At least you've got a long, uninterrupted evening ahead of you.

As she popped bread into the toaster and heated up a small can of beans for her supper, she found herself wondering if the snippy Ms Rest and Recreation would be among those present tonight. Not, of course, that it was any concern of hers. And even if the lady stayed over afterwards, the bedrooms were quite far enough apart to avoid any awkwardness.

Although any embarrassment would undoubtedly be all on my side, she admitted, chewing her lip again. What I have to learn is to be more relaxed about these things.

Not that it would matter once she was back under her parents' roof. They were old-fashioned about morality, and she supposed she'd inherited their attitude. Or thought she'd done so before Gareth had entered her life, she added with a faint sigh. If only he'd wanted her in return…

She ate her meal at the breakfast bar, then washed her plate and cutlery and put them away, making sure the kitchen was immaculate before she poured herself a mug of freshly brewed coffee to take to her room.

As she walked out into the passage, Mark was approaching from the sitting room, talking on the cordless phone.

'Look, don't worry about that,' he was saying. 'I'm just thankful that you and Milly are all right. No, it's fine. I can handle it. I'll book a table somewhere.' He listened for a moment, then nodded. 'Make sure you both get properly checked over. Goodnight, Fran. I'll be in touch.'

He saw Tallie and grimaced ruefully. 'My caterers,' he said. 'A car came out of a side street without stopping and ran straight into them. They're not badly injured, they reckon, just bruises and shock, but their van's a write-off and so, of course, is tonight's meal.'

'Oh.' Tallie stared at him. 'So what will you do?'

He shrugged. 'Try and find a restaurant that can feed six of us, although frankly I haven't much hope at this short notice.'

'Can't you cook something yourself?' She glanced at her watch. 'You've surely got enough time.'

'Sadly, I lack the skill,' he said. 'Eggs are my cut-off point—scrambled, boiled or fried. Hardly adequate under the circumstances.' His brief sigh held irritation and frustration in equal amounts. 'I don't suppose you number a chef among your London acquaintances—someone who'd like to earn a few extra bob before the evening shift?'

Out of nowhere, Tallie heard herself say, 'I can cook.'

There was a silence, then he said politely, 'I'm sure you can. What were you going to suggest—spaghetti Bolognese?'

'No,' she said. 'And you're being patronising again, just when I'm trying to help.'

She paused, then added levelly, 'In any case, a really good *ragu* sauce would take far too long to make. My mother's emergency stand-by dish—Mediterranean chicken with saffron rice—is much quicker, and it tastes fantastic. I suggest something really simple like smoked salmon for a starter, and a fruit flan from the deli round the corner as dessert. Chantilly cream would make it a bit more special.'

He said slowly, 'You're quite serious about this, aren't you?'

'You were entitled to throw me out a week ago,' she said, 'but you didn't. This makes us quits.'

Mark Benedict took a deep breath. 'Then I can only say I'd be eternally grateful. Write down all the things you need and I'll get them.'

Tallie raised her eyebrows. 'You mean you can cope with supermarkets?'

The green eyes glinted at her. 'Now who's being patronising?'

He took the list she eventually handed him, reading it through in silence, then glancing at her, brows raised. 'Anchovies? I don't think Sonia likes them.'

'Is that Miss Rest and Recreation?' The words were out before she could stop them. 'Oh, God, I'm sorry,' she added, flushing as she saw his mouth harden. 'It's really none of my business.'

'Hang on to that thought,' he suggested unsmilingly.

'Yes—yes, of course. And the anchovies dissolve in cooking.' Embarrassment was making her gabble and she knew it. 'Your—your friend won't even know they're there, I promise. Or me either, for that matter,' she went on hastily.

'You're planning to dissolve too?'

She bit her lip. 'No,' she returned stonily. 'Just maintain my usual low profile.' She paused. 'After all, you have to admit that I've hardly been obtrusive this week.'

'That,' said Mark Benedict, 'is a matter of opinion. But we won't debate it now because I have to go shopping.'

When he'd gone, Tallie went into the dining room. She found the elegant linen table mats and the napkins that matched them, gave the silver cutlery and the tall wineglasses with their impossibly slender stems a careful polish, and set places for six people.

There were three dinner services in the tall cupboards that flanked the fireplace and she chose the simplest one—plain white china delicately edged in silver. Because she couldn't be sure how long it was since it had been used, she tied a tea towel round her waist in lieu of an apron and gave the plates, cups and dishes a swift but thorough wash.

She was just drying the last piece when Mark Benedict returned.

'You've been busy,' he commented, pausing at the dining room door before joining her in the kitchen.

'You did say six people?'

He nodded. 'My cousin Penny, with her current companion, Justin Brent, two pals of mine, Charlie and Diana Harris, plus Sonia, of course, and myself.' He paused. 'Although, you are naturally welcome to join us,' he added courteously.

'You're very kind,' she returned with equal politeness. 'But I've eaten already.' *And even if I was starving, I'd still say no.*

She began to unpack the heavy carriers, almost disappointed to discover that he hadn't forgotten a thing.

'Is there anything I can do?' He was propped in the doorway, watching her, his presence making the kitchen seem oddly smaller and more cramped.

'No, thanks. It's all down to me now.' She hesitated. 'Although I wasn't sure if you'd want to use those lovely candlesticks on the sideboard, and whether or not there were any candles for them.'

'A romantic thought,' he said. 'But I think we'll stick to the wall lighting.'

'Just as you wish.' Tallie began to chop onions, praying at the same time that his frankly disturbing scrutiny wouldn't cause her to lose a finger. As she reached for the garlic press, she said with faint asperity, 'There's no need to stand over me. I didn't include rat poison on my list, so don't worry.'

'Do I give that impression? Actually, I'm simply admiring your efficiency.'

'And checking at the same time that I really know what I'm doing.' She gave him a steady look. 'However, I'm not accustomed to an audience, so if you're sufficiently reassured, maybe you could go and see to…wine and things.'

The firm lips twitched. 'Wine and things it is, then,' he murmured. 'May I bring you a drink, Miss Paget, to assist in your labours?'

It occurred to her that she felt slightly drunk already and that she had the way he'd been watching her to thank for it.

She said rather primly, 'I think I need all my concentration, thank you. But I do need some white wine for the sauce. Nothing too fancy,' she added hastily.

Mark Benedict gave an easy shrug. 'I was thinking of continuing the Mediterranean theme with some rather nice Orvieto. Will a slightly cheaper version do for cooking?'

She nodded, staring rather fiercely at the chicken joints she was extracting from their packaging.

'And please try to relax, sweetheart,' he added quietly. 'You're doing me a big favour, remember, not passing some crucial examination.'

Easy for him to say, thought Tallie. He hasn't got, *Don't mess up—don't mess up* unrolling through his mind like a banner as I have. And I lied when I said I wasn't used to an audience. At home, there were always people in the kitchen and it never bothered me. So why is it different with him?

But she couldn't answer that, any more than she could explain to herself why she'd volunteered to cook this meal. It had been an absurd thing to do, especially when she owed him less than nothing. She could so easily have left him to sort out his own dilemma—and been perfectly justified in doing so.

Yet, maybe, in some weird way, she'd wanted to prove to Mark Benedict that she wasn't simply a freeloader with grandiose ideas about her own talent and an aversion to working for a living. That she was, in fact, as practical as the next person.

Maybe she also wanted to show him that she was large-minded enough to overlook his past behaviour. Heaping coals of fire on his head, as the saying went, instead of pouring petrol over him and chucking a lighted match.

And now all she had to do was prove her point, she told herself, determinedly turning her attention back to the task in hand.

Within the hour, her Mediterranean chicken was flawlessly assembled and already sending out a mouth-watering aroma of tomatoes, garlic and wine as it simmered slowly in the oven.

The smoked salmon would be served with a simple lemon wedge, a watercress garnish and little rolls of paper-thin brown bread and butter. She'd already whipped up the Chantilly cream to go with the tarte tatin that Mark had bought, arranged a platter of cheese flanked by a bunch of green grapes at one end and some celery sticks at the other, and spooned a rich Colombian blend of coffee into the cafetière.

All that was left was the saffron rice, which she'd cook at the last minute.

She looked down at her plain top and boring trousers, wondering if she should change into a skirt, make herself rather more presentable for the arrival of Mark Benedict's guests.

Don't be silly, she adjured herself crisply. You're the skivvy. You belong in the kitchen and no one's going to give a second glance at what you're wearing. Least of all the host.

Promptly, at eight o'clock, the door buzzer sounded and she heard voices and laughter in the hallway. Then, a minute later, she was joined by a tall, dark girl with an engaging grin. 'Hi, I'm Penny Marshall, Mark's cousin. I gather you're Natalie Paget, otherwise known as our saviour—rescuing us from the queue at the local pizza parlour.'

Tallie smiled back. 'I don't think it would have come to that.'

'But I'd like to have seen Sonia's face if it had.' Penny lowered her voice conspiratorially. 'It might almost have been worth it.' She glanced round. 'Is there anything I can do?'

'Thanks, but I think everything's under control.'

'In that case, why not come along to the sitting room and have a drink with us?'

Tallie moved restively. Picked up a spoon and put it down again. 'That's…kind, but I'd really rather not.'

'We don't bite, you know. Well, one of us might, but she's not here yet, so you're quite safe.'

Tallie smiled with an effort. 'I see. Do I take it that you don't like your cousin's girlfriend?'

'Let's just say that, for me, she comes pretty low down on his current list of playmates.' Penny shook her head. 'Mark, of course, is a total commitment-phobe, which is probably why he spends so much time abroad when he has good people who could take his place perfectly well.

'And he seems to have rounded up every female in London who shares his views—or lets him think she does, anyway. I think a few of them have their own agenda, much good may it do them. So if Sonia believes she's extra-special, she's fooling herself.'

Tallie became guiltily aware that she was paying too much attention to these indiscreet disclosures.

She said firmly, 'Well, I must get on.'

'But you just said everything was fine.' The other girl gave Tallie a coaxing smile. 'So come and meet the others, while the coast is clear.'

'It just—wouldn't be appropriate.'

'Because you happen to be doing the cooking? Oh, come on now…'

'No.' Tallie met the other girl's gaze squarely. 'Because I'm only staying here temporarily, and very much on sufferance, and Mr Benedict wouldn't like it.'

'My dear girl, it was Mark's idea, or I wouldn't have dared, believe me. He said you might be more amenable if the invitation came from someone else.'

Tallie bit her lip. 'And I feel that things are best left as they are.'

'Ah, well,' Penny said with a sigh, and walked to the door. Where she turned back. 'As a matter of interest—and because I'm irredeemably nosy—how do you come to be here? Mark's the last person in the world I can envision taking in a lodger.'

Tallie's smile was wintry. 'I'm the one who was taken in. The offer came from Kit Benedict, who made me think the flat belonged to him.'

'Kit the Curst, eh?' Penny gave a short laugh. 'Now, why didn't

I guess? Egged on by his ghastly mother, no doubt. Sticking like glue to Ravenshurst clearly isn't enough. It must really gall her to know there's another desirable piece of real estate that she can't stake a claim on.'

'Ravenshurst?' Tallie queried.

'The family home in Suffolk. Lovely old house where Mark was born, and was growing up perfectly happily until the frightful Veronica got her hooks into his father and played the "I'm pregnant" card.

'Which was bloody clever of her, because Mark's mother couldn't have any more children. My parents have said it was the most frightful, heartbreaking time, but after the divorce Aunt Clare put herself back together and bought this flat with some money Grandfather had left her. And she got custody of Mark, although he had to spend part of each school holiday under the new regime at Ravenshurst.' She grimaced. 'You can imagine what that must have been like.'

Tallie thought of the love and security she'd always taken for granted, and shivered. 'Yes—I suppose I can—almost.'

'And as soon as his father died, Veronica sold the house without reference to Mark, who was abroad at the time. She moved to London on the proceeds and had a high old time. Then, within six months she'd got married again—to Charles Melrose of Melrose and Sons, the wine people.'

'Oh,' Tallie said slowly, 'I see.' *So that was where Kit's job had come from.* 'Did Mark mind very much about the house?'

'He doesn't mention it. But I don't think his memories of the latter years were good ones.'

She paused. 'And he had another problem too.'

'And what problem is that?' Neither of them had heard Mark's approach but he was there, just the same, standing in the doorway, making Tallie wonder apprehensively how much he'd heard and, at the same time, be thankful she hadn't contributed her own viewpoint to the topic under discussion.

He'd changed, she realised, into close-fitting black trousers and a matching shirt, open at the neck and the long sleeves rolled back over his tanned forearms.

He looked stunning but dangerous, she thought with a sudden intake of breath. Like a panther.

Penny sent him a wide-eyed look. 'Why, the late Sonia Randall, of course. Can't you get her better-trained, darling?' She sent him an impish grin. 'Although I suppose punctuality's hardly her most appealing attribute where you're concerned.'

Mark reached for a tress of her dark curling hair and tugged it gently. 'Behave.' He looked across at Tallie. 'However, I do apologise for this delay. Will the food be ruined?'

'No.' She turned away, putting the jar of oregano back in the cupboard. 'It—it's very good-natured.'

'Unlike dear Sonia,' Penny added. 'So how is it she's joining us tonight at some point? What happened to Maggie? I liked her.'

'Working in Brussels for three months.'

'Well, Caitlin, then?'

'Got engaged to her boss.'

'Decided to cut her losses, eh?' Penny enquired dulcetly, then pulled a repentant face as she encountered Mark's cold glance. 'Okay, I'm sorry—I'm sorry, and I'll write out a hundred times "I must mind my own business."'

'If I could only believe it would work.' He paused. 'Have you persuaded Tallie to join us while we wait?'

Penny shook her head. 'Cinderella refuses point-blank to come to the ball. You seem to have turned her into a recluse—one of the few women in the world who finds you undesirable, cousin dear.'

He said dryly, 'Perhaps that's just as well, under the current circumstances.'

'You mean someone you can't send home in the morning?' Penny's eyes danced. 'Now there's a thought. And you've persuaded her to cook for you, too. What next, I wonder?'

'We're going to leave her in peace,' Mark said with great firmness. 'Before she misunderstands your warped sense of humour and walks out on me altogether.'

He looked at Tallie, who was standing in rigid silence, her face warming helplessly.

He said lightly, 'Tallie, I apologise for my female relative. There's no excuse for her.'

She found a voice from somewhere. Used it with an approximation of normality. 'I feel much the same about my brother.'

She watched them leave, heard him say something that she couldn't catch and Penny's gurgle of laughter in response as they walked away down the passage.

Stayed where she was, leaning back against the work-top, looking ahead of her with eyes that saw nothing.

Undesirable…

She tried the word tentatively under her breath. Was that really how she thought of Mark Benedict? Or how she wanted to think?

And found herself remembering with odd disquiet the way her pulse had quickened when she'd seen him standing in the doorway. And how her mouth had suddenly dried…

But I was startled, she told herself defensively. He gave me a shock by…suddenly appearing like that—as if he was some kind of Demon King.

On the other hand, he does it all the time, so there's nothing to get stirred up about.

All the same, she was sharply aware that the sooner she was away from this flat and out of his life altogether, the better it would be for her—personally if not professionally.

And, in spite of the warmth of the kitchen, she realised she was shivering.

CHAPTER SIX

ANOTHER forty minutes passed before the door buzzer signalled the arrival of the final guest.

'About bloody time,' Tallie muttered as she lowered the oven temperature yet again. Her chicken dish might indeed be good-tempered enough not to resent being kept waiting. She, however, felt no such obligation.

There was a murmur of conversation in the hall and then a woman's remembered voice rising effortlessly above it, pitched just right to reach anyone who might be listening, especially in the kitchen. 'Mark, honey, you're actually letting this waif you've acquired do the cooking? Are you crazy? My God, we'll be lucky if we don't all end up in Casualty having our stomachs pumped.'

If there was some way I could arrange for it to happen to you, and the arrogant Mr Benedict, without the other guests being affected, the ambulance would be already on its way, Tallie thought grimly. 'This waif' indeed.

'But I need drinkies first,' the newcomer added with decisive clarity. 'And I've brought some lovely fizz to celebrate the success of my most recent shopping expedition. Yes, darling, I absolutely insist. A few more minutes won't matter, for heaven's sake. You see, I heard this whisper that Maddie Gould wasn't terribly happy…'

A door closed and the rest of the revelation was lost.

Maddie Gould…Tallie repeated to herself as she took the

smoked salmon from the fridge and arranged it carefully on the plates before adding the garnish. Now, why does that name seem familiar?

She was still trying to remember when a voice from the doorway said, 'Can I carry anything into the dining room?'

Tallie glanced round and stiffened, her eyes widening. Because, for one shocked, ludicrous moment, it seemed to be Gareth standing there smiling at her.

But of course it wasn't. This man might be the same height, with blond hair cut in a similar, slightly dishevelled style and blue eyes, but there, she realised, the resemblance ceased.

He was built on broader lines than Gareth and his features were pleasant rather than classically handsome.

He said ruefully, 'Oh, God, I've startled you, and that certainly wasn't the intention. I was lured here by this heavenly smell of cooking.'

Tallie added the final bunch of watercress to the plate in front of her. She said coolly, 'You're not worried about food-poisoning?'

'Oh,' he said. 'So you heard that?'

'Wasn't that the intention?'

He pulled a face. 'Yes, of course. That's why I'm here, really—to make sure you haven't thrown a wobbly and dumped the whole meal in the bin.' He looked at her solemnly. 'Promise me you haven't—not when I'm starving.'

Tallie found she was smiling. 'No, you're quite safe.'

'I'm Justin Brent, by the way,' he went on. 'And you're—Tallie? Is that right?'

'My full name is Natalie Paget,' she said. 'But Tallie will do fine.'

'My sentiments exactly,' he said, and his own smile warmed he unexpectedly, making her wish she wasn't flushed from cooking, with untidy hair and still wearing a damned tea towel.

No, she thought. Not Gareth, in spite of the physical resemblance, but someone very different, with kindness as well as charm. Someone she could possibly learn to like, given the opportunity.

'Let's take in the starters,' he added, seizing a couple of plates and starting towards the dining room. 'Maybe other desperate refugees will realise and join us before I pass out.'

As Tallie followed him in, he paused, looking round the table. 'Six places? You're not eating with us?'

'No, I'm quite definitely below the salt this evening. My own choice entirely,' she added hastily as his brows rose. 'I'd already eaten when I volunteered to cook.'

'Wow,' he said. 'That's awfully generous of you.'

She said stiltedly, 'Well, Mr Benedict has also been very kind, allowing me to stay here.'

His mouth slid into a grin. 'And I'd say that response lacks real conviction. But Mark's an old mate, and if he's…wary about being used, then it's fairly understandable.'

'So I gather,' she said wryly, then paused as she remembered that her information had come from Mark's cousin. And that this man she was chatting to was Penny's—what? Partner? No, that wasn't it. 'Current companion' was the phrase Mark Benedict had used, whatever that meant.

And just being agreeable to the help did not make him available—something she needed to remember unless, of course, she was planning to take a leaf from Josie's book, which she would not dream of doing. Even if she looked halfway decent.

Your place, she told herself firmly, is back in the kitchen, cooking rice.

She made a business of looking at her watch. 'Heavens, I must get on. Perhaps you'd tell Mr Benedict that dinner is served.'

As she turned to go, her smile was brief and impersonal. And, she intended, final.

All the same, she found herself hoping, now that the dinner party was actually under way, that it would be Justin who'd bring the used plates from the first course back to the kitchen and collect the platter of chicken, in its thick delectable sauce of tomatoes, peppers, olives, with tiny spicy cubes of Spanish sausage, and the bowl of perfectly fluffy golden rice.

But of course—inevitably—it was Mark Benedict.

He looked at her, brows lifting. 'Is something wrong?'

'Not a thing,' she denied too swiftly, angry that she'd allowed even a glimpse of her disappointment to show. She indicated a pair of oven gloves. 'Be careful, the dishes are very hot.'

'Thanks for the warning.' His glance was ironic. 'I thought you'd prefer me to burn myself to the bone.'

She shrugged. 'But then you might drop something, and I've worked too hard to see my food end up on the floor.'

'I should have known,' he murmured. He picked up the platter with care, breathing the aroma with lingering appreciation. 'God, this looks fantastic.'

'I hope it passes muster.' She sounded prim, she thought as she busied herself taking the fresh plates from the warming drawer and putting them on the counter top.

Or maybe she was just being wary. It wasn't a small kitchen by any means, but once again his presence in a room seemed to make it shrink in some inexplicable way, making her feel as if she needed to edge round it, pressing herself flat against the units in order to avoid physical contact with him. Which was absurd.

Yet it was only when he'd finally departed that she felt she could breathe properly again.

She hadn't used all the wine in her casserole, and she poured the remainder into a glass and took a reviving sip of its cool Italian splendour. In reality, her job was done now, she supposed, but the missing caterers wouldn't have left the kitchen in a mess with used pots, pans, knives and chopping boards, so she wasn't planning to do so either.

I owe it to myself, she argued defensively, as she began to load the dishwasher. I want to see the thing through to the end. Everything like clockwork.

Besides, that wonderful glazed apple tart would be even nicer if it was warm, she reasoned, hunting for a pretty glass bowl to contain her whipped cream concoction.

And also, if she was honest, it would be good to rub Mark Benedict's nose in her thoughtfulness and efficiency. Prove once and for all that she was no one's 'waif'—least of all his.

An hour and a half later, with the kitchen totally restored to order, Tallie filled the cafetière with a thankful heart. Mission accomplished, she thought. She could now vanish to her room and set about rescuing Mariana from her current dangerous predicament, trapped upstairs in a Spanish inn, which was little more than a house of ill fame, while Hugo Cantrell played cards in the room below with a bunch of equally villainous-looking locals, thus blocking her only means of escape, and, even worse, as a prelude to sampling the charms of the ladies on the upper floor.

Which now, of course, included Mariana—someone he was unlikely to have forgotten after their encounter at the waterfall.

It was annoying how easily this heroine of hers kept going off at a tangent, she thought restively, when she ought to be focusing far more on finding William, the man she loved, instead of allowing herself to be sidetracked so easily. Especially when, yet again, that track seemed to lead directly to arch-bastard Hugo.

But then I can hardly allow the course of true love to be too smooth, she reminded herself, or there'd be no plot. And Mariana had managed to dodge him unnoticed on the last occasion, which meant there would have to be a confrontation between them now…

'We're a coffee cup short.'

Tallie jumped and turned to face Mark, who was standing in the doorway, realising she'd been too deep in thought to hear his approach. 'I'm sorry. I was sure I put out six.'

'You did, but we need another for you, plus a brandy glass.' He smiled at her and she felt the charm of it like the unwanted stroke of a hand on her skin. 'We're all waiting to drink your health.'

'I already feel fine, thanks,' she returned tautly, annoyed at her reaction. 'And, as I've now finished here, I'd prefer to go straight to my room.'

'I was hoping for a more gracious response.' The green eyes

narrowed. 'Not that it matters. You're coming with me to be properly thanked, even if I have to pick you up and carry you. Understood?'

It was as if Hugo Cantrell himself had suddenly materialised— walked off the printed page, she thought, aware that her heart was thudding like a roll of drums. And threatening to carry her— where? Off on his horse, thrown ignominiously over his saddle? Or across a darkened room to a waiting bed...?

She swallowed, then lifted her chin. 'Do you never take "no" for an answer, Mr Benedict?'

'I'd say that would rather depend on the question, Miss Paget,' he drawled, as he collected the extra cup and saucer. 'Now, shall we go?'

As she moved rigidly past him, he loosened the tea towel round her waist and removed it in one deft gesture.

And to offer any kind of protest would only make her look ridiculous, she thought, seething as she walked to the sitting room.

'There's nothing to be shy about,' he told her quietly as she hesitated in the doorway. 'You're the heroine of the hour.'

But not in all quarters, Tallie thought, as her eyes rested on the woman seated on the sofa facing her, who'd signally failed to join in the general round of applause at her appearance, and was now looking her over with eyes almost the colour of turquoise that missed nothing.

For the rest, she had hair like burnished copper cut in a severe bob, skin like milk, plus long legs and full breasts, emphasised by the black silk slip of a dress that she was wearing.

'I'm Di Harris.' A sweet-faced blonde girl with serene grey eyes came up to Tallie, smiling. 'And that's my husband over in the corner struggling to decide between armagnac and Drambuie. What terrible choices men face all the time.'

She put a hand on Tallie's arm and drew her unresisting into the room. 'Charlie says you have to give me the recipe for that wonderful chicken,' she went on, handing her a cup of coffee. 'And I'm to use bribery if necessary.'

Tallie flushed. 'It's really very simple.' She was about to recite the list of ingredients when she remembered the forbidden anchovies and paused awkwardly. 'I'll write it all out for you and ask Mr Benedict to pass it on.'

'Or you could come round and cook it for us yourself,' the other girl tempted. She looked around her, eyes dancing. 'I'm sure everyone here would like a repeat performance.'

'I hardly think the child's experienced enough for that, Diana.' Sonia Randall's tone was chilly, cutting across the murmur of assent. 'And if she's thinking of cooking professionally, her presentation could certainly use some work. I'm not used to having my food just…thrown on to a dish. Also, she needs to hire help with the serving. It's ridiculous expecting the host to trail backward and forward to the kitchen.'

Tallie's flush deepened. 'That was Mr Benedict's own idea,' she defended. 'And I've no ambition to cook for a living.'

'No?' The supercilious gaze swept over her again. 'Then how do you earn your crust?' She added impatiently, 'I suppose you do have a job?'

'Not…exactly.' Tallie bit her lip. 'You see—I'm writing a novel.'

There was a silence, then Sonia Randall gave a harsh laugh. 'Yes, I do see. You and a thousand others, of course, who don't have this golden opportunity to meet socially with a commissioning editor for a major publishing house.'

She paused. 'But if you've been persuaded to set me up so that this young woman can try and ingratiate herself with me, Mark darling, I assure you I shall not be amused.'

Tallie thought she heard Justin murmur, 'Now there's a surprise,' but she couldn't be sure. She couldn't be certain of very much at all—not when she felt as if she were a biological specimen pinned to a board for examination.

Mark said curtly, 'There's no question of any set-up. Tallie has no idea who you are, Sonia, or where you work. The topic has never been raised.' He added coolly, 'And I don't suppose she'd have mentioned the book at all if you hadn't started interrogating her. She simply doesn't discuss it.'

'Well, I'd like to talk about it.' Justin moved to Tallie's side. He gave her a coaxing smile. 'You must tell us what it's about.'

'Oh, spare us,' Sonia intervened impatiently. 'I'm here to relax, not take part in some…busman's holiday.'

'Yet you're always telling us you're looking for the Next Big Thing.' The ironic reminder came from Penny. 'This could be it.'

'I doubt that very much.' Sonia examined perfectly manicured nails, her expression bored. 'Anyway, there's no chance of it coming to me. Alder House only takes scripts recommended by agents.'

'Tallie has an agent,' Mark said quietly. 'Alice—Morgan, isn't it?'

'Well, yes.' Tallie bent her head in embarrassment, wondering at the same time how on earth he'd remembered that.

Sonia's head lifted abruptly and she studied Tallie again, her eyes sharpening. 'My goodness,' she drawled. 'I'd heard rumours that poor Alice was getting past it, and now it actually seems to be true.'

'But didn't you tell us earlier that she represents Madeline Connor, your latest acquisition?' Mark asked coolly. 'Presumably she was still sharp enough to negotiate that deal.'

Sonia's crimson lips tightened. 'She didn't have much choice in the matter,' she said curtly. 'Maddie really wanted to work with me.'

Whereas I'd rather be boiled in oil, Tallie informed her silently, taking a gulp of hot coffee. But I should have recognised that Gould is Madeline Connor's real name, because she rang up when I was in Mrs Morgan's office.

Sonia's gaze was still fixed on her. 'Have you read any of her books?'

'Yes, of course,' Tallie returned. She'd devoured all the emotional, sexy, modern blockbusters that epitomised Madeline Connor's work. 'I look forward to them.'

'And imagine you're going to be just like her, I suppose.' Sonia sighed. 'Alice really shouldn't encourage you in that when Maddie's her client.'

Tallie looked back at her calmly. 'She doesn't—because I'm writing something completely different.' She drank the rest of her coffee and put the cup down on the table. 'And now I should be getting back to it, so I'll wish you all goodnight.'

She flashed a swift smile at the concerned faces watching her—not including Mark Benedict, who simply looked amused—and walked to the door.

She'd just arrived at her room when Justin's voice reached her. 'Tallie—wait a minute.'

She paused reluctantly, waiting for him to join her.

'I've come to apologise.' His expression was wry. 'I feel responsible for all that, because I asked about your book.'

'It's not your fault. She had it in for me before she got here.' She drew a deep breath. 'What on earth can he see in her?'

Justin gave a faint grin. 'Believe me, that's a question no man would ever need to ask.'

'Oh,' Tallie said, flushing a little, remembering the voluptuous breasts revealed by the skimpy chic of the black dress, and the full crimson mouth. 'Yes, of course.'

'But, forgetting Sonia, and how I wish we could,' Justin went on, 'I'd be seriously interested to hear about your book. So may I call you—take you out to dinner one night next week?'

She didn't look at him. 'I really don't think that would be appropriate. Besides, I'm not even sure…' She broke off, biting her lip. 'Not that it matters,' she added with an effort. 'And now I must ask you to excuse me.'

She was aware of real disappointment when she closed her bedroom door behind her. He seems so nice, she thought wistfully, so how can he be propositioning me when he's seeing Penny?

She sighed. But then, what do I really know? she asked herself almost resignedly. Maybe two-timing is just a way of life for men these days. And, if that's how it is, I'm going to be spending a lot of my time alone.

She nodded, almost fiercely, as she crossed the room to her table and sat down in front of her laptop. Her vigil in the kitchen had been productive, and she knew now how Mariana was going to elude the advances of Hugo Cantrell, fuelled this time by his desire for revenge as well as lust, so doubly dangerous. It was going to be a terrific scene, she thought, and nothing Sonia Randall could say or do was going to spoil her belief in her story and her ability to finish it.

What happened to it after that was in the lap of the gods, but maybe she should warn Mrs Morgan that Alder House was definitely a no-no, she told herself, grimacing.

Determinedly, she relegated Sonia Randall's dismissive remarks to the outskirts of her mind and turned her attention to the job in hand.

The words seemed to be flowing out of her as she wrote, then rewrote feverishly, building the tension as frantic minutes passed, with Mariana crouching on the bed, the ancient, filthy bedcovering ripping like paper in her hands as she desperately tried to fashion it into a rope to lower herself from the tiny window. Knowing, as she threw it aside, that even if the fabric held by some miracle, it would still be inadequate, leaving her with a dangerous drop to the street below, and certain serious injury.

As she stared around her, looking for some alternative means of escape and realising it did not exist. As she thought of William, prayed absurdly for him to come and find her—rescue her—when she knew it was impossible because he didn't even know where she was and would never guess, even in his worst nightmares, that she'd ever embark on such a foolhardy escapade.

When he'd be encamped wherever Lord Wellington was and assuming that she was safe in her father's house, living for—longing for—his return.

Then the terror of hearing the sound of a man's boots ascending the stairs, stumbling a little because he'd been drinking, swearing softly in English in the voice she'd never forget.

Finding the darkest corner of the room and shrinking into it, trying to use the shadows for camouflage as the door was flung wide on its creaking hinges, and she saw him, standing there, his silhouette grossly exaggerated by the flickering light of the candle he was carrying.

His glinting eyes scanning the room—searching, and inevitably finding.

The gloating triumph in his voice as he said, 'The runaway nymph at last, by God. I've been waiting for this moment, my beauty, and here you are, the delicious end to a perfect evening.'

The way he crossed the room, his stride long and steady, as if the sight of her had rendered him sober and grimly, wickedly focused. How his hands descended on her shoulders, jerking her towards him, and the insolent sensuality of his mouth.

And as he bent to her, Mariana, struggling to push him away, her heart pounding unevenly, suddenly heard someone knock on the door…

Except—it wasn't supposed to happen that way, Tallie thought, staring in bewilderment at the words on the screen. There was going to be a diversion when the Spanish ruffians from downstairs, realising that Hugo Cantrell had been cheating them with marked cards, came looking for retribution, dragging Mariana away from him when he tried to use her as a shield, and enabling her to make her getaway while he went down like a fallen tree under the murderous barrage of their fists and boots, and his choking, agonised cries followed her as she fled.

It was the second, louder knock that brought her back to full reality. This was fact, not fiction. Someone was at her bedroom door, trying to attract her attention.

She glanced at her watch and stifled a yelp as she saw the time. She'd been working for almost three hours and, if it was Justin, back for another attempt at persuasion, she could only hope he was sober.

She opened the door warily and stepped back with a small, startled gasp when she found herself instead facing Mark Benedict.

'For God's sake,' he said, an edge to his voice, 'do you have to leap away every time you see me, as if I was a mad axe-murderer?'

'Do you have to come banging on the door at this hour?' she threw back at him shakily. 'I might have been asleep.'

'With the light on?' he asked mockingly. 'As a prudent landlord, I'd have felt bound to intervene.'

'Or getting ready for bed, anyway.' She glared at him.

'You mean undressed?' He grinned at her. 'My luck's never been that good, or not twice in a week, anyway.'

Do not blush, Tallie told herself stonily. Do not give him the satisfaction of seeing you embarrassed yet again.

'Is there a reason for this visit?' she asked coldly. 'Apart from checking if I'm wasting your electricity, of course.'

'I've made some hot chocolate,' he said. 'I thought you were probably still working, and might like some.'

She stared at him, her lips parted in sheer astonishment. 'Hot chocolate,' she said at last. 'You?'

He shrugged. 'Why not?'

'I thought you'd have preferred something more exotic.'

His grin widened. 'To match my taste in women? But you've only met one of them.'

And that was more than enough. The words hovered unspoken between them.

She said stiffly, 'Please believe your…lady friends are no concern of mine.'

'Bull's-eye,' he approved. 'I'd be so grateful if you could talk Penny round to your way of thinking.' He paused. 'But most men have a weakness for chocolate in some form or other, and I'm no exception. So, do you want yours or shall I pour it away?'

She hesitated, realising reluctantly how long it had been since that gulped-down coffee.

'Thank you,' she said stiltedly. 'It's…very kind of you.'

'Call it conscience,' he said, his mouth twisting. 'I should have known better than to put you in the same room as Sonia. Although the kitten turned out to have claws of her own,' he added musingly.

'We waifs learn to fight our corner,' she returned, adding, 'However, I'd still prefer not to encounter her again—or intrude on your privacy in any way.' And bit her lip as she met his sardonic look.

'You won't. She left when the others did.'

Deep within her, she felt a disturbing stir of pleasure at the news. She said coolly, 'She must be very disappointed.'

'Well, she's not alone in that,' he said. His hand casually cupped her elbow, guiding her, to her surprise, towards the sitting room rather than the kitchen. 'You dashed poor old Justin's hopes pretty finally.'

'What else did you expect?' Tallie wrenched herself free and faced him hotly. 'You may not care about your cousin's feelings, but I think Penny's lovely and she deserves better than her boyfriend trying to date another girl behind her back.'

'Well, we agree about one thing,' he said, closing the sitting room door behind them. 'Penny is indeed a great girl. But you've got Justin all wrong. He was Penny's escort tonight, but only because he's her See If I Care Man.'

Tallie sank down on a sofa, staring at him. 'Am I supposed to know what you're talking about?'

Mark was pouring chocolate from a silver pot. 'It's quite simple. Up until a few weeks ago, she was seeing a guy called Greg Curtis. Serious stuff, with talk of an engagement. Then Greg's former girlfriend unexpectedly came back from Canada without the husband she'd gone there to marry, demanding sympathy, attention and the place in his life she occupied eighteen months ago. With the result that, suddenly, his future with Penny was in the melting pot.'

'But that's awful.' Tallie's brows snapped together. 'She must be devastated.'

'Pretty much.' He handed her a porcelain mug full of steaming chocolate. 'But she's also a practical girl and she suspects this may be just a wobble, induced by some pretty intense emotional blackmail from the ex-lady.' He smiled faintly. 'And that he'll soon remember why he was so thankful that the beautiful Minerva eventually opted for someone else.

'At the same time, my cousin's not the type to wear her heart on her sleeve, or sit round waiting while Greg sorts himself out. If he ever does, of course,' he added, frowning. 'However, for her own self-respect, she needs to be seen out and about with an attentive man in tow so that Greg will get the message loud and clear. Hence Justin, an old friend of mine, who has some bruises of his own and isn't looking for a heavy relationship right now.'

'Making him Penny's See If I Care Man,' Tallie repeated slowly.

I wish I'd found someone like that, she thought wistfully, when Gareth dumped me. So much better than moping around like a wet week, letting everyone see how much it mattered. As it is, I'll always feature as some naïve saddo. Not least with the man facing me now.

'But Pen doesn't have exclusive rights, if that's what you're afraid of.' Mark was watching her over the top of his mug. 'Plus, he's a nice guy and it would do you good to go out—flutter your wings a little.'

He paused. 'After all, you know what they say about all work and no play.'

'I have heard it before,' she admitted tautly. 'But even if Justin isn't messing Penny about, it makes no difference. I—I shan't be accepting his invitation. And I'll take my drink to my room, if that's all right.'

'It isn't,' he said laconically. 'To use a cliché—we need to talk.'

She lifted her chin. 'If it's about Justin, it's pointless.'

'May I know why?'

'I'd have thought it would be obvious—especially to you.' She shrugged. 'I'll be moving very soon. End of story.'

'But I'd be happy to pass on your new address.' Those amazing green eyes were watching her steadily. 'Except, of course, you don't have one—do you? Because you haven't been able to find anywhere else to live in London. Isn't that the truth of it?'

She looked down at her hands, clasped round the mug. 'No.' It hurt to have to admit her failure and to him of all people. 'No, I haven't.'

'So what are you planning to do?'

She hunched a shoulder, still not looking at him. 'Go back to my parents' home.'

'But that isn't what you want.'

'I don't really have any other choice.'

He nodded. 'And, of course, you think Justin may hesitate over pursuing you back to whatever rural fastness you came from.'

'It's hardly likely.' The fragrant chocolate was smooth comfort against the sudden tightness in her throat. 'But, as we've only just met, it's not a major concern. And I'm sure someone as attractive as Justin won't feel too put out.'

'Possibly not.' He was leaning back against the cushions, those endless legs stretched out in front of him, his gaze meditative. 'But it seems a pity to reject him out of hand. So why don't you forget the looming deadline for your departure and stay on here?'

She almost spilled her chocolate. 'Stay—here?' Her voice was hoarse.

'Why?'

'Because I think you deserve a chance.'

Her mind was reeling. 'With—Justin?'

'No, to finish your book, you little idiot. Your love-life's your own business. But you need peace and quiet in which to work, and I can provide that.' He paused. 'Besides, I'm seriously grateful about tonight.'

'But I already said—we're quits.'

'Well,' he said, 'maybe I'll ask another favour some time, if that makes you feel better.'

She wasn't sure how it made her feel, so she sipped at her chocolate as she tried to collect her random thoughts.

Eventually, she said, 'I don't think Miss Randall will be very pleased when she finds out.'

He shrugged. 'Why should she care? You're being invited to continue your occupation of my spare room, sweetheart, not move into my bed.'

The muscles in her chest seemed to clench oddly. She had to control her voice. 'But you don't want me here. You've made that clear.'

'I won't be here a great deal myself. I have several trips abroad coming up, and maybe a flat-sitter isn't such a bad idea.' He smiled at her. 'And you like the place, don't you? I've noticed the way you move round it—the pleasure with which you look at things— handle them as if they were precious.'

She tried for lightness. 'I didn't realise I was under such close observation.'

'Security.' He echoed her tone. 'I had to be sure you weren't a burglar's moll.'

He finished his chocolate. 'So—are you going to stay? I'm offering the same terms as Kit.'

She hesitated. 'In that case, yes, please.' She tried a smile. 'Although I could always cook you the occasional meal.'

He shook his head. 'This evening was a one-off. Same roof—separate lives. That's the deal.'

'Of course.' She put down her empty mug and rose. 'In that case, thank you, Mr Benedict, and...I wish you goodnight. It seems it's my turn to be grateful.'

'One other thing.' As she reached the door, his voice halted her. 'My name is Mark. Think you can remember that?'

She said huskily, 'I...can try.'

And, as she went away from him, down the passage to her own room, she found herself wondering if she'd found the perfect solution to her problems—or just made the biggest mistake of her life. She realised she could not find an answer.

CHAPTER SEVEN

TALLIE woke the next morning, uneasily aware that she was still unsure whether she'd made the right decision.

She sat up slowly, looking round her tranquil, sun-filled room, telling herself it was perfect—the ideal working environment. Reminding herself how much she'd written there over the past week in spite of everything.

Why, even last night, instead of going straight to bed, she'd sat down and finished the scene she'd been working on, although not in the way she'd originally intended, she admitted wryly.

Because after The Kiss which Hugo Cantrell had inflicted on the kicking and struggling Mariana, they'd been interrupted by the sound of feet thundering up the rickety stairs and furious voices baying for blood. And, instead of using her as his shield, Hugo had inexplicably picked Mariana up in his arms and strode with her to the window.

'Here.' He pushed a leather purse heavy with coins into her hand. 'My winnings. Now, go while you can, because they won't spare either of us.'

And, before she could scream in protest, he'd pushed her slender body through the narrow casement, dropping her into a hay-wagon passing below.

And as she lay, winded but otherwise undamaged, she heard from the inn the crashing of splintering wood and the chilling sound of a man shouting in pain.

That, at least, was what she'd originally planned.

Well, maybe even the nastiest pieces of work had their moments of weakness, Tallie conceded reluctantly. As Mark Benedict had surprisingly demonstrated last night.

But even if she'd let Hugo slip out of character for a few minutes, and she wasn't sure why that had happened, he was still the villain of the piece and nothing was going to change that.

And Mariana was definitely not going to return at some point, to find him broken and bleeding, so that she could bandage up his injuries with her torn-up petticoat and nurse him back to health in some remote barn.

Because any spare petticoats she had would be devoted to William, wounded during his gallant actions at Salamanca, probably by a sabre cut during Le Marchant's charge, she thought. Because he was the hero, and she must make sure the reader knew it.

But it was last night's decision that was still at the forefront of her mind as she showered and dressed. The flat seemed deserted when she emerged from her room, and for a moment she thought Mark had already left to pursue whatever he'd got planned for the day, but then she detected the murmur of his voice from behind the closed door of his office.

She was in the kitchen, just finishing her tea and toast when he came striding in, dark brows drawn together in a frown and his mouth set grimly.

Not a good sign, thought Tallie with sudden apprehension. Maybe she wasn't the only one having second thoughts about their new agreement. And it might be better to jump before she was pushed.

She said quietly, 'If you've changed your mind about letting me stay, I quite understand.'

'What?' He seemed to become aware of her for the first time. 'God, no. I've something else on my mind entirely.' He refilled the mug he was carrying from the percolator and leaned back against the counter top. He was wearing beautifully cut jeans and a plain white shirt, open at the throat, its sleeves turned back over his tanned forearms.

He said abruptly, 'I hadn't intended to ask so soon, but I rather need that favour I mentioned last night. It seems my stepmother is paying me a visit.'

'And you want me to cook lunch for her?'

'No,' he said. 'Just to be here. She claims she's coming on a business matter and I need backup.'

She hesitated. 'What do you mean exactly?'

'I mean I'd prefer not to be alone here when she comes calling.' His tone was blunt.

'Oh,' she said, as unwelcome light dawned, 'so that's what…' And stopped, flushing guiltily.

'That's what Penny was undoubtedly about to tell you when I interrupted,' he supplied, his face lightening into amused resignation. 'Are there any details of my life my dear cousin has withheld? For instance, did you get a recital of my childhood ailments, including how she gave me chickenpox when I was thirteen?'

'No—' Tallie's own mouth quivered into amusement '—but she might be saving that for another time.' She put her used breakfast things carefully into the dishwasher. 'So you want me to play gooseberry, is that it?'

'Not exactly,' he said carefully. 'I want you to pretend that you're my girlfriend, and that we're sharing a damned sight more than just our living space.'

She bit her lip. 'But surely you shouldn't be asking me. It ought to be…Miss Randall, or someone…'

'Actually, no.' A sardonic note entered his voice. 'I've no wish to send out misleading signals to Miss Randall—or anyone.' He paused. 'And as you and I have nothing going for us apart from an uneasy truce, that makes you the ideal choice.'

He looked at her. 'So, will you do it?'

'I…don't know.' She glanced down at the workaday jeans and top she was wearing. 'I hardly look the part of anyone's live-in lover, least of all yours.'

'That can be fixed.'

'And I'm not a very good actress.'

'Pretend it's a scene from this book of yours,' he said casually, and Tallie bit her lip, wondering if that wasn't a little too close for comfort.

'Very well, then,' she said. 'I'll do my best. What time is she getting here?'

'Mid-morning, she tells me.' His mouth twisted. 'And, as she appears to want something, she may even be on time.'

'Fine.' She summoned a smile. 'Then I can get some work done while I'm waiting.'

But an hour later she couldn't pretend she was satisfied with what she'd produced. Even while hurling himself on the French lines, William still seemed oddly remote. Maybe he would become warmer, more human, when Mariana came back into his life, she thought, and the sooner the better.

But maybe she was just tired. She hadn't slept very well the previous night, her mind invaded by disjointed words and images. 'Mark, of course, is a total commitment-phobe'…Mariana struggling in the arms of a man she hated, and, more than once, Mark's voice asking, 'Why don't you…stay on here?' And herself, fighting to find a reason and put it into words.

She was reluctantly saving what she'd written when there was a rap at her door.

'Come in.' She got to her feet, wondering apprehensively if she was being summoned because Veronica had arrived ahead of time.

But Mark walked in alone. 'I've brought you something.' He tossed a couple of carrier bags emblazoned with the name of a well-known department store on to her bed. 'I hope it all fits. I'm not intimately acquainted with your measurements, so I had to guess.'

Tallie opened the first bag, extracting a deceptively simple cream skirt and a scoop-necked silky top the colour of horse chestnuts. The second held a pair of high-heeled cream sandals.

When she could find a voice, she said, 'You bought these—for me?'

'I hardly plan to wear them myself. I suggest you change into them now. Practise walking in those heels.'

She gasped. 'I'll do nothing of the kind.' She tried to stuff everything back into the bags. 'You have no right—no right at all…'

He sighed. 'Please don't fuss. You admitted yourself you're not dressed for the part. Now you can be.'

She said, 'I could live for a month on what you've just paid for this stuff.'

Mark shrugged. 'Then tomorrow you can sell it on eBay,' he returned. 'But I suggest that you hang on to it. Wear it when you meet your publishers. You might get a better deal if they think you're not hungry.' He looked her over. 'And leave your hair loose.'

She was quivering with temper. 'Any other instructions—sir?'

'Not at the moment, but that could change.' He glanced at his watch. 'I'm going to put some coffee on while you get dressed. We haven't got all day.'

As he went to the door, she said, 'One thing occurred to me.' She hesitated. 'You don't think Kit may have told her about moving me in here? That she might recognise my name?'

'Unlikely,' he said. 'Even if he did share the joke with her, your actual identity would be far too unimportant a detail to mention.'

'Oh,' she said with false brightness, 'that's all right then.'

'No,' he said, more gently. 'But I'm afraid it's as good as it gets, with that precious pair.' He grimaced. 'As you're about to find out,' he added, and went.

The new clothes, she had to admit, were becoming. Even more annoyingly, they were a perfect fit. And the sandals made her already slim legs racehorse-slender.

She found herself wondering what Mark would say when she went to join him in the sitting room, but he merely looked her over, then nodded abruptly.

And a moment later the imperious sound of the buzzer announced that their visitor had arrived.

Tallie turned to him, apprehension twisting inside her. 'Shall I—answer the door?'

'We'll do it together,' Mark said. 'And—relax,' he added as they walked down the passage. 'Remember you're not here to make a good impression.'

The woman confronting them on the doorstep was tall and stunningly attractive, with blonde hair caught back in an immaculate chignon. Her complexion was flawless, her nose short and straight, and she had enormous blue eyes fringed by curling lashes heavily enhanced by mascara. Her reed-slender figure was moulded closely by a suit in royal blue, the skirt displaying shapely legs and the short jacket revealing rather more than a hint of cleavage.

Tallie, who'd been expecting a hatchet-faced harridan, found herself almost gaping. Kit's mother? she queried in silent incredulity. She doesn't look old enough.

She thought of her own mother—warm, pretty and adored by her husband, but with comfortable curves, a few first touches of grey in her hair and laugh lines around her eyes and mouth. Tried to imagine her in an outfit like that, and failed utterly.

'Mark, darling, how wonderful to see you.' Veronica Melrose's voice was low and husky. The astonishing blue eyes rested on Tallie. 'And who is this?'

'This, my dear Veronica, is Natalie.' He put an easy arm round Tallie's shoulders and drew her against him, giving her no option but compliance, she realised mutinously. But she could hardly accuse him of taking advantage of the situation when she'd agreed to this charade.

She was also aware that the older woman's harebell gaze had carried out a lightning assessment of everything she was wearing, costing it to the last penny. But she still wasn't sure she'd passed muster.

I'm just not glamorous enough, she thought, and swallowed.

'Do come in,' Mark went on. 'May we offer you some coffee?'

'That would be pleasant.' Mrs Melrose walked into the sitting room and deposited herself decoratively on the sofa. Not many women of her age could pout and get away with it, thought Tallie, but she managed it somehow. 'I did hope that our conversation would be a private one. Is there any reason for your…little friend to be present?'

Mark looked surprised. 'She lives here,' he said. 'With me. Perhaps I should have made that clear.'

'Perhaps you should.' The husky voice had acquired a metallic edge. She gave a little laugh. 'Well, well. The eternal bachelor caught at last. And in such a young and charming trap. How fascinating.'

Tallie said coolly, 'I don't think Mark feels particularly trapped. I'll fetch the coffee.'

'You seem to have made yourself quite at home,' Veronica commented as she returned, placing the tray on the table. 'Although you clearly haven't had a chance to put your own stamp on it yet— whatever that might be.' As she accepted the coffee Tallie handed to her, she flicked a disparaging glance round the room. 'But it so needs updating.' She looked at Mark. 'Kit told me he was astonished you hadn't brought in a decent decorator by now.'

'And is he equally amazed by Australia?' Mark enquired politely. He reached up a hand and pulled Tallie down on to the sofa beside him. 'I assume you've heard from him.'

'Indeed I have.' Veronica jerked upright as if a steel pole had suddenly replaced her spine. 'He's been telephoning me nearly every day. He's having the most appalling time, stuck at this vineyard which seems to be miles from anywhere else. The weather's disgusting—apparently it's winter—and he actually saw a snake.'

She shuddered. 'He should never have gone there.' She gave Mark a look that wasn't remotely seductive. 'But I have you to thank for that.'

'Difficult to see how,' he returned indifferently. 'When I was at the back of beyond myself, and in a totally different continent. Besides, didn't you sweet-talk poor Charles into taking him on at Melrose and Sons?'

Her crimson mouth tightened impatiently. 'I meant Kit should have taken his rightful place by now in his father's company.'

'I didn't tell him to abandon his engineering course at university,' Mark said shortly. 'That was all his own idea. But if he'd stuck to it, he'd have found himself in places he'd have liked even less than Australia.'

'There must be projects in this country too.' She waved a vague hand. 'Hotels, leisure complexes, shopping malls. Something he could have enjoyed.'

'But we're committed to roads, bridges and hydro-electric schemes,' Mark said gently. 'Long-term developments which will help rather more people.'

Veronica shrugged. 'Until they choose to blow them up, of course.' She added with a touch of malice, 'Isn't that what happened on your last site?'

'A temporary set-back,' Mark drawled. 'And now that the fighting seems to be over, we'll be going back to the Ubilisi to finish what we started.'

Tallie stared at him. When she spoke, she found her voice was shaking. 'But that's dangerous, surely. The previous government's been overthrown, and the new regime tried to kill you when you were there before. You only just got out last time.'

There was an odd silence, then Veronica gave a tinkling laugh. 'Why, Mark, the child is seriously concerned about you. How terribly sweet.' She looked at Tallie. 'But a complete waste of time, my dear. Mark is a law unto himself, and he actually revels in charging off to remote corners of the globe, turning disasters into triumphs. No one woman could possibly offer a viable alternative to that sort of buzz.'

She paused. 'But that does not mean Kit has to do the same. He can't possibly stay where he is, when he's so wretched. He needs to come home, and find work in this country.'

She paused again. 'So, I thought you might offer him a job. It's full time he learned about the company, especially when you're still hurling yourself into the world's trouble spots. After all, Kit is your nearest male relative, and if something were to…happen, he'd be your heir.'

'You think so?' Mark's tone was dry. He slid his arm round Tallie's waist, smiling down at her. 'But all that might change very soon.'

'Good God.' Veronica's eyes swept over Tallie's slim figure with disbelief. 'You mean…'

'I mean nothing yet,' Mark returned easily, as Tallie sat rigidly beside him, not knowing where to look. 'But we're working on it.' He paused. 'And there are no vacancies at Benedicts that would pay Kit the kind of salary he'd clearly expect, or make use of his extremely limited skills.

'We market our expertise, Veronica, trouble-shooting difficult engineering projects all over the world. Believe me, your son is better off where he is. And, if he works, he might even get promotion eventually.'

'I see.' The coffee cup rattled in its saucer as Veronica replaced it on the table. 'Then there's nothing more to be said.' Her look lasered Tallie. 'However, I do hope you're going to make up for my disappointment by offering me a bed for the night. I'm dining with friends this evening and I have an early dental appointment tomorrow morning.' She looked from one to the other. 'You do have a spare room? I'm sure Kit has mentioned it.'

'I'm certain he has.' Mark shrugged. 'But Natalie's currently using it as an office. Besides, I thought you always stayed at The Ritz.'

'I do, but Charles is being very difficult at the moment. Says we have to cut back on our spending.' The pout reappeared and the blue eyes rested smilingly on Mark. 'I didn't think you'd begrudge me just one night.'

'Except,' Mark said gently, 'that Natalie and I are enjoying our privacy, and really don't wish it to be interrupted, not even by the most understanding guest.'

'My dear Mark—such unwonted concentration on one woman. I can hardly believe my ears. I think the best thing I can do is go, and leave you in peace.' At the door, she turned. 'And please don't worry. There'll be other nights, I'm sure.'

When Mark returned from showing her out, Tallie was still seated on the sofa, staring into space.

She said, 'That was awful.'

'It's also over.'

'Is it?' She looked up at him. 'Your stepmother doesn't seem to think so. If I was genuinely involved with you, I'd be starting to wonder.'

'But as you're not,' he said coldly, 'you need not concern yourself.' He picked up the coffee tray and carried it to the kitchen. After a moment or two, she followed.

'I'm sorry.' Her voice faltered a little. 'That was wrong of me. I don't really believe that…you…that you and Veronica…'

'Thanks for the vote of confidence.' His tone was dry. 'It's slightly gutting to find someone thinks you can be that much of a bastard.'

'Yes.' The word had a hollow ring, the image of Hugo Cantrell large in her mind.

'Well, don't look so stricken.' His mouth twisted. 'Because I'm no saint, and at times it's been a damned close-run thing. Veronica can pack quite a punch, especially when you're sixteen and not nearly as sexually experienced as you like to think.'

Tallie gasped. 'She came on to you—at that age?'

'She'd correctly figured I wasn't a virgin. Also, she was only nineteen when she married my father, and he was already in his mid-forties. Maybe that side of their relationship was on the wane, or perhaps she was simply feeling the seven year itch.'

He paused. 'I've wondered since if she also saw it as a way of establishing a hold over me—insurance for the future, perhaps.'

He added lightly, 'On the other hand, she may simply have found the idea amusing. All those raging adolescent hormones at her disposal—if I'd proved amenable.'

'But surely she can't still think…'

'No?' he asked. 'When you admitted you began to wonder.' He shook his head. 'Veronica is not a woman to allow her marriage vows to stand in her way.'

'She's vile.'

'She's also sad.' He paused. 'But thank you for saving me from a potentially awkward situation. I owe you big time, and I won't forget it.'

'I wish I could say it was a pleasure.' She got to her feet. 'And now I have some awkward situations of my own to deal with, so I'd better get back to work.'

'You won't allow me to express my gratitude by taking you for an expensive lunch? It seems a pity to waste the new gear.' His voice followed her to the door.

She didn't look back at him. 'No, thanks.' She sounded faintly brittle. 'Veronica seems to have killed my appetite stone dead.'

Back in her room, she found she was leaning back against the panels of the door, panting as if she'd been running, angry with herself and bewildered at the same time. After all, she was undeniably hungry, so where would have been the harm?

She caught a glimpse of herself in the mirror—a girl she hardly recognised in the smart, unfamiliar clothes, her eyes unnaturally bright and her cheeks flushed.

And knew exactly why she wouldn't take the risk.

She wrote steadily for the rest of the day, her unaccustomed finery restored to its carrier bags and stowed at the back of the wardrobe. Out of sight, out of mind, she told herself.

And when eventually she ventured out to heat a tin of soup and make a sandwich, the flat was deserted.

She'd just cleared away her makeshift meal when the buzzer sounded. What now? she wondered, groaning silently as she obeyed its summons. Don't tell me Veronica's come back to say all the hotels are full.

But when she opened the door, she found Justin smiling at her.

'Hi,' he said, too casually. 'Is Mark around?'

'No,' she said, her own lips twitching reluctantly. 'But I suspect you knew that already.'

'So, are you going to let me in? I promise I'm safe and house-trained.'

'Also difficult to keep away.' Tallie stood aside to admit him and led the way to the sitting room. 'The choice is tea or coffee. The alcohol belongs to Mark.'

Justin opened the briefcase he was carrying and produced a

bottle. 'Cloudy Bay,' he said. 'Taste it and fall in love. But only with the wine, naturally.'

'Naturally,' Tallie agreed dryly, and went to fetch the corkscrew.

Although unexpected, it was a relaxed and convivial interlude, taking away the sour taste of Veronica Melrose's visit. They talked about books, comparing favourite authors, found they had broadly similar tastes in music, but differed widely on films. And the wine was wonderful.

By the time he left an hour later, she found she'd agreed to accompany him to the theatre the following week, and when he paused at the front door, cupping her chin gently in his hand and bending towards her, she allowed his kiss, which was brief, undemanding, yet undeniably pleasant.

Alone, Tallie smiled as she re-corked what was left of the wine, preparatory to putting it in the fridge, and began to wash the glasses.

There was no denying that Justin was an extremely attractive man. And, with his fair hair and blue eyes, exactly her type, as well as being practically a template for William in her book.

I based him originally on Gareth, she thought. And when Gareth turned out to be not the person I'd hoped, I think I may have stopped believing in William too, and that's why I'm having all these problems in bringing him to life. But maybe it will be easier to put him centre stage from now on.

As for Hugo Cantrell, who was becoming almost too real, and who might have to be killed off in some unpleasant way...

'You look very fierce,' Mark commented from the doorway. 'Is something wrong?'

She almost dropped the glass she was drying. 'I—I didn't hear you come in.'

'Evidently. You were lost in thought.' He looked at the wine bottle on the counter top. 'Been entertaining?'

'Yes, as it happens.' Her tone was defensive.

'May I guess the identity of your visitor?' The note of amusement in his voice was not lost on her.

She stared at him. 'Did you tell him to come?'

'As if.' He leaned a shoulder against the door frame. 'So where's he taking you?'

'To the new Leigh Hanford play,' she admitted unwillingly.

'It's had good reviews,' he said casually. 'He's lucky to get tickets.'

She frowned. 'Did you have anything to do with that?'

'Why, Miss Paget,' he drawled, 'what a suspicious mind you have. I suppose it comes from working out plots.'

'Probably,' she said. 'And now I must go and work out some more of them. Goodnight, Mr Benedict.'

'Goodnight to you, Miss Paget.' He added softly, 'I hope your dreams are sweet.'

Tallie hoped so too as she headed towards her room, but they would have to be delayed. First she would have to find some way of dealing with Hugo Cantrell. After all, the wretched man seemed to be taking over the book, and that was the last thing she wanted. So he would have to go. Painfully and permanently.

At the same time it occurred to her that, although she might be able to remove him from the manuscript, it would not be so easy to erase his dark-haired, green-eyed image from her mind.

Not when she was living with the real thing.

A disturbing reflection that pursued her for the remainder of the night, so that the dreams that eventually punctuated her sleep were restless and uneasy.

CHAPTER EIGHT

'So,' LORNA said eagerly, 'tell me what he's like.'

'Arrogant,' Tallie said coldly. 'Serial womaniser. Fortunately, I don't have to see much of him.'

Lorna gaped at her. 'Then why are you taking all this trouble, if he's so frightful?'

'Oh—' Tallie flushed '—you're talking about Justin.'

And I should be too, she told herself. Talking about him, thinking about, dreaming about him. And not sparing Mark Benedict a second thought.

Especially when he's barely addressed two consecutive sentences to me since his stepmother's visit three weeks ago. He said he owed me, she thought. Yet now he seems to have cut me off completely. Iced me quite deliberately.

'Damn right I'm talking about Justin,' said Lorna.

'Well…' Tallie considered '…he's…lovely. Just as nice as I thought, and I'm having dinner with him tomorrow night at Pierre Martin.'

'Very smart,' her friend approved. 'Also expensive. And you need me to help along the good work by lending you something to wear.' She waved at the open door of her wardrobe. 'Take your pick.'

'I just don't know,' Tallie said, peering wildly along the rail. 'You choose for me.'

'Hmm.' Lorna gave her a shrewd once-over. 'Do you want "Touch me not" or "Come and get me"?'

Tallie blushed more deeply. 'Maybe somewhere in between,' she hedged.

'Wimp,' Lorna said, not unkindly. She paused. 'Tallie, you're not nervous about this dinner date, are you?'

'I think I could be,' Tallie admitted. 'Up to now, it's all been pretty low-key, but I have a feeling that's going to change. And I don't know what to expect.' She sighed. 'Or what he'll expect either.'

'Well, being a man, he'll undoubtedly be hoping,' Lorna returned dryly. 'Especially after dinner and a bottle of wine at Pierre Martin has cost him an arm and a leg. Presumably, he's attractive.'

'Very,' Tallie said emphatically.

'And you trust him?'

'Absolutely.'

'Then what are you waiting for?' Lorna demanded robustly. 'Just—go with the flow.'

She took a dark red dress from the wardrobe and Tallie's eyes widened. 'That's fabulous.'

'It's a good simple style, not too low-cut, not too short.' Lorna held it against her to demonstrate. 'And the colour should be good for you as well. Stop you looking like your own ghost.'

She rummaged in the bottom of the wardrobe. 'And there are shoes to match, plain and not too high. You don't want to risk taking a nosedive, or spraining your ankle.'

That, Tallie thought, could be the least of my problems.

She wasn't sure why she felt so edgy, she thought, as she got ready for her date the following evening. Up to now, she'd enjoyed the moments she'd spent in Justin's arms, for heaven's sake, and she was sure he was far too decent a man to apply undue pressure, or push her into something she wasn't ready for.

But he'd been letting her go with more and more reluctance. Which seemed to indicate that he now wanted their relationship to be more than just friendly. And maybe she should stop worrying and regard the night ahead as simply a step on the way to falling in love with a man she liked.

But with some bruises of his own.

Or that was what Mark Benedict had said, anyway. And if they'd still been having even some rudimentary form of conversation, she might have asked him what he'd meant. But she wasn't risking another snub, as he stalked past her on the way to heaven knew where.

Clearly, she thought, he didn't like being in her debt, and regretted the impulse that had caused him to ask for her help. And any hint at a new understanding between them had relapsed once more into the silence of that first week. A silence she didn't know how to break, and which was clearly intended to keep her at a distance.

Which was how matters between them still stood, and she'd probably been a fool to expect anything different.

'Same roof—separate lives.' That was what he'd said, and what he meant.

But the situation was less embarrassing than she'd feared, because most of the time he wasn't around. He'd been off to Germany, Canada for three days, and Venezuela for four, and in between he'd been fitting in meetings all over Britain.

'Doesn't he ever slow down?' she'd asked Penny, who'd turned up quite unexpectedly one evening during one of his longer absences, bringing a Chinese take-away—on the off-chance, she said cheerfully, that Tallie hadn't eaten yet.

'I only wish he would.' Penny sighed. 'He's got a terrific team working for him, and he could delegate far more. For instance, there was no need for him to be caught up in that hideous African mess, but he knew there was trouble brewing and he didn't want to risk anyone who had a wife and family.'

'And now he's going back there,' Tallie said, half to herself.

'He has a job to finish.' Penny shrugged fatalistically. 'That's the way he is.'

And they'd turned to other topics.

Tallie had enjoyed seeing Penny again, but had backed off when further meetings were suggested. However, it wasn't simply the lack of time or money that she'd used as her excuse, and which

Penny had reluctantly accepted, which had made her demur, but more the suspicion that Mark might not approve of any burgeoning friendship between her and his cousin.

That it might impinge on his 'separate lives' ruling.

But I wish I'd asked her about Justin, she thought. Except that it might have revived unhappy memories about her own bruises.

She zipped herself into her dress, wondering doubtfully if it had been stupid to spend money on a new broderie anglais bra and briefs set from her favourite chain store.

But if—something was going to happen tonight, she would need all the confidence going, and some pretty lingerie could only boost her self-esteem.

She was on her way down the passage to the front door when Mark emerged from the study, stretching wearily. He paused, his gaze travelling over her, taking in the demure charm of the red dress with narrow-eyed speculation.

'Ah,' he said softly. 'Big date tonight.'

An almost civil remark, thought Tallie furiously, and just when it was needed least. How very typical. And if she'd left five minutes earlier, she could have avoided him altogether.

She lifted her chin, saying coolly, 'I am going out, yes.' And tried to ignore how his glance seemed to be lingering on the way the dress clung to her small high breasts and the slender curve of her hips.

'Then clearly I won't bother to wait up,' he murmured and sauntered off in the direction of the kitchen.

And Tallie made her escape, thankful he hadn't hung around to watch her blushing.

Justin was already at the restaurant, and he stood, taking her hand and kissing her on the cheek as she joined him at their table.

'You look lovely.' His eyes were warm with admiration, and possibly more. 'Is that a new dress?'

New to me anyway, she thought, basking in his appreciation. It will be all right, she told herself. Everything will be fine.

She looked about her with interest as she took her seat beside him on the cushioned bench against the wall. Most of the tables were occupied, and waiters moved between them with quiet efficiency. There was no canned music, just the hum of contented conversation, punctuated by the occasional pop of a cork.

She sat back with a sigh. 'What a nice place this is.'

'I came to the opening about a year ago,' he said after a brief hesitation. 'So I know the food is good.' His mouth quirked. 'After the meal you cooked for us that night, I felt nothing less would do.'

Tallie laughed, and after that everything became easier. It was fun to sit close to him and chat over a shared menu, which was short but crammed with delicious possibilities. Rather like the evening itself, she thought with sudden shyness.

Because Justin's gentle flirting had a new and definite purpose since their last encounter, and it was exciting to realise that, for the first time in her life, she was being seriously propositioned.

She recognised, too, that before long she would need to make a decision, and therefore it would be better not to drink too much of the wonderful wine he'd picked to accompany the food, in case it clouded her judgement.

Or had her choice really been made from the moment she'd accepted tonight's invitation? She couldn't be sure.

For dessert, Justin ordered two of the restaurant's famous chocolate soufflés.

'And coffee, m'sieur?'

'I think we'll decide that later.' Looking at Tallie, he added softly, 'Shall we?'

The moment had arrived. He was asking if she'd go back with him to his flat and he required an answer, she thought numbly, staring down at the white linen tablecloth. She could say yes or no. Nod or shake her head. Anything rather than sit as if she'd been turned to stone, her heart the only part of her body that seemed to be working, as it pounded unevenly away against her ribcage. As she tried desperately to *think*...

She was aware of the waiter moving away, but only realised someone else had taken his place when he spoke.

'Good God, Justin. You're the last person I expected to see here.'

Tallie glanced up, startled by the challenge implicit in the harsh drawl.

The newcomer was a youngish man, with a round, pug-like face, unbecomingly flushed as he stood over them.

'This is a restaurant, Clive, and we all have to eat,' Justin returned coolly. 'Even you,' he added, with a fleeting glance at their visitor's overweight body snugly encased in its dark blue suit. 'Please don't let us keep you.'

'Oh, I'm over there.' He waved a vague hand. 'Family party. They couldn't believe their eyes either, so I came across to check.'

He paused. 'Life treating you well, is it? Job...all tickety-boo and no regrets? You certainly seem to be recovering in other ways.'

Tallie found herself the unwelcome target of small, leering brown eyes. 'Although, to be honest, she's a little young for you, isn't she, old boy? Bit fresh from the makers? I didn't know you were into cradle-snatching.'

Justin beckoned to the nearest waiter. He said quietly, 'I think Mr Nelson wishes to rejoin his friends. And cancel the soufflés, please. We'll just have coffee.'

'Oh, don't run away on my account. Okay, sunshine, I'm going.' This to the waiter, before he turned back to Justin. 'Always a pleasure to see you, old man. And good luck to you, poppet.'

When he'd gone there was a long silence.

Justin didn't look at her. 'Tallie, I must apologise for that.' His voice sounded odd, as if it were coming from some other, far-distant world. 'I...I don't know what to say. But I think... maybe...it would be better if I just...got the bill and found you a cab.'

He added, his face bleak with embarrassment, 'I wish I knew how to explain, but I can't. You see, I—I just didn't realise...'

How young I am?

But you must have done, she argued silently as his voice tailed away. You had to know when you met me—the first time you took me out—that I wasn't very old, or very experienced. Yet you asked to see me again. You let me think it didn't matter...

She swallowed past the tightness in her throat. It hardly seemed possible this was happening to her again. That he was rejecting her as Gareth had done, and for the same reason. When, only a few minutes before, it had seemed she would be the one to choose how the evening should end.

He couldn't have wanted her very much, she thought, if he was allowing some snide comments from some passing half-drunk acquaintance to tip the balance against her. To prompt him to take another long look, and realise he was making a big mistake.

So maybe it was for the best, and she should even be grateful to the obnoxious Clive for intervening before she'd had a chance to commit herself, thus saving her from the possibility of even worse embarrassment later.

But I won't think about that now, she told herself with determination. I'll just concentrate on getting out of here with a little dignity. I can do that. I've had previous practice.

She lifted her chin, forcing herself to smile.

'Heavens, there's nothing to explain.' She kept her tone bright and friendly. 'It's getting late, and we both have to work tomorrow. I—I've had a lovely evening, and you were absolutely right about the food. It's amazing.'

She kept up a flow of chatter until they were outside, and a passing cab drew up obediently beside them in response to Justin's signal.

'But there's really no need for you to come with me,' she told him as he gave the address to the driver. 'I'll be fine.'

'If that's what you want.' He looked at her, his face troubled, as he handed the driver the money for the fare, then paused. 'Tallie—I'll call you.'

'Well—that would have been nice,' she said, still smiling. 'But I'm afraid I'm not going to have much free time for a while. It's been terrific, but I have rather been neglecting my book. But—thanks, anyway.'

And she shot into the back of the cab, closing the door smartly behind her, just in case he was contemplating kissing her goodnight, as some sort of consolation prize. Even sent him a cheery wave as the vehicle moved off.

Before slumping back, shivering, into the corner.

All that inner heart-searching, said a jeering voice in her head. All that panic-stricken debate about whether he was the right man, and if you were doing the right thing. All for nothing.

She bit her lip. In fact, totally wasted on someone who'd suddenly decided, when push came to shove, that she didn't suit his requirements after all, even if he wasn't as overtly brutal about it as Gareth had been.

But she still felt stranded, and very foolish, her fragile confidence in herself yet again torn to ribbons.

In the end, the red dress hadn't helped at all. It had just been another error of judgement, along with the new underwear, she thought, flinching.

And when she returned it, Lorna, of course, would be eager to know how the evening had gone, although a simple, 'I didn't fancy him enough after all,' would probably deal with that particular problem.

She trailed slowly up to the flat, letting herself in quietly and with deliberate care, just wanting to reach the sanctuary of her room.

But her luck was still out because, as she closed the door, Mark's voice said sharply from the sitting room, 'Tallie, is that you?' And next moment he appeared in the doorway, staring at her, his brows drawn together.

'Back already?' He checked his watch, then glanced past her. 'So, where's Justin?'

'Well, I'm not hiding him in my handbag.' She managed a degree of insouciance. 'He went home. Isn't that what most people do at the end of the evening?'

He was still frowning. 'But I thought…'

'Did you? And so did I for a while. But we were both wrong.'

'Evidently.' He paused, then said almost abruptly, 'I've only just got back myself. I've opened a bottle of wine. Would you like to share some with me?'

She hesitated, surprised. After his recent aloofness, she'd hardly expected any kind of friendly overture from him. Or did he just feel sorry for her because she'd obviously been dumped?

Instinct told her to make a polite excuse and escape into her room, to nurse her wounded feelings and damaged pride in private. On the other hand, did she really want to be on her own? And, besides, she'd spent a relatively abstemious evening and some alcohol might help her sleep.

She tried to smile. 'I thought it was supposed to be tea and sympathy.'

'Who mentioned sympathy?' He motioned her past him into the sitting room. 'I'll get a glass for you.'

The room was softly lit by a single lamp. The wine, a St Emilion, was standing open on the coffee table, his half-filled glass beside it.

Tallie kicked off her shoes and curled up on the sofa opposite, her feet tucked under her. When he returned, she accepted the glass he handed her with a murmur of thanks.

'However, a toast hardly seems appropriate under the circumstances,' he remarked, resuming his seat, lounging against the cushions. He was barefoot too, she noticed, and casual in a dark blue V-necked sweater over his close-fitting jeans. Then, afraid he might notice that she was looking at him, she hastily transferred her attention to the glowing ruby in her glass.

'Probably not,' she agreed stiltedly. 'Did…did you have a pleasant evening?'

'I went to the cinema,' he said, 'to see a film so enthralling that I came out halfway through it, deciding that life was too short to remain any longer.' He shrugged a shoulder. 'But maybe I wasn't in the mood.'

'You went alone?'

'Well, don't sound so surprised,' Mark returned. 'I do spend the occasional few hours in my own company.'

'I just thought you'd have gone with Miss Randall.'

He said dryly, 'Sonia only likes films where you need subtitles to understand the subtitles. Tonight's effort was rather more basic. Now is there anything else you want to know about my relationship with Miss Randall, or can we file the whole subject under "Forget It"?'

'Willingly,' Tallie said shortly, and drank some of her wine.

'And don't sulk,' he added.

She was forming a dignified denial of any such intention, when the sheer absurdity of it struck her and her mouth twisted into a reluctant smile.

'That's better,' he said. 'So, now we've discussed my disappointing evening, let's talk about yours. Did you and Justin have a row?'

She shook her head. 'No, nothing like that. We had a marvellous dinner, then he decided, as he had every right to do, that I wasn't old enough or sufficiently sophisticated for him. End of story.'

'I can't honestly believe that.' He was frowning again. 'Are you sure there wasn't some kind of misunderstanding?'

'I'm certain,' she said. 'I think "cradle-snatching" is frank enough to remove any lingering doubt. Don't you?'

'Cradle-snatching?' he repeated slowly. 'But that's ludicrous, bordering on crazy. Because you, Natalie Paget, are not a child by any stretch of the imagination.' He paused, then added quietly, 'And when you look as you do tonight, I'd have said you were irresistible.'

Startled colour invaded her face and she felt her breathing quicken. The silence that followed his words seemed to be growing, thickening in some inexplicable and disturbing way, and it needed to be broken.

She said hurriedly, 'But clearly Justin is aware of…of the age difference between us, and it…worries him.'

'Age difference,' he echoed derisively. 'God in heaven, the poor bastard's thirty, a year younger than I am. Neither of us is looking forward to drawing his pension quite yet.'

'I didn't mean that.'

'I'm relieved to hear it.' His voice held a touch of grimness as he refilled his glass.

'Because my lack of…worldly wisdom is probably a more important issue.'

'My God,' he said. 'If this is how the debate went, I'm not surprised the evening ended early.'

'There was no debate,' she said. 'I'm just trying to make some sense of it all.'

He said slowly, 'Maybe it just wasn't meant to be. Consider that.'

'I could,' she said. 'I would. Only this isn't the first time it's happened. As I once mentioned.'

'I hadn't forgotten.'

She forced a smile. 'Yes—well, I'm beginning to feel as if I have two heads.'

'Not from this angle. And, as I think I also once mentioned, maybe you should consider your innocence a bonus rather than a burden.'

She said in a low voice, 'But it isn't as easy as that. I feel like a total anomaly—a freak in a world where girls, years younger than me, have forgotten more about sex than I'll ever know.'

He contemplated his wine. 'You consider that a good thing?'

'Not particularly. Just—the way it is. And for some reason, I'm out of the loop.'

'Maybe that isn't a bad place to be,' he said. 'There are far worse, believe me. And now I think it's time you went to bed.'

She stared at him, a few feet away from her in the lamplight, taking in the incisive lines of nose, the firmly sculpted mouth and the cool brilliance of his eyes. Allowing the imprint of the long, lean body with its broad shoulders and narrow hips to burn into her mind. Really—looking at him in a way she hadn't done before, as a thought was born. And became a resolve.

She said in a voice she didn't recognise, 'Will you come with me?'

His head lifted sharply and for a moment he was utterly still, looking back at her in silence.

Then he got to his feet, walked across and took the glass from her hand. He said quite gently, 'You've probably had more than enough to drink. So I'll pretend you didn't say that.'

She stared up at him. 'Mark, I'm not drunk. Not on two glasses of wine over the entire evening, for heaven's sake. I'm just someone who's sick of being thought of—dismissed as a child. And I'm asking…you to help me become a woman.'

'Offering yourself to the nearest man is hardly a sign of maturity,' he returned curtly. 'And, anyway, what you ask is impossible.'

'Because of your "same roof—separate lives" ruling?' As he turned away, she caught at his hand, halting him. 'But that needn't change because…because of anything that happens tonight. It will begin and end here, and afterwards things will go back to exactly the way they were between us. I swear it.'

She swallowed. 'I just want to lose my virginity, not embark on any kind of relationship.'

'Dear God, Tallie, that's exactly what you should want,' he said harshly, releasing his fingers from her clasp. 'Just be patient. Things may not have worked out with Justin for some reason, but you'll meet someone else—someone you'll fall in love with, and you'll be glad you…waited for him.'

'But if and when I meet this man, it has to be on equal terms,' she said vehemently. 'No hang-ups or feelings of inadequacy because I'm embarking on unknown territory.'

'Unknown?' he repeated. 'How can it possibly be that, when films and television make it graphically clear what goes on? But if you're still in any doubt, buy a good sex manual.'

'I don't mean—the mechanics of it, but how it relates to me. How I'm going to feel while it's happening. For all I know, I could be frigid.'

'Doubtful,' he said. 'In the extreme.'

'But I need to be sure.' She took a gulp of wine and set down the glass. 'Also there's far more chance of it being…good with him—the man I love—once the…the first time has been dealt with. You must see that.'

He'd resumed his seat opposite. 'I'm not sure that I do.'

She bit her lip. 'Well, I know—at least I've been told—that sex is usually pretty much of a disaster to begin with—painful, messy and even downright embarrassing. So I'd like…all that to be over and done with before I really…make love with someone who actually matters to me.'

'Ah,' he said. 'And just how have I come to feature in this unappealing scenario?'

She lifted her chin. 'Because you owe me,' she said bluntly. 'You said so.'

'Yes,' he said slowly. 'But this is not the kind of recompense I had in mind.'

'And also because we…we don't care about each other,' she went on. 'You said that too—that we have nothing going for us but an uneasy truce. So it won't actually matter if it turns out to be…' She hesitated.

'A catastrophe of epic proportions,' he suggested.

She gave him a suspicious glance. 'Are you laughing at me?'

'No,' he said. 'I've never been further from amusement in my life.' He got up and walked to the window, pulling back the curtain to stare into the darkness. 'You're making me see myself in a whole new light, sweetheart,' he tossed back over his shoulder. 'The unfeeling bastard who walks away, leaving innocent girls crushed and bleeding.'

'I never thought that for a minute.' She bit her lip. 'Oh God, I've said this all wrong, haven't I? I just wanted you to know that, if you agreed, I'd have no expectations afterwards—wouldn't make any waves. You'd have nothing to worry about on that score. We'll just…resume the truce, until I can find somewhere else to live and get out of your life for good. Which was always the plan, anyway.'

She paused. 'As for…for the rest of it, I assumed you'd know…what you were doing. That you'd probably try not to hurt me. After all, you've had enough experience…' She stopped with a gasp, realising this remark was hardly felicitous either.

'Women by the cartload,' Mark agreed expressionlessly, his back still turned to her. 'But, unfortunately, it's not Tuesday, which is my usual day for deflowering virgins.'

She said quietly, 'Now you are making fun of me.'

'Yes—no. Hell, I'm not even sure any more.' He swung back to look at her, pushing a hand through his hair. 'For God's sake, Tallie, let's forget this grotesque conversation ever began. You don't know what you're asking.'

'Would it really be such a hardship?' She got to her feet. 'Earlier, you said I was…irresistible. But that's not true, is it, Mark? Because you don't seem to have any problem in resisting me. So why say it, if you didn't mean it?'

'Because at the time I wasn't fighting some latent sense of decency, damn you.' His voice was harsh, goaded. 'But perhaps I should give up the battle.' He paused. 'Turn round—slowly.'

Bewildered, she obeyed him, her skirt brushing against her legs as she performed a complete circle. Aware, as she did so, of a faint, disturbing smile playing round his mouth as he watched her.

He said softly, 'Now, take off your clothes and do that again—even more slowly. Just to refresh my memory.'

She stared back at him, her lips parting in shock, and saw his smile widen.

'Losing your nerve, sweetheart?' he gibed. 'Wondering if you really want to be naked in front of me again? Especially when you know this time I'm going to do a damned sight more than just look.'

Tallie swallowed. She said, 'If it's…what you want…' And fumbled for the zip at the back of her dress.

'No,' he said sharply, halting her. 'It isn't—merely a final attempt to bring you to your senses, which doesn't appear to be working. Therefore…'

He walked over to her, pushing a tumbled strand of hair back from her face, his thumb lingering almost ruefully on her cheek-bone before tracing the curve of her face and the line of her jaw.

It was the lightest of touches but somehow it seemed to burn through flesh and bone and down into the very core of her, and Tallie found herself swallowing back a gasp.

He said quietly, 'This is a new situation for me, so maybe you should just go along to your room and I'll join you there presently. When I've had a chance to think a little.'

She nodded. Tried to smile. Failed. And slipped away—to wait.

And waiting, she realised, as she sat rigidly on the edge of the bed, might well turn out to be the worst part of it all. This tense anticipation of the moment when the door would open and he would come to her. When she would finally...know, and be known.

Because, hopefully—mercifully—*that* would probably be over quite quickly.

In the meantime, the uncertainty was getting to her. What should she do? Undress—lie down on the bed? Like some maiden sacrifice on a pagan altar, she thought, crushing down the bubble of appalled hysteria rising in her throat.

Only it wasn't like that at all. Just a calculated, clinical solution to a problem. Or would be, when it happened.

She got up and began to pace restlessly round the room, rearranging things on the dressing table. Closing the lid of the laptop. Picking up the clean skirt draped over the back of the chair and hanging it in the wardrobe.

Somehow it was essential to have the room totally neat and tidy, she thought, even if she herself was in turmoil.

She stared at the door. Oh, where was he? Why was he taking so long? Or had she simply misheard him? Did he want her to go to his room instead? Perhaps that was it.

Well, there was only one way to find out.

She walked quietly up the passage, past the silent office, the deserted sitting room and the darkened kitchen. His door was ajar and she knocked quietly at first, then more firmly.

'Mark.' She swallowed. 'Mark, are you there?'

But the room was empty, the bed unruffled. No shower running in the adjoining bathroom either.

In fact, no sound in the entire flat. She looked around, feeling suddenly very cold as she realised that he'd gone. That he'd walked away, leaving her quite alone.

Realised, too, as pain gripped her, that this was the worst re-

jection of them all, because it was one that she'd brought entirely
on herself. And that, somehow, she would have to deal with the
shame of that as well.

If I can, she thought, without breaking into a thousand pieces.
And turned away.

CHAPTER NINE

THE shoes she'd discarded earlier were still on the sitting room floor. Tallie picked them up and sank down on the sofa, gripping them tightly. Pretty shoes, she thought. And a pretty colour. She remembered admiring them as she had dressed that evening. While she'd been getting ready for the important dinner date that she'd thought she would remember always.

And so she would, but not for any of the reasons she'd expected.

And now she'd made everything a hundred times worse by throwing herself at yet another man who didn't want her. At Mark Benedict, of all people in the entire world.

A chance to think. That was what he'd said. And he'd gone away and thought, and obviously decided it was impossible. That he couldn't go through with it.

But why hadn't he told her so? Tallie wondered numbly. Did he really think he was letting her down lightly by—vanishing without even an attempt at explanation?

Yet what could he really have said?

And what on earth could she say, or do, when she saw him again? She'd have to think of something—another salvage job. Maybe she should apologise, be contrite, even a little sheepish as she admitted that the whole thing had been madness. That she was nothing but a child, after all, hell-bent on making a fool of herself. And she was only glad he'd recognised that in time to stop her careering blindly into the mistake of a lifetime.

And, if she was really lucky, he might even believe her.

She shuddered. I'd like to run too, she thought. But where can I go—and at this hour?

The wine he'd taken from her was on the table. She let the shoes fall back on the carpet and reached for the glass instead. She would drink the contents and follow them with whatever was left in the bottle. She hoped wearily that there'd be enough to get her drunk, or at least impose some kind of oblivion so that she would stop hurting so much.

It was the memory of pleading with him, she thought. The searing, scarring knowledge that she'd begged him to take her that somehow made all this so much worse than anything that had gone before.

That was the only explanation for the icy pain that was consuming her. Making her want to bury her face in the cushions and weep.

But she must never let him know it. Never give a sign that his decision had caused her even the slightest pang. It was essential that he should think it was simply guilt and embarrassment that would be keeping her so determinedly out of his way while she stayed under his roof.

And that could not be for much longer, whatever the cost. Because she knew now that the price she would pay if she stayed would be even higher.

In the stillness, the slam of the front door brought her unhappy reverie to an abrupt end. Tallie's hand jerked, spilling a few drops of wine on her dress as she turned in disbelief to see Mark stride into the room.

'Tallie?' He halted, brows lifting sardonically. 'Not cowering under the bedclothes, waiting for me to blight your girlhood? I'm surprised.'

She said, 'I—I thought you'd changed your mind.'

'Far from it,' he said. 'I went to find an all-night chemist.'

'Oh,' she said, biting her lip as light belatedly dawned.

'Oh, indeed,' he echoed with faint mockery. 'Poor Tallie, is safe sex a little too much reality for you?'

'No.' She lifted her chin, a mass of conflicting emotions at war inside her. 'I was hardly expecting romance. I'm not that stupid.'

He came across to her. Removed the glass from her hand again. 'Anaesthetic?' he asked and shook his head. 'You don't want your senses dulled, sweetheart, and I certainly don't. I need you completely awake and totally aware.'

He took her hands and drew her to her feet. 'Now come with me.'

If ever there was a moment to tell him that she'd had second thoughts herself and he was off the hook, it had to be now.

And yet, somehow, she was being led unresistingly by him down the passage to her bedroom and he was shutting the door, closing them in together in the softness of the single bedside lamp.

Tallie stood there, hands at her sides, watching as he removed his jacket, then extracted a packet from his jeans and put it on the night table.

It was all so—practical, even casual, she thought, swallowing, and maybe she should try to be equally matter-of-fact. Especially as he was here by her invitation.

He pulled his sweater over his head and discarded it and, as his hands went to the waistband of his jeans, Tallie turned away, reaching for the zip on her dress, struggling unsuccessfully to tug it down. Telling herself, as she'd done earlier, that undressing in front of him didn't matter because he already knew what she looked like naked. Except now it wouldn't stop at looking. He'd told her so and, now the moment had come, the prospect of what lay ahead of her was drying her mouth and making her fingers clumsy.

'Having problems?'

Too many, and all of my own making. Aloud, she said huskily, 'I—I think there's some material caught in it.'

His voice was quite gentle. 'Come here.'

She went to him slowly, observing with a kind of relief that he was still wearing his jeans. 'I feel so stupid.'

'Why should you?' he asked. 'After all, I shall enjoy undressing you, darling, far more than you seem to be doing.' He added with faint amusement, 'Or do you intend me to share your lack of pleasure in what's about to happen? If so, I can guarantee you'll be disappointed, because I plan to savour every minute.'

She tried to think of something to say, some clever answer, but her mind seemed suddenly blank and it was easier to stand in silence under his hands.

Deftly, he released the scrap of fabric and undid the zip to its full extent. Then he slipped the dress from her shoulders, allowing it to slide easily down her body to the floor.

Tallie waited, head bent, during the endless pause as he looked at her, clad in nothing but those two pretty scraps of broderie anglaise. Then he said quietly, 'Just seeing you like this, Tallie, makes it all worthwhile.'

And, taking her rigid body in his arms, he kissed her.

His mouth was warm as it moved on hers, and gentle in a way she had not anticipated.

After all, he'd not set out to seduce her. Apart from that first hideous encounter in his shower, he'd never by word or gesture indicated even a fleeting desire for her. And while there'd been brief moments that approached understanding between them, there'd been no tenderness.

He didn't want to be here in any real sense, so she'd expected him to demand rather than ask, and to take rather than seek, wasting no time on any kind of wooing.

And that was fine, she told herself, because she, too, wanted the entire process over and done with quickly, her body and her bed all her own again. Their uneasy truce restored.

Which was why she found the deliberate restraint of this first caress faintly disturbing. But if he was playing some private waiting game, hoping for a response, he could think again, because it wasn't going to happen.

So she stood passive in his embrace, her lips unyielding to his delicate pressure.

He was holding her lightly too, his fingertips merely brushing her skin as they stroked its cool and silken texture and began an initial exploration of the planes and curves of her slenderness. Making her aware of an unwelcome answering quiver along her nerve-endings that she had never experienced before. A confusing reaction which made her heart pound unevenly and set her suddenly racing towards panic.

She pulled away from him. She said huskily, 'You don't have to treat me as if I'm made of glass. I—I know why we're here.'

He looked at her for a long moment, the green eyes narrowing. 'You prefer the more direct approach. Fine.' He picked her up and threw her across the bed, following her down and kneeling over her. He unzipped his jeans with one hand, then hooked two fingers into the fragile band of Tallie's briefs with unmistakable and deliberate purpose.

'No.' Her hands lifted, pushing at him frantically, her voice hoarse. 'You can't—not like this—oh, God, please…'

'I could,' he returned grimly. 'And I'd enjoy it and persuade you to do the same—under the right circumstances. But not, I admit, for your first time.'

He lifted himself away from her, lying beside her in silence. Eventually he sighed and turned back to her, his hand sliding under the soft fall of her hair to cup the nape of her neck, his touch sending another immediate *frisson* rippling down her spine.

He said quietly, 'Tallie—you told me you wanted this.'

'I did.' She didn't look at him as her breathing quickened. 'I do. It's just…'

'Then please accept that we're batting on the same side here, and try to trust me.' He paused. 'Now, I'm going to finish undressing and get into bed. If you really intend to continue, I suggest you do the same.'

He swung himself to the edge of the bed, turning his back to her, while Tallie wriggled to the opposite edge and sat there for a moment, trying to steady herself.

And recover my nerve as well, she thought wryly. Up to now, I've behaved like a complete idiot, and it would serve me right if he'd walked out on me. But he seems prepared to stay if I—I…

Behind her, she was aware of movement, the soft creak of the mattress. And his voice saying, 'I'm waiting.'

She allowed herself no more hesitation. After all, she was here for a purpose which was about to be fulfilled, so she simply unhooked her bra, dropping it to the floor, then sent her briefs to follow it before she slid hurriedly under the covers, lying on her back, her arms at her sides and staring up at the ceiling.

Mark propped himself on an elbow, looking down at her. He said, a ghost of laughter in his voice, 'I get an overwhelming impression of teeth being gritted. I know it's what made England great, but it doesn't work quite so well in bed.'

He added more gently, 'And, in spite of anything I've said, Tallie, if you decide at any time that you want me to stop, you only have to tell me.' He paused. 'From my personal point of view, I'd prefer it to be sooner rather than later. And definitely well before the point of no return. I don't want to ache for a week.'

She said in a low voice, 'I—I won't ask you to stop. You're being very patient with me. I know that and I'm—grateful.'

'I can be more patient than you've ever dreamed,' he told her quietly. 'And I'm hoping for a damned sight more than gratitude.'

He smoothed her hair back from her face. 'Now, stop fighting me, my sweet, and start listening to what your body's already begun to tell you. Will you do that?'

'I'll—try. I really will—Mark.' She pronounced his name carefully, as turned towards him, lifting a hand, shyly, tentatively to rest on his bare shoulder, feeling the muscles flex under her hesitant touch.

And as he bent towards her, she raised her mouth to his.

This time his kiss was harder, as he explored the softness of her mouth, then probed more intimately, the silken invasion of his tongue allowing him to taste all the inner honeyed sweetness that he sought, and draw from her a first diffident response.

With a murmur of satisfaction against her lips, he gathered her closer, so that her body touched all the warm, lean nakedness of his, her breasts grazed by the roughness of his chest hair, his hands splayed across her back.

When at last he raised his head, they were both breathless. Mark glanced down to where the concealing sheet had fallen away, baring her rose-tipped breasts to his gaze.

He said softly, 'Exquisite.'

She flushed, turning her head away. 'They're too small.' Her voice was husky.

'No,' he said. 'They're utterly adorable. Because I can do this.' He cupped one soft mound in his palm, stroking the nipple gently with his thumb, watching as it puckered and hardened into throbbing life. 'And also this,' he added softly, taking the pink, aching peak between his lips and teasing it with his tongue.

Sensation pierced her, a glancing pleasure shockingly akin to pain, as it arrowed its path through bone and blood to the secret centre of her womanhood, and Tallie heard herself make a small bewildered sound that was almost a moan.

His mouth returned to hers, lingering there, while his fingers continued their delicate erotic teasing of her breasts, arousing them to an intensity of need that was almost anguish.

Tallie found she was reaching for him in turn, her hands gliding over his shoulders, learning the strong line of his throat, and the hollows at its base. Pressing her palms against the flat male nipples and feeling the vibrant power of his heartbeat. Aware too of the potent male hardness pressing against her thighs, and not knowing whether to be scared or exultant over this undeniable proof that he wanted her.

He was questing further now as he caressed her, taking all the time in the world and making her whole body tremble under the subtle play of his lean hands. And where his fingers touched, his lips followed, delineating the blue tracery of veins in wrists and arms, and the delicate structure of collar-bone and ribcage, then marking the indentation of her slim waist and the slight concavity of her belly. Whispering soft words of pleasure against her skin.

There were tiny sparks dancing behind her closed eyelids. He'd told her to listen to her body, she thought, her mind reeling, and it was telling her with shocking, almost terrifying frankness how much she already—incredibly—wanted him in return.

And when he turned her in his arms so that his mouth could trail tiny kisses down the length of her spine, her body arched in shivering, gasping delight, mutely, blindly seeking more, her breasts swelling into his hands, the nipples aroused to acute tumescence by his touch.

He let his hands move down, gliding over her flanks and the swell of her buttocks, stroking them rhythmically, almost soothingly, except that it was arousal he was offering, not assurance, and her body was already in tumult, her bewildered senses fainting.

Because this was not the soulless learning procedure she'd bargained for and might have dealt with—not this sweating, sticky ferment of sensation, where she was lost, drowning in feelings she hadn't realised could exist. Scared by the sheer force of her own needs.

Mark drew her back against him, his lips caressing the side of her throat, one hand moving to pleasure the taut mounds of her breasts, while the other began a leisurely traverse of her stomach, skimming the hollow of her pelvis to reach, with tantalising slowness, her slender thighs, and linger there, fondling their pliant softness, before sweeping his fingers from her knee to the curve of her hip and back again.

Building on the insidious torment he'd already created, forcing her to writhe in his arms with urgent, impotent need, because he was touching her everywhere but *there*—those soft, hidden places where, to her shame, she most craved him. Where she was burning for him, melting for him, her breath sobbing from her throat as she whispered his name.

At last, just when she thought she would have to beg, his hand moved, cupping the silken triangle at the joining of her thighs for one heart-stopping moment, then drifting inwards, brushing like gossamer over her secret flesh and the tiny sensitive bud it concealed and pausing there to coax it erect, before gliding onwards to let his fingers penetrate the molten core of her with one sure and gentle thrust.

She said, 'Oh, God,' her voice choking, almost extinguished, as she felt her body flood with delight and she lifted herself against him not merely accepting what he'd done, but inciting him deliberately to deepen his exploration of her most intimate being.

Realising at the same time that his thumb had rediscovered that small nub of damp, heated, responsive flesh and was skilfully continuing its arousal, stroking it with a delicate, yet sensual mastery that made it difficult for her to breathe. Driving her, urging her far into that dark and unknown place that she'd feared.

Because Tallie was aware of a feeling growing inside her that transcended excitement, an inexorable spiral of intensity threatening her last remnants of control, and she was close to panic because what was happening to her now was already too much and she couldn't bear any more. Couldn't...

She tried to say, Stop—please stop...but the only sound emerging from the tightness of her throat was a small frantic moan that spelled desire, not protest.

And then it was altogether too late, because she was caught, swept irresistibly away on a rising tide of sensation that was almost an agony. Finding herself lifted to some pinnacle, then flung from it, crying out as her straining, panting body convulsed in spasm after spasm of helpless, exquisite pleasure, before she was sent spinning, back down to a reality that had changed for ever.

And as she lay, limp, wrung out, the only immobile element in a still trembling universe, she became aware that Mark was moving her, placing her gently back against the pillows.

Opening dazed eyes, she found him beside her, leaning on one elbow and watching her—just as he had been, she thought, when it all began, minutes, hours, aeons ago.

She said in a shadow of a voice, 'I thought I was going to die.'

'Yet here you are, alive and incredibly well.' His hand stroked her cheek, then moved lightly down the line of her throat to mould the curve of her shoulder and rest there. 'Maybe your scare-mongering friends should have extended their terms of reference—mentioned the amazing power of the orgasm.'

She said shakily, 'Perhaps they didn't know.'

'That might well be true.' He sounded faintly amused. 'Which puts you ahead on points, my sweet, and definitely not frigid.'

A sudden wave of shyness swept over her. She tried to think of something appropriate to say. In the end, all she could manage was a feeble, 'Thank you.'

He was grinning openly now. 'Happy to have been of service, ma'am.' He paused. 'But it's not all over yet. As you must have realised.'

'Yes—yes, of course.' How could she not, she thought, swallowing, when he was lying close to her, naked, the evidence impossible to ignore? And it seemed they were back to matter-of-fact again. Well, that was fine with her. She said, aiming for casual, 'I—I'm perfectly willing.'

Mark shook his head. 'I don't think so,' he said. 'Not at this precise moment, but soon. And I can wait.'

She could have asked what he meant, but she suspected she already knew because she could feel her skin warming, beginning to tingle under the hand quietly smoothing her shoulder.

Oh, God, she thought, shaken, as realisation dawned. This can't be true. It just isn't happening to me, not again. He can't make me feel like this so soon. It's wrong…

He said softly, 'You're gritting your teeth again, Tallie.' And, drawing her back into his arms, he kissed her. For a moment she tried to resist, but the warm, sensuous movement of his mouth on hers was altogether too shamefully enticing and instead her lips parted, sighing her surrender.

Immediately, his kiss deepened, turning gentleness into passionate, almost ruthless demand, and she twined her arms round his neck, answering him with all her new-found ardour, pressing her body against his in open invitation, and he groaned softly as his hands found her eager breasts, caressing the swollen peaks to throbbing glory.

At last he tore his mouth from hers with open reluctance, moving out of her embrace, and Tallie murmured in breathless protest, reaching for him again.

'Yes, darling.' His own voice was husky, ragged. 'But first I have to take care of you.'

She waited, her body melting for him, longing for his return in a way that left no room for pretence or embarrassment at the realities of desire. And she looked up at him, her eyes widening endlessly, as he moved over her, covering her with his body. He entered her slowly, his gaze searching her face for any sign of discomfort or dissent as, with infinite care, he sheathed the hard strength of his manhood in her yielding woman's flesh.

And for an instant she braced herself, expecting to be hurt, but it didn't happen. Instead of the pain or difficulty she'd believed would be inevitable, however willing she might be, there was only acceptance—and a sense of completion, as if she'd been created for this moment—and this man.

She lifted her hands almost languidly to his shoulders and gripped them, a smile wavering on her lips as she answered the unspoken question in his eyes. He bent his head in silent acknowledgement, then began to move unhurriedly inside her, his long, even thrusts, Tallie soon realised, tempered with deliberate restraint.

She murmured, her breath catching, 'Mark, I told you before—I'm not made of glass, so I don't think you need to be...so patient...any longer.'

He said hoarsely, 'Tallie, I could hurt you.'

'You won't.'

'You don't know...'

'Then show me,' she whispered and, obeying an instinct she hardly understood, she raised her legs, and clasped them round his hips, locking herself to him. 'Show me.'

Mark groaned softly, fiercely, his rhythm altering with stark immediacy, his hard body driving powerfully into hers with a new imperative, and she clung to him, gasping, carried away by its sheer sensual force and the intense sensations it was already beginning to engender within her.

She began to move with him, learning the cadences of his passion and matching each stroke. Eagerly echoing the raw physical ebb and flow of their bodies' union. Striving to reach the coil of pleasure deep inside her and feel it gloriously unwind. Knowing it was there, but finding it strangely elusive.

She heard his breathing change and realised the momentum of his lovemaking had changed too, becoming faster, and threatening to leave her behind.

But, in the next instant, his hand slipped down between them to the joining of her thighs, finding her, touching her there— *there*—the caress of a fingertip enough to bring her, suddenly and fiercely, to sobbing, frenzied rapture.

And, at the very apex of her delight, she heard him call out harshly as he reached his own climax.

Afterwards, she lay wrapped in his arms, his head pillowed on her breasts, her body still glowing in the aftermath of consummation, and thought wonderingly—I'm a woman. Mark's woman.

Except that wasn't true, she reminded herself with a sudden pang, and she could not pretend otherwise. Because he'd simply done what she'd asked, no more, and now it was over.

And, almost as if he'd read her mind, he lifted himself carefully away from her and, without a word, left the bed, and then the room.

Tallie turned on her side, feeling desolation twist in the pit of her stomach. She put up a hand to touch her mouth, still tender from his kisses, then her throat tightened uncontrollably and she felt the first slow tears trickle down her face. And with a little sob she buried her face in the pillow.

The first inkling she had of his return was his hand on her shoulder, turning her towards him.

'Tallie?' He looked at her damp face and sighed as he rejoined her in bed, taking her swiftly in his arms. 'Oh, God, I did hurt you after all. I was afraid of that.' His voice was remorseful.

'No—no, you didn't.' Her head was against his chest, and his hand was stroking her tangled hair. 'I'm just being—stupid.'

'And probably in a state of shock too,' he said dryly. He was silent for a moment, then added quietly, 'Now, I think we should both try and get some sleep.'

Sleep? Tallie thought. How was that possible with her body, her mind and her emotions in such turmoil? And yet there was something ineffably soothing about his hand on her hair, and the steady beat of his heart under her cheek. And maybe she might rest—just a little—if she closed her eyes, and let herself drift on this warm, tideless sea of contentment…

When Tallie awoke there was daylight coming through the curtains. She lay for a moment, luxuriating in the feeling of well-being that was permeating her entire being, then turned, smiling, to look at him sleeping.

Only the bed beside her was empty, the pillows straightened and the covers tidy, as if she'd spent the entire night alone instead of in his arms.

And as if those unforgettable moments in paradise had never occurred. Were simply a waking dream. Except her body was telling her a very different story.

She slid her feet to the floor and fumbled her way into her robe.

Maybe he was just being considerate, she thought. Perhaps he'd decided his presence in her bed might prove an embarrassment in the cold light of day. That she might be regretting her recklessness of the previous night.

If so, she would soon set his mind at rest, she thought, and laughed softly to herself.

It was still early, she reasoned, so a visit to his room could bring its own rewards. And there was only one way to find out.

But he wasn't in his room. He was in the kitchen, fully dressed in dark suit, silk shirt and tie as he glanced though the newspaper.

'Good morning.' His voice was polite. No more. There was no hidden laughter there, or any shared knowledge in the cool green eyes that met hers. 'There's fresh coffee in the pot if you'd like some.'

She tried to think of something to say, but her mind was numb. She was icy-cold too, aware of an overwhelming need to wrap her robe ever more tightly round her, not simply for warmth on this sunlit morning, but to hide herself, just as if there was still one inch of her that he hadn't touched and kissed.

He picked up his briefcase and walked towards the door, and she felt herself shrink against the frame to avoid contact with him.

He added crisply, 'I'm off to Brussels. I shall probably be away for two to three days.'

She couldn't speak, couldn't find one rational word to say, so she nodded instead.

As he passed her, sending her—oh, God—a brief, impersonal smile, she could smell the faint aroma of his cologne and the warm, clean scent of his skin. The familiar essence of him that she'd breathed last night. Now—suddenly alien.

And, in spite of this, to her shame, Tallie found her body clenching in renewed desire.

As the front door closed behind him, she let herself slide down until she was sitting, huddled on the floor.

The floor where she knew she would have given herself to him again, if he'd shown any such inclination.

Only that wasn't the deal, she thought, staring blindly ahead of her. No part of the bargain she'd made with him.

What she had left—what she had to live with—was the resumption of their truce. Because that was what she'd promised him—that afterwards there'd be no expectations—no demands, so he was making absolutely sure that those terms were strictly adhered to.

Same roof—separate lives, she thought, just as before. His point made and thoroughly underlined a few moments ago. And nothing that had happened between them during that wild and beautiful night was ever going to make the slightest difference.

We were having sex, she thought, not making love, and I was a fool if I thought otherwise, even for a second.

And it was wonderful sex, because he wouldn't allow it to be anything less—not after those awful things I said to him. He was angry, and he had something to prove. Nothing else.

And I—I not only asked for it, I made it so easy for him, it was almost a bad joke.

Only I can't laugh about it. Because I'm angry too—with myself.

It would have been far better, she told herself bitterly, if he'd stayed away the first time he'd left her, reminding her of their agreement, and what she could expect. But he'd come back and held her while she'd slept, and somehow that was the cruellest thing of all.

She got to her feet and trailed to the bathroom, turning on the shower and standing under it, drenched and drowning, as she washed away any lingering traces of her abysmal folly and the subsequent humiliation that she so richly deserved.

Some of the water on her face was salt from the tears she couldn't control, but they were the last ones she would shed. She'd made a fool of herself, and worse than a fool, over Mark Benedict, but it was all over now.

And she had his absence of two—three days—to pull herself together. So that when he returned, he would find the positive avoidance of the last weeks re-established. She would be civil if they were forced to speak, and silent if they were not. Because pride alone demanded that she show him she could keep her word—and her distance.

As it had been, so it would be. Until the day she would thankfully go, and never have to see him again.

And if he insisted on intruding on her thoughts, she would deal with that too and also find some way of assuaging the quite ludicrous sense of hurt at this self-inflicted wound that was gnawing away at her.

I need to hate him, she thought slowly as she stepped out of the shower, wrapping her towel around her. And I think—in fact, I'm certain—I know exactly how I can achieve that.

And I may even find it a pleasure.

CHAPTER TEN

TALLIE stood watching the sheets of paper emerge from the printer, aware that she was shaking a little.

Because she'd finished it at last—the charged, ugly scene where the terrified and weeping Mariana was ruthlessly raped by Hugo Cantrell in revenge for losing the money he'd left with her. It was powerful stuff, probably the most dramatic piece of writing she'd achieved so far, pouring into it all her own pain, bitterness and disillusion about her night with Mark, and the total humiliation of its aftermath.

Although what they'd done together wasn't rape by any stretch of the imagination and she couldn't—wouldn't—pretend it was for an instant. On the contrary, she thought, wincing, she'd committed the ultimate act of lunacy in surrendering to him willingly, joyously, followed by the ultimate in self-deception—the brief and fatal hope that their encounter might mean something to him too.

Yet, at the same time, there'd been that telling moment when she'd been lying on the bed where Mark had thrown her, totally at his mercy, and she'd been scared. So she'd taken the feelings that had assailed her then and built on them, imagining the anger she'd sensed in him driving him on to some irrevocable and unforgivable conclusion.

Except it was Hugo, of course, who stripped the clothes from the frightened, struggling girl beneath him and took her with a cold brutality that spared her nothing, and left her shattered and alone.

Hugo, whom she'd made in Mark's image, originally as a joke. But which had suddenly become a far more serious issue.

At first, she'd been half-tempted to delete the whole thing, shocked at the anger and passion that screamed from her words. But then she reminded herself defiantly that she'd chosen quite deliberately to do this. To allow her story to give the pain inside her some sort of focus, and show Hugo Cantrell as the cruel and soulless creature he really was.

And she'd used him to some effect, although, as an exercise, she wasn't sure it had really made her feel any better. But while she wrote, she managed to provide herself with a mental barricade against unwelcome reality.

Because Mark Benedict was no loathsome fictional invention but a living, breathing man who would shortly be coming back into her life.

A man who had done exactly as she'd asked, and accepted her absurd assurances at their face value. And who'd promised nothing in return. A fact she could not escape.

But how could she possibly have foreseen how her night in his arms would make her feel—how her perspective would alter?

Yet she could not in reality blame him for that. It was entirely her own fault and, if she was angry, then she knew exactly where her rage should be directed.

The hurt and sense of loss were a different issue. And their intensity bewildered her. Even frightened her. And made her wonder how she would react when she saw Mark again.

He'd been away for over three days already and she told herself the longer his absence, the better, because it gave her more time to recover, and prepare herself to match his own indifference.

Brave words in daylight, but the nights were another story altogether.

Following his departure, she'd gone straight back to her room, stripped the bed completely and remade it, rigorously banishing every trace of him. At least that had been the intention. But, as she soon discovered, she could not remake her mind and her memory or erase the new hunger in her awakened flesh.

She woke constantly in the darkness from restless, tormented dreams, reaching out to him, yearning for him, her lips eager for the taste of his skin, her hands recalling the dynamic of every bone and muscle in his lean, hard body. Only to find herself solitary and the bed beside her a wasteland.

But she should not—could not—allow herself to feel like that.

During the past twenty-four hours, she'd been particularly on tenterhooks, expecting at any moment to hear the front door open and his incisive step coming down the hall.

Especially, she acknowledged dryly, as, on practical terms, she was in his study, using his printer without permission.

But how could she ask someone who wasn't there? And, anyway, he'd be unlikely to object, she reminded herself. Because anything that would help her to finish the book and remove herself from his space would be fine with him.

Perhaps he was staying away so long because he half-expected her to break her word and confront him with the embarrassment of some girlish, emotional scene.

But that was a trap she would avoid at all costs.

Tallie turned away from the steady swish of the printer and looked around her. The room was no longer in the same pristine state as when she'd arrived. Even its atmosphere seemed to have changed, imbued with that restless energy that was so much a part of him.

The long table at one side of the room was littered with paperwork, as files and reports jostled for space with blueprints. While pinned to the wall above was a detailed map of the Buleza area, including the Ubilisi River.

It seemed he really intended to go back there, in spite of the increased risk from the new regime, Tallie thought, biting her lip. But he was his own man, with his own life, and if he wished to endanger himself it was no concern of hers. Nor could she allow it to become so.

When the printer was finally silent, she read through the final section, wincing a little, then added it to the folder with the rest of her completed pages. She'd written about two thirds of the book now, and for the first time she wasn't altogether certain of the direction it should take. Or not after the trauma of that last scene, anyway.

So the time had clearly come for the professional second opinion on the work in progress that Alice Morgan had offered.

'Yes, do let me see it,' had been her encouraging response to Tallie's tentative phone call earlier that day. 'You'll bring it round? Well, I shan't be here later, so leave it with my assistant and I'll read it as soon as I can.'

Which is going to be like waiting for sentence to be pronounced, Tallie thought as she fitted the folder into a padded envelope and added a covering note before setting off to the agency's office in Soho.

Her mission there was soon accomplished. The assistant, not much older than herself, said, 'Oh, yes, Miss Paget,' as if she was known and valued, instead of a floundering beginner, Tallie thought with amusement as she handed over the precious package. But it was gratifying just the same.

She didn't rush back to the flat afterwards, but went for a walk instead, lingering in front of shop windows and pausing to study the posters outside theatres, imagining a time when she might not have to count every penny.

Besides, now that she'd handed over the manuscript, she felt slightly bereft, she thought wryly. But until she heard from Mrs Morgan and was able to discuss with her the shape the book's ending should take, there was little she could do.

She stopped to read the menu outside an Italian restaurant but it only served to remind her that she was getting hungry, and it was time to return to Albion House and make herself some lunch.

She was just about to walk in the main entrance when a voice behind her said, 'Tallie, I thought—I hoped—it was you.'

She swung round, her eyes widening. 'Justin?' She forced a smile. 'What a surprise.'

'Not a horrible one, I hope.' His voice was rueful. 'I do realise

I may be the last person you want to see, but I think we need to talk. And I've brought lunch.' He held up a bag. 'A couple of chicken wraps. So may I come up to the flat?'

As she hesitated he added swiftly, 'Please, Tallie. Because you must be wondering about my weird behaviour the other night.'

'No,' she said hastily. 'Really. I—I quite understand.'

'You do? Did Mark explain?'

'No,' she said, wretchedly aware that her face was flaming. 'No, he didn't. It—wasn't necessary.' *But because of it I've done a crazy thing that I'll probably regret for the rest of my life.*

He sighed. 'I suppose you saw my reaction to Clive and guessed the rest.'

'Yes,' she said. 'Something like that.' *And I do not need to be having this conversation.*

'But not all of it,' he said. 'And that's what I need to tell you.' He paused. 'So will you listen?'

'Yes, I suppose so.' Her agreement was openly reluctant and she heard him sigh faintly as he followed her into the lift.

They sat in the kitchen to eat and, to her astonishment, she found she'd demolished every crumb of her wrap. Then she filled two mugs with fresh coffee from the percolator and sat down to listen, her face guarded.

At last, Justin said slowly, 'Firstly, I have to tell you that if I'd had the least idea Clive might be at Pierre Martin, we'd have gone somewhere else, but I didn't even know he was back in Britain.'

'Maybe you should also tell me why he seems to matter so much.'

'He was going to be my brother-in-law,' Justin said after a pause, his voice bitter. 'I was engaged to his sister Katrin, officially engaged with the diamond solitaire and a potential wedding date. We'd met six months before at a party, and she was the most beautiful thing I'd ever seen. She knocked me out, and when she agreed to marry me I told myself I didn't deserve to be so happy.

'I'd encountered Clive a few times, and not liked him much, but I told myself I was marrying Katrin not her relatives and, as they spent nearly all their time on a yacht in the Caribbean, they wouldn't be around to trouble us a great deal anyway.

'Her father I hadn't met at all up to then, but it wasn't a problem. I only had to convince him that I loved Katrin and was able to support her financially. Done deal. Or so I thought.'

He swallowed some coffee. 'I was fairly surprised to get a summons to Miami for our first meeting, but I'd already gathered from Katrin that Daddy was a high-powered fellow with his own way of doing things, so I didn't let it faze me.

'But I was disappointed that Katrin wasn't coming with me. She told me it was going to be man-talk, and that she'd be superfluous.

'So I flew to Miami and met Oliver Nelson at one of those vast luxury hotels. He seemed friendly enough, but I could tell he was sizing me up. Later, over dinner in his suite, he told me he was in the market for more than a son-in-law. That he wanted a business associate, and with my background in banking and accountancy I'd be ideal.'

He shook his head wearily. 'And then he told me what he wanted. Oh, he dressed it up a little, but it was money-laundering and we both knew it.'

He paused. 'So I told him—no, and I didn't dress it up at all. I also said I'd bring the wedding forward and make sure that Katrin saw as little as possible of him in the future.

'He—smiled. Who did I think, he asked, had suggested me in the first place?'

'No.' Shocked, Tallie put her hand on his. 'He couldn't have meant it.'

'Oh, but he did. And Katrin admitted it when I confronted her on my return. And what was so wrong anyway? she wanted to know. Wouldn't I like to be fabulously rich instead of just—well-paid?

'She said I was being offered an amazing opportunity, and she found my attitude—disappointing. And, by implication, I was disappointing too.

'When I was stupid enough to mention that our own plans seemed pretty wonderful to me, she looked at me without smiling and told me that, unless I did the deal with her father, we had no future. And, later that night, she moved out.'

Tallie swallowed. 'Justin—I'm so sorry. This is—unbelievable.'

'I thought so too, until I found out she'd taken the next plane to Miami, joining Daddy for a cruise on *Golden Aurora*. I realised then she'd meant every word.'

He looked at her. Smiled with an effort. 'That…was nearly a year ago. I've been working ever since at getting my life back together. I thought I was succeeding. And that meeting you—liking you, as well as fancying you rotten—was a major step towards full recovery.'

She said huskily, 'Justin, you don't have to say that…'

'Yes, I do.' His voice was urgent. 'Because it's the truth. God, Tallie, you must have known I had plans for that night. A new beginning with a bright lovely lady.'

She too forced a smile. 'Not just your See If I Care girl?'

'God, no,' he said. 'Far from it. In fact, I was so confident I was cured I even took you to Pierre Martin.'

'Of course,' she said slowly. 'You were with Katrin at its opening, weren't you, so it was a kind of test for yourself.'

He nodded. 'And everything was fine—wonderful—until Clive came up to the table. I thought I could deal with him, but it was his mention of a family party that did the damage, opened up the wound again. I had this overwhelming feeling that if I looked across the room, I'd see Katrin there.'

He looked ahead of him, his face blank. 'Of course, I knew it was bound to happen eventually. That, one day, we'd run into each other, but I truly believed that, by then, I'd be able to handle it.

'Only I suddenly realised I was fooling myself. That I didn't dare look across the room because I wasn't over Katrin at all. Because she was still there in my heart, and my bones. And I was scared, Tallie. Terrified I'd walk over to that table and agree to do any damned crooked thing her father wanted if I could just— *just*—have her back again.'

'And that's why you wanted to leave?' Tallie asked faintly. 'Not because of the other things he said?'

'By this point I wasn't really listening to the poisonous little bastard,' he admitted moodily. 'I just knew I needed to get out of there before I did something monumentally stupid and wrecked the rest of my life.'

She didn't look at him. 'I wish you'd told me at the time what was going on.' *Oh, God, if only—if only you had…*

'I should have done. I suppose I was too confused, and ashamed too. And that's why I came round today—to set things straight, if possible. And ask you to forgive me.'

'Of course I do.' She managed to speak lightly, crushing down the incipient hysteria that was bubbling inside her. 'Apart from anything else, I had a terrific meal, and there were no bones actually broken.' She held out her hand. 'So—friends?'

'I'd really like that.' He didn't release her fingers immediately. 'Tallie, I want you to know that if things were different…'

'Yes.' She freed herself gently. 'You're a lovely guy, Justin, and I know that in time you'll be ready to be happy again. With us, it was just too soon.'

I must have sensed that, she thought, as she came back after seeing him to the door. *And that was why I felt so uncertain about the prospect of sleeping with him. Because there couldn't have been any other reason.*

She went into the sitting room and dropped limply on to the sofa, sinking her teeth into her lower lip until she tasted blood. Wanting it to hurt.

How wrong, she asked herself numbly, was it possible for someone to be? She'd only been concerned with Clive's crude jibes about her age. But Justin, sinking back into the misery of the past, hadn't even heard them, and wouldn't have cared if he had.

But she'd jumped to conclusions and, in the process, had totally and fatally misunderstood the situation.

As Mark, of course, had suspected, even without hearing the full story from her. Because, of course, she'd never mentioned Clive. Which had been a mistake of the first magnitude.

Because, if I had, she thought. *If only I had—then he'd have* explained it all to me. Made me see that it was Justin's problem and had nothing to do with me. Would have told me that I must stop being paranoid about my age and lack of experience, sending me off comforted. I know he would. But I never gave him the chance.

Instead, I—I...

She gave a little choked cry, wrapping her arms tightly round her shaking body.

One of these days, she thought with anguish, Justin will tell his friend Mark all about that evening at Pierre Martin, and how Clive's intervention ruined everything. After all, why wouldn't he?

And Mark will think I simply invented everything I told him in order to get laid. A touch of illicit excitement to make up for my disappointing evening.

So now I don't just feel stupid. Because I've had sex with him under false pretences, and now, just thinking of the way he's going to look at me, I feel...dirty too.

And I just pray I'm long gone before that has a chance to happen.

She went slowly along to the bathroom, ran herself a hot tub and soaked in it for nearly an hour, wishing the soothing warmth could dispel the chill inside her.

Once dry, she wrapped herself in her dressing gown and lay down on top of the bed, her mind turning in endless circles without reaching any kind of resolution as regret, shame and every other negative emotion she could name went to war within her.

And this time she couldn't even hope for an uneasy truce, she thought with a pang.

She just had to hope that Mrs Morgan liked the book enough to show it to a publisher, and maybe get her some money up-front. Not a great deal, naturally, but enough to get her out of Albion House before Mark learned the truth.

Because if he thought badly of her already, his contempt would reach stratospheric levels after he'd talked to Justin.

And what could she say in her own defence?

But why do you need to defend yourself, argued a small voice in her head, when he's the Owner, the bastard, and the inspiration for Hugo Cantrell? What can his good opinion possibly matter?

I can't explain, she thought wearily, closing her eyes and turning on her side with a sigh. Not even to myself. I only know that it does matter—terribly. And I wish I knew why.

Tallie woke with a start, realising she must have dozed off, but assuring herself quickly that, if so, it could only have been for a few minutes. But the light in the room seemed to have changed quite fundamentally, and when she looked at her little clock she was startled to see that the supposed minutes were actually hours.

She sat up, listening intently. It was quiet everywhere, but even so she knew instinctively that she was no longer alone in the flat. That, at some point, Mark had returned.

And would, somehow, have to be faced.

Well, she told herself, swallowing, as she lifted herself off the bed, there's no time like the present.

But not in her robe, she amended quickly. That was what she'd been almost wearing the morning he'd left, and she didn't want to remind him of it.

She pulled on clean jeans and a sleeveless top, then, bracing herself, went to find him.

He was in the sitting room, stretched back on the sofa, a glass of whisky in his hand and a file of papers open but disregarded on the table in front of him, his brooding gaze fixed on space.

And then, becoming aware of her hesitating in the doorway, he rose coolly and formally to his feet.

'Hello.' Tallie came forward. 'I didn't hear you come in.'

'I've been back for some time. I'm glad I didn't disturb you.' His voice was expressionless, but she sensed a tautness about his tall figure, as if he'd also been dreading this first encounter.

Keep it friendly, she adjured herself. Keep it normal. Don't sound awkward or embarrassed. Above all, don't sound hopeful.

'I wasn't working,' she said. 'Actually, I was having a rest. I've done quite a lot to my book since you've been away.'

Now why had she told him that? she demanded silently and restively. Did she want him to recommend her for a Queen's Award
for Industry?

He made no response, just stood watching her, the green eyes
faintly narrowed.

She found his scrutiny disconcerting and hurried into speech
again. 'So perhaps you'll soon have your flat to yourself once
more.' Adding brightly, 'How was Brussels?'

'Much as usual,' he said. 'As far as I could judge between
meetings.'

'So we've both had a busy time.' God, she thought, I sound like
one of those talking dolls. Pull a string for today's cliché.

She waved a hand towards the file. 'And you're trying to work
now, so I won't disturb you any longer.'

As he seated himself, his mouth seemed to twist in a faintly
sardonic quirk. As if, it seemed to be saying, you could possibly
disturb me on any level.

At the door, driven by some death wish, she paused again.
'Have you eaten?'

'I'm going out later.' His tone was crisp, warning her that she
was straying on to forbidden ground. That food offers were still
not part of the deal. Or friendly overtures, for that matter.

'Of course,' she said. *Of course, Sonia would be waiting.
And, if not her, then someone else. Always someone else for the
commitment-phobe.*

She was about to add, See you later, but refrained, reminding herself how unlikely it was that he'd be spending the night
in his own bed.

Or in hers.

The thought came from nowhere, and with it a shaft of pain so
swift and so deep that she almost cried out, needing all her self-
command to take her out of the room, and out of his sight.

She made it back to her bedroom on unsteady legs, leaning
against the closed door as she fought to calm her uneven heartbeat.

She said aloud in a voice that shook, 'Oh, God, what's happening to me? And how am I ever going to bear it?'

The summons from Alice Morgan came a week later. After what Tallie had mentally categorised as seven days from hell.

Since Mark's return, the tension between them had become almost tangible, exacerbated by his decision to work at home most days. In fact, the only respite had been provided by the visits of the cleaning lady, Mrs Medland, a cheerful, down-to-earth body, and the exact opposite of the dragon Kit had described.

At least Tallie had the odd friendly remark to look forward to when she was around, and it was like balm to the soul when Mark was barely acknowledging her presence.

It wouldn't be so bad, she thought, if she was still able to work on her book, but, for the time being, she was in limbo and, although she'd read and re-read her own copy of the manuscript every day, she still hadn't come up with any firm idea about how Mariana would deal with the terrifying trauma of her ordeal, or how she could take her story to a satisfactory conclusion after what had happened.

She tried to get out of the flat as much as possible, exploring London by long, rambling bus rides and going for lengthy walks. And in the evenings she spent much of her time in the breezy, crowded chaos of Lorna's flat in Hallmount Road, playing silly card games, listening to music, drinking cheap wine and talking about every subject under the sun, except her personal affairs.

But her carefree mood had usually dissipated by the time she got back to the flat, knowing that she would find it deserted and Mark gone for the night, leaving her to imagine in searing bitter detail who he was with and what they were doing.

Although it might not be Sonia's bed he was sharing, as Penny had ebulliently announced in another of her unexpected flying visits. 'Rumour has it that he cooled it a while ago, and she's peeved,' she'd said, her eyes dancing. 'Let's pray it's true and that he's found someone marginally human this time.'

Tallie could manage nothing more than a constrained smile in reply.

She was nervous about Mrs Morgan's verdict on her book, but at least it would give her mind a much-needed change of focus, she thought as she walked into the agency office.

Alice Morgan greeted her with a pleasant smile and an offer of coffee, which she gratefully accepted.

'Firstly,' the older woman began, 'let me say I'm excited about the way you've tackled this. There are a few places that could be tightened, but you seem to have a real grip on the story, and the action scenes you handle well. I was relaxing and thoroughly enjoying myself, then—whoosh, suddenly the whole thing careered off the rails into disaster.'

She shook her head. 'Tallie, my dear, I don't want to impose any modern political correctness on a story taking place two hundred years ago, but even so you *cannot* allow the hero to rape the heroine.'

Tallie stared at her. 'But he doesn't.'

Alice Morgan's brows lifted and she thumbed through the manuscript lying in front of her. 'Well, I don't know what else you call it, when a man ties a girl's hands together and forces himself on her repeatedly. When he hurts and degrades her in a way that, frankly, made my hair stand on end.'

'Yes, but it's Hugo Cantrell who rapes Mariana,' Tallie said with a touch of desperation. 'Because he isn't the hero—he's the villain.'

'The villain?' Mrs Morgan's voice was incredulous. She cast herself back in her chair. 'Oh, but he can't possibly be. He's absolutely gorgeous—to die for—and Mariana's clearly more than half in love with him already.

'No, he's clearly the hero, and has been ever since he rode up and caught her under the waterfall. You could have done rather more with that scene, by the way.'

She favoured Tallie with a long look. 'Promise me you're not still clinging to the idea of Mariana ending up with William the Wimp.'

'He's not like that,' Tallie said defensively. 'I—I realise I've neglected him rather, and he hasn't featured much in the story so far, but I can work on that. He has to be the hero. Mariana's loved him since childhood, and she's come all that way to find him.'

'She has indeed come a long way,' Mrs Morgan agreed. 'On a journey of self-discovery, no less. And, in the process, she realises where her heart truly belongs.'

She rolled her eyes to the ceiling. 'My dear girl, I can't believe you didn't realise this was happening. But I suppose the sub-conscious can play strange tricks.' She smiled. 'I won't ask what private fantasy inspired you to invent Hugo, but I'm very impressed.

'And, by the way you portrayed him, I thought you'd fallen pretty heavily in love with him yourself.'

'On the contrary,' Tallie said very clearly. 'I think he's absolutely vile.'

'Well, very few of your potential readers will agree with you there,' Mrs Morgan said briskly. 'And, whether you intended it or not, Hugo's taken centre stage in the book, and you have to leave him there.

'Besides,' she added practically, 'if he's genuinely so evil, why did he bother to save Mariana at the inn, when he could have got through the window himself and escaped? It makes no sense. Unless you want me to believe he was simply keeping her safe so he could rape her himself, which is nonsense.'

'But he's not just a rapist,' Tallie protested urgently. 'He's a traitor and a deserter, and he's going to murder someone, and be hanged for it.'

'I've no real objection to Hugo killing someone, if it's in the defence of the girl he loves.' Mrs Morgan tapped a finger thoughtfully against her teeth. 'Besides, the victim could be an Afrancesado—one of the Spanish who collaborated with Napoleon's troops, as could the men he cheated at the inn.

'As for him being away from the army, you could make him one of Wellington's exploring officers—military spies who infiltrated behind enemy lines for information on French plans. My brother's a military historian and he says it was highly dangerous work and they took the most appalling risks. The real stuff of heroes.'

She looked at Tallie and frowned. 'My dear, you look absolutely stricken. You've gone quite white. Are you ill?'

'No,' Tallie said hoarsely. 'Just—thinking.'

'And worried, I suppose, that you'll have to rewrite the whole thing?' Mrs Morgan's tone was understanding. 'A pretty daunting prospect, I agree, but I promise it's not necessary. Naturally, you'll need to change the emphasis in a few places, signalling Mariana's growing attraction to Hugo. No need to hold back on that any more.'

She paused thoughtfully. 'And, of course, the rape must go. But you can always replace it with a very different kind of love scene. Why not make it a seduction—with Mariana's full co-operation?'

She smiled at Tallie. 'I do realise it's not the story you set out to write originally, but it's going to work brilliantly.' She handed her a sheet of paper. 'I've made a note of some of my suggestions for you to work with. You don't have to go along with them all, but Hugo, I have to tell you, is not a variable. He has to be your hero.'

She rose. 'So I'll have the old script shredded and look forward to receiving the revised version. And if you have any problems, I'm on the other end of the phone. Good luck.'

Outside in the street, Tallie stood for a moment, dazedly gulping the thick, fume-laden air.

Mark and Hugo, she thought. Hugo and Mark. One fact, one fiction, who'd somehow become a single entity. Someone she'd wanted to dislike, had fought to hate, when every instinct had told her the opposite, as she'd travelled on her own unwitting journey of self-discovery. While she had battled to stifle the truth.

I thought you'd fallen pretty heavily in love with him yourself...

And so I did, she thought, as she began to walk slowly and aimlessly, struggling to come to terms with this hopeless, anguished self-revelation. So I always did—right from the start, when Tallie in the shower became Mariana under the waterfall, and found I was writing about feelings and desires that were totally alien to me, and that had to be denied.

But why didn't I realise they were happening to me?

Or have I've been lying to myself all along? And especially—that night…

Because I know now that I didn't simply want a lover, she told herself bleakly. I wanted *him*. Wanted him to belong to me and think only of me, even if it was just for a few short hours.

Because I believed that I could somehow make that enough. But I was wrong—so very wrong.

Pain twisted inside her as she remembered, too late, a favourite saying of her father's: 'Take what you want. Take it, then pay for it.'

So, I took, she thought, achingly. And now I shall end up paying in loneliness and unhappiness for the rest of my life.

CHAPTER ELEVEN

TALLIE delayed her return to the flat for as long as possible, knowing it would be harder than ever to face Mark now she'd been forced to confront the reality of her own emotions, and the pain this had engendered.

But at least she had the barrier of work to shelter behind once more, she thought as she made her way to the library and found a quiet corner where she read and re-read Alice Morgan's notes, her heart sinking. Re-creating Hugo as Mariana's beloved instead of her enemy wouldn't be that difficult, she thought wistfully. All she had to do was jettison the deliberate denial she'd been practising throughout the story so far, and write what was in her heart.

But providing the requisite happy ending for the lovers was a different situation altogether, because she'd be attempting to fulfil a dream that she knew was impossible. And she would need all the emotional strength she possessed, knowing that, with every word, she would be pressing down on the agony of an open wound.

Especially when the moment came for Hugo to look into his lady's eyes and say, 'I love you.'

But she would deal with that when she had to, she told herself with resolution. For now, she would look through the stock of books on the Peninsular war for references to exploring officers and their adventures. Concentrate on the practical stuff.

She stayed in the library until it closed, by which time her notebook was half-full of useful material, and Hugo's transformation didn't seem quite such a daunting prospect.

He would be faced with the terrible dilemma of trying to protect the girl he was growing to love without jeopardising the secret mission entrusted to him by Wellington.

While Mariana, of course, would be struggling to maintain her loyalty to the fading vision of William, and fighting her shameful attraction to a man she still believed to be totally unworthy.

Thinking it over, now that the first shock had worn off a little, Tallie had to admit that Mrs Morgan was quite right and the story would undoubtedly work much better like this. And, from now on, she told herself with determination, she would put out of her mind the reasons why Hugo had come to be invented and treat the whole thing as the pure fiction it always should have been.

As she waited to cross the road to Albion House, she saw Mark come out of the main entrance. He was walking with his head bent and, even from a distance, Tallie could see his expression was preoccupied, almost brooding.

She stood feasting her eyes on him, secure in the knowledge that she was unobserved. And realising, as she did so, that there was a kind of freedom in not having to pretend dislike or indifference any more. Except, of course, when he was standing in front of her, when the charade would have to be maintained. Even intensified.

She watched him hail a cab and drive away, trying hard not to speculate about his destination. But failing. Jealousy, she thought sadly, was one of the most negative emotions, but sometimes it was inevitable.

Because no one was fireproof and one day Mark would fall in love. Indeed, it could even be happening right now, and perhaps that was why he'd seemed so deep in thought—because he'd suddenly realised that 'commitment' was no longer a dirty word in his vocabulary. And maybe he too was struggling to come to terms with his discovery.

But, if this was so, it might be rather easier to bear when she was no longer around to be reminded on a daily basis that he had a life in which she couldn't hope for a part.

I need my independence, she told herself, swallowing. My own place to live, far away from here, and friends who have no connection with this period in my life. A whole new beginning. And, in order to achieve that, I have to stop confusing my emotional life with the necessity of earning my living, and offer Alice Morgan a book that she can sell.

So why don't I stop this futile hankering after a man I can't have, and get down to some work instead?

And squaring her shoulders, she crossed the road and went up to the flat.

By the time she fell into bed that night, Tallie could feel quietly satisfied with her evening's output, although making the required changes was not going to be an easy process and she still had a long and tortuous way to go. But she'd deleted all reference to the rape scene and felt oddly cleansed as a result.

After all, Mark had not asked her to fall in love with him, so it was wrong to denigrate him so appallingly in order to feel better about herself. Especially as it hadn't worked, anyway.

And she could use her own experience and emotions more usefully to illustrate Mariana's confusion of mind.

Although she was tired, sleep did not come easily. Instead, Tallie found she was dozing restlessly in fits and starts and around one a.m. she gave up the battle and lay wide awake, staring into the darkness.

Which would not do at all, considering the amount of work waiting for her. Maybe a milky drink would help, she thought, sighing.

She slid out of bed and put on her robe. As she opened her door and peeped into the passage, she realised that the kitchen light was on.

But maybe she'd forgotten to turn it off after she'd made herself the late toasted cheese snack, which might be to blame for her insomnia.

At the door, she halted, stunned by the sight of Mark, also in his robe, turning from the fridge with a carton of milk in his hand. And, before she could beat a hasty and silent retreat, he'd seen her too.

'Tallie.' He paused, frowning. 'Is something wrong?'

'No.' She moved forward hesitantly. 'I...I couldn't sleep, that's all.'

His mouth tightened. 'Nor could I.' He poured the milk into a pan waiting on the hob. 'I thought I'd have some chocolate. Do you want any?'

'Oh,' she said. Then, 'Yes—thank you.' She reached into the cupboard and took down the tin, but, when she held it out to him, he indicated silently that she should place it on the work surface and turned away to get the mugs.

My God, Tallie thought, her throat tightening, he doesn't want me anywhere near him. Not even to touch his hand in passing. And I cannot—must not—let him see that it matters—or if I've even noticed.

When all I want to do is run away and weep.

Instead, she went to the table and sat down, arranging the skirts of her robe decorously round her.

She said, making her voice casual, 'I didn't think you'd be here.'

'I'm catching an early plane.' His voice was clipped. 'I needed to pack.'

'Yes,' she said. 'Of course.' She paused. 'Is it going to be a long trip?'

'Possibly,' he returned. 'It's difficult to tell at this stage.' He poured the milk into the mugs and added the chocolate. 'But you know how to contact the lawyers if there's any problem.'

Suddenly her alarm bells were ringing as Tallie stared at him. She said quietly, 'It's the bridge, isn't it? In spite of everything, you're really going back to Buleza.'

'I never pretended otherwise.' He put her chocolate on the table in front of her and returned to lean against one of the fitted units. He added harshly, 'And you have no Veronica to impress this time, so you can drop the white-knuckled fears for my safety.'

She said huskily, 'I'm not even allowed to ask why you're de-liberately putting yourself in danger?'

'It's not your concern,' Mark returned brusquely. 'But, for the record, there's nothing wrong with my sense of self-preservation. And the risk is minimal, or I wouldn't be going.'

He seemed to read the question in her eyes, and sighed impatiently. 'The new regime in Buleza is trying to make friends and influence people in the outside world, and they're not managing it particularly well. So, they'd have nothing to gain and a hell of a lot to lose by harming me, or any other foreign visitor. And, at the first sign of trouble, I shall be gone by the route we used last time.'

He put his mug down and left the room to return almost at once with the map she'd seen on his office wall, which he spread on the table in front of her.

'Buleza is frighteningly poor,' he said. 'And the people in the north are the worst off, because they're separated from what are laughingly thought of as the more affluent parts of the country by this—' he stabbed the map with a finger '—the treacherous and unpleasant Ubilisi River, which, as you can see, practically bisects the place. The bridge we were trying to build was no solution to their problems, but it was a first step.

'I need to see if anything can be salvaged from the original project, and if the new Democratic People's Republic wish to improve life for their northern compatriots by authorising the building of a replacement.'

He folded the map. 'I suspect I know the answer already, but I have to try.'

He paused, then added more gently, 'Now do you understand?'

'No.' Tallie got to her feet. 'But, as you've pointed out, it's hardly essential that I should.' She picked up the mug. 'I think I'll take this to my room and leave you in peace.'

'A curious choice of word,' he said. His smile grazed her. 'But probably a wise decision.' He looked her up and down, his mouth twisting cynically. 'Unless, of course, you were thinking of sending me off to my potential doom with a beautiful memory. And that's not very likely.'

'Not likely at all,' she agreed, keeping her voice bright. 'So—goodnight, and…good luck.' And went.

The chocolate was smooth and creamy, but it tasted as bitter as gall, and Tallie only managed a couple of mouthfuls. She could only think of Mark and the journey he was about to make.

He'd made comparative light of the risk involved, but she couldn't do so.

One of the broadsheets had profiled the new Bulezan president, and it had made grim reading. He'd had himself elected for life, and was dealing ruthlessly with anyone he saw as an enemy, apparently determined to rule by fear. And Mark had been rescued before by people he'd see as his opponents.

She lay on top of the bed, staring into space, her mind caught on a weary treadmill of love, loneliness and fear.

With Mark's departure went any immediate danger that she might betray herself to him, but that could be no comfort. Not any more. Because if the worst happened, she knew she would regret for the rest of her life that she hadn't been brave enough to confess to him her true feelings, chancing his mockery or his indifference. Enduring them if she had to.

And, as the sky began to turn light behind the curtains, she heard him walking quietly down the hall and knew what she had to do.

She was across the room in a flash, dragging open the door. At the sound he turned, his leather travel bag slung across one shoulder, his briefcase in his other hand. His surprise was evident.

He said tautly, 'I didn't mean to disturb you. I'm sorry.'

'You didn't,' she said. 'I was waiting.'

'Why? To say goodbye?' Mark's brows lifted. 'I thought we'd covered that already.'

'No, not—goodbye. That's too final. To ask you to take care, because if you...don't come back...if I never see you again, I won't be able to bear it.'

She saw the incredulity in his face and hurried on. 'And I'm sorry if that isn't what you wanted to hear, or if I've embarrassed you, and made you angry because I've broken our agreement.

'I...I just needed to tell you...to let you know how I feel, that's all, and now I've done so, it doesn't have to matter any more.'

She added huskily into the continuing silence, 'And I won't talk about it ever again, if that's what you want.'

'What I want?' The harsh query seemed torn from him. 'God almighty, Tallie, you pick your moments. All this wasted time—all those hellish lonely nights, and not one word—one sign until now—when I have to go and catch a bloody plane.'

He flung the travel bag and briefcase to the floor and came to her, pulling her roughly into his arms, his hands parting her robe to find the warm nakedness beneath it as he kissed her.

He was not gentle and she responded deliriously in turn, pressing herself against him, her arms locking round his neck as she gloried in the stark hunger that drove him, her body surging to his touch.

When he raised his head, they were both breathless.

He looked down at her, touching a rueful fingertip to the reddened and faintly swollen contours of her mouth.

He said, his voice unsteady, 'When I return, Natalie Paget, you and I are due for a very serious conversation.'

'Don't go.' She reached up to him, offering her eager lips, and he groaned softly as he kissed her again, his hand tangling in her hair, his mouth sliding down to the racing pulse at the base of her throat.

'I must, darling, and you know it.' He detached himself with open reluctance. Took her hand, touching her palm to his mouth. 'But sleep in my bed while I'm away—please,' he whispered against the soft flesh.

Then he stepped backwards, away from her, and walked across the hall to pick up his belongings.

At the door he turned. 'And I am coming back,' he told her, his sudden smile glinting in his eyes. 'So make sure you're here, and waiting for me.'

'Yes.' Her voice was a breath. 'I promise.'

After he'd gone, Tallie stood for a long time, staring at the closed door, feeling the blood sing in her veins, at the same time as the faint but potent ache of unsatisfied desire began to uncurl inside her.

But I can live with that, she thought, now that I have so much to hope for. When Mark comes back.

And, smiling in her turn, she went down the hall to his room. Discarding her robe, she slid under the covers of the big bed, then, turning her face into the pillow his cheek had touched, she fell deeply and dreamlessly asleep.

It wasn't always that simple, of course. There were nights when she couldn't shake off her anxieties entirely and lay for hours staring into the bleak darkness that his distance from her imposed.

By day, work came to her rescue. The astonished realisation and candid acknowledgement of her real feelings for him seemed to have opened some creative valve in her mind, allowing the words to pour out of her.

And it was surprisingly easy, she found, as the time following Mark's departure lengthened inevitably into weeks, to transpose her own emotions on to Mariana, burdening her with the frantic knowledge that Hugo, now her lover in every sense, was apart from her only because he was still deliberately endangering himself in Lord Wellington's service.

But, on the lighter side, there was also William, the book's erstwhile hero, to be dealt with. So, when Mariana eventually achieved her objective by reaching the British cantonments, Tallie enjoyed making him priggishly stuffy, and shocked to stiff-backed silence by what he regarded as the sheer and unforgivable impropriety of her quest. A totally unworthy object of her affection.

Unlike Hugo, who loved his wayward girl for what she was, rather than some dimly perceived pattern of feminine respectability.

And Tallie had worked out the book's ending too, forcing Hugo to face a firing squad at the demand of Wellington's Spanish allies for having murdered one of their number, a dashing young officer and sprig of the nobility whom he'd discovered was secretly in the pay of Bonaparte.

Which meant putting Mariana through the agony of witnessing Hugo facing his executioners, head high, his eyes unbound, before falling under the rattle of fire.

Except that none of the musket balls reached him, because the powder that dispatched them had been mixed with other less lethal substances at Wellington's order.

Something Mariana only learned when, listless and numbed by shock and grief, she entered the inn at Lisbon where she would stay before returning to England, and found Hugo waiting to go home with her, his work in the Peninsula over and done.

And Tallie was smiling through her tears as she sent them into each other's arms for the last time.

But she would have to wait for her own happy ending, it seemed, because Mark would not be returning any time soon.

The new President, it seemed, was graciously willing to meet him, but strictly in his own good time, as being measured for a wardrobe of new and splendid uniforms of his own design was taking precedence over everything else.

Or so she gathered down the crackling and echoing lines that suggested he was phoning from another planet. Because of this, their conversations were usually fairly abbreviated, and hardly romantic, but Tallie hadn't expected him to call at all, and so the regular sound of his voice, however brief and distorted, made her brim with shy delight. Especially as he tended to ring her late at night, as if deliberately waiting for a time when he knew she would be curled up in his bed.

But perhaps that was simply her imagination running riot, she thought wryly, and if so she needed to haul it back into line because it was needed for other purposes.

Alice Morgan had given the revised manuscript a brisk and unqualified commendation and announced she would be sending it out at once to selected publishers. Then, while Tallie had still been basking in the glow of that, she'd completely floored her by asking what her next book would be about.

'Because whoever buys it will want to know before offering you a contract,' she said. 'And almost certainly they'll be looking for another romantic adventure. So start thinking, my dear, and fast.'

Tallie had done precisely that, and had come up with a glimmer of an idea about a girl who takes to robbing stage coaches in order to clear her brother's name of some still amorphous wrongdoing, and finds herself facing a far more formidable adversary than the vagaries of British justice in the notorious highwayman Captain Moonlight.

She'd been to the library one afternoon to research crime and the underworld in the eighteenth century, and returned to the flat just as Mrs Medland was preparing to leave.

'You've a visitor, Miss Paget,' she said in an undertone, jerking her head significantly towards the sitting room. 'I told her no one was home, but she said she'd wait. Wouldn't take no for an answer either.'

Penny, was Tallie's immediate thought as she deposited her bag of books by the hall table. But, if it was, then Mrs Medland would surely have said. And Lorna, the other likely candidate, would still be at work.

Even so, she wasn't prepared to find Sonia Randall sprawled on the sofa, her hard eyes fixed on the doorway.

'So,' she said, 'if it isn't the budding authoress at last. Although that isn't quite accurate any more. Because I hear on the grapevine that you've bloomed—that your book is finished and starting to do the rounds. You must be very pleased with yourself.'

Tallie came forward warily. 'Good afternoon, Miss Randall,' she said, forcing politeness. 'I—I'm afraid Mark's still away.'

'Yes,' the other woman said. 'Playing the Good Samaritan in Africa again. But actually it was you I came to see.'

'Oh.' Tallie's heart sank like a stone. 'Then may I offer you some coffee—or tea, perhaps?'

'The perfect hostess.' Sonia's tone bit. 'And I'd have thought milk and water would be more appropriate—coming from you. However, I now realise one never can tell.'

Tallie lifted her chin. She said clearly, 'I don't know why you're here, Miss Randall, but I don't have to put up with your rudeness. Kindly see yourself out.'

As she turned, Sonia's voice halted her imperatively. 'I think you'd better sit down and listen, my girl. This is business, not social, and I have a lot more to say. I promise you're not going to like any of it.'

Tallie came back slowly and sat on the edge of the sofa opposite. She said coldly, 'If you're telling me Alder House isn't going to make me an offer, that's hardly a surprise. You made it clear you wouldn't be interested, and I informed Mrs Morgan accordingly.'

'I have no commercial interest in your scribblings, certainly, but I admit to being slightly curious—especially when we seem to share so much in other ways.'

The jibe was hardly unexpected, but Tallie winced inwardly all the same. She made her tone dismissive. 'I hardly think so.'

'Oh, don't be coy. I had a look round while the cleaning woman was busy in the kitchen, and I noticed that the spare room is now just an office. I also saw there were things of yours in Mark's room.'

Tallie moved restively. Much as she disliked the other woman, she realised that she must be hurting too. 'I—I'm sorry.'

Sonia shrugged. 'Why? It's no surprise. It was perfectly obvious at the dinner party from hell that he was planning to bed you. Unless, of course, his mate Justin managed to get there first, but Mark enjoys a challenge, and my money was on him.'

Tallie stared at her. 'You mean—you don't care?'

'What is there to care about? Mark likes variety in his bedmates—I've always known that—and you must have been a real novelty.' She added softly, 'But although I also know he likes to play rough at times, the fact that you appear to share his taste really has surprised me.' She laughed. 'I'd have said you were much too prim for those games.'

Tallie suddenly felt cold. 'I don't know what you're talking about.'

'Then let me refresh your memory.' Sonia reached into the large suede bag at her feet and extracted a bulky file which she placed on the table between them. 'After all, it's here in black and white. Or should I say in vivid, glorious detail. Tell me something.' She lowered her voice intimately. 'Was it Mark's idea to tie you up, or yours?'

Tallie stared at the file in horrified recognition. It was her original manuscript, she thought, nausea rising within her, complete with that dreadful rape scene—the one Alice Morgan had promised to shred. Yet—somehow—here it was.

She said hoarsely, 'Where did you get that?'

'From your agent's office. I had it collected by messenger. Apparently it was the very last copy, and I read it with total fascination, especially the final chapter. Does Mark actually know that his more unusual sexual proclivities are going to appear in print, or are you planning to surprise him?'

'But it's fiction,' Tallie said wildly. 'I—I invented it. All of it. Everything.'

'Not quite everything, my dear,' Sonia drawled. 'Your description of the Cantrell character is Mark to the life, including those very distinctive scars. Certainly no fiction there, so why shouldn't the rest be true?'

Tallie tried to steady her voice. 'Because you of all people should know that it isn't. That Mark never...' She drew a breath. 'That he wouldn't—*couldn't*...'

Sonia leaned back, smiling. 'I only know he didn't with me. But then he didn't see me as a victim. Maybe that makes a difference.'

Tallie said quietly, 'You're vile. Utterly beneath contempt.'

'And you're Snow White, I suppose.' The older woman's tone grated. 'Except she never found herself in court facing an action for libel.'

Tallie gasped. 'What are you talking about?'

'About Mark's reaction when this garbage—' she pointed at the folder '—is made public.'

'But it never will be,' Tallie said desperately. 'I rewrote the whole thing and it's completely different. Hugo Cantrell has become the hero. That...episode has gone.'

'Gone?' Sonia echoed. 'When I've read it, and other people can too? I hardly think so.'

'But no one else is going to read it,' Tallie argued. 'This is the only copy.'

Sonia shook her head slowly. 'It was, perhaps. But not any longer, because I can think of a couple of seriously downmarket tabloids who'd love to get some dirt at last on the great Mark Benedict.'

'On Mark?' Tallie queried in bewilderment. 'But why should they care about him?'

Sonia looked at her for a long moment, then began to laugh. 'Why, Natalie Paget, I do believe Mark's been holding out on you. I admit this run-down pad isn't the kind of environment you expect for someone who's a millionaire several times over, but it belonged to his mother and he feels sentimental about it. God knows why.'

She shrugged. 'He doesn't make a fuss about his money, of course. Likes to see himself as a co-worker in all those companies of his, and not just the boss. And, in his way, he's quite a philanthropist, although he invariably denies it because he loathes publicity.

'He refused point-blank to do any "millionaire hero" interviews after he got his men out of Buleza, and wasn't terribly polite about it, according to a friend of mine who's been looking to get her own back.

'So imagine how he'll feel when he finds himself the centre of a sordid sex scandal—featuring as the incredibly rich man who raped his cook, the innocent virgin he took off the streets. And how she got her revenge by detailing her ordeal in a cheap bodice-ripper.'

'But there isn't a word of truth in it,' Tallie said stonily. 'And I shall say so.'

Sonia laughed again. 'Oh, you've said too much already, my child.' She leaned forward, tapping the manuscript with a crimson nail. 'And it's all here. And even if Mark can get the all-powerful lawyers he employs to stop the papers printing the story, the word will still get around—my friend will see to that—and the damage will be done.

'Because some people will actually believe it, some will always wonder, and some will laugh. And I wonder which reaction Mark will hate the most?' Her smile lapped at the cream. 'But, more importantly, what's he going to say to you, little Miss Paget, and what will he do? You've invaded his precious privacy, dented his reputation and made him look ridiculous, which is something he'll never forgive. And if you think otherwise, you don't know him. And it won't matter a damn what you're prepared to do with him in bed.

'So, he may well decide to teach you a lesson through the courts. I hope your family has money, because the damages could be substantial.

'And as Mark won't want to feature as either hero or villain in your adolescent ramblings, he'll probably get an injunction to stop you publishing the other version too.

'Not that you'll find a market anyway,' she added. 'Publishers cringe at the word "libel" and your precious agent won't be too pleased to know that the ludicrous Hugo is based on a real life model.'

She gave a contented sigh. 'So, my dear Natalie, I'd say your little romance is dead in the water, and your writing career is toast. What do you think?'

CHAPTER TWELVE

'YOU want to withdraw the manuscript?' Alice Morgan repeated, her tone and expression aghast. 'But my dear child, why?'

Tallie looked down at her hands, twisted together in the lap of her cream skirt. She'd been reluctant to wear the outfit Mark had bought her, but she'd forced herself to put it on because it was important to be dressed properly for this crucial interview. To look as if she was actually in charge of her own life, and not the pathetic loser she knew herself to be.

'It's just the decision I've reached,' she said in a low voice. 'I've realised I don't want to make writing my career after all, so there won't be another book, and I can hardly offer the first one under false pretences.'

'But you were so eager,' Mrs Morgan said unhappily. 'And you have real talent too. It's turned out to be a splendidly rip-roaring read.' She paused. 'Are you sure you're not just suffering a sense of anticlimax now that the book's finished? Or worrying, perhaps, in case no one wants it? Because you're quite wrong about that, I assure you. I have two editors interested already, and a third is telephoning me this afternoon. It may even go to auction.'

Tallie suppressed a shudder. 'Then stop it—please. I...I can't let that happen.'

Because she had to live with the possibility that Mark might do exactly as Sonia had suggested, and take some kind of legal action, with the kind of far-reaching consequences that night-mares were made of.

Mrs Morgan sighed. 'I wish you'd tell me what the problem is. Perhaps we could solve it together.'

And I wish I could explain, Tallie thought desolately, but I can't. This is the deal I've been forced to make with Sonia Randall and, for Mark's sake, I have to stick to it. I must do exactly as she says, because anything else—seeing his name dragged through the gutter press—knowing that people are talking—laughing about him—is unthinkable.

I can't bear to think what I've done to him already, or that she knows about it. I could have ruined everything for him, made him an object of ridicule. So, instead, I have to kill off my book completely and get out of his life. Never see him again.

That was what Sonia eventually demanded, and I—I had to agree. I didn't have any other choice.

Not that he'll want anything more to do with me once Sonia shows him that original manuscript with that cruel, horrible scene in it. And she intends to. I couldn't talk her out of it, even though I begged. And he'll hate me for it—*hate me*…

But will he like her any better? She'd certainly seemed to think so, Tallie thought, remembering the gloating triumph in the older woman's face.

'Mark can be completely ruthless when crossed,' she'd said as she'd prepared to leave. 'And don't think spending a couple of nights in his bed will make him any more merciful when he discovers the truth. He's always been well out of your league, my dear, so find some children of your own age to mix with in future, and be thankful you're getting off so lightly.'

But, thought Tallie, it didn't feel like a fortunate escape. Quite the opposite, in fact.

Through the sudden tightness in her throat, she said, 'I've changed my mind, that's all. Decided to get a real job instead of wasting time indulging my adolescent fantasies.'

She got a shrewd look from the other side of the desk. 'Now

that sounds as if you're quoting someone else's opinion. Is that what it is?'

Tallie forced a smile. 'Or maybe I've discovered what hard work writing is, and realised that it's not for me.'

Mrs Morgan sighed. 'I certainly don't believe that—not when you turned round the book so quickly after our chat. And came up with another idea at once. But clearly you've taken a hell of a knock for some reason.'

She paused. 'However, I urge you not to do anything rash. To set your mind at rest, I'll recall the scripts that I've sent out and put the whole thing on hold for a while. Will that do?'

'Because you think I'll change my mind?' Tallie shook her head. 'I won't. In fact, I'm leaving London altogether. Today.'

And going home to hide. If I tell them I couldn't hack it, they'll accept that and, because they love me, they won't press me about it.

'If I never see you again, I won't be able to bear it.' That's what I told him, and now I'm having to face the stark reality that I've lost him. Face it—and somehow deal with it.

And one day this pain—as if someone has put a hand in my chest and wrenched out my living heart—will begin to get easier.

At least I have to believe that, or I couldn't go on.

Mrs Morgan rose. 'In that case, all I can do is wish you luck.' She clasped Tallie's hand for a moment. 'But I still wish you'd felt able to confide in me, my dear.'

Tallie muttered something incoherent and turned to the door. She couldn't confide in anyone, she thought wretchedly. Not now. Not ever. And knowing that there'd been a real possibility of her book being published only added to her burden of unhappiness. And her sense of failure.

She hadn't even asked why the original version hadn't been shredded as arranged, because she knew. Mrs Morgan's usual assistant was off sick and there was a harassed temp manning the outer office, so it was pointless trying to apportion blame.

Her case, containing everything she possessed, was also in the outer office with her laptop. Before leaving the flat, she'd left money for her share of the bills as she'd always intended. Plus a note that said simply, 'I'm sorry.' Which she hadn't intended, or ever thought would be necessary.

After telephoning her mother to say she was returning, she'd called Hillmount Road and left a message on Lorna's answering machine saying merely that she was going away for a while, and she'd be in touch. Apart from that, she spoke to no one.

Penny might wonder what had happened to her for a time, she thought, but London was a shifting community. People came and went, and were eventually forgotten.

And maybe it was those who left who took their memories with them.

Memories that were already haunting her as she sat on the train, staring at the fleeing countryside with eyes that saw nothing.

I'm sorry...

What exactly was she apologising for when she'd scrawled those two desperate words? she wondered drearily. For breaking her promise to be there when he returned, her body eager— yearning for his hands—his mouth? For re-inventing him as Hugo in a fit of childish resentment? Or for that fatal desire to punish him for hurting her in the icy aftermath of that one glorious night they'd spent together?

The list seemed endless. Not that Mark would care. Not once he'd heard what Sonia had to tell him. She could imagine his face hardening implacably as he crushed the note in his fingers. No man liked to be made a fool of, and powerful wealthy men would hate it most of all.

And she would be easily replaceable.

There would always be willing women to share his bed. Women who would not expect—or hope—for too much from him in return, as she'd been in danger of doing.

And perhaps it was best that it should end now, before she could damage herself even further. Because, as Sonia had pointed out, she was not in his league.

Besides, nothing he'd said in those last passionate moments

before his departure, or in those brief exchanges from Buleza's col-
lapsing phone system indicated anything more than his desire to
make love to her again.

She remembered the last time they'd spoken, only two evenings
ago, when he'd paused before saying goodbye to ask what she was
wearing, and she, stretching languidly against the cool sheets, had
told him, 'Nothing.'

And heard the rueful amusement in his response, 'Oh, God,
another sleepless night.'

And she'd smiled too, cradling the phone against her cheek, as
her own need ran like wildfire through her veins and tingled along
her nerve-endings.

But she doubted whether the thought of her naked in his bed
would keep him awake for too long. Any more than she could
honestly believe in the 'wasted time' or 'hellish lonely nights' that
he'd spoken of. He must have spent them somewhere, she thought
unhappily, and with someone. It might even have been Sonia…

And she was totally naïve to think otherwise.

If only I'd stayed in my room that morning, she whispered
silently. If I'd remained in control of my emotions and let my head
rule my heart, instead of giving way to my longing for him.

But it was too late for this, or any of the vast multitude of
regrets that were eating away at her like acid into metal.

And at least she would spend tonight in her own bed, she
thought, and not lying on the mattress in the spare room, wrapped
in a duvet. And there would be no need to clamp her hands to her
ears in an effort to shut out the sound of the phone ringing and
ringing down the hall in Mark's empty bedroom.

Had he wondered why she didn't reply, and why the answering
machine was switched off? Or had he simply shrugged and turned
away, his mind already switching to other, more immediate problems?

And would it ever occur to him, when he found her gone, that
she hadn't taken his call or let him leave any message because it
was impossible for her to endure the knowledge that she'd be listening to the sound of his voice for the last time?

No, she thought. That aching awareness would be hers alone.

And, like so much else, would have to be kept hidden behind the smiling face she needed to show when her journey ended, and she was home again.

'You've lost weight, darling,' Mrs Paget chided, and Tallie pulled a face.

'You always say that.'

'Because it's always true,' said her mother, adding cheerfully, 'but some decent food will soon have you back in top condition.'

'Like a prize heifer on her way to market,' Tallie teased, and hoped that the forced note in her voice wouldn't be noticed.

'You also need new clothes,' Mrs Paget went on, frowning a little. 'I'll get Dad to give you your birthday cheque early, and we'll go shopping.' She tutted over the meagre display taken from Tallie's case and laid out on her bed. 'There's nothing fit to keep. Not even the charity shop would give you thanks for it—apart from the skirt and top you're wearing, of course, which are lovely—and pricey too, like those gorgeous sandals. How on earth did you manage them?'

'They were on special offer,' Tallie said, and turned away to hide the tell-tale warmth invading her face. 'But I'll keep my working skirts and blouses. I'll need them when I find a job.'

'Well, there's no hurry for that,' Mrs Paget decreed. 'As soon as I saw you get off the train, I noticed your eyes were really peaky.' She shook her head. 'No, you're in need of a good rest, my love, and that's what you're going to have. I never thought London was healthy,' she added dismissively, and departed to make the steak and kidney pie she'd promised for supper.

Oh, God, Tallie thought, sinking wearily down on to the cushioned window-seat. Her attempt at a jaunty façade seemed to be cracking already. But then mothers could make the average eagle seem positively myopic.

But getting herself into full-time employment, and soon, was essential.

I have to keep busy, she thought desperately. Have to do everything possible to stop myself thinking—brooding. Grieving.

And there'd be other problems too. On the drive back from the station, her mother had mentioned over-casually that she'd seen David Ackland's mother in the supermarket earlier.

So I can expect a call from him, no doubt, she decided resignedly. And what possible excuse can I make? Sorry, David, but I've given myself body, heart and soul to a man whose life I nearly destroyed, and whom I'll never see again, is hardly a viable option, with Mum probably not far away, checking discreetly on her attempt at matchmaking.

But I doubt if he'd be prepared to be my See If I Care man either, even if I felt brave enough to consider it.

Sighing, she leaned her forehead against the cool window pane.

'Mark,' she whispered achingly. 'Oh, Mark, why did I have to love you, when it hurts so much to let you go?'

And knew she would never find an answer.

The days dragged past. The weather turned to rain and there was a morning chill in the air that spoke of autumn. In spite of the weather, or maybe because it matched her mood so closely, Tallie spent as much time as possible out of doors, taking the grateful dogs for longer and longer walks.

She was aware that her mother had begun to watch her with puckered brows, and feared that soon there'd be some form of gentle, but searching inquisition about the past months in London.

Naturally the subject of her abortive writing career had been raised—over supper on her first evening—but her parents had seemed to accept her explanation that things simply hadn't worked out.

'Such a pity when that lady agent seemed to think so highly of you,' had been her father's quiet comment. And after that the matter, thankfully, was allowed to drop.

In between helping to make blackberry jelly, pick apples and gather hazelnuts, Tallie tried to infuse some zip into the CV accompanying the job applications she doggedly sent off, but was not surprised when she was not interviewed for any of them. Maybe her lack of enthusiasm was as obvious as a finger mark on wet paint, she surmised wryly.

And maybe she should seriously consider her father's suggestion that she consider her time in London as a gap year and return to some form of higher education.

It was a supremely sensible idea, if only she'd been able to contemplate what shape her future might take, but, at the moment, that was beyond her. She couldn't think further than the next day.

In the meantime, she'd managed to get evening work, waitressing in the local pub which had a popular restaurant, and this had the added advantage of keeping David Ackland's gently persistent phone calls at bay, as well as earning her some money.

She'd been at home for nearly a fortnight when a large cream envelope arrived in the morning post, and Mrs Paget's eyebrows shot up as she examined the flamboyantly engraved card it contained.

'Good God,' she said blankly. 'Your cousin Josie's getting engaged—and to Gareth Hampton, of all people. The one who was always so full of himself when his family lived here. I'd no idea they knew each other. In fact, I was rather afraid you were developing a thing about him yourself at one point.'

'Well, not any more, and everyone's allowed at least one deliberate mistake.' Tallie made herself speak lightly. 'I presume there's going to be a big party?'

'Yes.' Her mother gave the card a last dubious look and put it down. 'And you and Guy are invited to bring your partners.' She brightened. 'Why don't you ask David to go with you? He's such a nice boy, and worth ten of Glamorous Gareth.'

'Or I could simply not go at all,' Tallie suggested, as she got up from the kitchen table. 'Anyway, we'll talk about it later,' she added, as her mother's lips parted in protest. 'It seems to have stopped raining for five minutes so I'll take the dogs out.'

It was an eventful hour, involving the pursuit of real or imaginary rabbits through a muddy copse, an encounter with a neighbour's cat, who simply climbed a tree and sneered at them, and a totally unscheduled dip in the river, before an exasperated Tallie called them sternly to heel and started for home. Upon which, the heavens opened, drenching her to the skin in minutes.

As she opened the back door, the dogs shot past her, skittering through the kitchen, with its seductive scent of home-baking, and down the passage to the front of the house, where she could hear them barking joyfully.

Her mother turned from the stove, looking unusually flurried. 'Tallie, there's someone to see you. He arrived a few minutes ago, so I put him in the sitting room, but it sounds as if Mickey and Finn have found him, so maybe you'd better rescue him while I make some coffee. And ask him if he'd like a hot scone.'

Tallie pushed back her tangle of sodden hair with a resigned hand. David Ackland, no doubt, she thought, missing out on his Saturday morning at the squash club to become the joint victim of a maternal conspiracy. The phone line between here and Myrtle Cottage must have been glowing red hot in the past hour.

Be pleasant but firm, she adjured herself as she walked down the passage. But make it clear that neither of you will be going to Josie's bash.

And then she walked into the sitting room and saw the tall figure standing by the rain-soaked window, the object of the dogs' vociferous welcome. And her mouth dried and the room swam dizzily around her as she realised exactly who was waiting for her.

'Mark.' The name emerged as a croak. 'You.'

'Full marks for observation.'

It was not a promising start. She said quickly, 'I'm glad you're safe. Are—are you going to build your bridge?'

'Not under the present regime. The new president is planning a palace instead, a cross between a brothel and the Taj Mahal.'

'You must be disappointed.' She took a deep breath. 'What...what are you doing here?'

'Looking for you.' His dark face was unsmiling. 'I did say I'd want a serious conversation with you when I came back. If you remember.'

'Yes.' Tallie swallowed. 'But the circumstances have changed since then.'

'I'm well aware of that.' The dogs were still leaping rapturously around him, but he snapped his fingers and they subsided, plumy tails beating the rug with rhythmic pleasure as they gazed up at him.

She heard herself say inanely, 'The dogs have been in the river.'

'You look as if you went with them,' he commented expressionlessly. 'Maybe you should dry your hair and change your clothes before we talk.'

She shook her head. 'If I leave this room, I may not have the courage to come back.' She lifted her chin. 'I'd much rather you said what you came to say—so I know the worst.'

'The worst,' Mark repeated slowly. 'Now, there's an interesting choice of words.'

She stared at the floor. 'I realise how angry you must be, and I accept the blame for that. Totally. And I'm terribly ashamed.'

Her mouth trembled. 'I suppose, for all my denials, I am still a child after all. A stupid, destructive child who takes something precious and smashes it, without realising it's gone for ever. And if I could go back in time and not write those horrible things, I would.

'But I can't, and I suppose you could still sue me for libel, because Sonia read what I wrote, and she's threatening to show other people. But—oh, God, Mark—my parents know nothing about all this. I…couldn't tell them, and if I end up in court, it will nearly kill them. And if there are damages, I won't be able to afford them.'

'Well, I wouldn't worry too much about that,' Mark said calmly. 'I believe a husband is still considered responsible for his wife's debts, and paying damages to myself seems a pretty futile exercise.'

The room swam even faster. Tallie made it to the sofa and sank down on the cushions. She stared at him.

'What—what are you talking about?'

'Marriage,' he said. 'You must have heard of it. Exchange of rings—till death us do part—a home—babies? Strike any chords?'

'But you don't want to marry me,' she said, her voice shaking. 'You can't.'

His brows lifted. 'Why not?'

'Because you could have anyone. Your—Miss Randall told me that you're a multimillionaire.'

'Yes,' he said. 'Although I wasn't actually planning to buy you. And I know a lot of people far richer than I am,' he added. 'I'll introduce you to a few and you can compare notes.'

She beat her hands together in frustration. 'Oh, be serious.'

'Tallie,' he said very patiently, 'this is the incredibly serious conversation I mentioned before I went to Buleza. Asking you to marry me. Didn't you realise that?'

'But you don't commit.' Her voice was almost a wail. 'Penny said so.'

'Pick a church, name a day, and watch me,' Mark retorted. 'You can ask Penny to be a bridesmaid. Now, my darling, will you stop talking to other people and listen to me? Please?'

He paused. 'I admit,' he said slowly, 'that marriage wasn't my priority when I first met you. Not until we made love, and I woke up at dawn with you in my arms and lay there, watching you sleep. You were smiling a little and I knew, as certainly as I drew breath, that was how I wanted to wake every morning for the rest of my life with you—my wife—beside me.

'And, for a few brief moments, I was completely happy, until I remembered that you didn't feel the same. That, to you, I was nothing but the tame stud you'd asked to ease you out of your inconvenient maidenhood. Also that you'd made it very clear this would be the only night we'd ever spend together.

'Which was when I realised I'd fallen into the appalling trap of loving a girl who didn't want me in return.'

'But when I came to find you, you were so cold,' she whispered. 'You hardly looked at me—or spoke.'

'I was terrified. I was praying that you'd smile again and come across to me. Or at least put out a hand.' His tone was matter-of-fact. 'But you just stayed in the doorway, without a word, looking at me as if I was an unexploded bomb.' His mouth twisted. 'So, no change there. And, as I walked past, you practically cowered. I was bloody devastated. I must have sleepwalked through those days in Brussels because I hardly remembered a thing about them when I came back.

'I could only think— She doesn't love me. She'll never love me…'

He paused again. 'And then there was Justin, of course.'

'Justin?' Tallie echoed. 'But nothing happened between us. You knew that.'

'But I saw him leaving,' he said, 'the day I got back. I was paying off my taxi when he came out, and I thought he'd—been with you. That he'd persuaded you to forgive him and you'd decided he was the man you wanted after all. That I'd been the rehearsal, but he was the main performance.

'I also realised I wanted to beat the living daylights out of him. So I got back into the cab and told the guy to drive—it didn't matter where.

'When I came back, the flat was full of the scent of that bath oil you use. I opened your door and you were asleep on the bed wearing nothing but that bloody cotton dressing gown.'

He drew a harsh breath. 'Christ, my imagination went into overdrive. All I could think of was—the two of you—together, sharing the pleasure we'd known. That you'd been mine, and I'd lost you. Let you go, when I should have fought for you.'

He shook his head. 'I didn't know I could feel quite so violent towards one of my best mates. Jealousy's a terrible thing.'

'You—jealous?' There was incredulity in her voice, and his smile was wry.

'It came as quite a shock to me, too. But then so did being in love.'

He paused again. 'By the way, who the hell is "poor David"?'

'Someone in the village. Why?'

He shrugged. 'Because when your mother answered the door

and I asked for you, she gave me a very long look, said "Poor David", then showed me in here. She also offered me some coffee,' he added thoughtfully. 'But it hasn't appeared.'

She said guiltily, 'I was supposed to ask if you want a hot scone.'

He smiled at her. 'I'd much prefer twenty-four hours of total seclusion, and you without your clothes. But, for now, I'll settle for food and drink. Thank you.'

'I'll tell her.' She stood up and moved to the door.

'And don't run away again,' he called after her. 'You've just given me the worst week of my life.'

Mrs Paget was sitting at the kitchen table absorbed in a book that she slid under a tea towel when she saw her daughter. But not before Tallie had seen the title, 'Cooking for Special Occasions.'

If she's reading the section on wedding cakes, she thought grimly, I shall stab her with her own icing nozzle.

She looked around. 'Didn't you make any coffee for Mr Benedict after all?'

'It can be ready in minutes.' Her mother rose. 'I thought you wouldn't want to be interrupted.'

'I've been flat-sitting for him while he's been in Africa,' Tallie said evenly. 'He—had some questions for me.'

'Then he's come a long way to ask them,' Mrs Paget said affably. 'Also he has the same lost, desperate look that you've been carrying around since your return.' She paused. 'When I bring the tray, I'll knock.'

Tallie went back to the sitting room, closed the door, leaned against it and said, 'Mark, I can't marry you.'

'Has your mother forbidden the banns?'

'Far from it,' Tallie said bitterly. "It's—just impossible, that's all. It can't happen.'

'Because you don't love me?'

She said in a low voice, 'You know that isn't true. I've been feeling only half alive since I left. But how can you want me— after what I did?'

'You haven't done anything.'

She gasped. 'You mean Sonia Randall didn't show you the first draft of the book. The one where I—I…'

'Described me as the epitome of evil?' Mark supplied. 'Yes, I read it, and was enjoying your portrayal of me as arch-villain until that last scene which, I admit, shook me.

'I realised you must have written it after we'd made love, and I asked myself if there was anything that had happened between us that could have been construed as rape. If I'd—disgusted you in some way.'

'Mark…' Her voice thickened.

'And then,' he went on, 'I recalled a moment when I could easily have lost all control—and I'd let you know it. I also remembered what I'd said to you, and felt sick to my stomach.

'It occurred to me, too, that when I was carefully distancing myself from you for my own self-protection, I might have hurt you very badly. That making me out to be a total bastard could be a defence mechanism on your part.

'Most of all, I realised how scared you must have been to break your promise to wait for me, and run away.'

Tallie wrapped her arms round her body. She said in a low voice, 'She—Miss Randall—said dreadful things. I was afraid she'd get her reporter friends to write stories to make it seem as if you'd actually raped me—and the book was my revenge. That people would think there was no smoke without fire, and you'd hate me for damaging your good name.'

He said very gently, 'Darling, I could never hate you, whatever you did. And the only opinion about me I value is yours.' He smiled at her. 'And I was glad to know that you redeemed me in the second draft.'

Her lips parted in shock. 'You read that too?'

'I certainly did.' His smile widened reminiscently. 'I particularly liked the scene at the waterfall. It reminded me that we've yet to take a shower together, something I feel we should put right very soon.'

There was a note in his voice that sent her colour soaring. She said hurriedly, 'But how did you get hold of the book? There wasn't a copy at the flat.'

'Alice Morgan gave it to me. Incidentally, her reaction when I walked into her office was even more interesting than your mother's. She sat back in her chair and laughed until she cried.'

'You went to see Mrs Morgan?' She froze.

'She was my last hope,' he said. 'No one else knew where you'd gone. I even steeled myself to go to Justin and check if you were with him. That note you left was pretty ambiguous. You might have been saying, Sorry—I've decided I picked the wrong man. I told myself that if you'd gone to him, I'd learn to deal with it somehow, because at least you'd be safe.

'However, after he'd put me right on a few points, he suggested I should try your agent. And when she'd calmed down and could speak, she said she could quite see why you'd developed cold feet. That the description of Major Cantrell was altogether too exact, and adjustments would have to be made.'

He grinned faintly. 'So the facial scars are going, and his eyes have turned an attractive blue. It seemed safer than risking the likes of Penny referring to us as Hugo and Mariana for ever and a day.'

He paused. 'Mrs Morgan also said that you were almost certainly clinging to the idea of Hugo as villain because you didn't want to admit your own feelings had changed. But once you'd come to terms with that, the whole book took off like a rocket.'

Her colour deepened. 'But it isn't for sale any more. Sonia…'

'Sonia is not an issue,' he said. 'Not if she values her job. And your book is for sale, my darling. I told Mrs Morgan that, as your future husband, I was authorising her to put it back on the market. And I bribed her for your home address with the promise that she can be godmother to our firstborn.'

There was a tap on the door and Mrs Paget entered with the coffee tray.

She looked from one to the other and her brows lifted. 'Mr Benedict, you seem to have made my daughter cry. I hope for your sake that they're happy tears.'

He said quietly, 'I intend to ensure they will be, Mrs Paget, for the rest of our lives together. And my name is Mark.'

She nodded. 'My husband has a surgery this morning, but he'll be back for lunch. Perhaps you'll stay and join us.' At the door, she turned. 'A nice hotpot, I think. Such a warm *family* meal.' And went.

When they were alone again, Tallie said shakily, 'I think the banns are safe, if you're really sure you want me.'

'I want you,' he said gently. 'And I always will. In fact I'm having a hell of a job keeping my hands off you, potential interruptions and snoring dogs notwithstanding. But more importantly, I love you, Tallie, and I need you to share my life.

'But it's your script, darling,' he added. 'This may not be an inn in Portugal, but you still have to supply the happy ending.'

He held out his arms and she went to him, the words springing to her lips as she looked up at him, smiling through the last of her tears.

'Oh, my love, my love,' she quoted softly. 'Please take me home.'

And, like Mariana, she lifted her mouth to his in trust and total surrender.

PUBLIC MISTRESS, PRIVATE AFFAIR

BY
MAGGIE COX

The day **Maggie Cox** saw the film version of *Wuthering Heights*, with a beautiful Merle Oberon and a very handsome Laurence Olivier, was the day she became hooked on romance. From that day onwards she spent a lot of time dreaming up her own romances, secretly hoping that one day she might become published and get paid for doing what she loves most! Now that her dream is being realised, she wakes up every morning and counts her blessings. She is married to a gorgeous man, is the mother of two wonderful sons, and her two other greatest passions in life—besides her family and reading/writing—are music and films.

To give and receive love is our highest purpose

CHAPTER ONE

'NASH! Good to see you, my friend. Thanks for dropping by at such short notice. I know you're a very busy man.'

His hand was gripped by the bearlike clasp of the tall, dark-eyed, bearded giant in front of him, and Nash Taylor-Grant's answering smile was brief but relaxed. 'No problem. You'd better tell me what all this is about.'

'I'll get my secretary to bring us in some coffee first.'

'You go ahead, but I'll take a rain-check, if you don't mind.' Nash grimaced as he peeled off his expensive coat and sat down in one of the leather club chairs opposite the long polished desk. 'Cutting down on the caffeine,' he offered laconically.

Nash hadn't known Oliver Beaumarche long, but in the relatively short time they'd been acquainted it had become clear that the wealthy and successful restaurateur was to be a good friend. Having regularly dined at both his upmarket London restaurants—for business and for pleasure—Nash didn't hesitate to recommend the establishments to his other well-connected friends whenever the opportunity arose.

Now Oliver had asked for Nash's help in a professional capacity, and although he hadn't hesitated to assure him that of course he would help, in whatever way he could, Nash was perplexed as to why the older man would need the kind of expertise that he particularly excelled in. 'Damage limitation' was how his stock in trade was known in the PR business—the protection of famous clients' reputations in the media—and it had made Nash's fortune. And, whilst Oliver Beaumarche was a respected and well-known name in the world of high-profile eateries, he was hardly an A-list or even B-list celebrity—and as far as Nash was aware he hadn't been involved in any scandal lately that would make his reputation in need of rescuing.

'Well, then.' Following his lead, Oliver lowered his large, impressive frame into a wing-backed chair and sighed heavily. 'Someone I very much care about has been going through the most horrendous situation and needs some help. Unfortunately it's not the kind of help that I can deal with on my own, and that's why I need to talk to you.'

His lightly tanned brow furrowing, Nash leant forward in his seat, loosely linking his hands together as he thoughtfully surveyed the other man. 'It all sounds a bit of a mystery, if you don't mind my saying. You know what I do…so how can I help?'

'The girl I'm talking about is my niece…my sister Yvette's only child. I'm afraid I've rather doted on her since she was a baby, and when she lost her father when she was only six—I suppose I took on a paternal role in her life.'

'You aren't making this any clearer, my friend.' Now it was Nash's turn to sigh. As much as he respected the other man, and genuinely wanted to be of assistance if he could, he had practically back-to-back appointments waiting for him at the office all the way up to seven o'clock this evening, and after that an important dinner with another valuable client. He sat back in his chair and swept his fingers through his hair, the floppily perfect dark blond strands falling back at an unconsciously rakish angle.

'Perhaps I should introduce her? Then no doubt all will become clear.' Getting to his feet, Oliver walked across to a door situated a few feet behind his desk and opened it. 'It's all right, darling…you can come in now,' he invited warmly.

The frown that was already furrowing Nash's perplexed brow deepened. He hardly knew what to expect before the slender dark-eyed brunette walked in. When she did, immediately he felt adrenalin pump through his insides, as though he was on a white-knuckle fairground ride. Although her exotic features were touched with just a mere application of make-up, and the plain dark grey suit she wore over a red wool sweater was not an outfit that was designed to demand attention, the face before him was immediately familiar. Freya Carpenter—an actress whose star had definitely been on the rise up until a couple of years ago, when there had been untold speculation in the press about her volatile marriage and her addiction to drink and possibly drugs.

Nash had met her once, at some celebrity bash he'd gone to, and although she'd looked more than sober enough at the time he'd been struck by how remote she'd appeared amidst the sea of well-known faces—as though the entire experience was an ordeal she'd really like to escape from. No…at that particular event it had been Freya's husband who'd been drinking too much and generally making a damn nuisance of himself. Nash remembered musing on how such a talented, beautiful girl could end up with such a loser. But if the rumours about her drinking and drug using were true, then clearly the woman's capacity for making good choices as far as her personal life was concerned was very definitely flawed.

Now, as he got to his feet and offered her his hand in greeting, of course he instantly knew why she might be in need of his help. Apart from the damage done to her reputation by accusations of drinking and drug-taking, two years ago Freya had also gone through the most horrendous divorce—an event that had been nothing less than trial by the media, and which had consequently lost her an important part in a major film because the producers had commented at the time that she was unstable. Then, just over a year ago, she had reportedly almost got herself killed in a car smash. Her ex-husband had very vocally reinforced the public perception that she'd been high on drink and drugs at the time. She'd been supposedly mourning their split, and the fact that he had left her for some nineteen-year-old fashion model who was pregnant with his baby.

Reading between the lines, and recalling her solemn face at that party whilst her husband had commanded most of the attention with his loud-mouthed antics, Nash now came to the conclusion that there was a hell of a lot more behind that story than the public had been led to believe. The young woman standing before him might have gone off the rails in her personal life, but she was still an actress with some highly notable roles to her name. She'd even graced the London stage a couple of times, and won critical praise bar none, so she was no bimbo just in it for the fame. That made it even more puzzling that she had wound up with a disaster like James Frazier.

The most recent slur to suddenly reignite frenzied interest in the actress had been speculation about her mental stability, and it had had the press camping out in droves on her doorstep for the past week. The story went that Freya Carpenter was all washed up: she'd suffered a major breakdown and was not likely to return to the stage or screen any time soon. Yes…it was obvious to Nash why Oliver Beaumarche's famous niece might urgently need the help of a man like him…

'Freya, this is Nash Taylor-Grant,' Oliver introduced her.

Warily, it seemed, she placed her chilled palm in his, and Nash saw her flinch as if contact with another human being—any human being—was tantamount to putting her hand into a tank of piranhas. Vaguely troubled, he volunteered a smile nonetheless. 'We've met before, Ms Carpenter…a long time ago at a party. I doubt that you'd remember.'

'I thought you looked familiar…although I have to say I can't recall the particular party.' Quickly withdrawing her hand, she pulled her glance away with it and went to sit in the seat that her uncle had positioned for her near his, her quick, light movements naturally graceful.

Once the men had resumed their seats, Oliver Beaumarche glanced very seriously at Nash. 'You will now have some idea as to why we need your help. I never told you about my connection with Freya before because naturally, as someone who cares very deeply about her welfare, my need to protect her privacy has always been paramount,' he commented, stealing a moment to smile at the reserved brunette. 'But now Freya wants to start rebuilding her career after the trauma she has been through, and she cannot do so unhindered while her unscrupulous ex-husband is still busy doing his utmost to undo every bit of good that she is trying so hard to achieve. Look at what has happened now, for instance! She has been nothing less than a prisoner in her own home after all this ridiculous nonsense in the press about her state of mind, and I do not doubt for a minute that the rumours were started by that good-for-nothing, unspeakable—'

'Please don't think that I am totally blaming my ex-husband for my recent lack of success, Mr Taylor-Grant,' Freya interjected quietly and her mesmerising, slightly smoky voice had the disarming effect of making all the hairs on the back of Nash's neck stand on end. 'I take full responsibility for what's happening in my life. It's my uncle who seems to believe that my reputation needs some help—though if you ask me after this latest fiasco I think it would probably be better if I just go quietly away somewhere and disappear until everybody forgets about me.'

An ironic little smile touched a mouth that was undeniably tinged with sadness yet still suggested the most riveting sensuality. As though hypnotised, Nash felt his gaze magnetised by it. He shifted ever so slightly in his seat. 'I don't think anyone who has read the papers or heard the news in the past couple of years would deny that your reputation has definitely taken a bit of a battering, Ms Carpenter. Nonetheless…I'm certain that there must be a lot of public sympathy out there for your predicament.'

A shadow of distress seemed to pass across her arresting features. Her slender shoulders stiffened beneath her unremarkable fitted jacket and her velvety brown eyes stared almost accusingly at Nash. 'I'm not looking for sympathy, Mr Taylor-Grant! And I'm not mentally unstable either! I'm angry, but then I think I have a right to be! Look…all I want is to be able to get on with my life again without interference. Can you imagine what it's been like being literally hounded by a pack of story-hungry reporters and photographers? If I did have a breakdown, could anybody blame me?'

'I don't think they could. It can't be pleasant,' Nash concurred.

'Besides…why should the public have sympathy for someone they believe had everything and then threw it all away because she let her private life go to rack and ruin? They probably think I got exactly what I deserved!'

'I'd hardly call a major car accident and defamation of character by someone I presume must have loved you once upon a time something that you "deserved"…. Would you?'

His words were like a cutlass, slicing her in half, and for a long, dreadful moment Freya was frozen by the wave of pain that throbbed sharply through her. Did he but know it, he was wrong about James loving her. Oh, his passionate words and declarations of being crazy in love with her had definitely convinced Freya that he was in earnest at the time, but she had quickly discovered that lies and deceit came very easily to him—especially when employed to get him whatever it was that would serve his own greedy ambition. But still Freya had to silently admit that she'd been complicit in all too easily believing his lies…

'Freya?' Her uncle's unfailingly kind eyes regarded her with more concern than she could handle right then. He'd been so good to her...so patient. And she wished that not even one single ounce of her predicament had ever visited its pain upon his heart.

'I'm fine...really. But if I'm honest...' She glanced at Nash and made herself endure the unflinching examination in his piercing blue gaze—an examination that seemed to reach deep inside her and see her soul laid bare... Was he looking to gain some advantage? she wondered. She'd learned the hard way to be wary in a profession that raised you up to the skies one minute and then sent you crashing back down to earth onto a bed of red-hot nails the next. Her uncle was too trusting for his own good sometimes. How long had he known this PR guru, anyway? Not long, was her guess. Though it was perfectly true that she remembered seeing Nash before...even though her comment about forgetting which party they'd met at had probably convinced him that she was probably too drunk or high at the time to remember.

Freya had been neither, and a flash of anger and despair assailed her. But, recalling the encounter with Nash, she remembered she'd certainly observed at the time that the man possessed an almost careless kind of male beauty and a sexual aura that was magnetising. She also recalled that the lissom beauty who had accompanied him that night had poured herself into the kind of tight-fitting dress that had made Freya wonder how she even breathed in it, let alone moved! The woman had spent practically the entire evening gazing up at her escort adoringly, as if there was no other man in the room but him.

It had been painful for Freya to witness such obvious adoration when her less than charming husband had been busy making a spectacle of both himself and her. Now, regarding Nash as he sat opposite her on the other side of Oliver Beaumarche's generous-sized desk, she guessed it would be all too easy to succumb to that frank, inviting demeanour of his and tell him everything…all the sordid little secrets of her disastrous soul-destroying marriage and the quite staggering mistakes she'd made along the way. The very thought was apt to make her doubly wary of the power he might so easily wield should she confess anything to him.

'I think this is a waste of time,' she continued. 'I'm in no hurry to get back into the limelight, Mr Taylor-Grant. I'm not saying I would never want to work in the industry again, but when I do it will definitely be behind the scenes. I've had my fifteen minutes of fame, and quite frankly I'd rather jump off a cliff than willingly submit my private life to the kind of vicious intrusion that I've had to endure ever again!'

'If you don't mind my saying so, Ms Carpenter, that's going to be a tall order under the circumstances.'

'How do you mean?'

'Well…' Nash crossed his legs at the knee of his dark

blue Armani suit, and rested his arms alongside the chair's dark cherry surround. 'So long as the press and the public keep speculating about you, and so long as your ex-husband keeps feeding them lies…I presume that they *are* lies?…then I doubt if you'll be allowed to get on with your life in peace and work behind the scenes as you desire. Have you even made a statement refuting your ex's most recent allegation?' he asked her. 'Not the one about you having a breakdown…the other one.'

Freya knew immediately what Nash was referring to, and she sensed heat rise in her face as his unwavering gaze locked onto hers with even more acuity than before.

'You mean that recent little slur about my sexuality? Do you think anyone really believes such salacious drivel?'

Nash said nothing. Although Freya's cheeks had turned slightly pink, he guessed it was more out of rage than embarrassment. Good for her! he thought privately. If she still had some fight in her after what her apparently malicious ex-husband had done to her then that would be all to the good in helping her work towards full recovery. Although if he was honest Nash still couldn't understand why she had given a waste of space like Frazier so much power over her life and her career in the first place. How people fooled themselves when it came to relationships. They took more care, it seemed, in choosing a car or a house than a life partner!

Determined to try and put his judgement aside—even though he privately thought she must have brought a lot of her disasters upon herself—Nash had no doubt that he could help Freya rebuild her career. He'd taken on many almost ruined reputations of people in the public eye before this, and helped restore them to a much more positive aspect. But if he accepted this job it would definitely be on the proviso that from now on her behaviour had to be far more exemplary than it might have been in the past.

'Well, I'm sure you don't need a lesson from me about people being easily manipulated by the media to believe almost anything they're told.' The broad shoulders beneath his beautifully tailored jacket lifted in a shrug. 'It's my view that you need to put an end to the publication of this "salacious drivel", as you so rightly referred to it. And to do that you need to lend the proceedings a little dignity, by making a very calm but firm statement refuting every defamatory remark that's been made by your ex.'

'Nash is right, Freya.' Oliver slid his big hand over hers and squeezed it. 'That man has got away with murder, and it simply can't be allowed to continue! If you cannot bring yourself to do something about this for yourself, then think about what your poor mother has gone through in all of this!' He directed his suddenly emotional gaze towards Nash and Oliver's dark eyes glittered. 'My sister has all but suffered a nervous breakdown because of what has gone on,' he explained. 'Where's the justice in that? James Frazier has no morals, and no remorse for anything he has done to our family, and he continues to carry on unchecked by anybody! Even the press is on his side! And even though he's maligned Freya's reputation, and all but bled her dry financially because of his lies in court—and because a well-known newspaper readily supplied him with some cutthroat lawyer from America, wanting to make a name for himself in the divorce—he still continues to cause havoc!'

The room seemed to spin a little. Freya was fine when she wasn't thinking about the devastating, almost unbelievable chain of events that had dragged her remorselessly down into the pits of hell, but hearing it stated out loud by her uncle, and registering the affecting passion in his voice, she wanted to find a remote desert island somewhere and remain there, forgotten by everybody until she died…

Why had she been so blind to the truth about James's character? she asked herself again in silent anguish. Why had she allowed herself to be so easily seduced by his lies? But again she had to consider that her downfall wasn't just due to her ex's bad behaviour. Some of the blame, if blame was to be apportioned, *had* to lie with her. Maybe if she hadn't fooled herself so convincingly that his regard was sincere because of her own desperate underlying need to be loved then none of this awful mess would have happened?

'Well…' Clearing his throat, and easing his striped silk tie away from his collar a little, Nash glanced briefly down at his watch. 'It seems to me, my friend, that only your niece can make the decision about what she wants to do. If you want me to help you, Ms Carpenter, then I will. But I will also need you to comply with how I suggest we proceed—to the letter.' Turning his gaze to Freya, he registered the stark unhappiness exposed to him in her coffee-dark eyes, and a genuine bolt of sympathy rippled through him. Lousy choices or no, she must have gone through hell, he thought. She was still going through hell, by the look of her…despite her initial insistence that she didn't need any help. 'Ms Carpenter?'

'This statement that you suggest I make…would you be willing to help me make it?'

There was the smallest flash of uncertainty in her dark-eyed glance, and Nash straightened in his chair. Satisfaction at the knowledge that she was going to relent to receiving some help pulsed through him, as well as gratification that he could do something to repay the generous friendship that her uncle had extended to him.

'Of course. If you decide to hire me to work on your behalf, Ms Carpenter, I can promise you that I will bring every ounce of expertise and assistance to your aid that is at my disposal.'

'Then I'll do it.'

Putting her hand up to her hair, she tucked a few silky strands behind her ear and looked as solemn as she had during that party where Nash had first met her. If he was any judge, right now she seemed to be garnering every ounce of steel she had left in her to face whatever was coming next—yet he also acknowledged that she must be dreading deliberately putting her life back under public scrutiny again.

In the absence of any further speech from his niece, Oliver leant across the desk and shook Nash's hand. 'Thank you, my friend. I have only known you for a short time, but I believe you to be a man of integrity and honour. Freya needs somebody like you on her side at long last… This dreadful situation has all but broken her.'

'What are you saying, Uncle Oliver? You know that isn't true!' Getting to her feet, Freya glared first at Oliver, then more pointedly at Nash. 'One thing I'd like to make very clear at the outset, Mr Taylor-Grant: I may have suffered a serious setback or two during the past couple of years—one or two broken bones in a car accident being the least of them, funnily enough—but I am not under any circumstances "broken". And even if I were…I'm not looking for anyone to "fix" me. I'm tougher than I look, and if I've survived what I've come through so far without going completely insane, then I'm quite capable of surviving more of the same without turning into some kind of pathetic jibbering wreck!'

'Well…it's my hope, and your uncle's too, I'm sure, that you won't have to endure too much stress and strain much longer, Ms Carpenter. Once you've made your statement to the press, we'll quickly get on with the task of helping you re-establish your career and getting you some very positive publicity for a change, so that you can do just that.'

The man in front of her appeared so utterly convinced

of what he was saying that something inside Freya—
some frozen little shard—seemed to break away from the
ice floe around her heart and suddenly start to melt in the
first hopeful feeling she'd had in a very long time. When
her uncle had first mooted the suggestion of seeing this
friend of his, who was a big name in PR, she had been
understandably reticent, uncertain that it would achieve
anything good. But now, having properly met Nash
Taylor-Grant, and in spite of her fear of ever placing her
trust in a man again…any man…she felt there was something about him that suggested the kind of rock-solid
strength and reliability that anyone in trouble would
welcome. Something that told her he could negotiate a
minefield on his wits alone if he had to, and get to the
other side intact. And it wasn't just the sharp, elegant cut
of his designer suit on a body that suggested he was a man
in his prime in every way, or the defiant hardness of his
jaw that threw out a challenge to 'do your worst' that convinced her. No…it was something innate in the man
himself.

Having found her ability to trust severely battered
after what James had done, Freya more than longed for
her assumption about Nash to be true. But she'd lost
faith in her judgement too…she couldn't deny that.

Sitting back in her chair, she smoothed her hand down
the side of her skirt and tried to hold onto some of the
previous hope she'd allowed herself to feel. When she
raised her gaze to re-examine Nash's strongly handsome

face, the blue of his eyes seemed to increase their potent wattage, and astonishingly Freya experienced a little dart of sensual awareness implode quietly yet devastatingly inside her.

'If you could really accomplish all of that...' She shrugged her shoulders a little, suddenly alarmed at the idea that he knew what that frank gaze of his had briefly done to her. 'I'd be in your debt, Mr Taylor-Grant.'

'Why don't you call me Nash? If we're going to be working together for a while formality only gets in the way...don't you agree?'

CHAPTER TWO

NASH cancelled his next two appointments and went
back to the office to do his homework. He needed to act
quickly if they were going to turn the tide of public
consciousness in Freya Carpenter's favour, and, frankly,
her loud-mouthed ex had had things his way for far too
long. It was time to redress the balance. Having seen
some of the evidence of the fine work that the actress
was capable of, Nash was of the opinion that it would
be a crying shame were she never to act in front of an
audience again. And, being a friend of her uncle's, he
felt a certain obligation to double his efforts in helping
her. But to say that he'd been surprised by the revelation that Freya Carpenter was Oliver Beaumarche's
niece was akin to being surprised to discover that the restaurateur was closely related to royalty! Not that Nash
was impressed…it was just that it had come as the most
unexpected shock. He'd known Oliver for a while now,
and never at any time had the older man indicated that

he had a famous niece. Or that she was a famous niece in deep trouble…

Tapping the end of his pen against his teeth, he leaned forward in his chair to more closely examine the glossy colour print that lay in front of him on the desk. He wasn't immune to the power of the darkly melting eyes that gazed back at him. Having seen them at close quarters for himself, he could see how a man would be apt to lose his sense of perspective if he looked into them too deeply and for too long… Their distinctly exotic slant helped to make them damn near unforgettable too. And when they were magnified up there on the big screen, as they had been in the past, would anyone be immune to their arresting impact?

Although in the picture before him her lips were parted in a smile, there was a vulnerability that lingered there too…a sensitivity that only the most hardened individual would be blind to. There were faces and people that scarcely left an impression…Freya Carpenter was definitely not one of those. With that amazing fall of rippling dark hair, as well as the slender, long-legged figure that she'd hidden almost primly behind that understated grey suit, her looks would guarantee her plenty of attention whether she was famous or not. A woman with that kind of stand-out sensual cachet could reel the men in like the most willing fish you ever saw… In light of that fact, Freya had certainly been unlucky in settling on a poor specimen like James Frazier to get hitched to.

Almost reluctantly setting aside the photograph, because its subject was frankly beginning to mesmerise him, Nash turned his attention to several different accounts of her headline-catching divorce, as well as the latest press speculation splashed all over the celebrity gossip pages, and he read them more carefully and avidly than a scientist reading the results of the most compulsive research…

The room had turned cold, and outside a fine drizzly rain was falling. Really, Freya didn't care one way or the other. Why should she care when the sky had already fallen in on top of her? The afternoon light was fading but, huddled into one of the deep corners of her once luxurious Fortnum and Mason sofa, she couldn't bring herself to move and switch on a lamp. Instead, she drew her legs towards her beneath the long wraparound skirt she wore with a baggy sweater and wrapped her chilled arms around her knees. It was definitely a 'hide under the duvet' kind of mood that had enveloped her, but she was too weary even to try and accomplish even that. She'd been endeavouring to read a long-time favourite novel—a kind of security blanket she reached for when times were tough and she needed to feel safe—but the words were a waving sea of hard-to-pin-down sentences, because her mind was too preoccupied.

What if she'd done completely the wrong thing in agreeing to make the statement Nash had suggested she make to the press? What if it just drew to her even more horrible and unwanted attention? Even now there were two or three photographers lurking around near her house, hoping to catch a glimpse of her. She could spot them a mile away! Returning to the idea of making a public statement, Freya groaned out loud at the prospect. What if her words came out wrong? Or she stumbled and they immediately concluded that she was indeed the 'wreck' that James had all but convinced them she was? A once bright star whose light had blazed all too briefly but had soon burned itself out, relegating her to the ranks of has-been.

Dropping her head into her lap, she squeezed her eyes shut tight and willed the world to go away. But, no matter how much she wished it, it never did. It was still there, in all the same washed-out colours, whenever she opened her eyes again. Her uncle was only trying to help her. She knew that. He believed in her talent even if the rest of the world didn't. He wanted her to work again, to express the gifts that he judged God to have blessed her with. But, in spite of her brave words in his office yesterday, when she had declared to Nash that she wasn't broken and that he shouldn't try to fix her, today was a different story. Today the twin demons of fear and self-pity had returned with a vengeance, like honed daggers attacking her in the dark, and all Freya wanted to do was hide.

The sound of the doorbell echoing through the house sent shockwaves flooding through her whole being and, lifting her head, she pushed back her hair from her whitened face. Uncurling her legs, she was almost disorientated by the primal river of panic that assailed her as she got shakily to her feet. The cold in the room and in her heart made her shiver almost violently. The only people who could possibly be visiting her legitimately would be her uncle or her mother—she didn't have an agent or a manager anymore, and most of her 'friends' had been conspicuous by their absence since her very public fall from grace. But both those two always rang her first, to warn her that they were coming.

Terrified in case the visitor was another mercenary reporter or photographer, taking the opportunity to catch her unawares—it had happened too regularly to be beyond a joke—Freya cautiously negotiated the crimson-carpeted corridor of the hallway in her bare feet, narrowing her gaze at the broad-shouldered shadow that hovered behind the opaque glass panels in the door. She froze for a moment, immobilised by fear. When she did finally move she hurried back inside the living room and, edging cautiously towards the large bay window, carefully moved aside a small section of the roll-down blind to peer outside.

The figure she saw standing on the wide front steps, his rain-dampened gilded hair a notable contrast against the expensive black cashmere of his overcoat, made her heart jump into her mouth. Nash! Her uncle must have trusted him enough to give him her home address, she guessed, but why hadn't he rung to warn her first?

Dropping the blind abruptly into place again, as though

it had suddenly turned into something unpleasant to touch, she smoothed her hands nervously down the sides of her rumpled skirt. Trying to banish the feeling of terror that gripped her at the thought of speaking to anyone today, she exhaled a long breath that was infused with both a kind of desperation and a sense of hopelessness. Dear God! Was she destined to spend the rest of her life hiding away from the rest of the world inside her own home? A home was meant to be a place of refuge…not a prison!

Her mouth feeling as dry as sawdust, Freya speared her fingers through her waving dark hair and reached a decision. She had no choice but to talk to him. After agreeing to make the statement yesterday, she couldn't now tell him that she'd changed her mind. There was always the danger that this man would also believe she was too unstable to be trusted if she told him to go away.

Reluctantly opening the door, she wrapped her arms across the beige coloured sweater that all but swamped her slender frame and briefly, jumpily, met the searing blue beam of Nash's immediately searching gaze.

'You didn't ring me to let me know to expect you,' she snapped accusingly. Although her words gave the impression that she was the one in charge of the situation, Freya's courage all but deserted her as she glanced up into her visitor's compelling visage.

'Yeah…I'm sorry about that.' He grimaced, but didn't appear overly concerned. 'Your uncle gave me your number, but I was nearby when he rang me in the car just now and I thought I wouldn't waste any time. I need you to fill me in on a few things, and I thought we could work on your statement together. Can I come in?'

Unable to think of an excuse in the world to deny him, Freya pressed herself back against the wall to let him pass her, then hurriedly closed the door again, her dark eyes making a swift reconnaissance of the street outside just before she did so, in case anyone should be taking a particular interest in her or her visitor. But, divertingly, the disturbing soft musk scent of Nash's masculine cologne impacted the air around her with unexpected sensuality, and she felt its potent effect immediately in the pit of her stomach and in her too-dry mouth. She told herself her reaction was simply down to nerves. All her responses were heightened by anxiety today, and she'd sell her last possession to access some calm from somewhere.

'Let's go into the living room.' Freya eased past him, making as much space between them as possible, before turning into the room she had so recently and reluctantly vacated.

Following her slender form, and wondering why she'd chosen to conceal it in clothes that seemed far too big, Nash was vaguely alarmed by the smudged mauve shadows he'd glimpsed beneath her fascinating eyes. Once inside the room he had another cause for alarm. There was a biting chill in the air that almost matched the freezing temperature outside. There was no evidence of heat at all, even though it was such a raw day. None

of the several lamps that he could see around the room
were turned on either, even though the evening's
shadows were threatening the pale afternoon light that
remained. The furniture seemed sparse, and apart from
the plush cinnamon-coloured sofa dominating the centre
of the room, and a matching high-backed armchair with
a scarlet cushion, there were very few comforts that he
could detect. A further disturbing bolt of concern shot
through him.

'Aren't you cold?' he asked, before he could check the
words. Freya regarded him as though his voice had just
aroused her from the deepest of drugging sleeps. A little
frown appeared in the softly pale space between her brows.
'I'm fine… But if you're cold, I'll switch on the fire.'

Before Nash could tell her it didn't matter, she had
crossed the room and switched on a modern electric fire
with fake coals in front of the old-fashioned fireplace.
In just a second the gas burners burst into warm life, and
he was glad for her sake that she had agreed to inject a
little heat into the icy room. The woman looked as if she
needed warming up in every way imaginable. Was this
how she spent her days now that she'd retreated into
near obscurity? he wondered. Alone in a big empty
house in near freezing temperatures?

The thought was apt to make him want to throttle
her ex-husband if this was what his mercenary deeds
had reduced her to. He'd been reading quite a lot
about James Frazier, and none of it did the man credit.
On a scale of one to ten, in Nash's book the man had

to score zero. As well as having sullied Freya's name as frequently as possible—both before, during and after their divorce—he had apparently been spending money like it was going out of style—money that, as far as Nash could ascertain, had come from the huge divorce settlement he'd won. And Freya had not retaliated either in word or deed. Not at any point.

He could scarcely understand it. What kind of legal advice had she been given? Why had her defence been so inept, and why had the courts decided in her husband's favour? Did he have some kind of hold over her? Nash had also learned that after their divorce Frazier had apparently invested huge amounts of money in unsound business deals that had more often than not backfired on him, losing him vast sums. But that hadn't curtailed his expensive lifestyle, it seemed. Having made some discreet enquiries late last night, and followed them up early this morning, Nash had discovered that Freya's ex was just about to leave for the Caribbean with his young blonde girlfriend and their baby, and he knew that it was time Freya made her statement and let the world hear her side of the story. After that, she could start to pick up the pieces and get her life and her self-respect back.

'How about turning on a lamp or two as well?' Nash suggested, keeping his voice low and friendly. As she seemed momentarily frozen into inaction he took the task upon himself. He moved towards the tall, fringed standard lamp by the window, and then over to another one situated on the opposite side of the room. Switching them on, he saw they made an immediate impact. With the fake fire now glowing, and the light from the lamps introducing a more amicable intimacy, Nash hoped that Freya might start to relax a little. He knew instinctively, even without regarding her worried features, that this whole business was going to be another huge trial for her, and he would have spared her any pain it might cause if he could. But he told himself that it was ultimately for her own good that they were doing this. The woman couldn't spend the rest of her days cloistered away like a nun who had taken a vow of silence.

'I'm a little rusty when it comes to entertaining visitors…I'm sorry. I should have offered you something to drink. I have some fruit juice—or perhaps you'd prefer some tea or coffee?'

'Why don't you just sit down and we'll talk?' Nash answered.

'Okay.' Clearly reluctant, as though his words had unhappily thwarted her instinct to escape into another room and get away from him, Freya resumed her seat on the couch. Taking off his overcoat, Nash sat down at the other end and stood his hide briefcase on the floor by his feet.

'So…what have you been doing today?' he asked interestedly. She blinked, appearing nonplussed for a moment—as though her brain could hardly compute the question, never mind find an answer.

'What do you think I've been doing?' she retorted, clearly annoyed. 'I'm under siege here…my whole life is under siege!'

'Then I guess the press have been making their presence felt in one way or another again? Well… tomorrow you'll get your chance to redress the balance and tell everyone the truth about things.'

'And do you think for one minute that they'll print the truth? You don't think that they might—just might— bend it a little, to suit whatever slant they've decided to take on that day?'

It was easy to understand why she was so angry. Nash would be too if it was his life that strangers were taking up a position on, manipulating information to sell newspapers. But then he hadn't entered a profession where fame was the currency that everyone secretly hoped for.

'I wonder that you want anything to do with the media…they're a bunch of vultures!' she added with feeling.

'You can't be blind to the fact that many artists and celebrities court the media? How else would they get their work promoted? Do you think film companies are in the business of making films to distribute to the public for free?' Shaking his head, Nash held her gaze with definite authority. 'What you've got to do is learn to play the media at their own game. Right up until now you've been the one that's clearly been wronged by your ex— and them—so the time is ripe to turn things around. The

British public in particular love an underdog. I'm sorry, Freya, but that's how you have to see it. After you've made your statement tomorrow, telling them your side of the story and refuting Frazier's slanderous allegations, you'll have everybody on your side again and that can't fail to attract more positive attention to help your career. Isn't that what you want?'

'I don't know…yes…I suppose.'

Her fingers intertwined and opened again several times as she said this, and Nash frowned at the sight. Never had a pair of slender hands appeared so pale and cold…almost as though they'd been dipped in ivory. He had the strongest urge to pull her into his arms so that he could hold her. He would have done it too, if he hadn't already known that to do so would probably propel him out of her life for ever. He owed it to Oliver, at least, not to risk such an outcome.

'All right, then… So, if I'm going to help you, I'll need your co-operation and not your hindrance. Don't think I don't understand your reluctance about appearing before the press again, because I do. This won't be easy, and I won't lie to you about that. But apart from what we have to do tomorrow there will be other things I need you to comply with…places I need you to appear, events I need you to attend…all in the name of achieving some positive publicity. And if you're reluctant to oblige then I can't do the job your uncle has asked me to do to help you…do you understand?'

There was a steely undertone to his calmly voiced reply, and Freya sensed that the man took great pride in seeing an assignment through and accomplishing it to the high standards that he no doubt exacted from himself and others. He did not appear to be someone who would let anything stand in the way of achieving that…no matter who they were. She told herself she should be pleased that he was prepared to be so diligent on her behalf, but right then—feeling the way she did—it was hard to be reassured by anything much. All she knew was that she was going to have to face the increased scrutiny of cameras and questions again, and her whole being baulked violently at the very thought—even though it was an exercise to help repair her damaged reputation.

Ceasing her fidgeting, Freya sat very still. Her expression was as calm as she could make it as she turned towards Nash.

'You say you understand my reluctance to appear before the press and the public again, but I wonder if you do?' Sighing, she swallowed hard before speaking. 'It's like a form of spiritual rape, you know? Like they can take everything from you and you can do nothing to protect yourself! Yes, I enjoyed my success when success came…but I never realised how essential my privacy was until all this happened. Should I be punished for that?' Stopping for a moment to glance towards the glowing fire, she brought her attention back to Nash again before speaking. 'Going through a marriage break-up is tough enough, without having to go through it in front of the media and the public. They all love you when your star is on the rise, but do you know how much they relish it when you start to wobble on that pedestal they've put you on?'

'You can't let anybody grind you down. You've just got to show them you're way too strong for that. Fight back, Freya! Don't let anyone relegate your existence to this house, this room, as if you're too afraid to live fully any more because you fear their judgement. That's just what they want you to do! Don't give them the satisfaction. Especially don't give your ex-husband the satisfaction of knowing that he's got some kind of hold over you.' His blue eyes narrowing, Nash compelled Freya to hear him out.

What he said struck an already very tender nerve. She'd fought James's lies up to a point, but after that he'd worn her down with his accusations and insults, and when his deliberate lying to the press about her had started to make some serious inroads into her self-esteem and personal confidence Freya had been too hurt and too mentally fatigued to fight him any more. Even in court she hadn't helped her own defence. Instead she'd blamed herself for everything that had happened…even told herself that she deserved it. She had the wonderful career she'd set out to achieve and now she had to pay. James Frazier was her nemesis.

'I have to ask this. Why didn't you sign a pre-nuptial agreement to prevent your ex from getting all your money? And why didn't you have a better lawyer to represent you? Surely your uncle could have—?'

Freya's hackles rose at that. Her almost translucent skin became very flushed. 'It's not my uncle's responsibility to do everything for me! I'm an adult…I make my own choices, even if they ultimately backfire on me! And as for a pre-nuptial agreement…' Her guilty glance was painful to witness. 'Suffice to say that James persuaded me that we didn't need one. I know you must think me the biggest fool that ever walked the planet, but what's done is done and I can't turn back the clock.'

'You say he "persuaded" you?'

Nash had honed in on that remark like an eagle swooping down on its far less swift prey, and Freya sensed the heat in her cheeks intensify. When that particular conversation had arisen between her and James it had ended with him throwing a frightening tantrum. He'd trashed her living room amidst threats of committing suicide, because she clearly didn't love him enough to trust him, and Freya had found herself trying to placate his wild distress by promising she would never bring the subject up again. Of course she'd been duped… She knew that now, to her everlasting shame.

'Did he hurt you?' Nash demanded.

'No…not physically. You'd be amazed at the creativity some humans can apply when it comes to inflicting pain. Anyway…what does it matter now? We both know how my marriage ended, and I can analyse where I went wrong until the cows come home, but it won't make the relationship any less of a catastrophe than it turned out to be!' she retorted defensively.

Was Nash judging her for marrying a man like James and not signing an agreement to protect herself financially? The idea that he was almost made her want to show him the door. Freya had had enough judgement from other people to last her a lifetime!

'The point is I've seen too many performers in your situation who have ultimately come to regret not signing a pre-nup,' Nash responded with a sigh, leaning forward and resting his elbows on his knees. 'Anyway, like you say, what's done is done...but if I'm going to help you I need to know that you're as committed to this enterprise as I am. I want to help you get your life back, but I want *you* to want that a hundred times more!'

'You have my word that I'll co-operate,' Freya replied softly, her dark eyes unable for a moment to hide the exquisite vulnerability that he'd witnessed in her photograph. 'I didn't lie to you yesterday, you know. I am tougher than I look. It's just that there are days when—there are days that I...'

'I know.' Nash knew what she meant, because he'd been there too. But that had been a long time ago when he'd been a very different person from the successful, confident man who sat here today. 'But the more you face the things you feel are impossible to face the stronger you'll become, Freya. Trust me...I know what I'm talking about.'

To Nash's intense relief, she dropped her shoulders

and stopped looking like a startled deer about to bolt. At some point in the not too distant future he was going to have to raise the thorny question of her alleged drinking and drug use… But he wouldn't hit her with that particular can of worms right now. Not that he didn't doubt she had great inner reserves… She might be feeling vulnerable, but he sensed strength there too. The woman couldn't have survived what she'd endured without it. A less strong person would have had a complete breakdown by now.

'Perhaps I will have a cup of coffee after all?' he suggested. 'Then we'll get to work on his statement.'

CHAPTER THREE

HE WAS getting ready to leave, and Freya found to her astonishment that she was strangely reluctant to see him go. For the first time in longer than she could remember she'd felt at ease in another human being's company, and she wanted to experience more of the same. As Nash's calm, almost hypnotic voice had drawn her out from behind the heavily guarded fence she'd erected between herself and the world she'd become afraid of returning to the morose mood that had afflicted her all day.

She didn't want to revisit that dark place. She'd lived in it for far too long and it was devouring her confidence. Already Nash had inspired her to want something different, something better. Listening to him read out the statement they'd prepared together, which she would read to the press tomorrow, she'd started to draw strength from the firmly assertive tone of the words. They made her sound in charge, not a victim any more. She was glad.

James had dictated how things would be for too long,

and her mistake in marrying him had been paid for a hundred times over—with too many tears, nearly all of her money, and a shattered career. This was where the tide started to turn. She wanted her life back. She wanted to be able to face people again and not shy away from them in case they judged or hurt her. She wanted to resume her career in some form or another that would give her satisfaction and help her support herself. And no longer would she foolishly pine for a love that was unconditional and lasting. Such a thing was as rare as orchids growing in the Arctic. It was simply futile and painful to even go there.

It stunned her that James seemed to hate her so much. Naively, Freya had believed that when he had won that huge settlement from her in the divorce it would be the end of his animosity and resentment towards her. But, no… The hints about her unstable state of mind, the vitriol with which he'd spoken of their 'dreadful and oppressive' marriage to all who would listen, the lies he had made up about her so-called addictions had all become worse. Freya was certain that the public's perception of her had been utterly poisoned by him. He'd painted her as a jealous bitch, an egotistical, demanding actress who constantly craved attention, when in fact the opposite was true. As a woman who was so insecure that she'd been jealous of every other woman James had looked at, especially if they were younger than her. Well, Freya was only twenty-eight years old herself…hardly over the hill!

The truth was that James had taunted her deliberately with his interest in other women to try and make her jealous. He'd hated his wife getting the attention, the adulation for her work that she'd eventually discovered he craved for himself. He'd never loved her. She wouldn't kid herself about that any more. He'd merely seen a chance to elevate himself by his association with her. An assistant cameraman when Freya had first met him, it had soon become evident that he had a driving ambition to be in front of the camera instead of behind it. She should have left him then, instead of agreeing to marry him.

When she looked back on what a gullible idiot she'd been, entering into such a disastrous relationship, Freya could hardly believe her own stupidity. The need for love, she'd discovered, could make sane people crazy. She might just as well have climbed into a barrel and thrown herself into Niagara Falls!

Reaching for his coat from the couch, Nash turned to Freya with a smile. There were two fascinating dimples in his hollowed-out cheeks when he employed that compelling gesture, and an intensely glowing heat seemed to inhabit her entire body as she gazed back at him. Because the points of her breasts had pinched shockingly inside her voluminous woollen sweater, she folded her arms protectively across her chest—as if Nash might see through the thick layers of clothing to the erotic reaction he had wrought underneath.

'One more thing before I leave,' he drawled.

'Yes?'

'What are you going to wear for this press inter-view tomorrow?'

'What am I going to *wear*?'

He considered her with the same kind of patience that a concerned adult might employ with a confused child.

'Whatever you decide, it has to be exactly right. Something plain, like that grey suit you wore yesterday, says "I want to hide". That isn't the image that we're trying to project, Freya. You want to show the world that you're done with hiding, as if you've got something to be ashamed of. Alternatively, something too glamorous might suggest false confidence… Do you see what I mean when I say it has to be just right?'

She did. 'I'll spend some time this evening choosing something suitable,' she promised.

Would Nash be shocked to see how sparse the contents of her wardrobe were? she wondered. She'd never had a stylist, or been an avid follower of fashion or anything, but she'd often been gifted glamorous clothing by eager designers wanting their designs promoted by a famous name. However, along with her antique furniture and jewellery, most of it had been sold to help meet the debts incurred by her court costs.

'Want me to come and take a look with you?' he offered.

Feeling sudden shame at her reduced straits, Freya lifted her chin even as her cheeks flooded with crimson.

'No, thanks. I know it might appear as though I've

let a lot of things slide, but I can assure you I'm still capable of picking out my own clothes!'

Her vehemence made Nash grin. It didn't hurt that his suggestion had piqued her pride. It demonstrated that she was still capable of displaying a little grit. Seeing the way she'd been when he'd first arrived—sitting alone in a freezing cold room without the light on—he had been concerned that depression had struck deep. Now he knew that it was only a low mood that had descended, and he was honestly relieved. It made him even more determined to help her return to the land of the living and claim the full life that was naturally hers.

'I've arranged for the press to meet you at my office, and I'll be here at about nine in the morning to pick you up and take you back there. I want to make everything as easy as I possibly can for you, and I don't want you veering off into fantasy land, imagining everything is going to be horrendous. I'll be right beside you, and you're going to be just fine,' he told her. 'Of that I have no doubt. When it's all over we'll spend some time talking about how it went. After that, I believe your uncle has arranged for us to have lunch with him at his restaurant.'

'He's always trying to feed me,' Freya quipped, with a little half-smile playing about her pale lips. 'He thinks I don't eat enough.'

'Do you?' Nash asked sharply.

'I don't look like I'm starving myself, do I?'

Nash let his gaze rove boldly down her body, in the

baggy sweater and floor-length skirt, and his blue eyes glinted with humour. 'How would I be able to tell in that outfit? Do you always cover up like that?'

Out of the blue a memory came to him of Freya playing the female lead in an action/adventure movie he'd seen about four years back. Her role had been that of a fiery slave-girl in a sultan's harem, and she'd been all long tanned legs and curves aplenty. Just the recollection alone helped Nash get hot under the collar.

'It's a cold day, and I was trying to keep warm,' she replied testily.

'Then put the fire on,' he advised, walking to the door. He turned to briefly face her again, his expression serious but not bereft of kindness. 'Try and get a good night's rest. You're going to need all the energy you can muster for tomorrow. If you need me for anything…anything at all…here's my number.' He handed her a small business card. 'Sleep well, Freya.' And with that he departed.

Unmoving for several minutes after he'd gone, Freya stared down at the little card in her hand as if it was the first lifeline she'd been handed in a long time. Nash might only be helping her because of her uncle's claim on his friendship, but she couldn't deny she was glad to have someone like him on her side. There was something about the man that told her he could handle almost anything…that nothing would faze him because he'd seen it all—both the light and the dark side of human existence. Now, what had brought on that belief?

Shivering, Freya headed determinedly for her bedroom. She needed to survey the somewhat diminished contents of her wardrobe and decide what she was going to wear during her big ordeal tomorrow, when she would voluntarily face the press after so long spent trying to avoid them…

Nash dropped into his office to check that everything was ready for the press visit before going to collect Freya the next morning. He'd hardly been able to sleep for reflecting on their meeting yesterday. She hadn't confirmed it in so many words, but the idea that she'd been living like a hermit for the past two years, with only her uncle and her mother to stand by her in the face of all that had happened, had elicited a fierce, almost physical protest inside him. Injustice of any kind was apt to raise his hackles like nothing else, and he never failed to be astounded at the base depths some human beings could sink to in order to exploit another. She was well rid of her grasping, loud-mouthed ex-husband, that was for sure, and the best revenge in his book was always success. Nash didn't doubt for a second that Freya's star would rise again once her confidence had returned—and return it would. He would make sure of that.

Raising a corner of the cream-coloured blind at the window, he glanced broodingly down at the gleaming black Mercedes with personalised number plates parked beside the kerb below. Then, turning his head, he considered the dozens of signed celebrity photographs that were displayed round his office walls. He felt the ease and luxury of the bespoke suit he wore, which perfectly complemented his strong, hard physique. His good fortune never ceased to gratify him. In the inauspicious beginnings he had had, dreams of the kind of amazing success Nash enjoyed now had been either delusions or fantasies in other people's book. Yet he had still dreamed, and he had turned his dream into a reality.

But the thought wasn't entirely benign. It immediately provoked a disturbed frown between his dark blond brows, and for a moment Nash was consumed by some of the darker memories of his past. He'd been at the top of his profession for nearly six years now, but it never failed to bring him back down to earth when he remembered the painful and arduous route that had got him there. The point was he had risen above his seemingly insurmountable difficulties and succeeded. Now he needed to show Freya that she could do the same.

In the privileged circles that he moved in Nash enjoyed an admirable reputation amongst peers and clients alike, and he'd no doubt been helped by a biography that boosted the credentials he already had…even if some liberties had been taken with the facts… Most people assumed that he came from a fairly privileged background, with professional people as parents, and had benefited from a top-class education at a British public school. After all, his enunciation was perfect, with no traces of a Swedish accent at all. But

Nash wasn't the best publicist in the country for nothing. He'd never resorted to out-and-out deceit—but he intimately understood people's tendency to put two and two together and make five and he knew how to use it to his advantage.

From very early on in his career he'd been able to get away with revealing very little information about his origins—just a half-truth here or there, helped along by allowing various untrue assumptions to go unchallenged. That being the state of play, eventually a story had built up around him that was now more or less accepted as fact. He was Nash Taylor-Grant, raised in Suffolk, England, by a Swedish mother who was a chemist and a British father—an eminent scientist who had unfortunately died from a heart attack abroad on a business trip. There was also some vague notion that following his school years Nash had naturally gone on to Oxford or Cambridge—or at least one of the country's other leading universities.

The reality could not have been starker…

He hadn't been raised in Britain at all. He had been raised in a poor suburb of Stockholm in Sweden, the only son of Inga Johannsson—a laboratory technician who'd been forced to give up her job when she fell pregnant with Nash and had eventually had to work as an office cleaner just to keep body and soul together for herself and her small son. Nash's father had in truth been British. Nathan Taylor had been a biologist at the same laboratory where Inga had worked, and that was how the two of them had met. Unfortunately, when Nash was only three years old, his father had been killed in a car accident. With no compensation because she'd been unmarried, and no family to whom she'd been able to turn for help, Inga had had to get by on welfare. There had followed a series of disastrous relationships with the kind of men who would easily have found a niche in horror movies.

Flinching now from possibly the worst memory of them all, the time he'd witnessed yet again his mother being verbally and physically abused, Nash couldn't help but shudder. He remembered lunging at the man— his mother's current lover—and pummelling him with blows so hard that he'd split and broken the skin on his bare knuckles. But that had been before the man had turned on Nash and, with his far superior weight and strength, all but beaten him to a pulp. It would have been bad enough if Nash's ordeal had ended there, but neither he nor his mother could have anticipated what had happened next. In one horrific, unexpected act his attacker had produced a flash of something silver from inside his jeans pocket and torn open Nash's flesh with a flick-knife.

He'd almost lost his life that night. He'd certainly lost a good deal of blood, and put the fear of God into his poor mother as she'd sat weeping and wailing beside him in the ambulance that had gone screaming through the streets to take him to hospital.

Shame, hurt and fury moved through Nash's body

in one relentless wave of white-hot emotion as he remembered. Somewhere at the side of his ribs the old wound throbbed with renewed pain, and for a moment or two he really struggled to regain his equilibrium. Moving restlessly away from the window, he picked up the file he'd started on Freya Carpenter to will away the distracting and painful recollections that were bombarding him.

Yes…he'd experienced first-hand how human beings could wilfully hurt and maim each other—whether physically or with words—and because of that he had a genuine ability to understand the kind of hell this woman must have had to endure. But although he knew deep down that he didn't deserve to feel shame about his past any more, there was a part of him that still couldn't allow himself to admit the truth to everyone. He wished he could get over his own mistrust and think to hell with it, but it wasn't proving easy. Only time would tell if he would ever be at ease with himself enough to adopt such an approach…

As the press and television cameras whirred away in the small courtyard of Nash's smart Belgravia offices, before Freya read out her statement, he moved his gaze from the blur of journalists and photographers gathered round to study the woman that was the centre of so much clamouring attention standing by his side.

Astonishing beauty like hers scarcely needed the adornment of fine clothes and cosmetics to enhance it, but Nash would be a liar if he didn't concede that the elegant pink Chanel suit she wore—along with the perfectly applied make-up—elevated her looks to the realms of stand-out gorgeous. He already knew that the camera loved her—he'd seen the results often enough in photographs and on film—but now he could intimately see why. But did anyone but him guess that beneath Freya's faultlessly applied make-up her skin had the same pale sheen as ice-cold ivory?

Even now he sensed her tremble, and he deliberately slid his arm loosely round her small waist and gave her a reassuring squeeze. At that moment he didn't much care how the gesture might be misinterpreted. All he knew was a genuine desire to let her know that she wasn't alone, that he was firmly in her corner and would be staying there for the duration.

She turned briefly to acknowledge him, and the glint of warmth in her dazzling dark eyes momentarily unsteadied him. Clearing his throat, Nash addressed the small crowd in the courtyard. 'Ms Carpenter will now read out her statement, after which I will allocate just five minutes for any questions. All she and I would ask is that you accord her due respect and politeness for the great courage it has taken her today to speak out after two years of dignified silence. Thank you.'

It was over, and Freya knew she was still alive because her heart was beating strongly in her chest and her taste-buds could easily distinguish the strong Italian flavour of the coffee that she was sipping. Now alone with Nash, sitting on the stylish sofa in his office, her glance taking in the celebrity photographs that adorned the walls—many of whom she'd met—she could almost attest to breathing normally again.

'First hurdle over,' he commented, reaching for his own coffee as he settled himself in the matching armchair opposite. 'How does it feel?'

'What do you think?' Grimacing, Freya crossed one long slim leg over the other and saw Nash's gaze gravitate there almost immediately. For a moment it distracted her to be the recipient of that brooding and arresting cynosure, and the words she'd been about to speak got temporarily lodged inside her throat. She coughed a little to cover her unease. 'I feel like I've done a fire-walk…only I don't have the elation flooding me that's supposedly the result of doing one of those! Instead I'm wondering what I've started and if anything I've said will make a difference. If you want me to be frank…I'm also concerned about how James will retaliate. What I said doesn't exactly put him in a good light.'

Her words made Nash sit up in his chair, his cup of coffee returned swiftly to the table in front of him. 'Has he threatened you in any way?' he demanded.

'Do you mean physically?' Freya answered quietly, looking pensive. 'No. He has a good enough command of the English language to do enough damage using words alone. If you've read any of the newspaper reports from the past two years you must have noticed that.'

'You cry wolf enough times in my experience and you're going to get a kickback. I think the public are already drawing their own conclusions as far as your vindictive ex-husband is concerned, Freya. People aren't fools... '

'Words can cut so deep. Sometimes I think they can pierce the skin far worse than any physical violence. They have a way of inflicting damage where you're most vulnerable. That was James's particular little trick, anyway.'

'Even so...you can fight back.'

'Fight fire with fire, you mean? That's not my way.'

'I meant by getting on with your life again...by being a success! If you give up your acting career because your ex made you feel so bad that you can't face the world then he's won, Freya! You've made your statement today, stating the true facts of the case, and I know there'll be a lot of sympathy out there in return for your candour. After this you're bound to be in demand for all kinds of interviews, and depending on who's organising them and what their agenda is I'd advise you to agree to some of them. But don't worry...I'll guide you on that. If it means more positive publicity, then that's ultimately what we want. Plus it would get you back into appearing before the public again, and it might also help you rebuild some confidence.'

'I'll have to think about it.'

Leaning more fully against the chair-back, Freya

looked reticent. Nash wasn't blind. He could see that the woman was hurting, and hurting badly. It was becoming evident to him that she had suffered greatly in the past two years, and right now it was probably hard for her to believe that anything good could ever happen to her again. For someone with all the amazing assets she had it was a crying shame. Still, Nash wasn't in the business of lost causes. He was in the business of putting reputations to rights again.

'Remember what we agreed yesterday?' he prompted her, leaning forward and resting his hands on his knees. 'You have to give this enterprise your all! And it's not as though you have to negotiate all the hurdles on your own. I'll be with you, backing you up all the way…that's a promise.'

'What if public reaction isn't good? What if people still believe everything James has said about me?'

'It won't happen. Public sympathy will be totally on your side, Freya. Trust me, I know this business intimately. After today they'll know the truth about Frazier at last, and any further interest will be because people want you to do well again. Anyone who saw you out there today could easily see that you were a million miles away from being on the verge of a breakdown. You looked and were…amazing.'

They were just words, and Freya knew that, but she didn't doubt in those few charged moments that Nash meant them. She was only human, and could she help it if they melted her a little? Made her want more of this man's honest regard? Yet, even so, she knew the regard she craved ultimately had to come from inside herself. She couldn't afford to make any more mistakes, or constantly search for validity outside. Such a useless endeavour was always going to put her in a weak position and ensure her continuing vulnerability.

'Thanks. The suit helped. Uncle Oliver bought it for me when I attended my first awards ceremony.' Uncrossing her legs, she leaned forward to place her cup on the polished wooden coffee table between herself and Nash. Her lips quivered a little as she tried to form a smile. She was anxious that he wouldn't think she was deliberately fishing for compliments.

'It's a nice suit,' he agreed, an enigmatic smile of his own alighting on his highly sensual mouth.

CHAPTER FOUR

'FREYA? You're hardly eating anything, darling…'

'Please don't take it personally, Uncle Oliver…the food is wonderful, as always. I'm just not very hungry today. Do you mind?'

Meeting the older man's concerned stare, Freya touched her white linen napkin delicately to her lips and laid it on the table beside her plate. They were sitting in a private part of the beautiful French restaurant that Oliver Beaumarche owned—a kind of plush anteroom, with red velvet curtains, set aside for high-profile guests who preferred not to be seen dining by the rest of the public. But, even though the room was private, it was hard to eat when everything inside Freya felt as though it had been exposed to the penetrating glare of the most powerful microscope.

Having her performances on stage or screen scrutin-ised was one thing—but having to admit personal failings, such as marrying a man who had neither loved nor respected her, who had betrayed her trust and financially ruined her, and having then been driven to explain her actions publicly to defend herself…well, it had left her feeling a bit like an ant squashed by a heavy boot.

She lifted her gaze to observe the man sitting opposite her. Nash did not seem to be eating much of the delicious food that had been placed in front of him either. That inscrutable brow of his seemed to denote that he was thinking hard about something, and Freya wondered if he was considering that she should have made more of a stand against her ex-husband's vicious slander? To a man whose demeanour and presence suggested he was capable of dealing with any disaster— whether personal or public—it was probably beyond understanding that a person's self-esteem and will could be so crushed by someone far more manipulative and clever that they were, almost paralysed into inaction. Well, he was wrong if he thought her heart wasn't really in this battle, Freya considered with force. She knew it was time to fight back and put things right in her life. It was just taking a little time to acclimatise herself to the idea of voluntarily putting herself under the public gaze again—especially when her experience of it during the past two years had been so relentlessly negative.

'I've been thinking,' he said now, his deeply blue eyes focusing intently on Freya's face. 'It might be a good idea if we got you away from here for a few days. Interest is already hot after your statement today, and it's going to get even hotter. I've already received a couple of text messages from my secretary saying the phone hasn't stopped ringing since the interview. It might help to get a little relaxation and some sun in before we proceed with part two of our campaign. How does the South of France sound to you?'

'I've been telling her that she needs a holiday for the past two years!' Oliver exclaimed, animation lighting up his eyes—eyes the same silky brown as his beautiful niece's. 'But will she listen? I think it's a wonderful idea, Nash! Do you know of a place that's private, where she won't be disturbed?'

'I have a place of my own in the Dordogne,' the other man replied, his glance somewhat guarded as he moved it to the woman sitting beside Oliver…as though he were still carefully weighing up the suggestion in his mind. 'It's right in the heart of the countryside, and about twenty miles from the nearest town. We can go there.'

'We?' Freya stared at Nash in astonishment. Did he really mean them to go to the South of France together, and stay in a place that was miles from anywhere? She barely knew this man and he barely knew her! Did he really expect her to run pell-mell into the unknown with him without so much as a by-your-leave? Coiling her hair behind her ear, she let her dark eyes duel bravely with his now disturbingly dancing azure glance. It didn't help that he seemed to be mocking her a little. Did he think she'd back down and refuse to go because she was too scared of taking such a risk?

'It will be the perfect opportunity for me to get to

know you better, Freya. It's important that I learn as much about you as I can, since we're going to work together. And besides that it will get you out of the eye of the storm for a while. As well as being able to relax a bit more, without constant press intrusion, there'll be plenty of opportunity for being physically active too. There's some stunning countryside to walk in, as well as a pool at the house.'

The South of France sounded highly tempting, Freya had to admit. It conjured up lazy sun-drenched days, tempting culinary aromas, and the kind of relaxation that her body and mind craved deeply. Her uncle was right—she did need a holiday. Yet there was still the knotty little problem of going with Nash. Could she trust him as much as he seemed to be taking it for granted that she should? It was a tall order after what she'd endured at the hands of her ex-husband and a bloodthirsty press.

Silently acknowledging that she was too mentally fatigued to argue the case any more, Freya came to a decision. She would go. At the end of the day, Nash was a friend of her uncle's, and Oliver Beaumarche was no mean judge of character. The people he befriended usually became friends for life. And he wouldn't have even considered asking Nash to help if he thought the man was untrustworthy in any way.

She picked up her glass of mineral water and sipped it before replying. 'The thought of getting away from this circus is definitely appealing. When would we go? Don't you have to arrange things at work and at home?'

'I've got no one to answer to at home, as I live alone, and as things turn out I'm due some free time. Plus…this *is* work for me, remember?'

He smiled, and the smile highlighted the two fascinating thumbprints in his cheeks…dimples! Freya wished she didn't keep noticing things about him that distracted her from the matter in hand, but it wasn't easy when the man exuded an aura that would stun a room full of people into silence merely because he had entered it.

Yet what did it signify that Nash was a highly attractive man? She'd been around enough of them to know that the outside packaging meant very little, and it certainly didn't follow that she had to succumb to that attraction in any way. She didn't want to sign up for any more pain or shock, and she didn't want the rest of her life to be like the car crash she'd suffered a year ago. From now on Freya wanted to make good choices…wise choices that served her and didn't sabotage her efforts to improve her life. Nash had been hired to help her achieve some positive publicity and to rebuild her damaged reputation so that she wouldn't have to resume her career under a cloud. Other than that, their relationship would remain purely professional and platonic…she was absolutely certain about that.

'We'll leave the day after tomorrow, if that suits?' he suggested.

'Good,' Freya answered with unguarded frankness. 'The day after tomorrow is fine with me.'

Oliver beamed at them both.

* * *

'Hello?'

In her bedroom that same evening, Freya answered the ringing telephone, expecting her mother to be on the other end of the line. They'd talked earlier, after Freya had returned from lunch, but she often rang more than once in a day, to ascertain that her daughter was taking proper care of herself.

'You silly little bitch!'

It very definitely wasn't her mother. Instead, a harsh-sounding male voice ripped into her, sending icy chills charging violently down her spine. James. She dropped down onto the bed with its neatly spread satin eider-down, her heart racing.

'I've changed my number…how did you get it?'

'I have my contacts, as I'm sure you know. Anyway…what the hell do you think you're doing, rubbishing me in public like you did today? I warned you about making trouble for me, didn't I?'

Freya heard the resounding thud of her own heartbeat in her ears, despising the fact that her whole body was trembling as though she'd just emerged from a freezing plunge-pool. Yet, thinking of her new resolve to turn her life around, she knew that she couldn't keep on letting this cruel, manipulative man belittle or frighten her. She really did have to start fighting back.

'Leave me alone, James! We're over! Remember? You're nothing to do with me any more! And I didn't rubbish you to the press earlier today…I merely spoke the truth—something I should have done a long time ago. And if you try to get in touch with me again, or threaten me, then I won't hesitate to call the police and tell them what you're doing!'

'Do you really think they're going to believe you? Everyone knows you're a crazy, spoiled little bitch!'

'It's not me that's crazy, James.' It was hard to keep her voice steady, but deliberately drawing upon her acting skills Freya managed it. 'And if you make any more defamatory remarks like that, my lawyers will be contacting you too.'

'Who's helping you? Is it that meddling rich uncle of yours? Tell him from me to mind his own bloody business and keep his nose out of where it isn't wanted!'

'Why don't you tell him yourself? Or can't you do that because the truth is you're not so sure about coming out on top in that fight? You're only capable of threatening women! Why don't you just get on with your life and let me get on with mine? You've got your girlfriend and your baby and most of my money…surely that's enough to keep you from feeling so dissatisfied?'

'I won't be satisfied until your name is dirt—until people say "Freya Carpenter? You mean that crazy, no-talent actress? What ever happened to her?"'

He slammed down the phone in a temper, and Freya shakily returned the receiver to its rest and covered her face with her hands. 'Please, no… Not again.'

Minutes later, she almost catapulted up to the ceiling when the phone rang again. Feeling sick with nerves, she snatched up the receiver and said loudly, 'Right! As soon as I put down this phone I swear I'm going to ring the police!'

'Freya? What's happening? It's me…Nash.'

'Nash?' She almost crumpled with relief. Sliding her fingers through her long waving hair, she couldn't stop shaking. 'I'm sorry about that…I thought it was James.'

'Have you talked to him? Has he been round there?'

'No, he hasn't been round, thank God! He rang me just now. I thought today might spark off something with him. I knew he'd be mad at me for speaking out.'

'Are you okay?'

'I am now.'

'According to my information, he's supposed to be flying out to Antigua today. Did the call sound like it was long-distance?'

'It might have been. I don't know…I couldn't really say.'

'Obviously he threatened you? What did he say?'

There was such command in Nash's voice that Freya didn't think to play down the truth. Besides, it was a relief to be able to tell someone what was really happening for a change, instead of pretending things weren't so bad and bearing the situation on her own.

'He said he won't be satisfied until my name is dirt, and that he's warned me about making trouble for him… Do I have to go on?' she replied, her skin feeling clammy now that the shock was slowly ebbing away. Dragging the silky blue eiderdown onto her lap, she spread it over her knees.

Detecting the weariness in her tone, Nash clenched his granite jaw tight. After the guts it must have taken for her to speak out to the press earlier on today, it must have been like a kick in the teeth to receive a threatening late-night phone call from that bastard Frazier, he thought. Examining the cut-crystal glass that he'd half filled with brandy, he swirled the darkly golden liquid round a little before placing it down on the windowsill untouched.

'No, sweetheart,' he conceded a little huskily. 'You don't have to go on. What you've just told me illustrates the picture perfectly. You should have rung the police straight away…did you?'

'No. It hasn't helped me in the past, so why should it now? Every time I reported anything James always got to them straight after and told them I was making it all up because I was lonely or drunk or high, and I craved attention.'

'How the hell has he still got your number? Didn't you have it changed when all this kicked off?'

'Of course I did! More than once. But he said he has contacts—whatever that means. How he gets my number, I don't know.'

'Well, I have some contacts myself, at Scotland Yard, and rest assured I'll be talking to them as soon as I get off the line to you! How are you feeling now? Do you want me to come over?'

'I don't think he'll try ringing again… Anyway, I won't answer the phone any more tonight. I'll be fine.

I've been dealing with this sort of thing for a long time now…I should be used to it. You don't have to come over, but thanks all the same for offering.'

Nash had real trouble accepting her assertion. He knew first-hand what it was to witness a man's intimidation of a woman, and nothing could unleash his fury more than that. She probably wouldn't sleep, he told himself, thinking of her walking round that chilly house all alone. And after a night with no sleep she was going to have the added challenge of dealing with a barrage of reporters and photographers waiting for her on her front doorstep in the morning. As he'd told her earlier at lunch—interest would be hot after today's statement.

Staring out of the sixth-storey window of his Westminster apartment, he contemplated the London skyline in all its twinkling late-night glory. It was a privilege he enjoyed most nights, and he never took it for granted. For a boy who had been raised in a tiny flat in the backstreets of Stockholm, it was the difference between a palace and a hovel. Rubbing his hand round the back of his neck, Nash quickly revised his plan of going to Freya's in the early hours of the morning to give her some support with the press and came up with a far better idea.

'Pack a bag,' he ordered bluntly.

'What?'

'Get your passport, throw some things into a suitcase and get ready to leave. I'm coming over there to pick you up and bring you back to my place. You can stay here until we travel to France on Friday morning.'

'That's a little extreme, isn't it?'

'Extreme? After what you've just experienced? Listen to me, Freya... I won't take the chance of Frazier bothering you again tonight, and this is the best way to ensure that he can't get to you. You already know that tomorrow morning there's going to be even more media interest, and probably a crowd of photographers and reporters waiting to catch you leaving the house... That's if they aren't there already?'

'I've got about a half a dozen of them camped out on my doorstep.'

'That clinches it, then. I should have thought of it earlier, but you'll definitely be better off at my place.'

There was silence at the other end of the line. Feeling his skin prickle with an acute sense of foreboding, Nash made his voice sharp. He knew she must be feeling at a pretty low ebb after that phone call, and he didn't want to risk her getting any lower and doing herself some harm. If she'd been addicted to drugs it crossed his mind that they might have been prescription drugs. What if she had a drawer full of powerful sleeping pills, for instance? Perhaps she'd never consider such a thing in a million years, but Nash didn't know her well enough yet to easily dismiss the possibility.

'Freya? Did you hear what I just said?'

'I heard you,' she answered, that mesmerising brushed-velvet voice of hers making a whisper-soft imprint on the part of him that wasn't entirely impervious to more tender feelings. 'This isn't normal, living like this…is it? I wonder if my life will ever be normal again? If I'll ever be able to have any peace?'

How often had Nash reflected on those very same thoughts when he'd been going through hell all those harsh years ago, when he'd lived in his hometown? Well, he had turned dark beginnings into a far brighter future, and so would Freya. Nash would show her how or die in the attempt! It was fast becoming clear to him that this woman could really benefit from some time away from the scene of all her unhappiness. Oliver had confided in him that his niece hadn't left the UK in almost two and a half years—apparently he'd tried to persuade her to take a break abroad many times, and the restaurateur had homes in Spain and New York she could stay at—but the mental cruelty that Frazier had visited on her had made her almost agoraphobic.

'You just need a change of scene, sweetheart. Going to France for a while will be good for you. Staying at home you've just got all the same things and associations that you face every day, and they're like permanent reminders of everything that seems wrong in your life. Leaving them behind for a while will help you see things in a new perspective.'

'You must think I've completely lost the plot—but I wasn't always like this.'

'I know, Freya. I've seen you up there on the silver screen, remember?'

'That was a long time ago. I was a very different girl then.'

'Not so very different.' Catching his reflection outlined in the huge plate-glass window that encompassed a stunning view of the Thames, Nash saw a brief flash of pain register on his face. He couldn't pretend her words had glanced off him without making a dent somewhere. 'Life's just knocked you about a bit... It will get better, I promise.'

'What makes you so sure?'

'Good instincts.' He grinned at his own sense of certainty. If only he could transfer some of it to the traumatised woman at the other end of the phone...

'Well, if you're so sure that staying at your place tonight and going to France is the right thing, then I'll go and pack my suitcase.'

He heard her sigh, but this time there was definite resolve in her much more steady voice and Nash was relieved. 'I'll be there in half an hour,' he promised, then rang off and straight away depressed the numbers on his cordless phone for Scotland Yard, thinking as he did so that an ordinary member of the public was probably accorded more protection from the law and from friends and family than this lovely, talented woman whose face had graced movie screens...

A faint misty light was coming through the slatted silk blinds, dappling the damson-coloured duvet on the bed, and, blinking her eyes open in surprise, Freya sat up in a flash, barely knowing where she was for a moment. Peering at the illuminated digits on the alarm clock on the cabinet beside her, she registered the time in amazement. Five past seven!

'I don't believe it!' she muttered, checking again. She'd slept right through the night without waking up once…something almost unheard of! She was shocked to her marrow, especially as she had been sleeping in a strange bed as well.

She glanced round the spacious, frighteningly neat room, with its definitely masculine décor—there was no hint of anything remotely feminine amongst the muted colours and expensive modern furniture that she could easily detect—and, drawing her knees up to her chest, wrapped her arms around them as she contemplated her situation. Last night she'd been too tired and mentally fatigued after the phone incident to enter into a protracted conversation with Nash about what had happened. As it was, her nerves had been even more frazzled by the clamour of photographers almost swamping her and Nash as he'd spirited her away from them to his waiting car.

On reaching his apartment, she'd declined the nightcap and alternative cup of tea he'd offered and asked if he would mind if she just turned in. Immediately he'd shown her into this bedroom, which was easily reminiscent of a suite at a top-class hotel, and told her to try and get a good night's rest. When he'd said the words Freya had hardly believed that such a thing was possible, but here she was, seven hours later, feeling more rested and more refreshed than she'd done in absolutely ages.

Was it the distinct feeling of security she'd received from knowing that she was in Nash's domain and effectively under his protection? Was that why she had slept so well? That late night call from James had shaken her up badly, and to be honest when Nash had mentioned her spending the night at his flat part of Freya had been utterly relieved that he'd suggested it. Should she now berate herself because her defences had been low and she'd accepted an offer of help? If she'd accepted more help during the past two years when she'd needed it, then maybe she wouldn't have ended up as mentally bruised and battered as she was.

Feeling suddenly guilty that Nash might be already up and about and starting his day while she was still in bed, Freya threw back the duvet and put her feet to the floor. Just as she did there was a soft knock at the door.

'Freya? Are you awake?'

'Yes…I was just about to get up. Come in.' She extended the invitation automatically, without thinking.

Pushing the door wide, Nash was hardly prepared for the sight of one very shapely brunette, scantily clad in a flimsy red silk camisole with spaghetti straps and—as far as he could tell—matching panties, sitting on the bed rubbing the sleep from her very seductive dark eyes while her glorious dark hair cascaded freely down over her shoulders. His blue eyes locked onto her startled gaze with undisguised heat, and he had to ruefully tear them away when, realising how she must appear, Freya grabbed the duvet and quickly covered her exposed lower half with it.

'I'm sorry! I should have grabbed my robe,' she muttered, clearly embarrassed.

'It's me that should apologise,' Nash drawled, helplessly admiring the sight of her again, and laying a hand against his chest in the pristine white shirt as if to somehow corral his suddenly thundering heartbeat. The corners of his mouth hitched upwards into a definitely roguish grin. 'Except that I feel I should be thanking you too.'

'Thanking me? What for?'

'What for?'

His blue eyes glittering like the most compelling sapphires, he shrugged in disbelief. 'Sweetheart, if you have to ask me that then you really *have* been leading a sheltered life for too long!' he teased.

CHAPTER FIVE

SHE hadn't been to France for years. The last time had been when she'd attended the Cannes Film Festival—not to promote a film she'd had a role in, but as moral support for a friend of hers who'd made a very engaging film short. They'd had a wonderful time, Freya recalled, reminiscing as Nash drove their hire car through deserted French country roads. She sat beside him, her eyes shielded behind the pair of obligatory black sunglasses to keep out the glare of the midday sun and also to hide behind should some opportunist paparazzi happen to spot her.

She had always intended to venture into the French countryside one day and see for herself the scenery and way of life that so many ex-pats were enthralled by, and Freya's gaze alighted on the gently lilting verdant landscape with a quiet yet discernible excitement blossoming inside her. If she had to give an opinion on what she'd seen so far she would say that rural France was like an elegant apple tartan while its English equivalent was more akin to a sturdy bread-and-butter pudding—both sublime in their own way, but meeting different needs for different palates…

Suppressing a grin at her fanciful foray into culinary metaphors, she chewed down almost guiltily on her lower lip. This was no time for levity. God knew she'd been in dire straits for the past couple of years, and her plight had been only too serious… But right then Freya felt strangely inexplicably light—as though some of the troubles weighing so heavily on her heart had suddenly somehow lifted.

Stealing a glance at her serious-faced companion, able to explore that firm chiselled jaw of his and those enviable long eyelashes at close quarters, she allowed herself a surprising and momentary fantasy. They could be any ordinary young couple, she mused… Husband and wife taking a romantic break away from their busy lives in London—going to a place they'd bought for a steal a few years ago in the Dordogne and done up bit by bit, just the way they liked. They were going to unwind, lounge by the pool, read intriguing novels upon which they'd eagerly share their opinions over a glass of good red wine, and companionably share the cooking of the odd meal at home together, while at other times they would eat out in local cafés or bistros. Charming little family-run places, where they would be made most welcome and then discreetly left alone to enjoy the most divine food and, more importantly, each other's company…

So deep in the fantasy had Freya allowed herself

to drift that she didn't realise she'd released a long, heartfelt sigh.

'Won't be too much longer now before we're there,' Nash remarked, turning his head to briefly glance at her. 'What were you thinking about just then?'

'What do you mean?'

'That sigh.' The faintest lift at the corner of his mouth denoting amusement, Nash gave his full attention to the road again, slowing the car on the approach to a crossroads and flicking his gaze towards the array of signs there.

'It's just nice to be away.' Shrugging almost guiltily when she thought of the compelling little daydream she'd just conjured up for herself—a daydream that was outrageous when she thought about it in the cold light of day—Freya moved her head to glance out of the window. 'I'm in the middle of nowhere and nobody knows I'm here…except you, my uncle and my mother.'

'Freedom,' Nash agreed.

'Yes—freedom. It doesn't happen very often.'

Not long after the crossroads, they arrived at the centuries-old renovated farmhouse that was Nash's favourite retreat in the world. Its solid stone and mortar well-rooted in the earth, it looked as though it had stood there as long as the land containing it. The moment he drove the new-looking Renault he'd hired onto the huge expanse of gravelled drive and the scent of sweet herbs and newly cut grass drifted in through the opened car windows his body and mind seemed to heave a collective sigh. He undoubtedly thrived on the challenges and demands of his work, but he'd be a liar if he said he never felt like having the occasional break away from stressful city life.

Soon, with the sun blazing down on his dark blond head, Nash stood outside the engaging blue-shuttered façade with Freya, satisfaction and pleasure flowing through him at the thought of spending the next few days there, speculating if the stunning Dordogne valley and this gracious old house nestled within it would effect the same timeless magic for her that it did for him. She was, after all, the first woman he had ever brought there. In fact, he couldn't even recall mentioning its existence to any of his previous girlfriends. He'd always thought of Beau Refuge, as he'd christened it when the renovations were done, as his private and secret bolt-hole—a haven away from the rat race, and a place where he could unwind and enjoy his own company after days filled to the rafters with wall-to-wall people… But where else could he bring a famous movie actress and accord her some much needed privacy as well? This had to be the perfect place.

'You're a lucky man.'

He turned and met the full force of Freya's dazzling smile. Although her eyes were still shielded behind her glamorous dark glasses, Nash could feel the sudden unguarded warmth from her gaze practically drilling a hole in his chest.

'I wouldn't argue with that,' he drawled lazily, his

glance making an admiring reconnaissance of her body in a candy-pink shirt and pale blue denim jeans. Even though very little flesh was on show, apart from wrists and ankles, and even though her fairly ordinary attire was not provocative in itself, it couldn't hide the soft, undulating curves of the very feminine body beneath it. And, remembering the mouthwatering picture she'd presented when he'd walked in on her yesterday morning in his spare bedroom—red silk underwear and all—Nash couldn't help the dizzying electrical charge that zig-zagged like lightning into the pit of his stomach.

'How long have you had this place?' she asked, turning her face quickly away to re-examine the thick white walls and sky-blue shutters facing them.

'About five years now. There's a couple who live locally that look after it for me…Victor and Didi. They should have stocked the fridge and the cupboards for us, and got the rooms ready. Want to go in and have a look around? I'll bring the cases.'

'Okay.'

After depositing their luggage in individual rooms, and telling Freya to explore the place at her leisure, Nash went outside to sit in the sun on a cane chair beside the glimmering aquamarine swimming pool. Before he made the couple of calls he had to make on his mobile he let his glance scrutinise the vale of lush woodland to the right of him, followed by the recently ploughed fields to his left.

Whilst they'd encountered no problem of being

pestered at either airport they'd travelled from and to, Nash knew he could not afford to rest on his laurels and be lax in his vigilance. Even though this place was remote enough—and he'd driven on as many back roads as he could to get there—he still had to be on his guard for possible intruders. It only took one person to recognise Freya and report her whereabouts to a local paper and before they knew it they would find themselves knee-deep in picture-hungry paparazzi.

It would be a damn shame after getting her this far without a hitch, Nash reflected, spearing his fingers through his hair. He wanted publicity for her, yes... But he wanted it to be positive, upbeat publicity—and to achieve that Freya needed the chance to rebuild her confidence away from the invasion of cameras and people. And of course the barrage of abuse she'd taken from her malignant ex-husband.

Yesterday Nash had learned with satisfaction that Frazier had been stopped and questioned by the police on his arrival in Antigua, and issued with a strongly worded warning straight from Scotland Yard. Nash's contact there had been only too obliging, and had done what he could to illustrate to James Frazier that if he so much as tried to contact Freya again he would be recommending a restraining order with severe consequences. When he'd related the events to Freya— Nash had been gratified to see some of the fear that haunted her leave her eyes. Now his hope was that she would relax sufficiently to start seeing the myriad possibilities of living a far happier life than she'd been living of late…

In the middle of unpacking, Freya glanced out the tall shuttered windows that she'd immediately opened wide on entering the bedroom and glanced interestedly across at Nash, sitting in a cane chair beside the swimming pool. His tousled blond hair was a halo of dark golden flame, and his lightly tanned, fit body was clad in long ecru-coloured shorts and a white T-shirt. As he sat with his mobile phone pressed to his ear, Freya saw the sinews in his muscular arms flex a little as he moved, and her mouth went as dry as tinder.

Impatient with herself, she turned abruptly away from the too-disturbing sight of him and stood in the centre of the room, with its high ceiling, cool stone floor and neatly made bed, frowning deeply. She had no business ogling him like some starstruck movie fan, she chided herself irritably. In effect they were both at the farmhouse to work. Nash to get to know her with a view to helping her professionally, and she to seriously think about how she was going to proceed with her career.

Her little fantasy in the car when they'd been travelling earlier—about them being husband and wife—had been totally ridiculous and unhelpful. Freya wasn't interested in having another relationship—and, not only that, the mere idea of getting married again was enough to make her shudder. No…she would avoid entanglement at all costs, she decided firmly, and concentrate on making her future as good as she could make it, knowing that she was going to stay a single woman for a very long time.

But even as she laid her folded T-shirts and under-wear into a lined drawer that smelled of lavender, Freya couldn't help wondering why it was that a man as dynamic and attractive as Nash lived alone. Was he in a relationship at the moment? she mused. Her hands stilled over the drawer to properly reflect upon the matter. Just because he lived alone it didn't signify that he wasn't seeing someone. Perhaps he had been married, divorced, or even widowed and at the moment was unattached? And what had happened to the daring beauty who had shoehorned herself into that outrageous dress at the party?

Before she knew what she'd intended, Freya found herself gravitating towards the window again, to rest her gaze on the man whose charismatic presence was so plaguing her mind. He'd left his chair and was now standing by the pool, gazing out at some distant viewpoint that she couldn't immediately fathom. As she continued to stare—her body only too intimately aware of the stunning impact of his tanned, golden good looks—Nash moved his head ever so slightly. In the next second he was staring back at her, his sensual lips unsmiling and his fathomless blue eyes locked onto hers as though he had discovered something far more compelling than whatever he had been looking at earlier to rest his gaze upon.

Hurriedly moving away from the window, Freya

suddenly felt as if her limbs had lost all their strength and she was standing upright by sheer will alone…

'What's that?'

'What?'

'That huge bird! It looks like some kind of bird of prey.'

'It's a heron…you see a lot of them round here.'

Reaching for his wine glass, Nash sipped a little of the dry red wine that was made locally and of which his rustic wine cellar contained a generous amount. They were sitting outside the front of the house, around an octagonal wooden table with matching chairs and a huge green umbrella they'd agreed to dispense with as the sun started to set. The air was swiftly cooling after a day of hot Mediterranean sunshine, but he was quite content to sit outside and bask in the scenery. He included Freya in that, and told himself he was only human.

She was wearing a pink thin-strapped sundress that showed off her slender arms and great shoulders to perfection. Never let it be said that a woman's shoulders couldn't be as sexy as hell, he thought with unashamed appreciation. Her sunglasses now positioned on the top of her head, she was squinting up at the sky—intent on watching the heron she'd spotted glide gracefully on the calm, still air. Just now she radiated the same excitement as a child who had discovered something new and fascinating—some amazing titbit of information that she could add to the growing storehouse of interesting facts and figures she was busy accumulating. He found himself smiling as he observed her.

'Isn't that an oak tree over there?' Lowering her glance, she pointed at a towering specimen just beyond the swimming pool.

'That's right.'

'I somehow expected the trees to be different to the varieties we have at home. Silly, I know.' She blushed and reached for a piece of baguette that had been left over from their alfresco supper. She had not, Nash observed, so much as touched a drop of the wine in her glass yet.

'You like trees?' he asked.

'I just love being out in nature.' She lifted her shoulders and dropped them again, carefully breaking some bread between her fingers, as if reflecting on something that belied the joy she had just expressed. 'Unfortunately my crazy life often prevented me from enjoying it as much as I would have liked to. I regret that.'

'Well, now you have it all on the doorstep. What would you like to do tomorrow after breakfast? Go for a walk? There's a little church not far from here that you might like to take a look at.'

'I'd love that!'

She had that little-girl joy on her face again, and Nash knew it wasn't just the wine that was warming his blood. Straightening in his chair, he settled his gaze into the same intense examination of her features as an artist about to paint her portrait.

'Why are you looking at me like that?'

'Do you have to ask?' he challenged.

'Yes, I do, as a matter of fact.'

'I'm looking at you because, inevitably, your beauty is distracting me.'

She dipped her head for a moment, clearly discomfited. Nash thought it seemed strange that receiving compliments might disturb her.

'Looks don't mean much at the end of the day...not really. I know the profession I was in doesn't really bear that out—especially where women are concerned—but it's what's on the inside that's important...don't you think?'

The way she asked the question made him realise she was anxious to have her view confirmed. Her insecurities about being accepted for herself were easy to detect. She didn't want to be admired for her looks alone. Freya needed to know that she was admired for the person she was. Nash didn't suppose for one second that her painful dalliance with James Frazier had helped her case any.

'True. But all the same I don't necessarily go with the "looks don't matter" argument. Everyone—man, woman or child—is engaged by beauty. You don't have to be defensive about the assets God gave you. They were bestowed on you...and the world...to appreciate.'

'That heron flying by just now...commanding the sky with such grace...that's real beauty.'

'Ever thought that he might be looking down at you and thinking the same thing?'

His teasing raised goosebumps on her bared skin, and Freya shivered. Not only did this man rob her of the ability to keep her mind on her train of thought, but his low, sexy voice, easily suggestive of smoky bar rooms and hot, no-holds-barred lovemaking in the most unconventional places, definitely drove the point home. Perhaps she shouldn't have so readily agreed to come to France with him after all? This breathtakingly lovely place that was clearly his own private refuge from the rest of the world was far too seductive to her already fascinated senses…as was he. Perhaps the situation—the two of them alone together for an indefinite amount of time in an isolated farmhouse—was simply asking for trouble?

'Aren't you going to drink your wine?' he prompted when she stayed silent.

Registering her untouched glass, Freya shook her head. 'I don't really drink much…just the very occasional glass.'

'No?'

'Don't you believe me?'

She was stunned by the intense wave of anguish that swept over her at the thought that he didn't. If that was the case, then why was he agreeing to help mend her reputation? Was it only to appease her uncle? If he thought she had a drink problem, as James had often told the press, maybe he believed she took drugs too? Her stomach recoiled in protest.

'I wasn't casting any aspersions.' Nash's voice was calm in contrast to the small riot that was going on inside Freya. 'But now that the topic has come up we do need to talk about some of the things that have been said about you in the press. If I'm going to help you then I need to know everything.'

'So you think I'm an alcoholic and a druggie? Is that what you're saying? What about a neurotic, demanding, crazy woman on the verge of a nervous breakdown? Do you think I'm that too?'

Jumping to her feet, Freya started to walk away from the table towards the house, but her desire for flight was halted when she felt her upper arm firmly commanded by a large forceful hand and she was hauled back to face a suddenly not so benign-looking Nash. Even when he dropped her arm her feet remained rooted to the ground in shock.

'We're going to get nowhere fast if you can't have an honest discussion with me about this! I'm not accusing you of anything. I just want to know the truth so that I can help you!'

'Are you sure it's not just so that you can judge me, just like everybody else has judged me?' she fired back, her dark eyes beyond hurt. 'Is your own life so beyond any taint of blame or scandal that you can have the nerve to act like some kind of moral jury on my past conduct?'

'I'm not looking to judge you! If you stopped being so damned defensive for a minute we might get somewhere!'

They were both breathing hard. Finally Nash dropped his hands to hips that were lean and straight as an arrow and sighed. As his glance regretfully roamed the expression of acute distress on Freya's face, he fired a question.

'*Do* you have a drink or drug problem? If you do then I have a responsibility to help you get some proper help to deal with it.'

'You mean rehab?'

At the look of resignation that appeared Nash couldn't deny the bolt of alarm that ricocheted through him. Following that, there was the sensation of utter bone-crushing disappointment. He had so hoped that everyone had been wrong about the drink and drug label that Freya had been tagged with, but now it seemed that the speculation in the press had some foundation after all…

God knew his own past was hardly without taint, and he might indeed be standing in judgement—but only because he believed that she was in effect throwing her incredible ability down the toilet if she was an addict of any kind. No matter how bad things had been for Nash in the past he had never resorted to drugs—medicinal or otherwise—to ease his pain…

'So you *do* have a problem?' Shaking his head, he started to walk away a short distance, thinking hard in the twilight.

'I don't take anything other than the odd paracetamol for period pains,' Freya asserted quietly behind him.

Turning to regard her, Nash saw her beautiful dark eyes glisten with tears. His mouth felt dry as gravel and sawdust combined at the sight.

'I barely touch alcohol and I have never in my life

smoked dope or snorted cocaine or done anything similar. My ex-husband, however, spent a frightening amount of our money on all those things. What I'm telling you is absolutely true. If you feel the need—why don't you come up and search my room? Just in case I managed to smuggle drugs on the way out here and have a secret stash squirrelled away!' Walking right up to him, Freya prodded her finger into Nash's chest. 'After all…I would hate to think that your own whiter than white reputation was in any way sullied by your association with such a loser as me!'

'Hey!' His hand locked onto her wrist as she spun away and held her tight. Before he could get out the words that were furiously backing up in his brain, pure primal instinct took over and he kissed her instead. For a moment she was soft and compliant in Nash's arms, and he felt her sag against him almost in a kind of hungry relief.

A passionately arresting moan escaped her—the sound raising all the hairs on the surface of his skin—and then, just as he warmed to the provocative sweetness of her satin-textured lips and the taste of her tongue swirling hotly against his own, she ripped her mouth away, pushing at him hard with both hands to put some distance between them. Her breasts were straining against the thin cotton of her dress with each agitated breath, and her dark eyes were flashing angry sparks of barely contained indignation.

'How dare you? Just what did you think you were doing?'

'In any language I think it would be easily understood that I was kissing you.' A throaty, gravelly cadence
almost locked Nash's throat.

'Why?'

'Why?' With a wry glance from his azure-blue eyes,
he crossed his arms in front of his white T-shirt. The
action made the muscles in his biceps bunch hard. 'Put
it down to the heat of the moment.'

Staring at him, her agitated breath appearing to slow
down, Freya closed her lips against what she might have
been going to say and looked at him instead like some
kind of little-girl lost.

'I don't need to come up and search your room for
drugs.' He sighed. 'If you tell me you're not using then
I'm going to believe you unless I see evidence to change
my mind. All I was trying to do was ascertain the kind
of help you needed, so that I could put you in touch with
the right people. That's all. I want you to be in good
shape when you pick up your career again.'

'Oh.'

'Pact?'

'I'm sure you can understand why I'm naturally a
little prickly about the subject. Wouldn't you be under
the circumstances? It's perfectly horrible, having people
tell lies about you. And as far as picking up my career
again goes…well, we'll see. I don't even have an agent
any more—much less am I in a position to be offered
any scripts to read!'

'That can easily be rectified, Freya. I know plenty of

agents in the business. I could ring any one of them tomorrow and get you an interview. But first you need to unwind and relax, get yourself feeling good again.'

'All right.' Smoothing her hands down the sides of her pretty cotton dress, she looked distracted for a moment, as if she didn't quite know what to do next. Even so, Nash couldn't attest to regretting that inflammatory kiss they'd shared just a few moments ago. Not when his whole body was still craving her touch as though it were indeed an opiate he was becoming addicted to.

'I think I'll have an early night, if you don't mind? I'm feeling rather tired after all the travelling and everything today.'

Without waiting for him to comment Freya turned and went back inside the house, leaving Nash to murmur a heartfelt expletive to the rapidly cooling night air…

CHAPTER SIX

She couldn't sleep. When the dawn finally broke, Freya got up, showered and dressed, then sat quietly on her bed making a half-hearted attempt to read the book she'd brought with her.

Once again the words blurred on the page and, more than a little exasperated, she pushed to her feet and went to the window. Opening it with as little noise as possible, she drank in the sharp cold blast of morning air and let her gaze roam the beauty of the surrounding countryside. But her mind wasn't really on the sublime scenery. After Nash had kissed her so hungrily last night it was practically impossible to concentrate on anything else.

She'd been so mad at him…not for the kiss…but for believing for even one second that she was some kind of unstable addict. Then, just when she'd thought he was like everyone else after all—quick to judge her and point out her faults—he'd completely confounded her with that kiss and made her melt. Freya had still been shaking when she'd climbed the stairs to her room in the aftermath.

There was no way she could lie to herself and pretend she had been offended, even though she'd acted so indignant at the time. How could a woman not like a kiss that made her feel feminine and desirable once more after she'd started to doubt if any man would ever desire her again? Almost immediately her own hunger had risen to meet his, and the sheer desperate ache that had built inside her, so avid for release, had terrified her. If it had carried on she might easily have ended up in Nash's bed… A breathless little sound escaped her into the freezing air. Had she completely lost her mind?

Distressed, Freya turned away from the window and, grabbing up her sweater, draped it round her shoulders over the blue shirt she'd donned with a pair of white jeans, then hurriedly vacated the room to go in search of some coffee…

She didn't mention the kiss and, taking his cue from her, Nash decided not to raise the topic either. However, from the moment he set eyes on Freya the next morning—sitting outside at the table, catching the sun's first rays as she sipped her coffee—he was immediately aware of the tension it had wrought. It was as though he had transgressed an emblazoned prohibitive notice whose instructions had screamed *Keep Out*—but he'd paid no attention and committed the deed anyway.

Now he couldn't help cursing himself for his self-restraint being so badly knocked off kilter that he'd ended up kissing her as he had. Even though he'd been so aroused it had been painful, he knew it hadn't been the best of moves. And he certainly didn't make a habit of hitting on his attractive female clients. In fact he'd always made it a strict rule not to. Also, after his unwelcome suspicions about Freya's alleged addictions, practically ravishing her on their first night away together was hardly going to help engender the kind of trust they needed to forge between them to work together. From now on, he decided, his own behaviour had to be exemplary too. And if Freya proved to become even more distracting, then Nash would just have to give her as much space as possible, so that temptation would not be put in his way too often.

Considering he had to protect her from the paparazzi as well—it was going to be a hell of a tall order...

Later, walking across the fields from the house on their way to the small country church Nash had spoken about, he watched her lithe figure moving just ahead of him— her straw hat hiding her mane of opulent hair and her hips swaying almost too provocatively to be borne. He clenched his jaw as a trickle of sweat meandered down the small of his back underneath his shirt.

'You okay?' he called.

'I'm fine. This is great!'

'The church is just up ahead. There's the spire.'

When they reached their destination, Freya found to her disappointment that the ponderous oak door that led into the building was emphatically locked. Several huge rusting padlocks attested to the fact that it was no longer regularly used, and both the grounds and building displayed signs of elegant dereliction.

'Oh, what a shame! I was looking forward to having a look round inside.'

'How do you feel about graveyards? This one is pretty interesting.' Nash smiled.

Appraising the opened wrought-iron gates, and seeing the tombs looming up beyond them amid long grasses and weeds, Freya nodded. Removing her glasses for a moment, she wiped away the perspiration that had accumulated on the bridge of her nose and her forehead with the back of her hand. The day was warm and steadily getting warmer. It was a far cry from the overcast skies of the drizzly London they had left behind.

'Why don't you lead the way?' she suggested lightly—if only for the chance to watch him unobserved.

All morning she'd had a restless tension simmering inside her—ever since he'd appeared to join her for breakfast. Over fresh coffee, French bread, fruit and cheese, Freya had eyed Nash discreetly but helplessly as they'd talked and eaten, her gaze often alighting on that sensual carved mouth of his and remembering how delicious it had felt against hers, a jolt of hungry need flashing through her insides as she did so. What was astounding was that she'd scarcely thought about her past ordeal at all—or the fact that at home stories would be appearing in the newspapers about her again, after the interview she'd given. She'd even stopped looking over her shoulder, expecting paparazzi to jump out at her from some unnoticed hiding place. It was a revelation.

Now, following Nash into the churchyard, she found her attention reluctantly diverted by the presence of the large tombs that lay all around them. The ponderous stone cases were worn and weathered and strewn with lichen and moss, and several of them had pictures of the deceased family members entombed inside them, along with ornate tributes that included fake flowers fashioned out of plastic. An oppressive feeling started to gather strength in Freya at the sight of them, and she found herself wanting to leave. The realisation that they were family tombs slightly disturbed her—especially when she saw that some of the pictures were of children.

'It's too sad…can we go?' she asked, a betraying quiver in her voice.

'Sure.' Waiting for her to precede him out through the ornate iron gates, Nash frowned. 'I'm sorry if that upset you,' he remarked, his jaw set as he considered her from behind the dark shades that shielded his incredible eyes. 'I just thought you might find it interesting how differently they do things.'

'It was the pictures of the children,' Freya admitted.

'Yeah…I know. You like kids?'

'Very much. I always wanted to have at least three or four. I suppose, being an only child, a part of me always longed to have a brother or sister to play with. How about you? Do you want a family one day? Or maybe you already have kids?'

Nash couldn't fail to sense her intense regard behind the huge dark glasses. He couldn't deny the feeling of deep-rooted resistance that rose up inside him on the subject of having children of his own. He was thirty-six, and time was marching on, but he didn't know if he'd ever be ready to face the daunting prospect of being a father. The gut-wrenching experience of his own childhood as far as substitute fathers were concerned was enough to put him off the idea for life. And whilst Nash very much enjoyed women, and had had a few relationships—admittedly not long-lasting ones—he really didn't view himself as marriage material. Perhaps the truth was that he enjoyed the single life of a bachelor too much? Anyway…he had not met a woman so far that he wanted to share the rest of his life with. It interested him deeply, however, that Freya had confessed to wanting several children.

'I don't have any kids of my own, and I haven't really thought about changing that status quo any time soon,' he quipped, his tone wry.

'You're not—you're not in a relationship?'

'No. I broke up with my last girlfriend about six months ago.'

'Why?'

'Why?' Nash shrugged, slightly taken aback that she should ask him why. He didn't usually discuss his personal life with anyone—not even his mother. 'She wanted a bit more commitment than I was prepared to give,' he said truthfully, not liking the sensation of being suddenly put under a microscope, and slightly regretting that the truth had slipped out so easily.

'So…you're the kind of guy that likes to travel light, as they say? Isn't that how they describe men who have trouble committing to a relationship and like to play the field?'

As he registered the contemptuous tone in her arresting voice, a stab of anger shot through Nash. Where the hell did she get off, making such crass assumptions about him?

'Let's get back, shall we? Perhaps you'd like a swim in the pool instead of a walk?' He started to walk on ahead, down the deserted road that led back to the fields they had crossed from the farmhouse, and didn't spare a glance to see if she was following.

'You don't like talking about yourself, do you?' she demanded.

Nash kept walking, the back of his neck prickling hotly.

'My life is an open book—people can say whatever they please about me and that's okay—but you—you can't even have a decent conversation with me about yourself!'

He stopped. Slowly he turned, his hands on his hips, knowing acutely that she'd pressed a very hot button as far as his private life was concerned. Not talking enough about himself was an accusation that had come up time and time again in nearly all of his previous relationships. But to Nash his past was not some light aperitif on a conversation menu. It caused him too much grief for it ever to be included casually in an exchange.

'I didn't bring you here to talk about myself, Freya,' he said evenly. 'I brought you here so that you could get out of the limelight for a while and think about your future. When we get back to the house I have to leave you for a while, to go into town, but when I return we'll sit down and discuss some ideas. Deal?'

He was deliberately being all business again, and something in Freya baulked at that—even though he was right and that's why she'd come to France with him.

'What happened to the girl at the party?' she asked mutinously, whipping off her straw hat and pushing her fingers through the long dark mane of hair that suddenly tumbled like heavy silk over her shoulders.

'What girl?'

It was clear he wasn't exactly thrilled with the question—especially when he'd probably assumed he'd successfully deflected any more personal enquiries. Freya chewed down a little on her softly shaped lower lip before replying. 'The very clingy little blonde who couldn't take her eyes off you!'

'She was nobody important.'

'How flattering for the poor girl!'

'I meant that we weren't dating. She was just a friend.'

'Did she realise that distinction?'

'What's it to you?'

Freya shrugged. 'I was just interested to know if you ever brought her here to the house?'

Nash's body visibly stilled. 'I don't bring anybody out here but myself,' he answered.

Digesting that reluctantly offered titbit, Freya refused to be satisfied with such provocative fare without wanting more.

'If that's so…then why did you bring me here?'

'You needed some privacy…this was the best place I could think of to get you some. Any more questions, or are we done?' With the flat of his hand Nash palmed the sweat away from his glistening forehead. Freya had no doubt she had irritated him intensely.

'Don't you miss having someone special in your life to share this lovely place with?' She surprised even herself with her dogged persistence to weasel out more personal information about Nash's life.

'Do *you* miss having "someone special" in *your* life?' he shot back, turning the tables on her.

'After James?' Unable to ignore the sense of futility that the echoed question had provoked inside her, Freya crossed her arms defensively across her chest. 'No. Of course not.'

'Then let's leave the subject alone, shall we? We ought to be getting back…some of us have work to do!'

Watching him stride even further ahead of her, Freya swiped her straw hat against her thigh in pure frustration. 'Fine!' she muttered under her breath. 'But if you think you're getting away with not telling me anything else about you while I'm here…then think again!'

Sitting on a wooden bench that overlooked the valley, enjoying a clear, unhindered aspect of the farmhouse,

Freya watched another heron elegantly cut a swathe through the cloudless blue sky, then closed her eyes to listen to the mesmerising distant chorus of frogs croaking in a pond somewhere. It was very soothing just sitting there. Peace and relaxation had apparently found her at last, and she prayed that this time it was no fleeting visitor.

Sighing with contentment as the sun warmed her skin, she let her gaze drift with pleasure over the restful landscape once again. But her contemplation of the soothing scenery was suddenly abruptly banished by the sight of Nash, emerging from the farmhouse and walking towards her. He was wearing a loose white shirt over light blue softly napped denim jeans and his feet were bare. As he approached, sunlight glinting off the darkly golden strands of his hair, his easy hypnotic gait had Freya momentarily catching her breath.

'Ever read this?' he asked as he reached her. He was holding out a slim hard-backed novel, and for a moment Freya just stared at him without speaking, transfixed by the stunning intense blue of his gorgeous eyes.

Accepting the book, she pursed her lips a little to moisten them. Examining the cover, and at the same time acutely aware of Nash standing over her waiting for her verdict, she found her throat suddenly dry as sand.

'As a matter of fact I have, and I totally loved it,' she admitted with undisguised pleasure. Lifting her gaze, Freya steeled herself to meet that too-disturbing glance of his, just then feeling completely inadequate to the task. 'Were you offering it to me to read?' she asked lightly.

'It's been adapted for a movie and they're still looking for an actress to play the lead,' Nash told her.

They were adapting it for a film? Once upon a time Freya would have known something as significant as that. The fact that she didn't know only served to emphasise how long she'd been out of the loop.

'So?' But even as she endeavoured to sound blasé her stomach executed an excited cartwheel at the news.

'I think you should audition for it...don't you?'

'I told you...I don't even have an agent any more!'

'Why don't you have an agent any more?'

Shaking her head slightly, Freya splayed her palm against the smooth, glossy book jacket. 'Who wants to work with someone that's become a liability? Whose private life is such a disaster that she can't get her act together to even read a script...much less audition for a part in a movie!'

'Well...' His broad shoulders lifting in an unimpressed shrug, Nash stared down at her, his expression unmoved. 'Don't you think it's about time you started to get your act together? There's no time like the present. Why don't you start rereading the book, and later on you can tell me what you love so much about it and why you'd be the perfect choice to play the female lead.'

'I think your confidence in me is a little misplaced, if you don't mind my saying.'

'Actually, I do mind—because I think that's the

biggest load of rubbish I've ever heard! You could play that part standing on your head, Freya, and you know it! Why don't you stop juicing all those old negative beliefs you hold and show people what you're made of?'

Indignation surged hotly through her bloodstream at his unflinching words. He knew what she had been through, that there were still bruises smarting from her ordeal, yet he was calmly standing there telling her to get her act together and show people what she was made of! How dared he? She pushed to her feet and thrust the book back into his hand.

'You're supposed to be helping me! Is telling it like it is the tactic you're going to be using from now on? Only I didn't think I'd signed up for boot camp when I agreed to come here!'

'It riles you, doesn't it? Why didn't you act like this when your ex was busy trying to destroy your life?' Nash demanded calmly, his handsome face as implacable as she had ever seen it. 'Why didn't you stand up for what was yours? And I'm not just talking about financial assets here... Why did you let him strip you of so much?'

His words affecting her deeply, Freya felt tears sting the backs of her eyelids like a swarm of lethal hornets.

'I don't want to talk about this.'

'Why not?'

'Because your question is hardly fair!' she protested. 'You make it sound as if I invited him to treat me badly!'

'Did you?'

Once again Nash didn't pull his punches, and inwardly

Freya reeled from the impact. But this time she refused to take the easy route and avoid giving him an answer.

'All right, then! Maybe subconsciously I didn't feel I deserved the success I had… Maybe I was always waiting for the other shoe to drop, and when it did I just resigned myself to the inevitable. But I didn't deliberately choose to sabotage my life, you know!'

'But if you believed you didn't deserve your success then you did. We all make choices, Freya—practically every second of our lives. You could make the choice of wanting a better life right now! You could totally embrace the fact that you deserve success and that you're going to get it no matter what anyone else thinks! Maybe all you need to do is learn how to make better choices so that the outcomes of your decisions reflect what you say you really want?' Pulling his gaze away from her for a moment, Nash held up the book in front of her. 'This is an opportunity you can't afford to turn your back on. You're a born actress, Freya… I've seen you perform on screen enough times to know that's the truth. So do what you were born to do! Yes, you've taken some knocks—but what you need to do right now is dust yourself down and take up where you left off. Trust me…it won't be half as difficult as you imagine it to be.'

'And what about getting another agent?' Her heartbeat was picking up speed even as she asked the question, because she couldn't deny the realisation of possibilities that was excitedly building inside her. Freya accepted the book from Nash and felt her fingers close almost possessively around it. He smiled, and after the severe admonition he'd just dealt her it was like wallowing in blessedly cool rain after a drought.

'Leave that to me. All I want you to do right now is to start reading that book again. I need to drive into town to pick up some supplies for us. Later on, when I've returned, we can talk more in depth about things.'

'Okay.'

'Oh, and—' another smile provocatively hijacked his mesmerising lips '—you need a bit more sunscreen on your face…your nose is starting to get a little red.'

She'd been hoping that he'd been about to say something a lot more complimentary than that, and embarrassed heat flooded into Freya's cheeks. As Nash turned and walked away, she heard his throaty chuckle.

'Can't play the part of a beautiful Russian doctor with a nose like Rudolph!' he teased.

'That's what they've got a make-up department for!' Freya indignantly called after him, just before he re-entered the house.

Pausing outside the door, Nash grinned. 'Well…it's going to take a hell of a lot of make-up to cover up vivid cerise if you don't get that sunscreen on quick!' He laughed.

CHAPTER SEVEN

IT DID cross Nash's mind that he might have been too hard on Freya with his unsympathetic attack. But then he recalled the distinct flare of genuine excitement in her revealing dark eyes when he'd told her about the film part, and he knew that she had been as grabbed by the possibility of auditioning for it as he had.

He had taken a big chance, but he'd already got in touch with the casting agents on the movie and told them that Freya Carpenter might be interested. The agent he'd spoken with just happened to be a man whom Nash knew fairly well through his business dealings, and so was definitely open to some negotiating on his part. Even so, Geoff had been only too delighted at the idea of arranging an audition for Freya. He'd read the statement she'd made the other day in the newspapers, and he professed to be in admiration for her courage at finally speaking out against her money-grabbing ex.

'I always guessed the woman wasn't the total flake that Frazier made her out to be,' he'd declared emphatically.

Now all Nash had to do was keep on convincing Freya that this part—should she get it—was going to be the start of her long-overdue return to acting. His hands tightened perceptibly around the leather-covered steering wheel of the hire car he drove. Again he thought about the angry words he'd used to shake her out of her stupor of pain and regret. Had his anger arisen not just because he suspected she was still resisting taking total charge of her life but also because her situation so reminded him of what his own mother had gone through?

It was no secret that he'd felt bitterly disappointed and betrayed that she hadn't acted with more discernment in picking the men she chose to share her life—and Nash's—with. Considering that Freya might have acted with the same apparent lack of judgement definitely provoked a silent fury inside Nash. Yet at the same time he sensed that the actress had far more resolve in her little finger than his less assertive mother could ever dream of having. He prayed he was right about that.

Slowing down into the approach to the charming historical town, with its straight blocks of narrow streets and well-preserved medieval buildings, and finding an empty space by the roadside, he parked the car, got out, and started to walk up the steady incline that led to the picturesque town square, with its plethora of cafés and shops.

The afternoon passed into the evening, but Freya barely even noticed that the sun was going down because she was so immersed in the story she was reading. Nikita Pushkova had been a brilliant young heart surgeon at the top of her profession in Moscow when she chose to treat a poor child from the backstreets with a degenerative heart complaint, in her wealthy practice. The complicating factor had been that the child had contracted HIV from his prostitute mother, and just the mere association with that misjudged disease had been enough to send Nikita's reputation-conscious colleagues into a furious and indignant state of panic.

Going against the warnings and advice of her fellow surgeons, Nikita had operated on the little boy anyway, so touched had she been by his plight. Unfortunately, during the operation the child had developed an unforeseen complication and died. Nikita's reputation as an esteemed surgeon had been left in shreds and the hospital had fired her for bringing such disgrace upon them. The newspapers had inevitably got hold of the story and published a damning report about her that had effectively helped to finish off her career altogether. Her heart already broken by the fact that she hadn't been able to save the child, and seeing no hope of a future in the profession she had so passionately been drawn to, Nikita Pushkova had taken her own life.

The story had touched so many chords inside Freya when she'd read it the first time. Now, reading it again, she was even more deeply affected. But, more than that, she was absolutely determined that this part was going to be hers… If she won it, it would be the coup of her career so far. It would also challenge her acting skills in a way that they hadn't been challenged up until this point. If Freya played this incredible but ultimately doomed young woman then she owed it to her memory to deliver a true and passionate portrayal of someone who'd risked everything to save the life of one poor, disadvantaged child.

She had just come to the end of a chapter in which Nikita had emerged from the operating theatre, having just lost the child she'd been so desperately trying to save, when Nash called out to her. She'd heard him return from town about an hour ago, but she had remained sitting outside beneath the shade of an abundant and gracious olive tree, totally wrapped up in her book. Now, his announcement that dinner was ready made Freya realise how hungry she was, and she was on her feet and heading thankfully towards the house with unashamed haste, her senses still profoundly affected by the story that had so gripped her.

'There's apple juice if you don't want wine,' Nash informed her as she pulled out a chair to sit down at the rustic kitchen table.

He'd laid out a veritable feast for the senses before her. There was an array of cold meats, pâté, fruit, French bread and cheeses—including Freya's favourite, Camembert. For dessert there was a tarte tatin with an almost full jug of fresh cream beside it. There was also a carafe of red wine alongside the matching one of juice. The mellow sounds of some sultry jazz played quietly in the background, and the female singer's voice that accompanied it unashamedly oozed sex and seduction.

As Freya sat down, she was aware of an uncharacteristic sense of well-being and excitement flowing through her, and she realised it was nearly all down to this man. Just being in his presence seemed to energise her.

'You've been busy.' She glanced up and smiled. She saw a muscle tick in the side of his smooth-shaven cheek, and for one highly disconcerting moment he just stared at her without speaking. Then, as if someone had thrown a switch, he smiled back and the action created a cascade of delicious shivers that fizzed like sparklers all along Freya's spine.

'A budding Oscar-winner has to eat,' he teased lightly, pulling out a chair for himself.

'Yeah…' Freya raised her shoulders in a shrug. 'Dream on…' Her mouth tightened a little. Reaching forward, she helped herself to some bread and Camembert.

'That's what it's all about, angel…dreams. If you don't even allow the dream to take shape and believe in it then how do you think you're going to make it come true?'

'Is that how you got where you are today? By dreaming about success?'

'We're not talking about me.' The shutters came down again, and Freya tried hard to quell her sense of frustration.

'No…I sense a definite aversion to that. Do you think I'm going to sell your story to the newspapers or something, Mr Taylor-Grant?' she quipped, her dark eyes mischievous.

A knife-flash of pure unadulterated lust riveted Nash. The things this woman could make a man feel with that dancing, dark-eyed glance of hers were more potentially lethal than dynamite. All Nash's thoughts were directed to fulfilling the explosive desire that had all but blown his self-control apart, and every muscle he possessed quivered to contain it.

'Touché.'

Desperately trying to restrain the profound ache that imprisoned his body every time he glanced at Freya, he found himself wondering what it could hurt to talk a little about his own path to career success if it helped encourage her own dreams. Maybe it was the effect of the softly playing jazz, or merely that he was enjoying being a man with a very beautiful, desirable woman, but something was definitely prompting him to let his guard down a little. Anyway, he didn't have to tell her everything. He could be selective.

'I grew up in a one-parent family, and a ready supply of money and opportunity were assets that were hardly part of my life.' He cut some more bread and released a sigh. The jazz singer's voice flowed over him like a warm, soothing waterfall and helped him ease some of the tension that had inevitably cramped his chest at the mention of his past. 'Dreams of a better future were what sustained me even through the worst of times. I thought about celebrity and fame a lot in those days.'

'You did?' Freya's brows knitted together in surprise.

'Like many other kids I imagined those people who had made it into the limelight having the most amazing and thrilling lives. I wanted an amazing life too. But the more I thought about the qualities of fame, and the "specialness" it conferred on the people it visited, the more I realised the downside too. I only had to glance at a newspaper or magazine or watch the TV news to see that. Then I speculated that those celebrities must need good people around them to help deflect some of the not so attractive results of their fame, and I started to think about how I could get into something like that. There was a reasonable library in the town not far from where I lived, and I used to walk there every day after school and read the kind of books that I thought could help me. I also found an ally in one of the librarians there, who eventually suggested that PR might be the career for me.'

Grinning suddenly, Nash shook his head, remembering. 'I'm sure he thought I was either insane or completely living in cloud cuckoo land, given where I came from, but he gave me the information all the same. From that moment on I mentally worked on the idea of working in that field. When I moved in with my aunt, in a different, more…shall we say "well to do" area?…my dream really began to take hold, and there wasn't a day or night that went by when I wasn't planning my route to realising it.'

'You were a man on a mission…clearly.' Smiling up at him, Freya was almost intoxicated by the fact that he had shared this very personal revelation of realising his dream with her. She sensed it wasn't something he shared very often with people…if ever. The fact that he had clearly come from humble beginnings and had overcome his difficult start in life to become the success he was now made her warm to him even more.

'And you have to be a woman on a mission if you want to win the role that will be one step closer to winning an Oscar,' Nash replied. 'And you can't ever let doubt or what other people think get in the way. So…how did you get on with the book? Feeling inspired?'

Seeming to reflect upon the question, Freya leaned towards Nash with her arms folded in front of her on the table.

'A passionate story cannot help but inspire…do you not agree?' she asked him, in the most perfect Russian accent.

A hot charge of intense euphoria catapulted through his insides like a circus act shot from a cannon.

'So…you won't mind, then, that I went ahead and arranged an audition for you?' He grinned.

'When? How?' The shock on her beautiful face was a picture.

'You're telling me that you're interested?'

'Don't tease me…please!' She grabbed his hand and her warm palm curled around it.

Sweet heaven! Nash wanted to tease her some more—but not here. The teasing he had in mind should most definitely take place in bed, where he would be able to hear her sweet moans of pleasure as he did the things to her that his mind and body were so avidly clamouring to do.

'Have you really arranged for me to audition for the part of Nikita?'

Her grip on his hand didn't lessen, Nash noticed with almost dizzying satisfaction. Her perfume filled the air and deluged his senses.

'I have. But we'll arrange the timing of it when we get back to the UK and you're feeling ready. I've got Geoff Epstein's promise on that.'

'Oh, I could kiss you!' She lifted his hand to her sweetly warm lips and did just that.

The pupils of his blue eyes turned to jet. Before she could say another word he detached his hand from hers and walked round to the other side of the table where she sat. Gazing deeply into her captivated glance, he reached out and impelled her to her feet.

'Before you ask, sweetheart…I'm not asking for payment for fixing you up with an audition. But I want you to kiss me. I want you to kiss me because I think I'm in serious trouble if you don't!'

And she found her lips as well as her will vanquished beneath the possession of his burning kiss. Her mind couldn't have swum more dizzyingly if she'd been on a carousel. The way his body pressed tight up against hers, as though they were one flesh, left Freya in no doubt about his desire for her. Iron-hard, his strength and need exploded onto her senses like a crescendo of fireworks—and if that wasn't enough his intoxicating masculine heat seemed to elicit the kind of weakness in her limbs that only a serious fever would otherwise accomplish. Every part of him seemed made to entice and seduce her, and resistance never even entered her head.

So when Nash lifted his head, and his mesmerising blue eyes branded her soul with his name in tongues of flame, Freya knew the outcome of this inflammatory exchange between them was nothing less than inevitable. Keeping her hand resting possessively at his back, she felt her excitement make her tremble—hard.

'What about our meal?' she asked, her voice hoarse.

'Are you serious?' His wicked toe-curling grin was pure sex, and she shook even harder. 'I want you in bed, Ms Carpenter…and I want you there right now.' Possessively catching her hand, he drew her through the open doorway.

In Nash's bed, Freya discovered a sensual haven and the kind of bone-melting seductive delight that even her most secret fantasies had lacked the power to conjure up.

Beneath them, the sheets were pale cold linen—but they could have been satin, velvet, the most sumptuously exotic materials from a Bedouin market for all her entranced senses knew. Nash's warm, commanding mouth became both an instrument of delight and torment to her, because every time he withdrew it from her lips Freya felt as though he'd withdrawn some vital component that her very nature needed to exist. She found herself begging him for more of the same, and her huskily voiced pleas stunned her with the welter of desire and need she heard in their register.

His palms came into full, devastating contact with her bared breasts, and his fingers teased and seduced their sensitive tips as a musical maestro coaxed the most exquisite heavenly sounds from his orchestra. Her hushed urgent moans as she yielded to his riveting attentions fell upon the air like pearls of morning dew clinging lovingly to lush blades of grass. His skin was so smooth and warm, and the soft hairs on his well-defined muscular chest rubbed delightfully against her as he claimed the right to cover Freya's body with his own.

Her moans became even more rasping and urgent as Nash lowered his head and started to rain explosive little kisses down the whole length of her, right to the tips of her pearl-coloured toenails. Such devastating lovemaking was a revelation to her, and she wished that it never had to end. Arching her body with a surprised cry as his mouth found the most sensitive core of her womanhood, Freya sensed the room spin crazily once more. Pure sensation drowned her in its spell, as though the air was filled with showers of tiny diamonds that kept exploding onto her body like shooting stars. Her fingers curled tightly into the stiff linen sheet beneath her as his silken tongue made her climax, and the scalding surge of wild emotion that inevitably accompanied it brought her to tears. It was as though some dammed-up body of water had burst its banks inside her and was now moving unstoppably through every sense, cell and limb she possessed—as though its force would not be denied any longer.

Returning to examine her face, Nash brushed back her hair and glanced with concern into the dark eyes that glittered moistly back at him.

'I didn't mean to make you cry,' he said softly, his palm touching the side of her velvet cheek.

'You didn't do anything wrong… In fact…you did everything right. I just can't help it. This kind of thing doesn't happen to me every day.' Freya bit her lip to try and stem the threatened onrush of fresh tears, trying to form a smile at the same time. 'I guess I'm just used to a man taking his own pleasure and that's it.'

Hearing her softly spoken confession, Nash found her unexpected revelation profoundly touching. It saddened him to think that she'd never really enjoyed the act of making love up until now because her ex-partner had never given her that ultimate pleasure. But then he supposed that tallied with what he already knew about the man. He shouldn't be surprised. Nash had never witnessed a woman cry when he'd brought her to climax. He was beginning to see that there were many undiscovered shades to this lovely woman that he had frankly been quite unaware of. It made him want to become acquainted with even more of the myriad facets of her personality.

'Well, right now your pleasure is right at the top of my list, angel,' he asserted tenderly, then kissed her with all the voracious need that had seized his body, the desire he had been able to exert such control over up until then almost threatening to overwhelm him.

'Nash…' She rubbed the pad of her thumb across his mouth, and smiled as he gazed down at her.

He thought that he had never seen such a mixture of innocence and lust on a woman's face before, or even guessed at the torrent of feeling that sight might elicit. Capturing her wrist with his hand to still it, he suckled the thumb she had been teasing him with, then applied his teeth to the tender part. Feeling her hips rise towards his in surprise and hunger beneath him, Nash moved away for a few moments to see to protection, then slowly—and with devastating care—inserted his aching shaft deep inside the warm cavern of her exquisite womanhood.

She was tight and hot, and her sweetly enraptured moan shattered him as it fell on the hushed air. There was not another house for miles, and right at that moment it was as though the entire world belonged just to them. A gravel-voiced groan was emitted harshly from his throat. With increasing urgent need Nash clasped her hips even harder with his strong muscular thighs and drove into her, bending his head to kiss her breasts, her neck, her quivering mouth and her eyelids. Sliding his fingers through her glorious hair. He knew his delight in her body was beyond measure as he sensed her climax again beneath him.

He had waited for that satisfying response from her, but now Nash finally gave his own mounting desire wings and let it fly.

As he let himself lie against her in the aftermath, the combined heat they'd engendered making them cling hotly together, he listened to her heart beating wildly against his ear and knew his own easily matched it, beat for beat. His lips curved into an unashamed smile of acknowledgement.

'I didn't realise you had even more talents than I first suspected, Ms Carpenter,' he teased gently, leaning up on his elbows and laughing into her eyes.

At that very moment Freya knew she had walked to the edge of a pretty high cliff and was poised to take that final leap. There seemed to be no going back after what had just happened, and she knew it. Watching that devastating sea of blue sparkle back at her, she thought she had never seen another man more beautiful. He was incredible. Right now her will-power was teetering crazily—balanced on a knife-edge as she warred with the desire to let herself fall for him, utterly and completely.

'My dad used to say I had lots of talents,' she heard herself reply, wondering how that poignant thought had somehow permeated her mind when it was still reeling from the devastating impact of Nash's lovemaking. Probably the emotion of the moment had jettisoned it up from deep in her unconscious. 'He used to say that I could be anything I wanted to be and that everything was possible if I only believed it.' She sensed Nash's gaze narrow with interest. 'You would have found much in common with him, I'm sure.'

'What happened to him?' he asked quietly.

'He got cancer and died when I was six.' She shrugged, trying to will away the desolation that almost closed her throat at the memory—feeling the old gnawing ache of missing the man who had meant the world to her rise strongly inside her. 'People say that I was far too young to remember him that well—to miss him as much as I do—but they're wrong. I remember every detail about him—the way he looked, the way he spoke, the way he smelt—as though someone injected the memory into my very cells so that I would never forget him. He made me feel like I was the most precious thing in the world. When I was with him I felt so…so loved…you know?'

Nash didn't know, but he would have liked to experience the same from his own father if he had lived. People said that girls often subconsciously looked to find men modelled on their fathers in character and even sometimes appearance. Had Freya been searching for someone to love her with the depth of feeling her father had loved her with all along? If so, she must have been totally blinded by the true facts of James Frazier's nature to be so misled.

'Those big brown eyes would melt any father's heart,' he teased lightly. 'I'm sure that you were very easy to love as a little girl.'

'But not as a woman? Is that what you're saying?'

'I'm not saying that at all!' A bolt of shock slashed

through Nash's insides. Did she really believe that she was unlovable? Even the mere notion astonished him. 'Where did you get such an idea?'

Her gaze sliding momentarily away from his, Freya wriggled out from beneath her lover and moved herself up into a sitting position. Getting hold of the sheet, she pulled it up to her chest as Nash leaned back against the pillows beside her. 'Men only generally admire me because I'm a fairly well-known actress. They don't ever seem to see the woman behind the roles I play. Then…when they get to meet me…I think that somehow they're disappointed that the "real" me doesn't somehow fit with the fantasy they've bought into. I think that's why James was so angry with me. I refused to play along with the role of this amazing movie star he thought he'd married. The parties, the whole celebrity circuit—they were all things that he craved and I didn't. He often accused me of being the dullest creature on earth!'

'The man's judgement must have been seriously defective!'

'Everyone has their little fantasy…don't they?' She bestowed a look on him of such unremitting anguish that Nash sensed his heart constrict. 'And when it's proved not to be true they feel let down.'

Her ex was even dumber than he'd first suspected, he thought vehemently. If the fool couldn't see the glittering diamond that was the real Freya Carpenter then he must indeed be blind! The true woman was so much more than any character she might portray on screen or on stage, and far more compelling and enchanting. Any man in his right mind would be honoured to know her…let alone have her regard!

The depth of his own feelings startled him. 'Remind me why you married him,' he heard himself comment wryly.

'Why?' Her dark gaze riveted Nash. 'Because I have a spectacular talent for not knowing who I can trust, that's why! Either that or I trust too easily. Also…I was frightened of being alone. I never spent one lonely day in my life until my dad died. He used to say that he'd never leave me—and if you tell that to a child they believe you! I felt like he'd somehow betrayed me—not just deserted me when he died. Maybe subconsciously I expect every man to eventually betray me? Anyway… You asked why I married James. Well…when a good-looking, attentive man who professes to think the world of me then tells me that he loves me…I…idiot that I am…believe him!'

There was shattering hurt in her voice now, and before Nash could react Freya had slid across the bed, grabbed her jeans and started to pull them on with her back to him.

'I guess I'm just one of those gullible women who always end up with the wrong man—the type that the press is so good at mocking!' Turning her head, her dark hair spilling across her naked breasts, hiding them from Nash's view, she nonetheless easily commanded his gaze—stunned by her actions though it might be. 'You can't be a one-night remedy for all my unhappiness, Nash. I know that. And let's be real here too. I know that you don't really want any more of me beyond a little sexual recreation. So…nice as just now was…it probably wouldn't do either of us any good to repeat it.'

Picking up her shirt from the chair where she'd thrown it, she quickly shoved her slender arms through the sleeves and did up the buttons. Then she collected the discarded scraps of silk underwear that lay there too and balled them into her palm. 'I'm going downstairs to get something to eat.'

'Hold on a second! Sexual recreation, Freya?' Nash regarded her with furious disbelief. 'Is that all you think this was?'

'Well…tell me what it was, then, if it wasn't that?'

Freya stopped at the door, with her hand on the edge of the frame, and her expression was one of weary resignation, clearly anticipating the worst. Feeling both regret and great frustration, Nash was suddenly hesitant to try and explain feelings that right then were out of his remit.

He knew the exact moment when her interest in hearing what he had to say withdrew, even before he'd said another word.

'I thought so,' she said quietly, and pulled the door closed behind her as she went out.

CHAPTER EIGHT

KNOWING that Freya had just come through a pretty horrendous time in both her private and professional life, and would naturally be wary of other relationships as a result, did not help lessen the sense of failure Nash had experienced when she'd walked out of his bedroom, he reflected.

Nursing a freshly brewed cup of coffee the next morning, he stared out at the azure horizon through the open kitchen doorway, deep in thought. Okay, he hadn't deepened their intimacy by readily talking about himself and admitting some of his own issues…but was that really such a crime? He hadn't deliberately withheld information…at least not consciously. But he'd be the first to admit that dealing with emotions was not something he particularly excelled at—especially in relationships.

Now he considered that he had been playing a role too. One that he'd hidden behind—and not just professionally. The disguise had also encroached upon his private life, and that was why he rarely talked about himself with intimate partners. All they ever knew was that he was a successful businessman with a textbook-perfect past that didn't really exist, and Nash silently admitted that he had disguised his true background through feelings of shame and regret. He'd even sometimes fooled himself into believing the fiction rather than revisiting the truth.

The fact didn't make him proud. Freya was braver than him by far. Openly discussing her issues with trust, she had frankly told him that she feared any man she got into a relationship with would probably eventually desert her…just as she felt her father had done. At last Nash was beginning to get a true picture of her make-up, and he had to admit that it rendered her even more appealing to him than she had been already. She was a sensitive, caring woman—nothing like the brittle, self-absorbed persona in the picture the press and her ex-husband had painted for the public.

Remembering the highly provocative sight of her as she'd presented her back to him to dress, and the way her long hair had spilled like a black velvet waterfall across her breasts, Nash had to contain a groan as a strong resurgence of last night's heady desire throbbed through him. To lessen its hold, he got up and walked out towards the swimming pool. Settling himself in a cane chair, he silently and perhaps bitterly acknowledged that the sense of failure hadn't dissipated in any way. After all, it didn't make him feel too good to have a woman gaze at him as if he'd just confirmed her worst fears about him… especially when they had just made love.

Shortly after Freya had left Nash alone, he'd joined her in the kitchen to finish the meal they hadn't even started, and—just as he'd envisaged—conversation between them had been stilted, punctuated by long, tension-filled silences. Not long after that he hadn't been surprised when Freya had declared she was going to have an early night. But today, in spite of this new unforeseen tension in their relationship, Nash had to focus on the reason why they were here together. He was supposed to be helping her build her confidence, as well as protecting her from negative publicity and working on strategies to help her make progress professionally—not having his own ego deflated by imagined disappointment.

'I've finished reading the book. You wanted me to tell you what I loved about it and why I think I'd be the right person to play the lead?'

She'd stolen up on him on silent feet, and Nash glanced up at her in a simple white sundress, her lovely shoulders bare and her soulful dark eyes piercing him with their melancholy and beauty. Once again he was struck by how this woman commanded attention as avidly as a spectacular sunrise.

'All right. Why don't you pull up a chair?'

The book in her hand, Freya did just that. With a soft sigh she opened the slim volume and flicked idly through the pages. Pages that already appeared well thumbed and scrutinised.

'I love the story because it's about a woman who was only too human—even when to the eyes of the world she was a frightening success. Then she made a mistake…a mistake that came about because she wanted ultimately to do good…not bad. And she was doubly punished for it…both by outside forces and herself.' Sweeping her hand through her long hair, Freya lifted her gaze to Nash. 'I know what Nikita must have felt like when she lost the one thing she felt she was good at…the passion that had driven her life for so long. And I know what it feels like to lose the respect and support of friends and colleagues because they've judged that you've made a wrong decision…a "bad" decision. I know intimately how that feels.'

'So you really want to go for this part?' Inside Nash's stomach was a curiously hollow ache. He had judged her too…he couldn't forget that.

'More than I think I've ever wanted anything else…yes. When we get back home, will you arrange it?'

'Of course…that's a promise.'

'So…' Closing the book, Freya met his gaze. 'What shall we do today?'

'Do you want to get out of here? Go some place for lunch, perhaps?'

'Can we do that?'

Now passion was replaced by hope, and Nash realised how difficult it must have been for her, feeling as though she was a prisoner in her own home—unable to accomplish even the simplest outing to the shops or an appointment, too afraid to go anywhere in case she was pursued by an insatiable story-hungry press. People who were generally looking to present her in an even worse light than they had already…

'As a matter of fact, we can. I've got some friends in town who run a small bistro. They're good people, and I think I can safely say they won't be ringing up the local newspaper as soon as you set foot in the place.'

'But what about the other customers? I don't want to feel as though I'm some exhibit in a freak show!'

'That won't happen. It's a very small bistro…just two or three tables. Celine and Denis will agree to close it to other customers for an hour or two while we're there.'

Freya visibly relaxed. 'Okay. So we'll have lunch there. In the meantime, I think I'll take advantage of the pool and do a few laps.'

Rising to her feet, she was about to turn and leave when Nash lightly grabbed her hand.

'Is everything okay?'

'Everything's fine. If you're referring to last night, you can relax. I'm not one of those temperamental women who sulk when things haven't gone her way. We're both here for very good professional reasons…let's not forget that. We don't want to sully our time together with any personal awkwardness that will make it difficult to work together, do we? Can I have my hand back now? I want to go and change.'

'I just want you to know that I didn't take what

happened last night lightly.' His voice was a little gruff, and Nash recognised his own awkwardness at being unable to adequately explain his feelings…to make Freya realise he was sincere.

'You don't have to explain.'

She tugged on the hand he held, and reluctantly Nash freed it.

'I think I do.'

His words almost made Freya stumble. She'd been torturing herself with the idea that he'd made love with her purely out of physical attraction alone, and she hated the way that made her feel somehow unworthy of any deeper regard than that. Now, finding herself the intense focus of his penetrating azure gaze, she prayed he wasn't going to explain away what had happened with some trite excuse that would make her feel even worse.

'You're an enchanting woman, Freya. Much more enchanting than I think you realise. And I'm not just talking about the beautiful actress here…I'm talking about the woman behind the roles she plays…the real you.'

Her breath hitched a little as Freya slowly let it out, silently hoping, praying, that the deeply touching words were sincere.

'I woke up this morning with your scent all over my body and I didn't want to shower it off…I swear to God.' His hand lifted to lightly touch her hip in the thin cotton dress.

Freya felt as if she'd received an electrical charge so

strong it had rendered her limbs as weak as a newborn lamb's. She found herself fervently hoping he would continue to touch her like that…to tease her and perhaps seduce her as he'd done last night. It wouldn't take long for her to be ready for him. The thought turned her cheeks scarlet.

Just then a light, tantalising breeze smelling of sweet herbs and Mediterranean sunshine stirred a lock of his sand-gold hair and lifted it away from a brow that denoted strength and passion in equal portions. To her intense surprise, Freya glimpsed what she believed to be a provocative suggestion of vulnerability, and her heart squeezed at the sight.

'Could you handle me wanting to know the real man behind the public relations expert, Nash?' she asked softly, all her senses begging her to touch him too—to reacquaint herself with the reassuring iron strength beneath that silken golden flesh of his. His hand stilled for a long moment against her hip, then he slowly withdrew it. Freya held her breath, believing he was going to deflect her attention yet again.

'The "real" man?' His wide shoulders lifted in a shrug. 'Forgive me if I'm a little rusty at knowing who that is.'

'You can trust me.' Now it was her turn to catch his hand and hold it. Bending a little towards him, she rubbed the pad of her thumb over the fine golden hairs crossing the back of his palm and gave him a cheeky grin. 'I promise I won't break your heart if you tell me all your secrets.'

'Oh, you do, do you?' Before she could glean what he had in mind, Nash had turned his hand to grip hers, and with a firm hard pull he'd tipped her straight into his lap. 'What if I don't believe you?' he suggested seriously, his warm breath drifting over her mouth.

Astounded by the very idea that she might be possessed of the power to ever accomplish such a thing—Freya automatically closed her eyelids as Nash tauntingly touched his lips to hers and kissed her—all disagreement and hurt forgotten as she surrendered to the captivating moment instead…

Celine and Denis seemed enchanted by Freya from the moment they saw her. They were not the kind of couple who were easily impressed by celebrity or success either. In their late fifties, they had raised a large family and run a lucrative eatery for many years now, and were known to take people as they found them. But Nash could see that as soon as Freya started to chat unselfconsciously with them—about the restaurant, their family, and their much-loved historical town—she immediately endeared herself to the couple.

Watching her—seeing her laugh and smile and be so complimentary about the admittedly great food they were served—Nash realised she had a gift for bringing out the best in people. The warmth of her nature couldn't be faked—no matter how good an actress she was—and again he thought it was criminal how low she had been brought by her ex. But she had come on in leaps and bounds over the past couple of days, he considered, and now, with the promise of that all-important audition for a much-wanted film part, Nash saw no reason why her life shouldn't be entering a new, much more positive phase.

As for himself, he was finding it extremely difficult to be as detached as he should be where she was concerned. Even more so since they'd made love. With every smile that came his way, every provocative grin, Freya was threatening to break down every damn barrier he'd ever erected. Now he was jealous whenever her attention was diverted by anything else…and that included even scenery as well as other people. It disturbed him to realise how involved he was becoming. Up until now Nash had never let emotions dictate where relationships were concerned, and that was the way he liked it. It was a way of being he understood…a way to have most of the pleasure and almost none of the pain. Now Freya was pushing buttons in him that he hadn't even known he had, and there seemed to be no let-up.

'You look like you have a lot on your mind today.'

Her glance was slightly quizzical as she faced him across the bright red and white gingham tablecloth, and he noticed that the sun had brought out two or three very appealing freckles on her nose. His attention further diverted by her pretty mouth, he felt heat swirl like a small but lethal cyclone inside him.

'You could be right.' He nodded slowly.

'Are you regretting taking me on?' she enquired

lightly, but she wasn't quick enough to hide the doubt that crept into her eyes.

'Where did that idea come from?'

'Well…you've brought me here, to your own private little hideaway, and you can't even go where you really want to go because you've got to think of me. That can't be much fun.'

Remembering that smouldering kiss they'd shared beside the pool this morning, followed by the blood-stirring sight of her in a scarlet swimsuit, and then vividly bringing to mind the way those endlessly long legs of hers had been wrapped round him only just last night, Nash seriously wondered if there was anything else that could possibly have given him more pleasure…or been more 'fun'.

'I take my work seriously, Freya. It's my job to think of you twenty-four-seven while we're here together.'

It was his *job* to think of her? Already sensitive to the way words could hurt, Freya sensed something inside her die at Nash's coolly voiced answer. She could hardly believe he'd described their relationship in such a detached and unemotional way. If she'd been in any doubt before that her sleeping with him had meant anything, then she had just had those doubts thoroughly confirmed. She was just another job to him—nothing else—no matter how enchanting he professed her to be. She'd be purely crazy to hope for more from him. Trouble was…she guessed it was already too late to tell that to her heart.

'How admirable that you're so dedicated!' she said

sarcastically, her stomach wrapped in a vice of hurt. 'My uncle certainly chose the right man for the job when he picked you to help me, Nash!'

'Hell!' His riveting blue eyes glittered with frustration as he threw his linen napkin down on the table.

'Yes… I've been there too… Shall we go now?'

'Sure…if that's what you want.'

'I do.'

'I'll tell our hosts that you said *au revoir.*'

Turning away from her, Nash got to his feet and went to find the couple before leaving. As she waited at a side door that led out into the narrow alleyway, next to a bright, eye-catching watercolour of the bistro with its blue and yellow striped awning, Freya tried not to let emotion overwhelm her. She told herself all she had to do was hang onto her composure and remember that ultimately Nash was in her life to help her gain some positive publicity to rebuild her career—not to have a personal relationship with her. Their having sex—she wouldn't call it making love now, after what he had said—was just something that had happened, some natural animal instinct that had arisen between them spontaneously because of their enforced closeness, and probably a one-time only deal. Her main focus now should be getting herself into a good enough frame of mind to go for that precious audition—and Freya was determined she would win the part too. There was no doubt in her mind that it was the opportunity of a lifetime.

'Ready?'

Suddenly Nash was at her side, opening the door for
her and placing a guiding hand beneath her elbow.
Freya wished she couldn't so easily detect the heat and
disturbing masculine scent of his body, because it made
it so hard to stick to her new resolve to be cool and
distant with him. But when she glanced at his too-
compelling profile she saw by the rigidity in his lean,
carved jaw that he appeared equally resolved to be aloof
with her. Already low, her heart sank even further. She'd
believed they'd been making such headway in their relationship, but now she could see she must have been
wrong about that.

They started to walk down the quiet street. Most of
the little shops with their typically French signs were
now closed for the traditional lunchtime break, and they
walked with notable space between them, careful not to
touch, as though they were indeed work colleagues
instead of one-time lovers...

'Freya!' The sound of her name on a stranger's lips
pierced the air, and before she realised her mistake Freya
had spun round to see where the shout had come from.

Suddenly she was surrounded by flashing camera
bulbs, the lights almost blinding her with their white-
hot glare, making her raise her hands to shield her face
from their almost violent intrusion, feeling dizzy and
disorientated.

A strong arm gripped her by the waist and Nash
started to lead her away from the gathering throng,
shouting furiously behind him, 'Give her a break, can't

you?' followed by what Freya imagined must be the same sentence in fluent, equally furious French.

'I thought you said we could trust your friends?' she burst out bitterly as they hurried over the uneven path, her sense of betrayal stinging worse than a cut from a blade.

'This isn't Celine or Denis's doing…I'd swear an oath on it!' Nash's arm gripped her even more tightly round the waist.

Suddenly they were jostled viciously from behind. Lashing out to protect Freya from the frenzy of invading bodies, Nash was caught up in a tussle with two thuggish-looking photographers. Without his support she lost her balance and pitched helplessly forward onto the pavement. Her hands went out just in time to save herself, but she still landed hard on her knees. The impact seemed to knock all the breath from her lungs, and for what seemed like interminable moments she lay there on the cold, damp concrete, her heartbeat going wild and her knees burning with fiery pain. Behind her Nash let out a torrent of enraged invective, then he was urging her slowly and carefully to her feet as she heard the paparazzi start to head *en masse* in a joint sprint back the way they'd come.

Freya couldn't stop shaking. Her white dress was covered in dirt and stained on the hem with the blood that was oozing from her cut knees. Her smooth palms were also embedded with grit from the road.

'Are you hurt anywhere else?' Nash demanded urgently, his blue eyes hard with concern and his face grey as his hand curled tightly and possessively around her bare arm.

'I don't think so. Please…' Freya begged, knowing that tears were dangerously close. 'Just take me home.'

He'd taken her back to the farmhouse, tenderly cleaned the blood from her cut knees and put dressings on them, then given her some brandy to help her get over the shock. He could hardly believe what had happened.

As soon as he'd got Freya to go and lie down for a while he was immediately on the phone to Fleet Street in London and to press offices in Paris and Lyon to try and discover who had sent out the order to pursue her. Heads would roll…he was determined about that. The look on her stunned face when Nash had picked her up from the pavement would probably be engraved on his soul for ever. It had been a stunned reflection of immense hurt and confusion at being betrayed yet again by the human race. Not that Nash considered some members of the paparazzi anywhere near human after what had happened today. With the uncontrollable way they had behaved—like some bloodthirsty, unintelligent rabble—it was a wonder that Freya hadn't been hurt even worse!

Now he knew they probably couldn't remain where they were. If the press had found out their general location already, then they would more than likely already know the whereabouts of the farmhouse…isolated though it might be. No. It was time to get back to London. His heart acknowledged his deep regret about that, but then sheer pragmatism took over and he realised that he could protect her better there. Nash would be insisting that Freya stayed with him at his apartment on their return. There was no way he was going to let her go home on her own and face a similar rabble unprotected. Already he felt more than responsible for her suffering injury…

She'd packed her bags as Nash had instructed last night, sad on two counts. Firstly that he hadn't sought to comfort her in the way she ached for and still seemed to be keeping her at a distance, and secondly because she wished they could stay longer. The sunshine had been such a balm after the depressingly rainy skies of London, and she wasn't in a hurry to relinquish it. The beautiful rustic farmhouse and the lush surrounding valley had indeed represented a kind of haven. But yesterday a serpent had entered her paradise in the form of invading paparazzi, and if they tracked her down to the farmhouse they would give her no peace.

Now Freya's only consolation on returning to the UK was the prospect of attending the audition. The thought rang curiously hollow for a moment but she refused to pursue the reason why.

Arriving in the kitchen for breakfast, she immediately settled her gaze upon the stack of newspapers piled on the tabletop. On the other side of the room some coffee was brewing in the canary-yellow percolator, sending out a delicious hunger-inducing aroma, but there was no sign of Nash. Wincing a little at the pain, and trying to ignore the aching stiffness in her legs and forearms—the result of yesterday's fall—Freya picked up the top newspaper and scanned the headlines. She saw the photograph of her and Nash before she could comprehend the accompanying words. Distress was clearly evident on her shocked face, but it was Nash's heart-stopping visage that riveted her even more. The photograph had captured him with his arm tightly circled round her waist, and he looked both possessive and fierce. All the moisture seemed to dry up inside her mouth.

'How are you feeling this morning?' he asked behind her, in that smoky bar-room voice of his.

She spun round, her heart bumping against her ribs at the sight of him in faded jeans and a pale blue shirt with the sleeves rolled back to expose his tanned forearms.

'Like I've been knocked down by a runaway horse!'

'I'm very sorry about that.' His expression suggested her words caused him some pain.

'It's not your fault. It goes with the territory... I should know that well enough by now.'

'I got up early to go and get those.' Nash jerked his head towards the newspaper she was holding. 'I wanted to see what they'd write.'

'And? Wait... Don't tell me. No doubt it's something along the lines of "has-been actress falls down drunk in the street"!' Angrily trying to field the fresh wave of injustice that ebbed forcefully through her,

Freya knew that she failed miserably. Was there no end to this torment of mind, body and soul? Was she forever to be judged by everybody? Resigned, she waited for Nash to tell her the worst. Her French was fairly inadequate; there was just a minimal amount of words she understood.

'It's nothing like that.'

'Then what is it?'

'They're suggesting that you and I are lovers.'

CHAPTER NINE

'OH.' CLOSING the paper, Freya threw it down on top of the others. It was to be expected that if she was seen with a man—and a very attractive man at that—the press would have a field-day speculating on their relationship. The fact that what they were saying was true this time didn't help. It only served to remind Freya how foolish she'd been when she'd succumbed to making her relationship with Nash more intimate. Being such an intensely private man, no doubt he must deplore the very idea that the details of his supposed love life were now splashed across all the newspapers. Well, perhaps it would help him understand the sense of violation that Freya had experienced when it was done so carelessly and thoughtlessly to her?

'What does that mean?' His shoulders stiffening, Nash contemplated her warily.

'You probably hate the thought of your private life being pried into because of your association with me...don't you?'

'I admit that it doesn't exactly fill me with glee, but it could serve a purpose that would be worth it.'

'What do you mean?'

'It could help you with some good publicity at last. I hate the fact that you got hurt yesterday, but at least if the press are speculating about your love-life then they're not maligning you by suggesting you're a drunk or an addict or your career is all washed up. In fact it suggests that you're picking up the pieces again and starting afresh.'

'So what are you getting at?'

'What I'm suggesting is that we play along with them for a while. Let them believe that we really are having a relationship.'

Scraping his fingers through his tousled blond hair, he gave her a boyish, lopsided grin…the kind of grin that could break a woman's heart with destroying ease. Somewhere in the silence that followed Freya heard hers crack.

'And that won't cramp your style? What if you want to go out with somebody else in the meantime?'

Even as she asked the question her chest tightened in anticipation of his reply. She really didn't want to hear him tell her they'd get around it somehow. The mere thought of Nash wanting to see another woman hurt enough on its own without having the idea validated.

'I'm too busy working to see anybody else,' he answered, looking slightly aggrieved that she should even ask.

'Of course.' With a disdainful toss of her head, Freya walked across to the percolator to pour herself some coffee. 'I forgot…I'm just another job to you, aren't I?'

'Will you drop that? You're *not* just another job to me, dammit! I would have thought you'd have realised by now that this is not something I make a habit of—becoming intimate with the women I work with.'

'How would I know that?' Freya shot back. 'I've only got your word for it after all!'

'Are you saying that's not good enough?'

As she saw frustration and anger cross his handsome face, she despaired that they were rowing. Only yesterday Nash had been so playful, almost tender with her by the pool, and when he'd confessed that he didn't really know who the real Nash was any more she'd seen past the outward façade of self-assurance and success and glimpsed a more complicated perhaps wounded man underneath. A man who carried hurtful secrets he could not bring himself to share…

'Well…' She lifted a dismissive shoulder, even though inside her courage and resolve to stay immune from his powerful attraction was rapidly deserting her. 'I think we're in danger of forgetting what's important here, aren't we? Getting back to the point in hand, if you think it's helpful to act out that we're having a relationship—and you don't mind the personal intrusion—then maybe it would be a good idea? It's already splashed across the newspapers so…like you suggest…we may as well play along with it. Do you want some coffee?' She'd swiftly changed tack when she realised she was in imminent danger of revealing feelings that he would in all likelihood reject should she do so, which would leave her feeling like the biggest fool that ever was.

'No…I think I'll go for a walk before we leave for the airport. I'll be back soon.'

Watching him leave abruptly, and wishing he'd invited her to go with him, Freya couldn't help but feel inexplicably abandoned…

Nash knew that after the reports in the French newspapers they would more than likely be besieged when they arrived back in London. He was right. He'd arranged for a car to pick them up and take him and Freya back to his Westminster apartment, but from the VIP arrivals lounge all the way to where their car was waiting they found themselves deluged by photographers and reporters, harrying them for quotes and pictures.

Freya said nothing, as Nash had instructed her to do, and he was the one to give the press the answers about their relationship that they were so voraciously demanding. As he did so he couldn't help speculating on what—in their avid enthusiasm for salacious facts— they would dig up about his own past.

Determinedly stemming the doubts and fears that ebbed through him, he let slip the information that Ms Carpenter would be looking at film scripts again in the upcoming weeks, and hinted that she was naturally back in demand by interested casting agents.

Once cocooned in the luxurious passenger seats of the chauffeur-driven Mercedes he had hired, Nash witnessed the signs of strain on Freya's beautiful face from this latest brush with the press. He deeply regretted that their sojourn in the South of France had had to be cut short, and he only hoped that it had not set her back in any way in terms of rebuilding her self-confidence. If she was going to give this upcoming audition her very best then she simply had to pull out all the stops to help her do so. She couldn't afford any more setbacks.

But as he examined the sublimely beautiful features he had come to know so well, Nash's mind went back to that scene in the kitchen this morning, when she'd told him that they were 'in danger of forgetting what was important here'—meaning the reason they had been brought together in the first place. Her words had seemed to be drawing some kind of line under their personal relationship, and Nash couldn't deny that it had disturbed him greatly. He didn't fool himself that once their time working together was over he would probably never see Freya again. She'd be swept back into that glittering world that seemed to bring her both anguish and pleasure, that set her apart from the lives that most ordinary people led. And apart from the severe blow to his pride, Nash realised that her words had set in motion an even deeper hurt inside him…a sense of rejection that he deeply abhorred.

'That wasn't so bad,' he commented now, referring to the events inside the airport.

'No…they were a little better behaved than when we were in France.'

Her dark eyes seemed to flicker apprehensively as she considered him, and Nash had cause to wonder if his making love to her had made her completely doubt his integrity. Damn! He needed Freya's trust in him if he was going to help put her career back where it belonged. More than that…he needed her to know that he would never betray the trust she'd put in him.

'Do you think they really believed that we're seeing each other?'

'They'll believe whatever they want to believe… whatever helps them sell more newspapers. And if I'm not mistaken they'll have a car on our tail even now, following us back to my apartment. That should confirm the idea.'

'I can't stay there with you, Nash.' Her disquiet about the matter was evident. 'I know you said it was a good idea, but I think I'd prefer to go home. You have your work to do, and I have to prepare for this audition—whenever it might be. Do you have any more news on that?'

'I rang Geoff this morning, while we were still in France, and he's getting back to me later. As for you going home…it makes more sense for you to stay at my apartment. After all, you are my priority right now, and I can help you deal with the press as well as taking you wherever you want to go. You'll also be able to rehearse for the audition without any distractions, and I can even stretch to a little cooking if you prefer not to eat out.'

'What about my clothes and the things I might need from home?'

'I can go and get them for you… Just give me your key and tell me what you want.'

'And what about—what about if you want to entertain a friend? Won't I be in the way?'

Seeing immediately what she was getting at, Nash felt a flash of profound impatience assail his insides. 'I told you! I'm not seeing any other woman but you!'

'But this is only pretend, isn't it? You're not really having a relationship with me at all.'

'What are you trying to say, Freya? Are you telling me that you *want* us to have a real relationship?' His piercing ice-blue gaze left her with nowhere to hide.

'No,' she said firmly, her stomach clenching in protest at the lie. Succumbing to the need to retreat after almost exposing herself, Freya moved further down in the butter-soft leather seat to stare out of the window at the passing pedestrians and the shops that flashed by. 'Of course I don't! We both know we're neither of us a good bet for any such thing.'

'Yeah,' Nash agreed grimly, turning to glance out of his own side window. 'You've got that right.'

Nash had gone and collected the things she needed from home and brought them back to his luxurious apartment.

He'd also given Freya some long-awaited good news…
The casting agents wanted to see her for an audition
tomorrow afternoon, so she had in effect about twenty-
four hours in which to prepare for the coming interview.
She planned to spend the time reading some more of
Nikita's story, to refresh her memory about the character
and delve as deeply into the woman's psyche as she could,
to give herself a real fighting chance to win the part.

In the past she'd insisted on auditioning for every role
her agent had set her up for—even the ones that had
been hers for the taking—just to prove to herself and her
employers that she could definitely deliver what they
were looking for. Tomorrow she would be exhibiting
that same passionate dedication. But that evening, as she
curled up on one of the comfortable deep-cushioned
sofas in Nash's living room with her book, she couldn't
help but let her thoughts and her gaze stray from time
to time to the man in whose apartment she was a guest.

At home, his shoes immediately came off, she'd
noticed, and he walked everywhere barefoot, his shirt-
tails hanging loose over his softly napped jeans and his
dark golden hair inevitably awry where he absently
drove his fingers through it. Contrasting that much more
casual look with the precision-perfect façade of his
office apparel, she knew the two appearances were chalk
and cheese—yet both were defined by a strong,
dynamic sensual undercurrent that Freya couldn't
ignore. And he looked almost as good from the back as
he did from the front… His shoulders were strong and

broad, his back and his hips lean, and his legs long and straight, with taut well-honed muscles in his thighs. He also had a rear end that she couldn't help but drool over whenever he walked away from her…

He was currently ensconced in the bright modern kitchen, preparing some salad and a pizza for their supper, and from time to time—to Freya's secret delight and surprise—Nash whistled as he went about the task. It seemed incongruous to her that a man with such innate charisma should do something so ordinary and endearing as whistle while he worked. It stirred renewed pangs of longing deep inside her heart for the chance to really get to know him, and for him to get to know her. But, telling herself that that could never be—and, more than that, she'd be crazy to risk another relationship when her previous one had almost destroyed her—she withdrew her gaze from the kitchen doorway, and the occasional tantalising glimpse of Nash moving back and forth between the worktops, and determinedly returned to the pages of her book.

'I've been thinking about organising an appearance for you at a local children's home I'm involved with.'

They were sitting on opposite sides of the long chrome and glass coffee table in the living room, having just finished their late-night supper, taking their time over coffee, when Nash came out with this announcement. Freya's dark eyes widened to saucers.

'They're doing a fund-raiser for some trips to the

seaside next summer. The home is very near where you grew up, as a matter of fact, and I thought it would be a good opportunity to get you some very positive publicity. What do you think?'

'A children's home?'

'Yes.'

'Do you mind if I ask how you got involved with such an organisation?' Her interest quickening at the idea of Nash revealing something previously unknown about his life—Freya barely moved a muscle as she sat waiting for his answer.

Hesitating, Nash told himself he should have known that she would ask questions about his association with the home, and couldn't see how he could avoid telling her at least part of the reason why.

Sliding his palms down over his knees, he felt his resistance momentarily forgotten as he became captivated by the rapt expression on her face. Whenever she was interested in something her features lit up like starlight. As diligent as he was about keeping his emotions in tight check, Nash couldn't kid himself that it hadn't hurt when Freya had answered with a firmly voiced 'no' when he'd asked her if she would want a real relationship with him. It had inevitably pricked at that sickening sense of rejection he'd borne since childhood—when his mother had more than once brought another abusive man into their home rather than take the chance of raising her son by herself and putting his welfare first.

'Is it really so inconceivable to you that I might have some involvement with a children's home just out of plain humanitarian concern?' he asked, an unconsciously rough edge to his voice.

'I wasn't suggesting that I found it hard to understand. I was only interested that you—'

'I didn't have one of the most idyllic childhoods. I think I already indicated that to you before, so let's just leave it at that, shall we?' He almost had to force the words from his lips they were so repugnant to him. They couldn't help but reignite the pain of old wounds he was in no mood to re-examine. Pushing to his feet, Nash couldn't disguise his irritation. 'Happy now?'

Freya got to her feet too. The smooth skin between her perfectly defined velvet brows puckered. 'That you suffered in childhood? No, of course not! But if you're asking if I'm happy that you told me so, then, yes! I can't help but feel it's a huge step forward with you being normally so reticent about discussing anything personal with me!'

'Well, don't get your hopes up that there'll be a repeat.'

'Why not?' she challenged, her dark gaze latching firmly onto his. 'What are you so afraid of?'

What was he afraid of? Staring at her as a man praying for divine aid stared at a vision of an angel, all his senses deluged by her dark exotic beauty and his whole body aching to go to her, to demonstrate to her without restraint what he really felt and thought, Nash didn't have to search hard for the answer to that question. Yet still he shied away from it, pushing it almost violently to the back of his mind, telling himself that such a conclusion was not for him.

'Let's just stick with the subject we were discussing, eh? Will you appear at the fund-raiser or not?'

'Yes…of course I will! But why won't you tell me a bit more about why you got involved with the home…about your childhood? I'd really like to know, Nash.'

'You're persistent. I'll give you that.'

'You don't get anywhere in life without being persistent… You'd no doubt back me up on that.' Venturing a grin, Freya silently admitted she would use every charm offensive she could to persuade him to open up.

He grimaced, clearly not happy, but at the same time looking as if he might just relent. 'Okay.' A sigh escaped him, and he was displaying the resignation of a reluctant patient when forced to take disliked medicine. 'I was raised by my mother after my father was killed in a road traffic accident when I was three.'

'Oh…I'm sorry.' Unable to hold back her feelings of empathy at the realisation that Nash had also lost his father at too young an age, Freya didn't take her eyes off of him.

'We weren't well off, and my mother struggled to hold things together. Not very successfully, I'm afraid.' Threading his fingers through his hair, Nash glanced briefly at Freya, then away again, as if the memories he was recalling were still too raw to contemplate. 'From time to time she thought that being with another man might help improve our situation, but it frankly made things worse…a lot worse. The men she got involved with were total nightmares…the kind of walking disasters that mothers warn their daughters about. They used her and abused her and a couple of them beat the hell out of me too. One of them attacked me with a knife, and I ended up in hospital, having a blood transfusion. I was just fourteen years old. You heard enough?'

The blue eyes that were so mesmerisingly flawless glimmered with clear disgust, and Freya sensed her heart swell with pain, shock and regret at the trauma he must have suffered.

'Oh, Nash!' Natural instinct made her go to him, but she froze in shock when he deliberately moved away from her, his raised hand indicating she keep her distance.

'I'm not looking for sympathy, Freya. You asked me about my childhood and I told you. Now just leave it alone can you?'

'But—my God! Your mother's boyfriend attacked you with a knife? That's dreadful!' She twisted her hands together, distressed that he wouldn't let her comfort him—even though she knew it was many years too late for the boy he had been. What had happened to Nash made her own story seem like a fairy tale in comparison.

'I'm going out for a while.' He backed towards the door, barely looking at her. 'Don't wait up for me. I don't know what time I'll be back.'

'Don't leave, Nash. Why don't you just stay and talk to me?'

'I've done enough damn talking, in my opinion! Just go to bed and think about something else, will you? How about the audition you're going to tomorrow? You need to concentrate on that. I'll see you in the morning.'

'No!'

She was at his side with her hand on his arm before he could reach for the door catch and go out. He was staring at her as a wounded animal stared at a predator that had just appeared and cornered it—most of the colour seemed to drain from his face at the idea he might be trapped. It took every ounce of courage Freya had in her to keep her hand wrapped firmly round his strong wrist, but instinct told her she shouldn't let him escape this time.

'I just—' She swallowed hard across the lump in her throat. 'I just want to hold you, Nash… Won't you let me do that?'

She saw him grit his teeth, registered the stark mirror of pain that glittered back at her, and before he could shake off her hold moved in close to his chest, slid her arm round his waist. For a second or two he remained rigid as a fence-post, but then…incredibly…she sensed him relent.

'Oh, baby, I hate that you got so badly hurt… I almost can't bear it.'

Reaching up, she kissed the side of his rigid jaw, felt his stubble graze her soft mouth then heard the harsh sounding exhalation he made at the contact. Euphoria and relief washed over her in a wild torrent when he caught her to him and held her so tight that her breathing was almost compromised. Sliding his hand up behind her head, Nash stroked her hair as he brought her face down onto his shoulder. Freya knew she didn't imagine the shudder of emotion that went through him. She didn't think she would ever forget it…

CHAPTER TEN

PACING the plush air-conditioned waiting room of the West End casting agents where Freya was having her audition, Nash mused that his position was not unlike that of an expectant father waiting for news of his newborn. An hour had passed already, and he thought if he had to wait another minute for her to emerge from Geoff Epstein's gargantuan office he would honestly go nuts.

Pausing for yet another glance out of the window, he saw that it had started to rain again. Watching the snail-like pace of the traffic inching down the long narrow street below, he rested a wary eye on the pedestrian access to the front of the building. So far he hadn't spied any evidence of paparazzi, but he knew that if Freya's audition hadn't gone well she would understandably not feel up to facing cameras on the way out. He sighed. His need to protect her went way beyond a purely professional requirement. That was blindingly obvious. And after last night, the way she had held him and offered him the kind of comfort he had never allowed himself to receive before, he was a man in turmoil. But telling her the truth about his background had been cathartic as well. Something frozen for too long inside him was indisputably melting, and he felt like a changed man.

Following the events of last night, Nash also couldn't help reflecting on how he was supposed to withstand having Freya share his apartment and resist touching her. Every time he held her at the back of his mind was the realisation that one day soon his agreement to help her would be at an end and she wouldn't need him any more. Perhaps he should try and start to let go of her from now on, to pre-empt any further pain her departure might cause him?

The door to Geoff's office opened at last, and the woman who had been commanding most of his thoughts came out into the waiting room. She was wearing slim black trousers with a classic white shirt, a black fitted jacket and a minimal amount of make-up. With her dark hair swept up on top of her head and kept in place by a tortoiseshell comb her graceful appearance resembled that of a svelte professional dancer rather than a well-known movie actress. Catching the dark-eyed glance that gravitated straight to him, Nash experienced the most incredible pleasure explode like a skyrocket inside him. The sensation was getting to be a habit as far as Freya was concerned, he acknowledged, silently and broodingly.

'Everything okay?' he enquired, when she didn't immediately address him. Before she could answer, a large middle-aged man with black wiry hair, wearing a striped shirt and braces on his trousers, emerged from the room behind her. He made straight for Nash and heartily shook his hand.

'Nash! Good to see you, my friend! It's been too long. We must have lunch together some time soon. How's business? Still burning the candle at both ends? A rich guy like you can afford to take his foot off the gas from time to time, don't forget!'

The words burst from his lips like machine-gun fire, and Nash couldn't help thinking it would be a good idea if he drew a breath from time to time…

'That's good advice. Business is good… How are you doing?' The younger man's smile was far from relaxed, and neither was he in the mood to indulge in polite chit-chat, even though it might be good PR. All he was really concerned about was how Freya's audition had gone and how she felt about the performance she'd given. Watching him across the other man's shoulder, her quiet steady gaze revealed nothing of what she might be feeling.

'I certainly can't complain!' Laughing at his own joke—the plush offices with the signed movie-star photos covering its walls and the framed business awards a vivid testament to his own personal success—Geoff Epstein turned suddenly to include Freya in the general banter. Moving over to her, he put his arm familiarly around her slender shoulders and gave them a squeeze.

Immediately Nash sensed rage boil up inside him at

the sight. Another man touching her like that was anathema to him, and he wanted to rip her away from Geoff's side immediately. But he didn't want to scupper any chances Freya might have of winning the role of Nikita by a jealous display of temper. He was certain she wouldn't welcome it, and might just think he was taking too much upon himself.

'And business is starting to look up even more now that we've got this young lady on board to play the starring role in our film!' the casting agent declared with avid glee.

Shocked and surprised, Nash focused his blue eyes even more intently on Freya. 'You got the part?'

The briefest smile of acknowledgement touched her perfect lips. 'It seems so.'

'I've seen about twenty other actresses and I've got to tell you…there was simply no contest! The director and I were blown away by her performance! Freya is the consummate professional…born to play the role of Nikita Pushkova. And the backers and producers will be absolutely delighted to have her join us. Thanks a million for arranging for me to see her, Nash… I owe you.'

At the bottom of the narrow elegant staircase, by the door that led onto the street outside, Nash laid his hand on Freya's jacket sleeve to make her pause for a moment. For someone who had just won what could turn out to be a career-defining role, she seemed almost too composed to be believed. Especially when he knew intimately just how much that part meant to her in terms of resuming her career.

'Congratulations. You must be elated,' he remarked.

She wanted him to hug her…or at least appear far happier than he did at that moment. But his expression appeared a bare degree warmer than stone-cold marble, and Freya wondered if he wasn't already thinking about the next client he would be taking on and was simply mentally letting her go. The thought made her feel sick inside, instead of elated by her good fortune. She didn't want Nash to let her go…or to think about anybody else.

Last night, when he had allowed her to stop him leaving and simply hold him after his reluctant confession about his past, she had been suffused with an overwhelming feeling of love for him that had made her want to hold onto him for life. It had taken great courage to tell her his story, and Freya knew intimately that it didn't come easy when a person had been so profoundly and destroyingly hurt. She'd wanted badly to make love with him, but had sensed his need to retreat and recoup after what had occurred and so had accepted his ruefully offered goodnight and watched him go to his bedroom alone.

Afterwards, she had mourned the too-great loss of his hard, strong arms around her, and the scorching 'lock the door' kisses that she'd so willingly become enslaved by. It had felt as if he was locking her out by keeping her at such a distance—even though he had finally accepted her need to comfort him. Now her only consolation was the surprising revelation that she still obviously had what it took to be a first-class actress and had won this coveted role...in spite of all her own personal anguish. Seeing as Nash seemed so resistant to allowing her into his heart, all the passionate feeling she was capable of would simply have to be focused on delivering a portrayal of the beautiful Russian doctor that would be faithful and true and show everyone what an amazing young woman Nikita Pushkova had been.

'I'm so overwhelmed I can hardly take it in,' she confessed now, smiling tentatively. 'I think I gave a good performance, but it's not always easy to tell. Anyway...it's all really down to you that I'm in this enviable position. If you hadn't brought the part to my attention and arranged for me to have the audition I'd still be wondering how I was going to get back into the business.'

'You did it all on your own merit, sweetheart.' The endearment slipped out before he'd noticed, and Nash followed it up by gently touching his palm to Freya's cold smooth cheek. Seeing the startled look in her eyes, he wryly withdrew it again and held up the long black coat he'd been carrying for her. 'You'd better put this on,' he advised, even as she turned round to slide her arms into the sleeves. 'It's raining outside.'

'I wish we could go somewhere and get a cup of coffee to celebrate.'

A soft, regretful sigh followed this somewhat forlorn remark, and Nash thought, Why not? She was hardly asking for the moon to go and enjoy a cup of coffee in a café, like any ordinary citizen had a perfect right to do! Yet he knew if they started walking openly down the street it wouldn't take long for someone to recognise her, and then the press would descend on them like a swarm of avid bees round the last blooms of summer. He frowned...then grinned.

'Wait here,' he instructed, taking the staircase two steps at a time as Freya spun round in surprise to watch him. Returning mere minutes later, he triumphantly produced a short blonde wig and a purple velvet scarf, courtesy of Geoff Epstein's casting wardrobe.

'Ta-da!' He grinned. 'Go up to the ladies' room and put these on,' he instructed, pulling his own coat collar up around his ears. 'If we're only out for half an hour or so we should be able to get away with it.'

Sitting in a packed corner of a well-known coffee outlet just off Oxford Street, Nash watched Freya sip her frothy cappuccino with a pleasure that could not be measured on any scale that he knew of. She put him in mind of an excited child playing dress-up. She'd entered into the spirit of her disguise with real zeal—even affecting a Swedish accent that in his opinion would have fooled his own mother, who was from that country. Her lovely face—framed by ash-blonde instead of its usual ebony silk—was no less beautiful, and Nash barely touched his own coffee for looking at her instead.

'I can't tell you how much I've missed this!' She

leaned towards him across the small round table. If it hadn't been for the fact she didn't want to attract unwanted attention. Freya could have hugged Nash right there and then in front of everyone. Her delight in this small, not insignificant pleasure almost overwhelmed her. 'Thank you.'

'My pleasure. You're a knockout as a blonde, by the way.'

His voice was a little husky, she noticed, and the bedroom cadence of it made her shiver.

'Am I?'

'I'll have to get you to play dress-up for me in private one day soon,' he joked, but the laser-like heat in his crystal blue eyes burned her, and belied the humour in his tone.

To deflect the answering swell of need that arose like a deep wave from the bottom of a deceptively calm ocean inside her, Freya quickly sought a less provocative subject to talk about.

'When did you want me to do the benefit at the children's home?'

His answering glance was no less intense. 'It's on Saturday…just a few days' time. I'm going to speak to the press soon, to let them know you'll be making an appearance there. Did Geoff say when rehearsals start for the film?'

'Next month. We'll spend two weeks in London rehearsing before we fly out to Romania to look at some locations with the director.'

'It's going to be amazing for you.'

'I know.'

It was hard for Freya to rest her gaze on Nash and know that some time in the not too distant future he would no longer be in her life. She would be once more immersed in her film career, and he would be protecting and arranging more conducive publicity for another fortunate client who was overwhelmed by their predicament. The thought was almost too painful to bear.

She'd believed that living with the day-to-day misery of a failed marriage, a ruined career and a mercenary and cruel ex who'd bled her dry every which way was the epitome of despair—but it would be as nothing to the pain of parting from Nash now that she knew she was hopelessly, emphatically, in love with him. Her love genuinely was hopeless, since she'd now discovered that the dynamic PR executive was a man who clearly kept any suggestion of love away due to the wounds of his horrendous past. How was such a man ever to be reached?

'We ought to be getting back,' she said jumpily, needing to disguise the sorrow that had insidiously descended and stolen her joy.

'Sure. As soon as you've finished your coffee we'll go,' Nash agreed, his glance leaving her to diligently scan the room for anyone taking a too obvious interest in them, and also to check that there were no reporters or photographers waiting to pounce on them as soon as they set foot outside the building.

* * *

Both the children and the staff at the home had come up trumps. As the applause for the final act of the afternoon's entertainment died away—a charming rendition of *Snow White and the Seven Dwarfs,* no less—Nash speculated on what Freya had made of it. Judging by the completely enraptured expression on her face as she sat beside him on a hard plastic chair, she appeared as touched by the children's bright shining faces, and their determination to excel in their performances despite the heartbreak that went on behind the scenes, as he was.

Warmth crowded into his chest and rendered him almost too emotional to speak. But then Freya turned towards him, smiling her delight at the show they'd just witnessed, and Nash was struck again by how right it felt to have this amazing woman by his side.

'That was just wonderful!' she exclaimed with enthusiasm. 'I was astounded at how perfectly they all remembered their lines! Especially the younger ones.'

'They've been rehearsing for weeks to make it look seamless.'

'Well, it definitely paid off!'

A sense of hard-to-contain excitement was building up around them in the rows upon rows of seats occupied by children and staff alike, but at the back of the room the waiting press had been warned not to take any pictures until Freya actually got up to speak. Catching the eye of the principal of the home, Nash covered Freya's hand briefly with his own.

'They're waiting for you to say something,' he said lightly. 'Do you mind going up unannounced?'

'Not at all.' She started to get to her feet, a vision of slenderness and poise in her pink Chanel suit, her perfume lingering in the air with seductive tones of amber and jasmine. 'Wish me luck!'

Nash's answering glance was perfectly serious. 'You don't need it, angel,' he murmured, and his keen gaze was unwavering as Freya made her way gracefully up the five wooden steps that led onto the small wooden stage.

Her smile of greeting dazzled everyone present in that tiny hall—from the domestic staff and the children to the eager press and the principal of the home herself. She looked every inch the perfect ambassador of her craft. Something told Nash that Freya Carpenter would never, ever be the has-been actress that she had so derogatorily called herself when they'd first met. She had way too much talent and charisma for that ever to be a reality.

Her short but enthusiastic speech—praising the children's and staff's efforts and pledging her support for any future fund-raisers in whatever way she could— all but brought the house down. Cameras whirred and flashed and, agreeing to pose with the children, Freya put her arms around the eager little bodies that pressed forward for her attention. She seemed to have a special smile for each and every child there, clearly not just making an appearance to help further her career.

Nash realised she was genuinely happy to be there, and then—like a thunderbolt out of the blue as he continued to gaze at her beautiful joyful face—the truth hit him. In those few almost unreal minutes, when time seemed to strangely stand still, Nash realised he was in love. The realisation throbbed through him in a relentless tide of powerful emotion, and he shook his head in wonderment to try and relieve himself of the giddiness that had somehow seized his brain.

After that, it was hard to concentrate on anything but the need to be alone with her, to somehow convey his feelings…if it wasn't already too late. He had pushed her away so many times when she'd tried to get close. Would she believe his sincerity when he told her that he would never keep her at a distance again?

When it was time to leave, and they had said their goodbyes to all, he led Freya out to the car park. Oliver Beaumarche was waiting in the driving seat of his BMW to take Freya back to his house for drinks, then out to dinner. Nash was going to follow in his own car and join them. He wished that they were going straight back to his apartment instead, but his need to talk privately to Freya would have to wait now until they could be alone…as frustrating as that might be.

As members of the press spilled out of the home behind them, continuing to call out to her and take pictures as she stood obligingly by the passenger seat of the car, Freya glanced up at Nash with shining eyes.

'I loved the kids,' she told him unreservedly. 'I'd love to go back and visit soon. Can you arrange it?'

'No problem.'

'I think you're wonderful to do the work you do here,' she whispered, for his ears alone.

Nash tipped up her chin, knowing that the picture the two of them made would no doubt feature highly in the following morning's papers. And, though he couldn't help wishing that the intimate moment could have been more private, nonetheless he was elated just to be able to touch her. 'I think you're pretty wonderful too, Ms Carpenter,' he teased, then planted a soft kiss on her surprised mouth. 'You've made their day coming here.'

She smiled. 'Not as much as they've made mine.'

'That's enough for today, folks.' Nash addressed the small crowd round the car as he briefly turned to open the passenger door for Freya. 'Ms Carpenter has another appointment to go to, and I think you've all had plenty of pictures to be going on with.'

'Thanks, Freya! Good luck!' somebody shouted out, just before she turned and got into the car.

The car park miraculously started to clear. Seconds later, after a brief exchange with Oliver Beaumarche, who'd waited patiently for the melee to finish, Nash was about to say goodbye to Freya when a tall, skinny boy with a shock of raven hair and piercing blue eyes hailed him from across the other side of the car park. Nash glanced round, smiling in genuine pleasure as the youth approached.

'Hey, Mark! How are you doing? I didn't see you inside.'

'No. I should've been at school today, but I've been to an interview for sixth-form college. Why d'you think I'm dressed like this?'

Nash's gaze took in the slightly shiny grey trousers, dull white shirt and ill-matched brown flecked tie beneath the habitual grey fleece that was the only jacket he had ever seen Mark wear, and his heart squeezed tight.

'Maybe I thought you had a hot date?' he teased, a twinkle in his smiling blue eyes.

'Fat chance!' Visibly reddening around the jaw, Mark grimaced. 'Is that Freya Carpenter in there?' He stooped down with awe in his voice to gaze at the glamorous woman in the back seat of the Mercedes.

'Why don't you say hello to her, Mark?' Nash smiled.

Hearing the invitation, Freya held out her hand to the youngster. 'Hello, Mark. I'm very pleased to meet you.'

'Wow!' Shaking her hand and turning to glance up at Nash at the same time, Mark went even redder in the face. 'She's gorgeous!'

'You won't get an argument from me,' Nash replied without hesitation, his own gaze moving to focus on a pair of exotic caramel eyes that could all but make a man's heart jump straight out of his chest with one beguiling look.

Mark dipped his head a little towards Freya. 'Nice to meet you too, miss.' He let go of her hand and straightened again.

'Can I talk to you for a second?' he asked Nash, his expression uncertain.

'Do you mind?' Encompassing both Freya and her uncle with his glance, Nash put his hand beneath Mark's elbow. 'Why don't you get going? I'll meet you back at the house…I know the address.'

'Take your time,' Freya said easily. 'We'll see you soon.' She pulled the passenger door shut with a brief flicker of concern in her eyes, then sat back in her seat as Oliver drove the car out of the car park.

Leading the boy to where his own Mercedes was parked, Nash let go of his elbow and folded his arms across his chest.

'What's up?'

'I saw my mum yesterday…in the hospital.'

Mark's mother was a registered substance abuser and an alcoholic who'd spent time in Holloway Prison for stabbing her abusive boyfriend. Feeling his heart start to race at what the boy might be going to tell him, Nash squeezed Mark's bony shoulder beneath the shabby grey fleece.

'What's she doing in the hospital?' he probed gently.

'She's been using again, hasn't she?' Anger darkening his brilliant blue gaze, Mark dipped his head in a bid to control his temper.

In an instant Nash saw himself reflected in the boy's

condemning wounded eyes. Because rewind to twenty years or so and the boy standing in front of him could have been him. Hurt, angry, and feeling betrayed by the very people who were supposed to look out for him. Nash recognised the crushing, bruising emotions only too well. His own father had deserted him by dying and his mother…his mother should have protected him better, he realised with a shock. Why had she prolonged both his and her own agony by living with man after man who'd abused and mistreated her and her son? Wouldn't it have been better if she'd struggled on alone until Nash was of an age when he could have gone out to work and helped her himself? Why had she sent him to England, to an aunt he'd never even met before, to make his own way?

Slowly, he eased out a breath. She'd sent him to his father's sister in Essex because her thug of a boyfriend had almost stabbed him to death with a knife. The wound in his side seemed to throb and burn as he reluctantly allowed the memory to linger for a moment. But…in the final analysis…by sending him away his mother had perhaps done the best she could think of to protect her son.

'Is she getting help?' Nash asked the boy now, his fingers curling even more firmly into his shoulder.

'She's got a new social worker assigned to her case. Won't make any difference, though, will it? She'll still go back to drinking and using and there'll be another

low-life waiting in the wings to take her back home…
Same old story.'

'But it can be a different story for you, Mark.' Letting
his hand drop away, Nash narrowed his blue eyes as he
studied the pale, haunted face of the young teenager.
'You get into sixth-form college and then maybe even
go on to university—the sky will be the limit for a bright
boy like you. I've seen your grades, remember? I know
what you're capable of. And any time you doubt that,
or just want to talk about stuff, ring me. Here.' Taking
one of his business cards from his wallet, Nash handed
it to Mark. 'You want to know the best way to help your
mum?' he continued. 'Do it by excelling in whatever
you do. Be the best you can be and she'll be the proudest
woman on earth.'

'Suppose so.' Appearing pleased, but embarrassed,
Mark nodded his head at Nash's car. 'I'll do it too, if it
means I get to drive a Merc of my own one day.'

'Want to go for a spin now?' Nash asked him, feeling
certain that Freya and Oliver would understand if he was
a little later than expected getting to the house.

'You kidding? Oh, man, that would be cool!'

'We've got to clear it with the powers that be first.'
Ruffling Mark's thick black hair, Nash slammed the car
door shut and walked alongside the teenager back inside
the children's home.

CHAPTER ELEVEN

FREYA had been wondering about the boy Mark she'd met so briefly before she'd left the children's home. Apart from his poor clothing, there had been a wounded look about him that had touched her heart. Noticing the way Nash had regarded him, with such interest and concern, had helped Freya see the indisputable goodness in the man she loved. Many people who had been hurt as badly as he had during their childhood instinctively wanted to retreat from the world somehow, and protect themselves from any reminders of the too shattering memories. But Nash had not behaved like that. He'd actively sought to use his success in helping others who'd had a less fortunate start in life…like he had had. She wondered if Mark realised what a potentially amazing friend he had in the older man.

Their dinner with Oliver at an end, Freya could hardly wait to be alone with Nash at the apartment. His gaze had scarcely left hers all evening, and a quiet but powerful anticipation was building inexorably through her at the thought that they might make love again. Her body yearned to feel his touch. Her skin was already hot and achy, as though she were incubating a fever at the mere idea.

When no press cars followed them from the restaurant, she felt like an elated escape artist who had pulled off a stunt previously thought impossible. At the apartment, after hanging his jacket on the chrome stand inside the door, Nash briefly excused himself to go and use the bathroom. Back at the restaurant a waiter had accidentally spilled red wine on his spotless white shirt, and he wanted to change out of it and put on a fresh one.

While she waited impatiently for him to return Freya wandered into the kitchen, then the living room, restlessly inspecting the immaculate, artistically designed rooms with an air that was definitely distracted. Selecting a Mozart CD to play on the state-of-the-art music system, she sat on the couch and shut her eyes to more fully concentrate on the music. They flew open again in surprise when the telephone rang. Hurrying to turn down the volume, she was just about to reach for the receiver when the answer-machine clicked into action. There was Nash's voice, telling the caller he wasn't at home and to please leave a message and he would get back to them.

A woman's voice, smooth and rich as opulent velvet, came on the line.

'Nash, darling… I'm so disappointed that you're not there! It's late in the evening, I know, but please ring me when you get this message. I miss you and love you lots, my angel. Speak soon.'

Freya had straight away identified the accent that filled the room as Swedish, and as the affectionate—she dared not think passionate—words echoed mockingly round her stunned brain—she levered herself off of the couch and found herself at the window that framed the twinkling London nightscape to such spectacular effect.

Nash was seeing someone else! Someone who spoke as if they were on the most intimate of terms! An acquaintance or even a close friend would hardly sign off their message with 'I miss you and love you lots, my angel'…would they? He'd lied to her.

Ice water seemed to seep into her veins as the terrible realisation sank in. It was just like a sickening replay of the horrible moment when she'd discovered that her new husband didn't love her at all and had only married her because of her fame and wealth. She and James had been at yet another tedious party and—his speech impaired by too much alcohol—he'd slurred the confession mockingly to a friend of his just as Freya had walked back into the room after visiting the cloakroom. But this was far worse than that repugnant memory.

Devastated tears slid down the softly smooth contours of her face and she cupped her hands across the bridge of her nose as though she were praying, catching them as they fell. How could Nash do that to her? How could he have made love to her—and he would have made love to her again tonight, she was certain—knowing that he was possibly in love with someone else? Was her judgement so impaired she could so easily be deceived by a man again? No wonder he'd sometimes seemed to keep Freya at a distance! No wonder he'd been so secretive about his past! He obviously had a hell of a lot to hide besides his background!

'Did I hear the phone ring?' he asked, strolling through the living room door just then, his hands adjusting the cuffs on his fresh white shirt.

Turning to face him, that chiselled arresting visage of his and tousled blond hair catching her on the raw, Freya strove to compose herself. 'As a matter of fact, you did. The woman who called left you a message. You'll find it on the machine.'

'Okay. I'm sure it wasn't important. I'll listen to it later.' His smile was relaxed and intimate, as if nothing could possibly be amiss, and as he started to walk towards Freya she could no longer control the turbulent emotion that was coursing through her at the idea he was seeing someone else.

'Oh, I would listen to the message now, if I were you, Nash,' she commented sarcastically. 'It sounded pretty important to me. The woman was practically desolate that you weren't in. And, by the way…she finished off by saying how much she loved and missed you! Who is she? Somebody you've been having an affair with, obviously!'

'What?'

Stopping in his tracks, Nash tried to assimilate the

sensation of driving head-on into a rockface at high speed. 'Of course I'm not having a damn affair!'

He was suddenly aware of the acute distress written all over Freya's lovely face, and saw that she'd been crying. His heart started to beat faster than an express train at the idea she believed he'd been seeing someone else all along.

'Then am I to deduce that it's quite *normal* that you receive phone calls late at night from some sultry woman telling you that she loves you?'

'Are you saying that she had a foreign accent?' Nash dropped his hands either side of his straight, lean hips and slowly moved his head from side to side in disbelief.

'Yes, she had an accent!' Freya burst out furiously. 'A Swedish accent, if I'm not mistaken! Why don't I play the tape and check to see if I'm right?'

Two things had hit Nash, like a force ten gale sweeping him nearly off his feet. Firstly, Freya had mistakenly thought his mother was some woman he was having an affair with…and secondly she was *jealous*! And if she was jealous then that must mean she cared about him…really cared. He hadn't left it too late to tell her that he loved her! If she knew how crazy he was about her then she wouldn't expect him to just walk out of her life now that she was on the brink of getting her film career back again. It was a revelation, and Nash's chest crowded with the kind of warmth that kindled forest fires.

'You don't need to do that.' He sighed. 'You're

right...the woman in question does have a Swedish accent. Her name is Inga Johannsson and she's my mother.' The corners of his mouth dragged up into a smile and he tunnelled his fingers restlessly through his inevitably mussed blond hair, hardly able to contain the sense of elation that was pouring through his bloodstream. 'That message you heard was from her. She was ringing from her home in Sweden.'

'Your *mother*?' He heard the doubt in her tone and for a few moments wrestled with the strongest urge to cross the room and go to her. He'd show her in no uncertain terms that she was the only woman he loved and wanted to be with, then he'd take her to bed and demonstrate it some more for the rest of the night.

'Why does your mother live in Sweden?'

'Because that's where she's from. Stockholm, to be precise. And until I was fourteen years old I lived there too.'

'And what about your father? Was he Swedish too?'

'No...British.'

Nash's heart swelled anew with the longing to go to her. He loved Freya. He had absolutely no doubts about that now. The thought of losing her made him experience the kind of dread he wouldn't wish on his worst enemy. She had become such an integral part of him that nothing in his life would make any sense any more if she weren't in it.

'Oh, Nash!' She ran into his arms then, burying her face in his chest as her arms twined tightly round his neck. 'I'm sorry I accused you of having an affair, but I was in pieces when I heard that message! Do you forgive me?'

Making her look at him, Nash gazed down into her passionate dark eyes with a slow, devastating smile.

'Yes, baby…I do forgive you. But you'll have to be very, very nice to me to make sure I don't hold any grudges.'

Freya's cheeks dimpled. 'How nice?'

'Come to bed and I'll show you.'

Taking her by the hand, Nash led her through the silent, spacious hall of the apartment to his bedroom. Outside the temperatures had dropped dramatically, and the sleeting rain that had been falling had long since turned to snow. After turning on a nearby lamp, the first thing Nash did was to close the blinds at the window and shut out the night completely. Then he returned to Freya and slipped her pink suit jacket from her shoulders. Laying it aside on a chair, he tipped up her chin so that he could see every contour and feature of the lovely face that was accentuated by the soft lamp-lit glow.

'I won't ever lie to you,' he asserted, and Freya sensed her heart stall, hardly daring to breathe. 'But don't expect me to go over every sordid little detail of my former life with you either. You already know some of the story, and for now that's enough. Right now I want us to focus on a different, far happier scenario…our own story.'

She loved him. Her heart grieved for every ounce

of pain and anguish he had ever suffered, but she understood enough of his character to know that it wouldn't benefit either of them for him to identify too freely or too frequently with the hurt he had endured. He had his own way of dealing with his demons and she had to respect that. All he needed to know was that it was Freya's heartfelt wish that they would meet any future challenges or hurt that came their way together.

How could I have lived alone all this time, Nash was thinking as he studied the beautiful face before him, and never realised how lonely I was until Freya came along? I never knew the thing that was missing in my life—the thing that could connect me back more fully to the human race—was her.

He hadn't told her yet how much he loved her. But he would. First he would take her to bed and demonstrate to her with every drop of passion and feeling he had in him how much he cared.

'Whatever you've endured, Nash,' Freya told him now, lightly pushing back a tarnished gold lock of hair from his forehead, 'you've obviously overcome to achieve what you've achieved. Look how much you've helped me restore my belief in myself…you should be proud.'

Remembering the boy Mark at the children's home, Nash allowed himself the faintest smile of agreement. Would he be telling him the same thing in a few years' time? He prayed that he would. In the meantime he would be proud enough to be his mentor and friend.

Glancing down at his watch, Nash smiled even wider as his gaze helplessly returned to Freya.

'I don't know how many hours it's been between kisses, but I don't intend waiting another second longer before I steal one.'

Angling his head to meet her lips, he kissed her full on the mouth, heat pouring through him in a blaze of hunger and desire as she opened for him and her tongue danced silkily with his. Then he led her to the generous king-sized bed that dominated the room, and with softly urgent sighs and eager touches they undressed each other and climbed beneath the duvet. Covering her delectable feminine contours with his own more hard-muscled form, Nash paid silent homage to her earthy, sensuous beauty. Then he showed her with his mouth, his tongue, his sex, just how much he desired her—just how much she had enslaved him and bound him to her with chains of love and passion. He intended to express that to her every day until they died...

And when Freya's sweet lips found that ugly ridged scar of his that was the cruellest legacy from his past, and kissed every inch of that seared flesh as though she were kissing the most beautiful thing on earth, Nash almost couldn't think any more for the powerful upsurge of emotion that arose inside him. Something broken in him seemed suddenly to reassemble, and he wanted to cry and laugh for joy all at the same time.

Later, after the storm of their loving, as Nash held Freya against him, her satiny behind pressed up close into the cradle of his hips, he covered her lovely breasts with his hands and placed a softly tender kiss at the side of her neck.

'Ever think about getting married again?' he asked.

Growing still at the question, Freya could hardly hear herself think for the sound of her own blood roaring in her ears.

'Think seriously for a minute about what you could be taking on, Nash,' she joked, biting back the sudden onrush of bitterness tinged with regret. 'James more or less left me stony broke. My house is mortgaged to the hilt, and I haven't earned any money in almost two whole years! And if you crave privacy then I'm hardly the best proposition for marriage, given the level of interest my life seems to invoke in the press!'

'I love you, Freya Carpenter. And I'd want to marry you whatever your life looked like! I didn't plan to fall in love with a gorgeous movie star, but hey…' she heard the grin in his voice '…we all have to make sacrifices in life…'

'Sacrifices indeed!' Turning round to face him, Freya was all but stunned into silence by the blaze of love directed towards her from those incredibly blue eyes of his.

'Just in case you didn't know…' he drawled thoughtfully, cupping her chin and drawing his thumb back and forth across that rather stubborn feature, 'given my own background, I'm hardly the most perfect proposition either.'

Warming to the subject, Freya snuggled closer. 'And

what can a less than perfect male specimen like you offer a far from perfect female like me if I were to marry you?' she teased.

'My heart,' Nash replied seriously, the fascinating hue of his eyes growing darker and deeper than a moonless night. 'Will that do for starters, Freya?'

'Oh,' she whispered, and for long, delicious seconds lost herself completely in his passionate and devouring kiss.

When she could finally bear to tear herself away from the delectably erotic promise his lips so tantalisingly offered, she gazed at him almost in awe. 'In case you hadn't already guessed…I love you too, Nash. And I'm not going to stop loving you…ever.'

'And when those adoring fans of yours try to trample over me to get to you, you can be sure that I'll be holding on real tight and won't ever let go.'

'Promise?'

'Promise.'

He pulled her round so that she was lying on top of him and proceeded to kiss her, until Freya honestly had no notion of being in the real world at all… Instead she lingered in a hypnotic sublime paradise that she never wanted to leave…

EPILOGUE

Two years later: Annual Film Award ceremony and dinner—the West End of London.

'AND the winner is…'

'This is your call, baby…are you ready for it?' Leaning confidently towards his wife across the glittering banquet table, where the candlelight lent even more of an incandescent glow to her alluring features than she possessed already, Nash felt his stomach clenched hard in a mixture of pride and emotion.

Freya had travelled so far to get to the unmatched position she held now in the eyes of the public and her profession, and nobody knew that better than he. Now she was a much admired and beloved actress whose star quality had blazed through when she'd played the incredible role of Nikita Pushkova, reminding the sometimes fickle viewing public just what this stunning woman was capable of. As soon as the nominations for the award of Best Actress in a Leading Role had come up,

Nash had not been the slightest bit surprised when Freya's name had featured head and shoulders above the rest.

Now, her dark, exotic eyes held his, as if she was terrified to look anywhere else in the crowded room, and she moved her lips in an urgent whisper for his ears alone. 'Please don't be so confident…I don't want you to be disappointed.'

But she needn't have been so cautious. People were already on their feet, cheering as her name was announced as the winner, and Nash immediately went to his wife's side and clasped her hard against him, in the shimmering red silk gown she wore, with its daring décolletage, kissing her full on the mouth in front of everyone before drawing back to bestow a tender, loving gaze.

'You did it, my angel! You *did* it! This is your moment, and I'm so damned proud of you!'

'I couldn't have done it without you.'

Her dark eyes were already swimming with tears, and she hadn't even made the podium yet! With her heart racing, and a sense of unreality the depth of which she'd never experienced before, Freya turned to walk the long red carpet towards the stage.

Accepting the coveted statuette from a handsome well-known actor, who'd flown in specially from the States to present the award to her, Freya was trembling so hard she almost feared she would drop the precious prize. Looking out at the sea of admiring faces, her gaze avidly searched the many smiling countenances for her husband's. When she found it, she let out a long, contented sigh.

'I feel like I've come back from the dead!' she quipped breathlessly, and the audience—already enchanted—cheered and applauded wildly. 'I won't say that playing Nikita has been the role of a lifetime, because I'm still only young, and naturally I hope to have a long and successful career doing what I love, but just the same it came along at exactly the right time— a bit like my husband, as a matter of fact!' She grinned happily, meaning every word with all her heart, and people cheered again. 'Nikita Pushkova was a truly amazing and inspirational woman, and I feel very privileged to have been allowed to play her in the film. I have so many people to thank, as I think you can guess, but before I do—' she once again searched for the arresting figure of her husband, resplendent in his midnight-black tuxedo '—there's one person I owe more gratitude to than I can ever adequately convey…my husband Nash, who did indeed help to bring me back from the dead and convinced me to resume my career when I seriously doubted if I would ever act again. He is the most incredibly good man, and two months ago—to add to our joy—I gave birth to our beloved daughter, Betsy.'

Her throat tightening at yet another display of delighted applause, Freya shook her head in disbelief at her own good fortune. 'I'm an incredibly lucky woman and I don't ever forget it. Nash…you and Betsy mean the whole world to me!'

Standing at the side of the glittering table with its

twinkling candelabrum, his handsome face visibly moved, Nash touched the tips of his fingers to his mouth and blew out a kiss towards the stunning brunette on the stage. He was the lucky one… He told her that every single night they spent together, and he would continue to tell her each and every night to come…

MISTRESS AGAINST
HER WILL

BY
LEE WILKINSON

Lee Wilkinson lives with her husband in a three-hundred-year-old stone cottage in a Derbyshire village, which most winters gets cut off by snow. They both enjoy travelling, and recently, joining forces with their daughter and son-in-law, spent a year going round the world 'on a shoestring' while their son looked after Kelly, their much loved German shepherd dog. Her hobbies are reading and gardening, and holding impromptu barbecues for her long-suffering family and friends.

CHAPTER ONE

IT WAS early, barely seven twenty-five, and London's morning traffic was still flowing fairly freely as Paul's pale blue Jaguar purred towards the city centre.

Normally, Gail knew, he would have been enjoying a leisurely breakfast before embarking on the day's business meetings. Judging by the look on his fair, handsome face, having his routine disrupted did nothing to improve his temper.

Sitting in the front passenger seat beside him, she sighed. She had told him more than once that she could make her own way to Jenson Lorenson's prestigious London offices. But, in spite of earliness of the hour and the personal inconvenience, he had insisted on picking her up and driving her there himself.

He had arrived early and, stressed and harassed when she'd changed handbags at the last minute, she had omitted to pick up her notecase. All she had with her was her purse, which contained her credit card and some small change.

When she mentioned the oversight to Paul, he said irritably, 'I don't see what you're worrying about. You won't need it.'

Perhaps he was right. With a bit of luck there would be just about enough to get a bus back home.

'Now don't look flustered, whatever you do,' he instructed

her as they stopped for a red light. 'Lorenson expects his personal staff to be cool and efficient. You've let this thing get to you and, now the crunch has come, you'll need to keep your composure.'

After a sleepless night, she felt washed out and on edge and in no mood to be preached to. 'I just wish there was some other way to achieve what you want,' she blurted out desperately. 'I hate all this lying and scheming.'

'There's no need to tell a lot of lies; in fact it's much safer to stick to the truth whenever possible. Your working background is solid and reliable, and you've got all the qualifications and experience Lorenson's looking for.

'Added to that, you've been recommended by a woman he trusts, so there's no reason for him to suspect anything. All you have to do is forget that we two have ever met and you can't go wrong.'

Glancing at her, he added, 'By the way, you did remember to take off your ring?'

'Yes.' The three stone diamond engagement ring that Paul had bought her was on a thin gold chain around her neck.

'Don't forget to emphasize that you have no ties and there's no current boyfriend. Lorenson has a massive office complex in Manhattan and he likes his Personal Assistant to be free and unencumbered, to be able to travel to his New York offices with him at the drop of a hat.'

'Oh, but I—'

'He's not an easy man to work for like Randall was. You'll have to be prepared for someone cold and arrogant and uncaring. Someone who expects his staff to jump when he says jump.'

'How do you know all this?'

'My sister, Julie, made a point of getting to know the woman who used to be Lorenson's PA. Apparently she'd been with him for over five years, and would still be working for him now if she wasn't planning to get married…'

As the lights changed to green, he went on, 'She told Julie that though he expects a twenty-four hour commitment, she rates him as a good boss…'

'When you say a twenty-four hour commitment,' Gail began uneasily, 'you don't think he'll…?'

'No, there'll be no funny business. Lorenson isn't known for mixing work and pleasure. Quite the opposite, in fact.'

'Then he's married?'

'No, and never has been. His ex-PA, who admitted she'd once been madly in love with him, told Julie she's convinced that there's no real place in his life for a woman.

'However, he's a good-looking devil,' Paul admitted grudgingly, 'and it appears that when he wants a woman to warm his bed there are always plenty only too willing to jump in with him. So you've nothing to fear on that score.

'Once you've got the job, all you have to do is be your normal efficient self and everything should be plain sailing.'

Gail wasn't convinced by his blasé attitude. 'But even if I *do* get it I'll be new, an unknown quantity. He may not trust me with—'

'The word is,' Paul broke in, his blue eyes impatient, 'that once he's chosen his personal staff he trusts them. He won't hire someone he doesn't trust. So you shouldn't have any trouble on that score…'

Somehow, knowing that only made her feel worse.

Oblivious to her mental discomfort, Paul was going on, 'I've had a report from someone I'd already planted—the plans for the Rainmaker project should be finalized in the next few weeks, which means we're just in the nick of time.

'As soon as you've managed to see those plans and get the latest gen, just let me know.'

He made the whole thing sound so casual, so innocuous, Gail thought helplessly, but to her it was spying, pure and simple, and she hated the thought of being involved.

But after days of unrelenting pressure Paul had made it a test of her love....

'There'll never be another opportunity like this. With his present PA leaving just as the Rainmaker project is going through, and you being out of a job, this is exactly the chance I've been waiting for.

'Lorenson has a reputation for being daring, for sticking his neck out when it comes to these really big deals. That's how he comes to be a billionaire at just turned thirty. If he intends to play it the same way this time *and I know about it in advance* I can be waiting with a hatchet.

'This is important to me.' He took her hand and squeezed it by way of emphasis. 'I have to know what's in those plans. I need to be at least one jump ahead.' Taking her hand to his lips and pressing a kiss to her palm he continued, 'That way, if I can't bring him down altogether, and he may be too powerful for that,' Paul admitted regretfully, 'at the very least, I can bring him to his knees.

'All I need is some reliable inside information, and when you're his PA it'll be a doddle...'

When Paul had first mentioned Jenson Lorenson, Gail had felt her heart stop, then start to race again uncomfortably fast.

'Jenson Lorenson?' she echoed warily.

'Don't tell me you've never heard the name. It's a big Anglo-American concern. It was started in the States by Richard Jenson just as the boom in electronics really got under way.

'When Jenson retired five years ago, he made the company over to Zane Lorenson, his nephew, who'd been his right-hand man for a number of years...'

So it was him.

Unbidden, a mental picture of Zane Lorenson filled her mind. Tall, black-haired, broad-shouldered and narrow-hipped... A lean, tanned face with strong features... A mouth like a fallen angel, and long, heavy-lidded dark green eyes. Handsome eyes. Eyes that seemed able to look into her very soul.

A shiver ran through her.

Paul went on, oblivious to her reaction. 'Lorenson, who had an American mother and an English father, is a clever swine and brilliant when it comes to business. He added the Anglo part, moved into Information Technology and Research and Development and trebled the company's profits inside two years...'

'But I don't see what—'

Paul cut in, speaking over her. 'He's an old adversary. That swine was responsible for my first company going down, and I've hated his guts ever since. Now, with your help, I've a chance to derail the Rainmaker project and get some of my own back.'

Gail turned to him, wide-eyed. 'With *my* help? Oh, but I—'

'Just listen. It should work like a dream...'

While he outlined the scheme her agitation grew. As soon as she could get a word in edgeways she said in a rush, 'No, Paul. I don't want anything to do with it.'

Once again, he dismissed her protest. 'It won't be difficult. Think about it. I'm sure you'll change your mind.'

'I won't change my mind.'

With a smile that would normally have melted her heart, he coaxed, 'Come on, sweetie, do it for me.'

Even if it hadn't involved Zane Lorenson she wouldn't have wanted to do it. But as it *did,* there was no way...

'I'd never be able to bring it off.'

Well aware that she was besotted with him, and wondering at her unusual reluctance to toe the line he had marked out for her, Paul demanded, 'Surely you could at least try?'

Her lovely mouth set in a determined line, she shook her head. 'I don't want to get involved.'

Paul turned to meet her gaze and said somewhat sharply 'You once said you'd do anything for me.'

'I said anything I *could* do. But this is something I *can't* do,' Gail pleaded.

'Why can't you?'

She shook her head, helplessly. 'I just *can't.*'

'There must be a reason,' he pressed.

Cornered, she blurted out, 'I once knew him.'

'How do you mean, you once knew him?'

'I met him when I was living in the States. He was…friends with Rona.'

'Your stepsister?'

Gail nodded. 'Yes.'

'I thought you'd been back in England for quite a few years?'

'I have—'

Paul brushed off her concerns. 'So it must have been some time ago?'

'Seven years.' She didn't add that for seven long years Zane Lorenson's image had haunted her. 'I was just seventeen.'

'Did you know him well?'

'No…' In spite of what had happened, she hadn't really *known* him at all.

Awkwardly, she added, 'But we met two or three times and I—'

His face impatient, Paul butted in, 'When your mother remarried after your own father's death, did your new stepfather adopt you?'

'No.'

'In that case you and your stepsister must have different surnames.'

'Yes, but—'

'Then what are you worrying about? Your name won't ring a bell, and if you only met each other two or three times he's hardly likely to remember you after seven years.'

'But suppose he did?'

'If by any faint chance he did, would it matter?'

'Yes, it would... You see I—'

'My dear girl,' Paul interrupted peevishly, 'do you seriously believe there's a cat in hell's chance of him recognising you after all this time...?'

The honest answer was no. She had been less than nothing to the young Zane Lorenson. Until Rona had turned that cruel spotlight on her, he hadn't even been aware of her existence.

'If you really think there might be a problem, for goodness' sake find some way of altering your appearance; get some glasses or something.

'But I'm quite certain you're worrying over nothing. In the last seven years you must have altered a great deal.'

She had.

In those days she had been just a gawky adolescent, a late developer, painfully shy and gauche, and still with the remains of a northern accent.

Then, goaded by Rona, and hopelessly in love with a man she had only seen from afar, she had set about changing her image.

Only to be laughed at and ridiculed by her stepsister who, at twenty-three, had been beautiful and glamorous and worldly.

But that hadn't been the worst...

She pushed the memory—still unbearably shameful and humiliating even after all these years—away and tried to concentrate on what she had become.

To all intents and purposes she was now a cool, self-possessed young woman with dark glossy hair, a clear skin, a good figure, a polished manner and no trace of an accent.

No, in all truth, Zane Lorenson was hardly likely to recognize her.

But remembering how he had looked at her the last time they'd met—his set lips, the cold fury in those green eyes—she still didn't want to take the risk.

'I don't want to have to see him again. I'm afraid…' About to say, *I'm afraid of him,* unwilling to have Paul laugh at her, she changed it to, 'I'm afraid I don't like him. I'd simply *hate* to have to work for him.'

Paul's fair face darkened. 'I think in the circumstances that's a very selfish attitude. After all, it wouldn't be for long. As soon as you've got the information I want, you can make some excuse and leave.'

Her grey eyes beseeching, she begged, 'Please, Paul, don't ask me to do this.'

Such a heartfelt plea ought to have melted stone. But his expression hard, unrelenting, he said, 'It's not as if it's *that* much to ask, and you'd do it for my sake if you really loved me.'

As, hating that look of censure, the feeling that she was letting him down, she wavered, he pressed, 'Of course if you *don't* there's not much point in our getting engaged.'

'I *do* love you.'

'Then prove it.'

Finally giving in to the pressure, she agreed unhappily. 'Very well, I'll try.'

Triumphantly, he drawled smugly, 'That's my girl. I always knew you wouldn't let me down.

'Now just one thing, no one else must know, so don't say anything to that flatmate of yours. Simply tell her you've got another job.'

She looked across at him, still worried about the plan. 'I might not get it.'

'Of course you will. It's practically a cert.'

As a reward for toeing the line, he had taken her out and bought her an engagement ring.

With his red-gold hair and Greek god looks, his bright blue eyes and long curly lashes, the boyish smile that added to his charm, most women he came into contact with were bowled over.

Gail had been no exception.

He had called one morning to see David Randall, her ex-boss, and after years of thinking she would never fall in love again, she had done just that.

A small, privately owned company, Randalls had been highly successful, coming up with some brilliant ideas that seemed set to revolutionize their particular branch of electronics.

They had been on the point of putting the new ideas into practice when David Randall had had a heart attack which had made him decide to sell out and retire at the early age of fifty-five.

The Manton Group, which Paul owned, had made an offer for the company, but it had been a derisory offer in David Randall's opinion.

As the negotiations dragged on, Paul had become a frequent visitor, often stopping by Gail's desk to have a chat. When one day he asked her to have dinner with him, she had been both flattered and flustered.

From then on he had taken her out a good deal and, though he had been both romantic and ardent, unlike her previous boyfriend, he had made no attempt to take her back to his place or get her into bed.

This restraint, as well as his good looks and his undeniable charm, had set him apart and deepened her feelings for him.

Finally the business deal had gone through and David Randall had left the company he had built up single-handed, satisfied that he had negotiated a fair deal for his employees.

But, as soon as Randalls was his, Paul had paid off staff and workers alike and closed the company down.

When, badly shaken, her liking and respect for Paul diminished, Gail had ventured to protest, he had answered that all the employees had received a generous cash settlement and most of them had been quite content.

'But it isn't what David intended,' she insisted. 'He spent a lifetime building up that company. He regarded his workers almost as family, and he wanted them all to keep their jobs—'

'My dear girl, you ought to know by now that there's no sentiment in business. Randalls was opposition we could well do without. A thorn in our side that had to be removed,' he answered dismissively.

'That wasn't what you told David Randall,' she said accusingly. 'You gave him to understand that nothing much would change.'

Paul shrugged. 'It was business, darling. He may have chosen to believe otherwise, but this was the best decision all round, I promise.'

Seeing she was still far from happy, and needing to keep her on his side for what he had in mind, he pulled her close and kissed her. 'Now let's forget all about work. If you really want another job, I'll give you one. But I thought you might prefer to be Mrs Paul Manton...'

Paul wanted to marry her. Still besotted by him, in spite of all that had happened, she floated up to cloud nine.

'But before we start planning the wedding, there's something I want you to do for me...'

She had come down to earth again with a bump when he'd explained what it was he wanted her to do and, even with his engagement ring on her finger, her joy had been marred by the thought of what was in store.

'This job you want me to apply for—' she broached the subject with reluctance '—how shall I go about it?'

'Don't worry about that. I know Mrs Rogers, the woman who runs the employment agency that Lorenson uses. I'll ask her to see you and recommend you for the position.'

Gail had found herself hoping that for once in his life Paul wouldn't succeed in pulling strings and manipulating people.

But, with the kind of looks and charm that made slaves of the female sex, he had, and she had been asked to call and see Mrs Rogers.

The following day the agency had rung to say that an interview had been arranged.

Though pleased that everything had so far gone according to plan, Paul had complained bitterly about the earliness of the hour.

'Lorenson wants you to be at his office at eight o'clock! Why the hell can't he work nine to five like most people?

'Well, you'll just have to take care not to be late. The swine is a stickler for punctuality and you'll need to look cool.'

Then, with a thoughtful glance at her face, 'Perhaps I'd better pick you up.'

'There's no need to do that. I can make my own way there. I'll get a taxi if necessary.'

After a moment or two's consideration, he said decidedly, 'No, it'll be best if I come round and collect you.'

She had strongly suspected that it was in case she chickened out at the last minute.

Whatever his reason, he had picked her up on the dot of seven fifteen, so now here she was, on her way to be interviewed for the position of PA to a man she had hoped never to have to see again.

Talk about being caught between the devil and the deep

blue sea, she thought miserably. If she didn't get it, Paul would be furious with her. If she *did,* she would be in an invidious position…

'We're almost there.' His voice broke into her unhappy thoughts. 'Lorenson's offices, as well as his own private apartment, are in the Clairmont Building on Lower Arlington Street. But, just to make certain no one spots you getting out of my car, I'll drop you at the corner.'

When they reached their destination, he drew in to the kerb and issued his last instructions. 'Now don't forget, try not to look flustered whatever you do, or all this planning and preparation will be wasted.

'And don't breathe a word about me. Lorenson would soon be on his guard if he picked up any suggestion that we know each other.' His gaze held a warning and Gail looked away as he continued, 'When the interview's over and you're well away from Lorenson's offices, you can give me a quick call and let me know for sure if you've got the job.'

Gail hesitated, still uncertain and unsure. 'But suppose one of his staff is doing the interviewing and is just compiling a short-list?'

'According to Mrs Rogers, Lorenson doesn't work that way. The people he wants on his own staff he always interviews personally, and usually he makes an on-the-spot decision.'

Gail's heart sank. She had held on to the faint hope that it might be one of his minions she would have to see, and that said minion would prefer some other candidate, thus giving her a let-out. But it seemed it wasn't to be.

Urgently in need of reassurance, she asked, 'When shall I see you? Lynne will be out tonight if you want to come round for a meal.'

'Once Lorenson knows where you live, it might not be safe.' Trying to keep the tell-tale tremor out of her voice, she suggested, 'Well, couldn't we meet in the park, or at a restaurant, or something?'

But, instead of softening, those eyes, blue as summer skies, looked at her dismissively. 'It's too big a risk. We can't afford to jeopardise our chances by possibly being seen together.

'After you've let me know the score it would be better if we don't have any contact until you've something to report.'

'Oh,' she said blankly.

'When you have, you'd better give me a ring at the office and we'll meet up somewhere.'

He leaned over and gave her a quick peck on the cheek. 'Now don't forget how much this means to me. Good luck.'

Feeling slightly sick, her stomach full of butterflies, Gail unfastened her seat belt, opened the door and got out.

Already the air was warm and the summer sunshine bright, glancing off the bodywork of passing cars and gleaming on pavements still damp from the early morning shower.

As the Jaguar drew away, she lifted her hand but, a slight frown on his good-looking face, Paul was staring straight ahead.

Opening her bag, she took out the pair of cheap low-strength reading glasses she'd bought in the local chemist and put them on.

Then bracing herself, she walked the short distance to the Clairmont Building, with its handsome Georgian façade, and through the imposing main entrance.

The clock above the reception desk showed it was ten minutes to eight, so she was in good time.

As, her heart beating fast and her legs feeling oddly shaky, she started to cross the marble-floored lobby, she caught sight of herself reflected in one of the long gilt-framed mirrors.

Wearing a smart charcoal-grey suit and an off-white blouse, her small heart-shaped face outwardly calm, her dark hair in a smooth coil, she looked every inch the cool, efficient business-woman.

No one would have guessed at her inner turmoil as she approached the desk and gave her name to the pretty blonde receptionist.

'You'll find the office complex on the second floor, Miss North. If you would like to go straight up, Mrs Bancroft, Mr Lorenson's secretary, will be waiting for you.'

When Gail stepped out of the lift on the second floor she was greeted by an attractive middle-aged woman with bobbed iron-grey hair.

'I'm Claire Bancroft. If you'd like to follow me, Miss North…'

As Mrs Bancroft led the way along the carpeted corridor to another lift, she remarked, 'Mr Lorenson is in his apartment this morning. He likes to keep the interviews he conducts informal.'

Entering a four digit code into a small panel, she added, 'This is his private lift.'

The lift took them up to the top floor, where they emerged into a quietly luxurious hallway. Opening the nearest door, Mrs Bancroft said, 'Please come in, Miss North…'

Gail found herself ushered into a large sunny room with an off-white and mint-green decor and an ornate plaster ceiling. To the left, a door into a neighbouring room stood slightly ajar.

Between two sets of windows was a desk with an impressive array of the latest electronic equipment and a black leather chair.

Apart from the businesslike desk, the room was furnished as a lounge.

'Perhaps you'd like to take a seat?' Mrs Bancroft suggested with a friendly smile. 'Mr Lorenson knows you're here. He'll be with you in a minute or so.'

When the other woman had gone, too nervous to sit and

cravenly grateful for even this short breathing space, Gail looked around curiously.

Along with some lovely antique furniture, there were a couple of comfortable-looking couches, several soft off-white leather armchairs and a large round coffee table.

A thick-pile smoke-grey carpet covered the floor and on either side of a beautiful Adam fireplace, which was filled with fresh flowers, there were recessed bookcases, their shelves overflowing.

Considering how very strongly she had felt about Zane Lorenson, aside from his appearance, she had known hardly anything about the man himself, what he was really like, what his tastes were.

This appeared to be the room of a man with eclectic tastes, a man who preferred his surroundings to be both simple and elegant.

On the walls several stark and dramatic snow scenes by Jonathan Cass rubbed shoulders with the vibrant colour and slumberous warmth of Tuscan landscapes by Marco Abruzzi.

Frowning a little, she studied them. With such diverse techniques and subject matter, they shouldn't have been hung together. But somehow the contrast worked, highlighting them both.

It seemed that Zane Lorenson was a man who knew precisely what he wanted and wasn't afraid to try the less obvious.

Her mother had always said that one could get a good idea of a person's character from what kind of books they read so, taking a deep breath, Gail moved closer to the bookcases and looked at their contents.

Classics and poetry, travel and adventure, mysteries, biographies, autobiographies, the best popular paperback fiction and Booker Prize winners jostled for space.

She had picked up a copy of a recent Booker Prize winner when, glancing up, she met a pair of brilliant dark eyes.

He was leaning negligently against the door jamb, his tough, good-looking face shrewd, calculating, an arrogant tilt to his dark head.

Wearing a smart light-weight suit, a crisp shirt and tie and handmade shoes, he looked every inch the billionaire businessman. He also looked fit and virile and dangerous.

Though she had braced herself to see him again, the shock hit her like a blow over the heart and in that instant her heartbeat and her breathing, the very blood flowing through her veins, seemed to stop.

She had remembered how he looked—of course she had, his face had haunted her for years—and, apart from an added maturity, he looked much the same now as he had then.

But in the intervening years she had almost forgotten just what a powerful impact his physical presence had on her.

While she stood rooted to the spot, endeavouring to pull herself together, he continued to stand and study her in unnerving silence.

It seemed an age, but could only have been seconds, before she released the breath she was holding and her heart began to beat again in slow, heavy thuds.

How long had he been standing there quietly watching her while she'd nosed amongst his personal belongings?

She felt herself shrivel inwardly. Her one consolation was that the cool green gaze fixed on her face held no sign of recognition. But she had known it wouldn't.

As soon as she had managed to regain some semblance of composure, she thrust the book she was holding back on to the shelf and said unevenly, 'I'm sorry; I was just...'

'Taking a look at what I read? What conclusion did you come to?'

His voice was low-pitched and attractive. It was a voice she had never forgotten. A voice she would have known amongst a million. A voice that could have called her back from the grave.

Shaken afresh, she said the first thing that came into her head. 'That you have interesting tastes.'

'Really? Do you?' he drawled nonchalantly.

'Yes, I believe so.'

'What about the pictures?' He nodded towards the impressive artwork.

So he had watched her studying those as well. 'I like them.'

His gaze narrowed. 'Do you know who painted them?'

'Yes.'

'How do you know?'

She raised her chin, trying to give an air of authority and calm. 'Though these are clearly originals, and I can only afford prints, Jonathan Cass and Marco Abruzzi are two of my favourite artists.'

He raised a dark, level brow. 'My, my, we *do* seem to have a lot in common. Wouldn't you say so?'

Clenching her teeth at the blatant mockery, she said nothing.

'So I take it you have the same pictures hanging in your living room?'

Aware that he thought she was making the whole thing up to curry favour, she answered briefly, 'No.'

'Ah, now you disappoint me. Do you actually have any by either of those artists?'

'I have two of Cass's and—'

'Which two?'

'*Snowfall* and *Winter Journey.*'

'Any of Abruzzi's?'

'Three,' she replied quickly.

'And they are?'

'*Olive Groves, Sunset* and *Fields of Sunflowers,*' she said, listing her three favorites.

'Do they all hang in the same room?'

'No…I would never have had the nerve to hang them together.'

'What do you think of the result?'

She wanted to say she hated it but, unable to frame the lie she admitted, 'It shouldn't work, but somehow it does.'

'I'm pleased you think so,' he told her sardonically. 'Well now we've established that when it comes to books and paintings we're practically soulmates, suppose you sit down and we'll see how you measure up on the business side.'

But she had had enough. If Zane Lorenson had realized who she was, he couldn't have been more unkind and derisive.

'Thank you,' she said stiffly, 'but I've decided I don't want the position after all, so there's no point in staying for the interview.'

Appearing totally unruffled, he asked, 'Why have you changed your mind?'

She had nothing to lose by speaking the truth. Lifting her chin and bravely meeting those green eyes, she told him, 'I don't like the way you're making fun of me. It's not business like and—'

'You can't bear to be teased?'

'I can't see the necessity for it.'

'As a matter of fact, how a person reacts to being teased tells me quite a lot about his or her character. Now sit down.'

Though he spoke quietly, his voice cracked like a whip and against all her inclinations, she found herself obeying a will stronger than her own.

CHAPTER TWO

As Gail sank into the nearest armchair, her heart hammering against her ribs so loudly she felt sure it must be audible, he commented, 'That's better.'

Then, with exaggerated politeness, 'How do you like your coffee, Miss North?'

Her empty stomach was churning and, about to say she didn't want any coffee, she thought better of it and answered, 'A little cream, no sugar, thank you.'

'Exactly how I like mine,' he observed. Adding provokingly, 'Now, isn't that strange?'

Refusing to rise to the bait, she put her bag on the floor and sat in silence while he filled two cups with the dark fragrant liquid and added a dash of cream to each of them.

Passing her a cup, he sat down opposite and looked at her with a gleam in his eye that showed he enjoyed being master of the situation.

Watching her bite her lip, he queried, 'Do I take it you're vexed because of a little gentle teasing?'

Without answering, she looked at him stonily.

'OK.' He sat back with a hint of a smile on his lips. 'Let's keep this strictly business—where are you from?'

Still riled, she answered quickly. 'I was born in the north-east—'

The moment the words were out, she could have bitten her tongue. She shouldn't have told him that. Rona had always teased her unmercifully about her Geordie accent and it was the one thing that he might possibly remember.

She risked a quick glance at him and the little flare of satisfaction in those handsome eyes made her heart sink.

Had he guessed her identity?

No, surely not. It must be because he had managed to provoke her into speech.

His expression bland now, he asked, 'Whereabouts in the north-east?'

'Tyneside,' she answered reluctantly, certain he was still mocking her.

When he nodded, clearly absorbing the information, Gail looked up at him and cautiously studied his handsome profile. She had forgotten just how devastatingly attractive his white smile was, and her heart lurched crazily.

Not that she was still attracted to him, she told herself hastily. It was just remembering the past that had affected her so strongly.

While she tried to steady herself, she made a pretence of sipping her coffee.

She was hoping that he had let the subject drop when he asked casually, 'How long did you live in the north?'

'We left when I was twelve.'

'Why?'

She paused, worried about how much information to reveal but replied honestly. 'My father died when I was ten, and two years later my mother remarried.'

Everything she had told him so far was the exact truth, but if he wanted to delve any further into her family background, rather than admit that her stepfather had been American and they had moved to the States, she would have to resort to lies.

However, to her relief, he changed tack by saying, 'So fill

me in on your personal details—full name, age, where you live, previous work experience…'

'It's all in my CV.'

He leaned back and crossed his ankles, perfectly at ease. 'I dare say it is, Miss North. But I'd prefer to hear it from your own lips…'

It was so in keeping with his attitude that she should have expected it.

'You can start by telling me your Christian name.'

'Gail.'

'Short for Abigail?'

'Yes.' She had been praying that he would take the name at face value and not make the connection.

Her parents had always called her Abbey, but after pointing out that in books Abigail was usually a servant's name, her step-sister Rona had used her full name, apparently in an unkind attempt to belittle her.

It was one of the reasons that, when she and her mother had returned to England, she had started to call herself Gail.

'A nice old-fashioned name,' Zane Lorenson commented after a moment. 'So how do you come to be called Abigail?'

'It was my maternal grandmother's name.'

'Would you believe me if I told you *my* maternal grandmother was named Abigail?'

'No, I wouldn't,' she said shortly.

He threw back his head and laughed. 'Well, at least you're honest. But, in this case, mistaken. It happens to be the truth.'

Her mouth went dry as he added, his tone reflective, 'It's quite an unusual name these days. You don't meet many Abigails.' His gaze held hers as if suggesting there was more meaning to his words.

So he had known who she was all along, and that was why he'd treated her the way he had.

If it had been at all possible she would have made a run for it, but her old fear of him was back in force and she was frozen into immobility, unable to either move or speak.

Quite a few seconds had passed before she appreciated that his lean, tanned face showed no sign of the anger or hostility she would have expected had he known who she was. She was being ridiculous, and she knew it. She had to keep calm.

His expression held a kind of studied patience as he waited for an answer to a question she hadn't even heard.

'I—I'm sorry,' she stammered.

'I asked how old you were.'

'Twenty…' she paused '…six.' It was her first white lie and the words almost stuck in her throat as she pretended to be older than she was. She had to make sure he hadn't made the connection.

'Which school did you go to?'

'Langton Chase.' She had gone to the well-known all girls school for just a year after she and her mother had returned to England.

He placed it immediately. 'So you lived in Sussex?'

'Yes.'

'With your parents?'

Though after the separation there had only been her mother she answered, 'Yes.'

'Do your parents still live there?'

She shook her head. 'They're both dead now.'

'Were you very close?'

'I was to my mother.'

'Any brothers or sisters?'

Family relationships were a minefield, and she answered briefly, 'No.'

He ran long, lean fingers over his smooth jaw before moving on to ask, 'How old were you when you left school?'

With a sigh of relief at the change of subject, she told him, 'Eighteen.'

'Then what?'

'I spent a year at St Helen's Business College before getting a job at Randalls.'

'And there you were…' he picked up her CV '…PA to David Randall.'

She nodded, then, all at once foreseeing a problem that Paul hadn't taken into account, she added hastily, 'After Mr Randall had a heart attack and retired, the company was closed down.'

Zane Lorenson's clear, long-lashed eyes pinned her. 'The financial news indicated that it had been bought by The Manton Group.'

Her heart sank but somehow she managed steadily, 'Yes, it was. They paid off the workers and closed it down as soon as it was legally theirs.'

'What do you think of Paul Manton?'

'W-what?' she stammered.

'I asked what you thought of Paul Manton. Presumably he did the negotiating and wielded the axe. Or was it someone else?'

'A Mr Desmond,' she said, seizing on the suggestion.

Mark Desmond, Paul's second in command, a bluff, hearty man she had disliked on sight, had come in with Paul a couple of times.

'I'm surprised. Manton usually enjoys doing his own dirty work… Tell me, what did you think of the decision to close Randalls down?'

'I thought it was totally wrong.' For perhaps the first time her tone held real conviction. 'It wasn't what Mr Randall had wanted or expected.'

He raised a brow, questioning her frankness. 'He couldn't have known what kind of men he was dealing with, otherwise he *would* have expected it.'

Then, with another swift change of subject, 'Where do you live?'

'In Kensington.'

'Which part of Kensington?' he pressed.

'Just off the West Brackensfield Road,' she answered reluctantly.

She had hoped he would leave it at that, but he asked, 'Whereabouts exactly?'

'Delafield House, Rolchester Square. I share a flat,' she went on, rambling a bit because she was nervous.

'Does that mean you have a live-in lover?'

She shook her head. 'No. It means I share with another girl.'

'Have you any ties or commitments at home?'

She shook her head.

'No steady boyfriend?'

She stuck as close to the truth as she could. 'I'm not seeing anyone just at the moment.'

Studying her heart-shaped face, with its small straight nose, beautiful almond eyes and dark winged brows, its flawless skin and pure bone-structure, he commented, 'That surprises me.' Then, drily, 'Or have you heard that I prefer my PA to be a free agent?'

Determined to avoid direct lies wherever possible, she said, 'I split up with Jason, my previous boyfriend, some six months ago.'

'And there's been no one since then?'

Forced into a direct lie, she surreptitiously crossed her fingers and said, 'No.'

'So you're still broken-hearted?' her tormentor asked, the old hateful mockery back.

'Are such personal questions really necessary?' she demanded, losing her cool.

'Oh, absolutely,' he assured her, his voice flippant. Then,

smiling a little at her indignation, 'You see I don't want to take on a lovelorn PA whose mind isn't on her work.'

'I am *not* lovelorn,' she informed him raggedly.

'Does that mean you've got over it? Or you didn't love him in the first place?'

The unholy gleam in his eyes telling her that this was just another attempt to bait her, she bit back the angry words, took a deep breath and repeated more calmly, 'I am *not* lovelorn.'

With an ironic smile, he saluted that show of anger management before asking, 'Do you have any objections to travelling?'

On firmer ground now, she replied, 'None at all.'

'Done much?'

'Not as much as I would have liked. Europe mainly…' After her mother's untimely death she had taken holidays with Joanne, one of the secretaries from Randalls.

'Ever been to the States?'

She should have seen that coming. Once again she crossed her fingers and lied. 'No.'

His cool green eyes studied her face and lingered there, and she had the strangest feeling that he knew perfectly well that she hadn't spoken the truth.

Unable to meet that probing gaze, she was forced to look away.

There was a long thoughtful pause, then he said, 'Tell me, do you usually wear glasses?'

Ambushed by the unexpected question, she hesitated fractionally before saying as steadily as possible, 'Why, yes.'

'Strange. When I asked Mrs Rogers to describe you, she failed to mention them.'

Leaning over, he lifted the glasses from Gail's nose and squinted through them, before asking, 'Why do you wear them?'

'Why?'

'Yes, why? As far as I can see, these are merely low-strength reading glasses.'

Feeling her colour rise, she said nothing.

He handed them back to her. 'So you don't wear glasses as a rule. You put them on especially for this interview.'

Both were statements rather than questions, but her failure to dispute either was answer enough.

'Why did you feel that was necessary?'

Cursing the impulse that had made her put them on, she stammered, 'Well I—I thought they would make me look more…efficient, more competent…'

His green eyes glinted. 'That reason hardly inspires confidence. It strongly suggests that you aren't at all sure of yourself or your capabilities.'

'I'm quite sure I'm capable of doing the job.'

'Possibly you are, but lying to me is hardly the way to get it.'

So she had failed.

All she could feel for a moment or two was a sense of relief that she wouldn't have to go through with something she had dreaded.

Hard on the heels of that relief came a leaden feeling of failure as she realized just how angry and disappointed Paul would be.

Then both those feelings were swamped by the urgent necessity to leave, to get away from Zane Lorenson's clear-eyed scrutiny, his condemnation.

Gathering up her bag, she thrust the glasses clumsily into it and jumped to her feet, babbling, 'I'm sorry to have wasted your time…'

He rose too and took a step towards her. At five feet six inches she was fairly tall for a woman, but at well over six feet he seemed to tower over her. 'Don't rush off.'

Ignoring the quietly spoken order, she was about to head for the door when his lean fingers closed lightly round her wrist and kept her where she was. 'I said don't rush off.'

He had said that same thing to her once before and she shuddered as, his touch burning into her like a brand, she made an effort to pull free.

It was to no avail and, panic-stricken, recalling that past encounter and desperate to escape, she tried harder. 'Please let me go.'

Ignoring her plea, he put his free hand on her shoulder and pressed her back into the chair. Then, releasing her wrist, he stood over her.

Her voice sounding high and frightened even to her own ears, she objected, 'You've no right to keep me here against my will.'

Clicking his tongue, he told her severely, 'Now you're being melodramatic.'

His words were like a dash of cold water and, realizing the justice of his remark, she took a deep steadying breath and apologized shamefacedly. 'I'm sorry. I really don't know what's got into me.'

'I dare say the prospect of being interviewed made you nervous,' he suggested with smooth mockery. Now, if you're still interested in the job, there are one or two things you ought to know…

'I expect my PA to be available for twenty-four hours a day if I think it's necessary. That's why I asked if you have any ties at home.

'More importantly, I always give my PA my complete trust and in return I expect discretion and one hundred per cent loyalty…'

His words made Gail feel hollow inside.

'Because of the occasional long hours, I'm flexible with

regard to the length and the number of holidays my PA takes, and the salary is generous…'

He quoted a figure that made Gail blink and she found herself thinking, no wonder his previous PA had been reluctant to leave.

'Oh, just one more thing. When we're away from the office I like a friendly, informal working atmosphere with the use of first names.

'Now, if you want it, the job is yours.'

She didn't. But the thought of Paul's anger prevented her from saying so. If there was still a chance, he would want her to grab it with both hands.

And, after the way Zane Lorenson had treated her, did she really care if he came a cropper? Wouldn't she be justified in cheering if he *could* be brought to his knees?

Yes, she would.

But the truth was that she didn't want to play any part in it. Didn't want to have to work closely with a man who had turned her whole life upside down once before, and who, she was forced to admit, might well have the power to do so again.

She had never met anyone else who had such an overwhelming effect on her. Just being with him was traumatic, turning the cool, competent woman she had become into a mass of nerves and making her feel like a gauche, insecure seventeen-year-old again.

If she didn't take the job, she knew Paul might never forgive her. But it was more than that—when it came to Zane Lorenson, Gail couldn't say no.

'Well?' There was the merest hint of impatience in Zane's voice.

Still she hesitated. If she said no, she would be free and Paul need never know that she had had the chance and turned it down.

Sorely tempted, she battled with her conscience. Her conscience won.

There was no way she could deceive the man she loved and was going to marry. It would be like living a lie...

Looking up and meeting Zane Lorenson's green eyes was like walking into a plate glass window.

She was still mentally reeling when he said silkily, 'You seem to be having a great deal of difficulty deciding.'

'Yes,' she stammered. 'Yes, I want it.'

She saw what appeared to be a look of almost savage relief and satisfaction cross his face.

It was gone instantly and she knew she must have been mistaken. He wouldn't care one way or the other whether or not she took the job. If she didn't take it, no doubt the next girl he interviewed would.

'Very well,' he said, his tone businesslike, 'it's yours for a three month trial period. I'll let my secretary know what's happening and get her to deal with all the details.

'I understand from Mrs Rogers that you're free to start at once?'

She nodded, though in truth she didn't want to start at all. The second the words, '*Yes, I want it,*' had been spoken she had regretted them.

'How did you get here?'

Momentarily thrown, she echoed, 'Get here?'

'Did you come by bus? Tube?'

After a brief hesitation, she answered, 'Taxi.'

'You have a current passport?'

She frowned, unsure where this conversation was heading. 'Yes.'

'Good. How long will it take you to pack a bag?'

'P-pack a bag? You mean to travel?'

'My, but you're quick,' he said with a hint of sarcasm.

She flushed. 'I'm sorry. It's just a bit sudden.'

Though Paul had warned her, '*Lorenson has a massive office complex in Manhattan and he likes his Personal Assistant to be free and unencumbered, to be available to travel to his New York offices with him at the drop of a hat,*' she hadn't expected to be going quite this soon.

'So how long?'

'Fifteen minutes.'

'Right. Let's get on our way. My private jet's waiting at the airport.' A hand beneath her elbow, he hurried her to the door.

Wits scattered by his touch, and feeling as though she had been caught up and swept along by a tidal wave, Gail found herself escorted to the lift.

As it carried them swiftly downwards, he said, 'I need to discuss something with my secretary, so perhaps you can get a taxi home to pick up your passport and luggage, then go on to meet me at the airport?'

'Of course.' She could always ask the driver to wait while she slipped inside for some money.

And this way, she thought with relief, she would have a breathing space, time to talk to Paul and let him know the score.

If she told him how Zane Lorenson had treated her, he might be concerned enough to forbid her to take the job…

She was warming herself with that small flicker of hope when—as though her companion knew exactly what was in her mind and was determined to thwart her—he said, 'On second thoughts, I'll only be with Claire for a short time so I might as well take you.'

Apart from needing to speak to Paul, she didn't like the idea of Zane Lorenson going anywhere near her flat. His knowing her address was one thing, his actually ending up on her doorstep another.

Just the thought made her feel vulnerable, exposed.

Biting back the panic, she said as levelly as possible, 'There's really no need for you to go to all that trouble. I can easily—'

'It isn't any trouble,' he told her crisply as the lift doors slid to behind them and they made their way down the corridor, 'and it makes more sense for us to go together.'

'Oh, but—'

'If you took a taxi to the airport you might have some difficulty finding me, so it'll save time in the long run.'

Knowing she couldn't keep arguing, she relapsed into silence, her teeth biting into her lower lip.

'Something wrong?' he queried, giving her a sidelong glance.

Damn the man, he never missed a thing. 'No, nothing,' she assured him.

'Quite sure? We don't want to start our relationship with any undisclosed issues or problems. I know it's the friction in the oyster that makes the pearl, but now you're my PA I'd like there to be harmony, complete trust and confidence between us.'

She was saved from having to answer by the office door opening and Mrs Bancroft appearing, a sheaf of papers in her hand.

'Ah, Claire, before we start for the airport, I need a minute or two of your time.'

'Of course, Mr Lorenson.' Turning on her heel, she led the way back inside.

Gail found herself shepherded into the office and given a seat.

Her thoughts busy, she paid scant attention while, quickly and precisely, Zane Lorenson issued his orders, ending, 'I may be gone for a couple of weeks, but I intend to remain incommunicado.

'If anything really urgent crops up that Dave can't handle you know how to get hold of me. Otherwise, I don't want to be disturbed while I'm away.'

'I understand, Mr Lorenson.'

'Good. Then we'll be off. Perhaps you'll ask John to bring the car round?'

'Certainly, Mr Lorenson.' She lifted the phone. 'Shall I ask him to pick up your luggage?'

'It's already in the boot, thanks.' Turning to Gail, he queried 'Ready to go, Miss North?'

The brisk question scattering Gail's thoughts like a gunshot scattered starlings, she got to her feet.

They went down in the lift without a word being spoken, but she was uncomfortably aware that he never took his eyes of her face.

As, his hand at her waist, they made their way across the foyer, the pretty blonde behind the reception desk smiled brightly and called an eager, 'Good morning, Mr Lorenson.'

'Morning, Miss Johnson,' he responded pleasantly. 'Settling in all right?'

'Very well, thank you, Mr Lorenson.' She gave him another sparkling smile and shot Gail a glance that was frankly envious

Judging by the way this attractive girl was practically drooling over him, Gail could quite believe he had no trouble getting a woman to warm his bed whenever he wanted one.

Outside the impressive entrance a stylish black limousine was just drawing up. A moment later the uniformed chauffeur had jumped out and was standing by to open the door.

As they approached, he said, 'Good morning, Mr Lorenson, with a respectful salute.

'Morning, John… On the way to the airport, will you stop at Delafield House, Rolchester Square? It's just off the West Brackensfield Road.'

'Certainly, sir.'

'How's the wife keeping?'

'Very well, considering, thank you, sir. The twins are due any day now.'

'Know what they're going to be?'

As Gail got into the luxurious car, she heard the middle-aged chauffeur answer proudly, 'A boy and a girl, sir.'

'Lucky man. When they arrive, I dare say your wife will be only too glad of some help, so take a couple of weeks paid leave. I'll be away, so you won't be needed here.'

'Why, thank you, sir,' the chauffeur exclaimed gladly. 'Jenny will be grateful. She's been wondering how she'd cope. But I told her, there's no need to worry, Mr Lorenson won't see us in a mess...'

Gail frowned. Though as far as *she* was concerned he'd been anything but easy to deal with, his consideration for his chauffeur didn't match the cold, uncaring image Paul had painted.

The thought of Paul made her wonder how she was going to manage to phone him. If Zane Lorenson stayed in the car while she went in to pack, it wouldn't be a problem. But if he decided to come in...

'You're looking worried,' he observed gravely, sliding in beside her and reaching over to fasten her seat belt. 'Something wrong?'

Feeling flustered by his nearness, the firm thigh pressing against hers, she moved away as inconspicuously as possible and said jerkily, 'No. No, nothing at all.'

The ironic glance he gave her confirmed that he had noticed her instinctive reaction to his closeness, but he merely observed, 'I thought you might have changed your mind about working for me.'

She longed to say that she had, but dared not until she had talked to Paul and got his blessing.

Instead she answered with what conviction she could muster, 'No, of course not, Mr Lorenson.'

'As I said, when we're away from the office I like a friendly, informal atmosphere, so make it Zane, and I'll call you Abigail.'

'I prefer Gail,' she said quickly.

'Then Gail it is.'

Very conscious of the fact that he was studying her profile, and struggling to keep her composure, she turned to look at him, remarking steadily, 'Yours is an unusual name.'

His white teeth gleamed in a smile before he told her wryly, 'I used to curse my father—who had a regrettable taste for Westerns and read a lot of stories by Zane Grey—until I discovered that my mother would have called me Tarquin.'

In spite of herself, Gail smiled. 'Yes, I see what you mean.'

His eyes on her face, he said softly, 'You're quite beautiful when you smile.'

If it had been his intention to destroy her hard won composure, he succeeded. Completely thrown by both by his words and his close scrutiny, she found herself blushing hotly.

A moment later she heard his quiet, satisfied chuckle, before he said with mock repentance, 'Dear me, now I've embarrassed you. I'm afraid I hadn't realized that some women are still capable of being embarrassed by a compliment.'

Gail sat as if turned to stone as he added caustically, 'Or anything else for that matter. Most of the females I've met, even as young as sixteen or seventeen, are able to throw themselves at a man without so much as a blush…'

Even as young as sixteen or seventeen… Oh, dear God, why had he said that unless he *knew?*

As she waited in an agony of fear and humiliation for the axe to fall, he went on, 'It's quite refreshing to meet a woman in her twenties who obviously doesn't belong in that category.'

So he *didn't* know. She released the breath she had been unconsciously holding. It was her own sense of guilt and shame that had turned a general reference into a specific incident.

Too wrung out to make any further attempt at conversation and wishing herself anywhere but where she was, she stared blindly ahead and made an effort to at least *appear* relaxed.

But while she remained taut as a drawn bow string she was well aware that her companion—who was leaning back, his long legs stretched negligently, his feet crossed neatly at the ankles—was completely at ease.

Nothing more was said until they turned into Rolchester Square and drew up outside the modern block of flats.

When the chauffeur opened the car door, as nonchalantly as possible, Gail told the man beside her, 'I'll be as quick as I can,' and hastily scrambled out.

She thought for a split second that she had succeeded in leaving him behind, but Zane followed on her heels, saying coolly, 'If you can rustle up a cup of coffee, I could certainly use one.'

'Of course,' she agreed hollowly.

It would be no use attempting to phone Paul now. The internal walls of the flat were paper-thin. Even if she spoke quietly, Zane was bound to realize she was talking to someone.

She could use her mobile to send a text, of course. But if Paul was busy he might not bother to pick up a text message until lunch time, and that would be far too late.

A second or two's thought convinced her that it would be better to wait until she reached the airport. Then she could slip into the Ladies' and phone him from there.

If he was willing to let her back out, she could tell Zane that she had had second thoughts and get a taxi home.

Feeling a shade happier, she fished in her bag for the key and let them both into her ground floor flat which, though small, was as pleasant as the two girls could make it.

Dropping her bag on the coffee table and indicating one of the linen-covered armchairs, she asked, 'Won't you sit down?'

But, ignoring the polite invitation, Zane followed her through to the tiny kitchen and leaned idly against one of the work surfaces while she put the kettle on and spooned coffee into the cafetière.

Feeling all thumbs because he was watching her, she said, 'I'm afraid we've only got milk. My flatmate's trying to lose weight and she refused to put cream on the shopping list.'

'Don't worry, I'm quite happy with it black.'

Seeing her get out, and fill, a single cup, he queried, 'Aren't you going to join me?'

Anxious to bring an end to this nerve-racking situation, she shook her head. 'I need to write a note for my flatmate before I start packing.'

If her appeal to Paul was successful, she could always tear the note up when she got back. If it wasn't—and that didn't bear thinking about—Lynne would need to know what was happening.

CHAPTER THREE

FINDING a pen and a piece of paper, Gail briefly explained the situation, adding that there was a possibility that she might be in the States for a week or two.

Then having propped the note against the kettle where her flatmate was sure to find it, she turned to go through to her bedroom.

'Don't bother to pack a flight bag,' Zane told her. 'There'll be everything you may need on the plane. But do remember to bring your passport,' he added as he took his coffee and returned to the living room.

She lifted her case from the top of the wardrobe and, hardly caring what she put in—as, hopefully, she wouldn't be needing any of it—packed it. Then, having zipped it up, she searched in the chest of drawers for her passport.

When she returned to the living room, her case in one hand, her passport in the other, Zane rose to his feet with a wholly masculine grace and said approvingly, 'You've been quick... Here, let me take care of those.'

He relieved her of the case and, before she could think of arguing, he'd taken the passport and slipped it into his pocket.

'Have you packed a swimsuit?'

'A swimsuit?' she echoed blankly.

Though a number of hotels boasted a swimming pool these days, she wouldn't have given it a thought even if she *had* intended to go through with the trip.

He shrugged dismissively. 'I can see you haven't. Never mind. I'm sure we'll be able to sort out the problem when the time comes. Now, all set?'

Picking up her shoulder bag, she nodded.

'Then let's go.' He shepherded her to the door.

During the drive to the airport he seemed occupied with his thoughts. Gail, who couldn't wait to get there, sat staring into space, silently repeating, *Please let Paul understand*...like a mantra.

Though they had a good run through, it seemed an age before they reached the busy airport and made their way to a special VIP parking area.

It was only as they drew up that Gail realized she had still forgotten to pick up her notecase.

As the chauffeur jumped out to open the car door, a young, smartly dressed man who had obviously been awaiting their arrival hurried over.

'Good morning, Mr Lorenson.'

'Morning, Derek. How are things?'

'Fine, thank you, sir. If you'd like to come through, your luggage will all be taken care of.'

Rather than striding ahead and leaving her to follow at his heels, as Paul was apt to do, Zane picked up his briefcase and, putting a hand at her waist, kept her by his side as they made their way into the airport buildings.

While he quickly dealt with the checks and procedures, Gail remained sunk in thought, doing her best to plan ahead.

When the formalities were over, instead of handing her back her passport, he put it in his briefcase with the rest of the documents.

Watching it disappear with a sinking heart, she realized that things had gone a lot further than she had intended and she might have to abandon both her passport and her luggage and make a run for it…

But first she had to speak to Paul.

'If you don't mind,' she said hurriedly, 'I just need to pay a visit to the Ladies.'

He put a restraining hand on her arm. 'We're running a little late—there's a perfectly good bathroom on the plane.'

'Oh, but I—'

'As we already have a take-off slot,' he added with a commanding edge to his voice, 'we shall be boarding immediately.'

Before she could catch her breath, she found herself escorted outside and across the tarmac to a sleek executive jet which was standing gleaming in the late morning sunshine.

The moment they had been welcomed aboard by a middle-aged, cheerful-faced steward, Zane remarked, 'Miss North is desperate to wash her hands, so will you show her where the bathroom is, please, Jarvis?'

'Certainly, sir. If you'll follow me, Miss North.'

Turning to Gail, Zane said, 'While you're gone I'll have a quick word with Captain Giardino and then we'll be about ready for take-off.'

Though his face was straight, she knew by the gleam in his eye that he not only knew how embarrassed she felt, but was amused by her discomfort.

Biting her lip and keeping a tight hold on both her temper and her bag, she followed the steward's white-coated figure to the rear of the plane, where she was shown into a small but luxurious bathroom.

She murmured her thanks and, the moment the door was shut and the bolt pushed firmly into place, unzipped her bag and felt for her mobile.

If she was quick enough there was still a chance she could talk to Paul and get off the plane before the luggage arrived and the main door was closed.

To start with, her fumbling fingers failed to locate it and, cursing the fact that everything was jumbled together in the bottom, she made a more thorough search.

The seconds were ticking away rapidly and when she still couldn't find it, frantic now, she tipped the entire contents of her bag into the sink and scrabbled through them.

It was a moment before she could really believe what her eyes were confirming. It wasn't there.

But she couldn't possibly have lost it. She had taken it off charge and put it in her bag that morning while Paul had stood and waited for her and she hadn't opened her bag since, apart from taking out and putting back the glasses.

Still, the hideous fact remained that *it wasn't there* and the only time the bag had been out of her sight was when she had left it in the living room while she'd gone to pack.

Suppose Zane had taken it?

Oh, don't be a fool, she told herself crossly. Why on earth should he take my phone?

Unless he had known precisely what she had in mind.

The thought momentarily sent her brain reeling.

But he couldn't possibly have known. She was being utterly ridiculous. If he'd had any idea of her link with Paul he would never have offered her the job in the first place.

Common sense having restored the balance, her mind went back to the more pressing problem of what she was to do now.

There were two options. She could throw everything away by telling Zane she didn't want the job after all and insist on leaving the plane. Or she could go through with this trip to the States and see how things worked out.

If she chose the former without consulting him, there was a

good chance that Paul, whom she knew bore grudges, might never forgive her. If she chose the latter, she would have to find some way of armouring herself against Zane Lorenson...

A tap at the door made her practically jump out of her skin.

'I'm sorry to disturb you, Miss North,' the steward's voice murmured discreetly, 'but Mr Lorenson asked me to let you know that any minute now we'll be starting to taxi in preparation for take-off.'

With a jolt, Gail faced the fact that she had left it too late. She no longer had a choice.

Somehow she found her voice and answered, 'Please tell him I'll be there in just a moment.'

Having transferred her belongings from the sink back into her bag, Gail hurried after the steward, much too harassed to be more than vaguely aware of her sumptuous surroundings.

They were already taxiing towards the runway, any minute now they would be airborne, and Paul didn't even know she'd got the job, let alone that she would soon be on her way to the States.

It was scant consolation when her common sense reminded her that if he didn't hear anything, he would no doubt get in touch with Lynne and find out what was happening.

When she reached the forward cabin, Zane was leaning against the bulkhead, waiting for her. He'd discarded his jacket and his crisp, white shirt made him look a little more relaxed, but just as ruthless.

'No problems, I trust?' he asked lazily.

'No, none at all,' she answered as levelly as possible and wondered what lay behind the question.

But she mustn't start attributing ulterior motives to everything he said, she told herself firmly, otherwise she would get paranoid.

Seemingly unaware of her worries, he helped her off with

her jacket, settled her into a window seat and fastened her bel▮ before taking his place beside her.

Feeling trapped, panicky, she very much regretted getting o▮ the plane. But it was too late for regrets, so somehow she woul▮ have to make the best of it. The thought failed to cheer her.

While they waited at the top of the runway, as though pickin▮ up on her feelings, Zane turned his head to ask, 'Scared?'

When she was younger she had been afraid of flying but▮ after Rona had teased her mercilessly about it, she had learn▮ to overcome that fear. Or at least hide it.

Now, in order to explain her only too obvious agitation, sh▮ considered agreeing that she was scared but, realizing that h▮ might tie it in with the past, she denied hurriedly, 'No.'

'That's funny. You give the impression you are.'

'I'm not at all scared.'

'Sure? If you are, I'll be more than happy to hold your hand.▮ He proffered a tanned, well-shaped hand with neatly trimme▮ nails.

Flinching, she insisted, 'Quite sure. I don't know why yo▮ think I might be.'

'Being scared is no disgrace. My previous PA was until sh▮ got used to being on a smaller plane.'

'Though I've always travelled on one of the big commercia▮ jets, being on a smaller plane doesn't really bother me.' Sh▮ tried to keep her voice level.

He smiled. 'Judging by your reaction, having me hold you▮ hand would bother you a great deal more.'

Realizing he was deliberately teasing her, she clenched he▮ teeth and stared resolutely out of the window while the plan▮ began to taxi down the runway, gathering speed.

Their take-off was smooth and effortless and, after climbin▮ steeply through a scattering of cotton wool clouds, they wer▮ soon at the right altitude.

When they levelled out, Zane unfastened both their seat belts and suggested, 'Would you like to come up front and meet the Captain?'

At her nod of acquiescence, he turned and led the way into the cockpit. There, while Gail stared in fascination at the banks of dials and instruments, he and the pilot briefly talked technicalities.

Then, with a smile, Zane made the introduction. 'Gail, this is Captain Giardino... Carlo, I'd like you to meet Miss North.'

She couldn't help but notice—and wonder why—he'd simply given her name without mentioning that she was his new PA.

Captain Giardino was a nice-looking, middle-aged man with dark, greying hair and light hazel eyes. Returning her smile, he said pleasantly, 'It's nice to meet you, Miss North.'

For all his Italian name he spoke perfect English with only the slightest of accents.

Then, showing he'd noticed her interest in the instrument panel, he went on, 'Believe me, it's not half as complicated as it looks. These days planes like this practically fly themselves.'

Gravely, Zane said, 'I'm not at all sure you should mention that. Though she won't admit it, Gail is a bit nervous of flying, so I'm sure she'd prefer an experienced pilot to be in charge.'

Giving Gail a sympathetic grin, the Captain said chivalrously, 'In that case, I promise I'll stay on the job.'

After the two men had had a short discussion about flying conditions, Zane and Gail returned to the forward cabin. As they reached it, he queried, 'What time did you have breakfast this morning?'

Much too worked up to eat, she had swallowed a cup of coffee at about six-thirty.

When she failed to answer, he suggested, 'Or maybe you didn't have any?'

'No, I didn't.'

'You couldn't eat because you were anxious about the interview?'

She nodded.

He disappeared into the galley, to return almost immediately. 'I've asked Jarvis to serve the food as soon as it's ready, so in the meantime let's go and have a pre-lunch drink.'

She found herself escorted into the sumptuous lounge area and seated in one of the soft, natural leather armchairs.

Crossing to a small, well-stocked bar, Zane queried, 'What would you like? A gin and tonic, perhaps?'

'A soft drink of some kind, please.'

'That might be wise on an empty stomach.'

While he put crushed ice and fruit juices into the thick glass tumbler, she watched him covertly.

As he looked down, momentarily absorbed in what he was doing, his lips were slightly pursed and long dark lashes seemed to almost brush his hard cheeks.

He hadn't the kind of film star, slightly effeminate good looks that Paul had, but a tough masculine face, his profile clean-cut and handsome, with a straight nose and a strong jaw. A fascinating face that had, from the start, moved her and made her feel a strange ache inside.

When he reached for a glass her gaze dropped to his hands, which were lean and long-fingered and, as she knew to her cost, had a whipcord strength. She recalled how they had held her, how they had…

With a shiver she snapped off the thought and looked away. In her present predicament it wouldn't help to dwell on the past.

As he put a tall frosted glass into her hand his fingers brushed against hers and what felt like an electric shock tingled up her arm, making her almost spill the contents.

'Still nervous, I see.'

'Not at all,' she denied huskily. 'I just thought for a moment that I was going to drop it.'

Though it was obvious he didn't believe her, he made no further comment.

Pulling herself together, she took a sip. It was cool and fresh and tangy, and she nodded her approval. 'It's very nice, thank you.'

Smiling a little mockingly at her schoolgirl politeness, he picked up his own glass and sat down opposite her.

As she sipped, starting to feel the tension, she tried to think of something to say.

Without success.

Then a soft tap heralded the steward, who wheeled in a loaded trolley, then quickly and deftly transferred everything to a small dining table by one of the windows and set a couple of chairs in place. 'Will that be all, sir?'

'Yes, thank you, Jarvis. We'll help ourselves.'

When the man had gone, Zane rose to his feet, pulled out Gail's chair and seated her, before asking courteously, 'Would you prefer seafood or sandwiches?'

She swallowed. 'Seafood will be fine, thank you.'

He filled two plates with seafood and salad and placed one in front of her. 'Make a start on that; you must be ravenous.'

Anxiety lying like a lead weight in her stomach, she had never felt less like eating and, though it all looked delicious, she picked up her knife and fork with reluctance.

Having helped them both to a glass of Orvieto, he lifted his own in a toast. 'Here's to our future relationship. May it be a good and lasting one.'

As she took a sip of the dry white wine, she wondered why he hadn't said *working* relationship.

But that thought was lost as, apparently making an effort to put her at her ease, he set the conversational ball rolling by saying lightly, 'It's time we started to get to know one anther, so tell me about yourself.'

When, wondering what she could safely tell him, she hesitated, he prompted, 'For instance, what kind of music do you enjoy?'

She paused, trying to gather her thoughts. 'Mainly classical, some middle-of-the-road, some pop, some jazz…'

'What about opera?'

She nodded a little nervously, aware of their close proximity. 'Yes, I like opera.'

'Do you have a favourite composer?'

'Puccini.'

'A romantic, I see…'

Their discussion continued, more often than not their opinions and tastes corresponded and the few times they differed it was on minor issues.

He proved to be an interesting and entertaining companion, easy to talk to and with a ready turn of phrase and an unexpected sense of humour.

It all seemed so normal, so unthreatening, that she found herself starting to relax.

They had moved to the armchairs to drink their coffee when there was a tap and the steward came in to announce, 'If you've finished your lunch, sir, there's something Captain Giardino would like to check with you.'

'Thanks, Jarvis. You can clear away now.'

While the remains of lunch were whisked away, Zane emptied his coffee cup and, rising to his feet, said politely, 'If you'll excuse me, I'll go and see what Carlo wants.'

'Of course.'

'There's a selection of CDs you can look at or, if you'd prefer to read, plenty of books.'

'Thank you.' She watched his broad back as he walked away,

...oting how his thick dark hair grew in a duck's tail in the nape of his neck.

It was one of the first things she had noticed about him all those years ago.

She had been living in her stepfather's downtown Seventh Avenue apartment then, and had been just about to leave her room one evening when she'd realized that Rona's latest boyfriend had arrived to collect her.

Disliking the kind of men her stepsister usually chose—men who thought it was fun to make smart alec remarks and pretend to flirt with her—she'd decided to wait until the pair had gone and, leaving the door slightly ajar, had peered through the crack.

He'd been sitting on the settee, his back to her. At first he'd seemed to be relaxed, at his ease, but then, as if he could sense her gaze, he'd turned his head. Although common sense had told her he couldn't see her, she had jerked back immediately.

After a moment or two she had taken another cautious peep. He had moved his position and this time she'd been rewarded by the sight of his clear-cut, handsome profile. A profile that had immediately bewitched her.

As though mesmerised, she had continued to watch until Rona had come in wearing a stunning scarlet evening gown and a white ermine stole, her blonde beauty as dazzling as the jewels her proud father had lavished on her.

The handsome young man rose to his feet. He was tall and broad-shouldered, she saw, and wearing immaculate evening dress.

Taking both Rona's hands, he told her, 'You look absolutely sensational.'

His voice was deep and attractive.

Well used to compliments, Rona appeared a little bored and, when he would have drawn her close and kissed her, she fended

him off. 'Not now, darling, you'll ruin my make-up and we'r
none too early as it is.'

As he opened the door and held it, Gail saw him full fac
for the first time and when he smiled at something Rona ha
said, her heart lurched crazily.

The pair left then, while she looked after them with a sigh

Most of Rona's boyfriends—the spoilt, decadent sons o
prominent society couples—appeared bored and effete.

But this man was different. Though he could have only bee
about twenty-three or -four, he had a maturity, a power, that th
others had lacked. Apart from his very masculine good looks
there was something real and vital about him, something char
ismatic that drew her like a magnet.

She discovered that his name was Zane Lorenson and ove
the next few weeks she lived for his visits, watching hin
covertly whenever she got the opportunity.

At first only her mother noticed her obsession. But the
Rona caught on and, with that inherent streak of cruelty, starte
to make her life even more of a misery than she'd made it fo
the past five years.

Her scarlet lip curling, she taunted, 'So you've got the hot
for him, have you? Go on, you might as well admit it. Your fac
gives you away.'

'I just think he's nice,' Gail muttered defensively.

'You just think he's nice?' Rona mimicked her Geordi
accent, which became more pronounced when she was stressed
'Then why don't you see what you can do to attract him?'

As Gail began to shake her head, Rona went on, 'I'll be fin
ishing with him soon.'

'Finishing with him?'

'Yes. It's a great pity he's not wealthy. Not only is he generou
but he's a fantastic lover.' She sighed. 'I must say it's been grea
while it lasted, but I'm on the lookout for a seriously rich man

'So, when I'm ready to give him the brush-off, would you like me to tell him that, as far as you're concerned, he's got it made?'

Looking horrified, Gail begged, 'Please, Rona, don't say anything...'

Rona laughed. 'Don't worry. Apart from the fact that you wouldn't know how to deal with a red-blooded man like that, timid little virgins aren't his style.

'If he needs consolation, glamorous blondes with model-girl figures are more up his street. He wouldn't look twice at a lank-haired, flat-chested, spotty schoolgirl...'

With Rona's derisive words ringing in her ears, Gail made up her mind to use the money she had been given for her seventeenth birthday to change her drab image.

She bought face-packs to clear her skin, had her straight dark hair turned into a frizz of long blonde curls and bought herself some make-up and a selection of pretty briefs and padded bras.

Only to find herself jeered at and made fun of even more by her stepsister.

Keeping a low profile, she did her best to ignore the cruel teasing in the hope that it would stop. But a few evenings later Rona walked into her room and, seizing her arm, almost dragged her into the living room.

To Zane Lorenson, who was standing there, Rona announced, 'This is my little sister, Abigail...Abigail is your secret admirer...'

Looking amused, he raised a dark brow.

'She fancies she's in love with you, and the hairdo, the make-up and the new padded bra are all for your benefit...'

Her face scarlet, Gail tried unsuccessfully to pull free.

'I'm sure she would happily give you her all. But, even with such an incentive, I'm afraid you'd soon be bored. She's a poor spineless creature. She'd never have the nerve to stand up to you...'

Looking anything but amused now, Zane ordered, 'Stop being bitchy, Rona, and let the child go.'

As soon as her stepsister's grip relaxed, Gail fled back to her room.

The feeling of shame and humiliation brought stinging tears and, for the first time since coming to live in New York, she gave way to them and cried.

Her only faint consolation was that Zane Lorenson had intervened on her behalf. Though it stung that he had referred to her as a child.

The unpleasant little scene had been overheard by her mother and stepfather, Martin, and caused the older pair to have yet another row.

This one was even more bitter than usual and Gail heard her mother threaten to leave him if he didn't stop Rona being so nasty.

In the days that followed, apparently on her father's orders, Rona left Gail severely alone and a couple of weeks passed without any further painful incidents.

Her stepfather went to 'have a drink' at his club most nights and her mother did voluntary work at their local church's Shelter for the Homeless. So on the evenings she knew Zane would be calling—though part of her ached to catch just a glimpse of him or hear his voice—Gail took good care to be out.

To have somewhere to go, she paid a subscription and joined in the Youth Leisure activities that took place in Greenwich Village. It was reasonably close to where they lived so most times, especially if it was fine, she walked there and back.

The theatre club were meeting that Friday to discuss their next production and, though Gail was far too shy to want a part, she was quite willing to lend a hand behind the scenes.

Earlier in the evening, before going their separate ways, her mother and her stepfather had fallen out yet again.

It seemed that Martin, who had turned out to be a petty dictator, had taken an unreasonable dislike to his wife's involvement with the Shelter and had ordered her not to go.

But this time she had dug her heels in and refused to let him rule her, and what had started as a minor disagreement had ended in a full scale row.

Upset by her stepfather's ranting and raving, and her mother's white, set face, Gail couldn't wait to get out of the apartment.

She was almost ready to leave when there was a perfunctory knock at her bedroom door and Rona came in, beautifully made-up and looking ravishing in a blue silk suit.

Handing Gail an envelope, she said shortly, 'When you go to the theatre club I want you to drop this in at Denver House, apartment 2B. You have to pass the end of Denver Street, so it's barely a block out of your way.'

Her mouth going dry, Gail stammered, 'B-but isn't that where...?'

'Zane lives? Yes, it is. I'd agreed to go to his place tonight but—'

'Well, if you're going there—'

'That's just the point; I'm not now. Something's cropped up and I've got other plans.'

Then, her aquamarine eyes impatient, 'Don't worry, you don't need to see him. Just push the envelope under the door.'

'Oh, but—'

'Denver House is an old place with just a janitor who lives in the basement. There's none of the tight security we have here. All you need to do is go on in and walk up.'

Far from happy, Gail asked, 'Why can't you just phone him?'

'A few minutes ago, while I was in my bedroom packing, I came across his Amex card and the key I gave him to this place.

They must have slipped out of his wallet last night when he was getting either dressed or undressed.

'Because of the way things are turning out, I've decided to keep the key. But I don't want him coming round here to collect his credit card—he's been a regular visitor and security know him, so they'd let him in even without a key—that's why I'm returning the card with a note to explain that I'm ill.'

'You don't look ill.'

Rona sighed. 'I'm not.'

'Then why lie about it?' Gail couldn't understand why she wouldn't want to see Zane.

'Because I'm flying out to spend a...shall I say *private* weekend on Johnny Chator's yacht.'

Appalled, Gail exclaimed, 'You don't mean...?'

'That's exactly what I mean,' Rona said with satisfaction, 'and I don't want Zane to find out. I imagine that if he knew I was two-timing him he could be quite formidable.

'One day he may well be rich himself, but I can't afford to wait. After some failed investments, Daddy's on the verge of bankruptcy, that's why he's started to drink so heavily.' Rona studied her immaculate nails.

'It's only a matter of time before the news becomes common knowledge, and I'd like a ring on my finger and a wealthy husband before that happens...'

Gail had known for some time that her stepfather was in difficulties and, though she had never liked him, she couldn't help but feel a certain sympathy for him.

'Now Johnny's back in circulation after his last trip to Reno,' Rona went on, 'and he may just be the answer to my prayers. It's rumoured that as well as a little fun and excitement, which I'm more than willing to provide, he's looking for wife number five. He likes his women young, and I'll soon be twenty-four so there's no time to waste.'

Shocked, Gail protested, 'But he's old and ugly.'

'I agree he's not exactly an oil painting, and he's known to be a bit of a rake, but he's reputed to be one of the richest men in New York.

'Even if the marriage didn't last long, the sort of alimony he pays would set me up for life—it's known as marrying well and divorcing better—so, if all goes according to plan and he takes the bait this weekend, I'll give Zane the brush.'

Incensed on Zane's behalf, Gail began indignantly, 'I don't know how you can be so—'

Rona gave her a disdainful glance. 'Save the preaching and, whatever you do, don't forget to deliver that note.'

Glancing at her watch, she added smugly, 'I must fly. Johnny's sending a limo for me and I don't want to keep him waiting.' She hurried away.

Looking down at the envelope in her hand, Gail clenched her teeth. She hated the way Rona had talked about Zane, hated her willingness to deceive him.

But of course it was more than that that was making her feel hollow inside, she admitted silently. The last thing she wanted was to have to go anywhere near Zane Lorenson's apartment.

So what was she to do?

She could either put the envelope in the post or do nothing.

But if she did either of those, when Rona failed to turn up at his place this evening, he would no doubt come round here to see what was wrong.

And when he found no one in, then what?

Doubtless he would keep coming until he got some kind of answer.

Which would put Rona in a spot. And if her weekend away hadn't gone according to plan and she wanted to keep Zane a little longer…

Well, if everything blew up in her face she only had herself

to blame, a little demon pointed out. Not only was she treating
Zane shabbily, but she shouldn't have tried to make someone
else do her dirty work.

So why not put her in a spot?

CHAPTER FOUR

No, Gail thought, sending the little demon packing, she just couldn't do it. Though from the start her stepsister had been as unpleasant as possible, and she owed her nothing, two wrongs didn't make a right.

She would have to deliver the envelope. And getting some kind of explanation for Rona's failure to turn up would spare Zane's feelings.

At least for the time being.

Having pulled on a light jacket, Gail thrust the envelope into one of the big square pockets, picked up her shoulder-bag and, apprehension hanging over her like a dark cloud, took the lift down.

She had started to cross the lobby when one of the blue-uniformed security guards appeared and she recognized a familiar face that she hadn't seen for some months.

Gail had always liked Patrick O'Brian and pleasure at seeing him well and on his feet again made her, for a short time at least, forget her anxiety.

The tall, thick-set figure approached, beaming at her. 'Well, well, I almost didn't recognize you. You've gone and altered the colour of your hair as well as the style.'

'Yes, I… I felt like a change.'

'So how are you, Miss Abbey?'

'Very well, thank you, Patrick… It's nice to see you back. I heard you'd been badly injured in a road accident,' Gail said, concerned.

'That I was, Miss Abbey. They practically gave me up for dead at one time, but I pulled through and now I'm back at work and nearly as good as new…'

In spite of living in the States for over twenty years, he still had the traces of an Irish accent.

'I wasn't expecting to start until next week, but both Frank and Ira have flu, so I'm holding the fort by myself for a day or two. It looks like it might be a busy time. I was told there'd been a security scare a couple of days ago—an intruder was spotted inside the building.'

Gail gasped. 'An intruder? How did he get in without a key?'

'When one of the tenants let herself in, this man just walked in with her, cool as you like, saying he was visiting someone.

'Then only yesterday Mrs Williams reported an attempted break-in in broad daylight. So warn your folks to be on their guard.'

'Everyone's out tonight, but I'll tell them when they get back. Though I do hope there won't be any trouble when you're on your own.'

Patrick laughed. 'Don't worry, the cops will be on hand if I need any help.' He checked his watch. 'Well, I'd best get on. Don't forget now, if you see anyone knocking about that looks suspicious, let me know straight away.'

'I will.'

As Patrick walked away, the dark cloud descended once more as Gail remembered the task in hand.

It was a fine summery evening, the streets crowded with traffic and pedestrians. There was a touch of *joie de vivre* in the air—New York at its best—and any other time she would have thoroughly enjoyed the walk. But this time apprehension walked with her and she couldn't wait to get the dreaded errand over.

But she was just being silly, she scolded herself, it was no big deal. All she had to do was slip the envelope under the door and walk away. He would never know she had been anywhere near.

When she reached the old house on Denver Street, she climbed the stoop and—not without some trepidation—walked straight in, just as Rona had said she could.

Though it wasn't in the least luxurious, everywhere appeared to be clean and well cared for and as she climbed the stairs she noticed that the air was fresh and smelled faintly of pine.

On the second floor she located the apartment she was looking for and held her breath as she crept up to the door and, stooping, tried to slide the envelope beneath it.

But the door was a much better fit than she had anticipated and she was forced to make several attempts before she finally succeeded.

Breathing a ragged sigh of relief, she was just turning away when the door opened abruptly and Zane stood there, the envelope in his hand, his handsome face alert, questioning.

Momentarily rooted to the spot, she stood and stared at him.

At first he didn't recognise her and then, as realisation dawned, he smiled, intrigued as to her purpose. 'Well, well, well, look who's here. Do come in.'

'I—I can't stop, really, I'm—'

Ignoring her protest, he took her arm, his touch, and the masterful look on his face, making her insides turn to jelly. 'I'm sure you can spare just a minute or two to tell me what this is all about.'

'There's a note from Rona that will explain everything,' she said desperately.

'I'd much prefer to hear it from you,' he drawled lazily.

Before she could make any further protest, she found herself drawn into a small inner hallway and the door closed firmly behind her.

'Through here.' Zane indicated a door opposite that stood invitingly open.

Having steered her to a couch and waited while she sank on to it, he stood for a moment or two looking down at her.

Part of her mind registered that the living room was light and pleasant and that a table had been set for a romantic dinner for two, but all her attention was focused on him.

He was wearing well-cut trousers and a toning dark shirt open at the neck to expose the strong, tanned column of his throat. His thickly lashed eyes were brilliant and a stray lock of dark hair fell over his forehead.

His gaze was piercing and it set her on edge. 'So what's going on, exactly?'

Her heart racing, her wits scattered by his nearness and the powerful effect he had on her, she couldn't have said a word to save her life.

As, her beautiful grey eyes wide and defenceless, she stared up at him, he remarked, 'There's no need to look quite so scared.' His voice was softer, but still held that quiet authority that had her so worried. 'I'm not the big bad wolf, you know.'

When she still said nothing, he sat down opposite her. 'Suppose you start by telling me why you're here instead of Rona?'

When she had found her voice, Gail began, a shade unsteadily, 'I pass the end of your street on my way to the theatre club and Rona asked me to—'

'*Told* you to, if I know Rona. But do go on.'

'To push a note under your door—'

He frowned. 'Why a note?'

'Because she can't come tonight and—'

'I mean, why didn't she phone me?'

'She said you'd lost your Amex card—' recalling *exactly* what Rona had said, Gail felt her colour rising '—and she wanted you to have it back.'

His eyes alight with amusement, as if he knew precisely why she was blushing, he said, 'I see. So why can't she come?'

'She's...' The lie stuck in Gail's throat and she was forced to swallow. 'She's ill.'

'She was fine last night.'

Then, as though reading her mind and picking up her feeling of guilt that she was concealing the truth, he demanded, 'What's wrong with her?'

'I—I don't know.'

He frowned. 'Surely you've some idea?'

Growing even more uncomfortable, she stammered, 'Not really... I m-mean she didn't tell me.'

Those clear forest-green eyes pinned her and it was obvious that he knew she was lying.

Jerkily, she asked, 'Why don't you read the note? That's sure to say.'

He opened the envelope, put the credit card to one side and, unfolding the note, scanned it quickly.

Seeing a chance to escape while his attention was distracted, Gail rose to her feet.

She had taken only a couple of steps when he glanced up and, tossing the note on to the coffee table, said, 'I must say that sounds like a load of claptrap.'

Though he looked anything but concerned, she could tell that underneath he was angry and, every muscle tense, she was ready for flight, when he queried, 'Wouldn't you agree?'

Wanting only to get away, she said shortly, 'I've no idea what Rona's told you.'

'She says that she's picked up some kind of bug and is too ill to get out of bed. She just wants to be left alone until she feels better.'

'Oh…' Gail stumbled over what else to say.

'You said you didn't know what was wrong with her, but if she really is as ill as all that, you must have known.' Then he paused, letting the silence hang in the air. Gail swallowed nervously. Then he continued, 'Of course, if *being ill* is just an excuse, then you *wouldn't* know, although, as her messenger, I do think she might have briefed you better…'

When she remained silent, his face sardonic, he added, 'But she was expecting you to just leave the note and run, wasn't she?'

Ignoring the question, Gail started for the door on legs that shook.

'Come back and sit down.'

Though Zane spoke quietly, his voice cracked like a whip. But, at the end of her tether, she kept going.

He easily reached the door first. 'I said come back and sit down.'

Though scared half to death, she lifted her chin and looked him in the eye. 'I can't. I'll be late for the theatre club.'

'Too bad. Now, are you coming back or do I have to carry you?'

There was something about the way he spoke that made her know he meant it and, terrified that he would carry out his threat, she retraced her steps and sat down.

'That's better,' he murmured, making no attempt to hide his satisfaction.

Riled by the way he was enjoying riding roughshod over her, she gave him a mutinous glance.

'So you do have some spirit after all,' he observed mockingly. 'I was starting to think that you might be the poor spineless creature that Rona called you…'

Gritting her teeth, she said nothing.

Looming over her, tall and dark and dangerous, he said softly, 'Now, let's have the truth. *Is* Rona ill?'

'Why would she say she is if she isn't?'

He smiled grimly. 'An intriguing question, to which I'd like an answer.'

'I've no intention of answering any more questions. I'm going to be late for the club and I want to leave this minute.'

'You can leave when you've told me exactly what Rona's up to.'

'I don't know what you mean.' Gail felt her voice break as tears threatened.

'You know perfectly well what I mean. What is she up to that she doesn't want me to know about?'

'I've no idea.' She hoped he would believe her but, naturally honest, she found it almost impossible to sound convincing.

'You're not a very good liar.' He smiled wolfishly and watched her soft mouth tighten. 'So why not try telling me the truth?'

Knowing she had reached the end of the road and that she would have to get out of there fast, in desperation she decided to carry the war into the enemy camp.

Rising to her feet, she said as steadily as possible, 'I've no intention of telling you anything further. I'm leaving now and if you try to stop me I'll scream the place down.'

He raised a brow mockingly. 'I don't believe you have the courage to make a scene.'

'Try me.'

When she reached the outer door without interference, she knew she'd won.

A feeling of triumph flooding through her, she had started to turn the knob when she was seized from behind and swung round.

She drew a deep breath but, before she could carry out her threat, he pulled her roughly into his arms and his mouth covered hers, skilled and masterful.

At first she held herself stiffly, but, pressing her back against the door, he kissed her until her head was spinning and her knees turned to jelly.

Feeling her slender body grow limp, he swept her up into his arms and, his lips still clinging closely, carried her back to the couch. Laying her on it, he sat down by her side, effectively trapping her there while he continued to kiss her.

Even though it was evident that she no longer had the breath to scream, it was a little while before he raised his head.

When, her senses reeling and feeling as if her soul had lost its way, she opened dazed eyes, he was staring down at her, an odd expression on his face.

His voice husky, he said, 'You may look like a child, but it was a woman I held in my arms, a woman who, in spite of that air of untouched innocence, responded to my kisses…'

She wanted to deny that she had responded, but couldn't. She hadn't been able to help herself. Though she had tried hard to resist him, the moment his lips had touched hers she had been lost.

'How old are you?'

'Seventeen,' she whispered. Wishing she was older.

'And still a virgin, I think?'

Quite a few of her school friends had been only too eager to lose their virginity to any boy who showed an interest, but Gail had been brought up to have good morals, to respect herself.

Though several boys had tried their luck, put off by their immature fumbling, their wet lips and sweaty palms, she had never even been tempted. Such coolness had earned her the nickname of Miss Icicles.

But, flat on her back and at a disadvantage, stung by what

she took as scorn, she scoffed, 'In this day and age? You must be joking.'

He lifted his shoulders in a shrug. 'I suppose, despite that virginal air, I should have expected it. A potential beauty like you must have attracted any number of boys.'

'Please don't make fun of me,' she said in a stifled voice.

'I'm not making fun of you.' His voice was dark and serious. 'Unlike Rona, you're obviously a late developer. At the moment you're like a rosebud that's too tightly curled. However, in a year or so…'

He let the words tail off and, getting to his feet, took both her hands in his and pulled her into a sitting position.

Feeling bemused and elated and self-conscious all at the same time, she straightened her skirt and jacket and looked anywhere but at him.

Sitting down again, his eyes on her flushed face, he said quizzically, 'Now, you know what happens if you threaten to scream; let's have an answer to my question. What is Rona up to that she doesn't want me to know about?'

'She's spending the weekend on a yacht,' Gail said in a rush.

'Well, if she wants to join a weekend party on a yacht, why didn't she tell me?' Then, his green eyes narrowing, he demanded, 'Whose yacht?'

'Johnny Chator's,' she told him reluctantly.

He cursed. 'No wonder she didn't want me to know. Still, there's said to be safety in numbers… So long as she takes care not to be left alone with him—'

Catching sight of Gail's expressive face, he stopped short. Then, with dawning comprehension, 'Don't tell me… This is going to be a private party, a party just for two.'

When she failed to deny it, he exploded, 'Damn it, Chator's more than twice her age and he's got a reputation for having some nasty habits.'

Standing quickly, he demanded, 'What time is she planning to leave?'

'She's already gone.' Seeing that he was genuinely concerned, she added, 'But I'm sure she can take care of herself—'

His face impatient, Zane brushed her words aside. 'Though Rona *appears* to know her way around, in some respects she's never really grown up; she's still something of an innocent...'

Then, shortly, 'Judging by your expression, you don't agree.'

'No, I don't,' Gail said quietly.

'Well, no doubt we see things in a different way. Rona may seem sophisticated and worldly to you, but at heart she's still Daddy's little girl.

'That's why she was so upset when he married for a second time. She was jealous of his new wife, jealous of you, afraid she was going to lose out...'

With a groan, he sat down and ran his hands through his hair. 'I hate to think of her alone with a swine like Chator.' Then, in obvious frustration, 'She can't have realized just what she might be letting herself in for.'

Gail gritted her teeth. 'I think she does.'

Zane's head came up. 'Then why on earth did she agree to go?'

Gail bit her bottom lip. 'She's hoping to find a rich husband and—'

'She's what?' His eyes blazed with fury.

Frightened by his anger, she whispered, 'Hoping to find a rich husband.'

'And she thinks Chator might fit the bill?'

'Yes,' Gail said miserably.

Zane shook his head, incredulous. 'Doesn't she know that he sheds his wives faster than most men shed their mistresses?'

'Yes, she knows.'

'What makes you so sure?'

'She said so.'

'Tell me exactly what she said.'

Agitation bringing her to her feet, she stammered, 'I—I really don't…'

He rose and, looming over her menacingly, ordered, 'Start from the beginning and tell me what Rona said.'

Bowing to a will-power stronger than hers, Gail took a deep, uneven breath. Then, quietly and with obvious truth, she repeated as well as she could remember exactly what Rona had told her.

While she spoke, Zane stood quietly, his eyes fixed on her face, making no attempt to interrupt.

When she had finished, a white line appearing round his mouth, he said bleakly, 'And here I was thinking Rona and I had a future together, but now it's clear that all the time she was just using me while she looked for someone with more money.' He laughed bitterly.

It was obvious that he was furiously angry, but mingled with that anger was the hurt and pain of disillusionment and loss.

Gail's heart went out to him as, for perhaps the first time, she appreciated that his feelings for Rona had gone far beyond mere sexual attraction.

Grieved to have been the one to tell him, she whispered, 'I wish I hadn't said anything.'

'Well, I suppose I had to know some time what a poor sucker I've been.'

His bitterness, and the desolate look on his face, shocked her. She rose to her feet and, tears gathering in her clear dark grey eyes, she whispered, 'I'm sorry. Truly I am.'

Standing on tiptoe, she made the bravest move she'd ever had the courage to make and went to kiss him, but he moved his head slightly and her kiss brushed only the corner of his mouth.

Flustered and embarrassed, she took a hasty step back,

caught her heel in the rug and, completely off balance, would have fallen if he hadn't gathered her to him.

The close contact with his hard, muscular frame took her breath away and turned every single bone in her body to water.

With no thought of the past or the future, conscious only of the love that filled her heart and the desire to comfort him, she melted against him and lifted her face blindly to his.

When his lips touched hers, she made a sound like a sigh and opened her mouth to him.

At first his kiss was deliberately hard and punitive but, instead of scaring her, as he'd half expected, she put her arms around his neck and, melting against him, returned his kisses with a passionate warmth that sent him up in flames.

At length, lifting his head, he ordered harshly, 'You'd better go.'

When, sensing the need in him, she made no move to obey, he said, 'Look, I'm only human, so unless you're prepared to end up in my bed, you'd better do as I say.'

He started to push her away but she clung closer, whispering, 'I want to stay.'

'Don't be a little fool,' he said roughly. 'Tomorrow you'll regret it.'

'I won't. I love you,' she said quietly and pressed her slender body against his.

As though his self-control had snapped, with scant regard for her youth and inexperience, he began to strip off first her clothes and then his own.

Laying her down on the carpet, he trailed his touch along her body. She shivered in response, begging him to make love to her there and then.

For perhaps the first time in his life, his passion fuelled more by anger than desire, he took without caring overmuch what he gave back.

Even so, Gail was swept away by his kisses, the touch of his skin on hers, and he carried her on a flight to the heavens, leaving her limp and quivering in the aftermath of such ecstacy.

But, though he had given her the kind of delight she had never even imagined, she felt a keen sense of loss, of sadness. While to her their lovemaking had been exquisite, she knew that he felt no tenderness or caring towards her.

Although what had she expected? She had thrown herself at him and, driven by anger and pain that the woman he loved didn't care, he had taken what she'd so freely offered.

But on the floor, as though she was just a common little slut, as though he couldn't bear to take her to the bed that Rona would have occupied.

She was filled with shame and humiliation, a feeling of disbelief that she could have acted so out of character and, rather than have to face him, she wanted to curl up and die.

When he rose to his feet she was still lying there motionless, the curly tendrils of blonde hair spread around her, her eyes shut tightly, her long, thick lashes like dark fans on her cheeks.

In his arms she had been all woman but, with her slender body and small breasts, she looked childlike and vulnerable, and, remembering her little gasp of pain at his first strong thrust, he felt callous and cruel.

But when he would have drawn back, she had tightened her arms around his neck, whispering urgently, 'It's all right. It's all right.'

Now, however, seeing the tears that squeezed themselves beneath her closed lids and trickled down her face in tracks of shiny wetness, he knew it wasn't and cursed himself savagely.

Angry with her for misleading him, for throwing away her virginity, and furious with himself for taking it, he began to pull on his clothes.

He was buttoning his shirt when, chilled and shivering, she scrambled to her feet.

Seeing his eyes fixed on her, she crossed her thin arms over her small breasts.

He found himself absurdly touched by her attempt at modesty and that made him even angrier.

His mouth compressing, he gathered up her things and, tossing them on to the couch, said curtly, 'You'd better get dressed and get out of here.'

As, with pathetic dignity, she began to pull on her clothes and shoes, he saw that her hands were shaking and, obeying the temptation to lash out, observed caustically, 'I should thank you for trying to console me.'

Only too aware that what had started as an attempt to comfort him had gone horribly wrong, she whispered, 'I'm sorry.'

'Why be sorry?' Now he was being intentionally cruel. 'Presumably you got what you wanted. But if you're hoping to take Rona's place, you'll have to think again. Inexperienced schoolgirls just out for a thrill aren't my style.'

Flayed, mortified, she snatched up her bag and jacket and, blinded by tears, fled.

Knowing she couldn't go on to the theatre club as if nothing had happened, she began to walk aimlessly, seeing nothing and uncaring of where she went, until at long last she succeeded in getting the worst of her misery and agitation under control.

Clouds had gathered and it was starting to rain—big, heavy drops of summer rain that plopped on to the sidewalk, making dollar-sized rings in the dust and the air smell of ozone.

Finding herself outside her own apartment building, like someone on automatic pilot, she took out her card-key and let herself in.

She was crossing the lobby when the sight of three men approaching stopped her dead in her tracks.

An angry-looking Zane was in the middle, flanked by Patrick and a burly policeman.

'Miss Abbey,' the security guard exclaimed, 'you're just the person we want. This man says his name is Zane Lorenson and he's a friend of your sister's; he was seen loitering outside your apartment…'

So he'd come to check that she'd spoken the truth, that Rona really had gone.

'When I asked him how he got into the building, he said your sister had given him a key, but he was unable to produce it, and there was no one home to verify his statement—'

Appearing to be holding on to his patience only with an effort, Zane broke in, 'I've already explained that I'd just mislaid it and that the regular security staff know me well.'

As though he hadn't spoken, Patrick went on, 'He then admitted that he'd walked in with one of the tenants. He said he was visiting you, but I knew you'd gone out, so—'

'For heaven's sake—' Zane appealed directly to Gail '—tell him you know me.'

Sounding surprised, the security guard asked, 'Can you vouch for him, Miss Abbey?'

Still raw and bleeding from the way Zane had humiliated her, the way he'd said, 'Inexperienced schoolgirls just out for a thrill aren't my style', and at that moment hating him for it and wanting to hit back, she shook her head and said jerkily, 'I'm afraid I can't.'

She saw the icy anger in his green eyes before she turned and hurried away.

By the time she reached her apartment, already bitterly regretting what she'd done, she was shaking so much that she could hardly open the door.

Feeling sick and hollow inside, she went straight to her room but, too agitated to sit down, she began to pace restlessly, going over and over the little scene in her mind.

Recalling that look of cold fury in Zane's eyes, she shivered.

He wasn't the sort of man who would take kindly to being made a fool of and sooner or later she would have to face him and answer to him for what she'd done…

The sound of the outer door opening and closing penetrated her thoughts and brought her heart into her mouth. Had she closed it properly in her agitated state?

But when she plucked up enough courage to go and look, it was her mother.

'You're back early…' They spoke in unison.

Catching sight of the bruises on her mother's face, Gail asked urgently, 'What have you done? How did you come to hurt yourself?'

The clear grey eyes that were so like her daughter's filled with tears. 'Earlier tonight Martin came round to the Shelter and caused a terrible scene. He was drunk and when I wouldn't leave with him he went mad.'

Elizabeth put a hand to her bruised face. 'It took three of the helpers to throw him out. Father Delaney brought me home.'

The tears spilt over and ran down her cheeks. 'I've had more than enough. I've decided to leave him. We'll go back to England.'

'But how will we manage?'

'Harriet knows there've been problems with the marriage, and the last time she wrote she said that if ever we wanted to go home we could stay with her for as long as we needed…'

Though Gail hadn't seen her aunt for several years she had always been extremely fond of her and the thought of the warm welcome they were sure to receive cheered her up considerably.

'…And I can get a job of some kind.'

'I'll get one too.'

Elizabeth shook her head. 'You've only got another year at school, and I want you to go on to college and finish your education.'

'Oh, but—'

'We'll manage somehow.'

'Are you sure you're doing the right thing?'

'Absolutely sure.' Then, a shade anxiously, 'You don't want to stay in the States, do you?'

'No. I love New York, but I've never really been happy living with Martin and Rona.'

'No, God forgive me, I know you haven't. The marriage was a sad mistake that we've both paid dearly for.

'I should never have married him, but I was lonely, I missed your dad, and Martin was a good-looking man who could be very kind and charming when he wanted to be. By the time I realized just what he was like, it was too late.'

'How soon do you want to leave?'

Dashing away the tears, Elizabeth said, 'As soon as possible. To save any further trouble, perhaps we could pack now and start for the airport before he gets home.'

As far as Gail was concerned, to be able to go at once and leave all the trauma behind was the answer to a prayer. 'Yes, let's,' she agreed eagerly.

A little over an hour later, they were in a taxi heading for Queens and JFK airport…

Just then Zane's voice broke into her thoughts and made her jump. She was forced to put the past behind her and remember why she was here. 'Sorry, I was miles away.'

'Reminiscing?' He had an unnerving knack of appearing to read her mind.

'No,' she denied quickly.

'Contemplating the future?'

She shook her head. 'I was just thinking about travelling in general.'

He sat back and observed the tension on her face. 'Earlier this morning you mentioned that you'd been to Europe?'

'I'm afraid they were only package holidays,' she explained depreciatingly.

'To one of the Costas?'

She shook her head. 'France and Switzerland a couple of times, and once to Austria.'

'Alone?'

'With a friend.' She sipped her drink, avoiding eye contact with him.

'Male or female?'

He watched her generous mouth tighten, before she asked shortly, 'Does the sex make any difference?'

His lips twitched, as if he was trying not to smile, before he answered, 'It might well to the people involved.'

'I mean, I don't see why you're asking. Why it makes any difference to you.'

'It gives me an insight into your character…'

Watching her like a hawk, he added, 'You see, I like to *know* my PA inside out. What kind of woman she is, how she handles her life, her attitude to the opposite sex, what makes her tick…'

CHAPTER FIVE

FEELING rather like some specimen on the end of a cruel pin, Gail repressed a shudder.

'So was it male or female?'

Rattled by his arrogance, she demanded, 'How can you be certain I'll speak the truth?'

'Because you have a very expressive face and I can tell when you're lying.

'Which was it?'

'Male,' she told him boldly.

He smiled wolfishly. 'I'm not sure I believe you.'

'As I consider that my private life is my own business, I don't—' She broke off, her grey eyes sparkling with anger.

'Go on,' he urged, 'say it.'

'I don't much care whether you believe me or not.'

'That's my girl!' he applauded. 'I do like a touch of spirit in a woman.'

Then with no change of tone, 'Do you speak any other language?'

A little surprised by what seemed an abrupt change of subject, she replied, 'During my last year at school I learnt French and a little German.'

'You don't speak Italian?'

She shook her head.

'Have you been to Italy before?'

Puzzled by the way he'd phrased the question, she said, 'No, I've never been to Italy. I've always wanted to go, but Jo preferred somewhere that would hopefully be a little cooler.'

'It can get very hot there in summer,' he agreed.

'I understand it can get quite hot in Manhattan,' she said carefully.

'Hot and airless at times,' he admitted. 'Though it's one of my favourite places.'

Wondering how long it would take a small plane to cross the Atlantic, how long they would have to be cooped up together like this, she asked, 'What time will we get to New York?'

He raised a dark brow. 'What makes you think we're going to New York?'

Nonplussed, she stammered, 'Well, I—I understood your offices were there.'

'So they are. However, that doesn't happen to be where we're going.'

With a stirring of unease, she asked, 'Then where are we going?'

'Italy. Tuscany, to be precise.'

'Tuscany?' she echoed, the feeling of unease increasing tenfold.

Apparently noting that unease, he queried, 'Does where we're going make any difference?'

She bit her lip. 'It just seems a strange location for a business trip.'

'Ah, but this isn't an ordinary business trip—'

Thoroughly alarmed now, she demanded, 'If it isn't a business trip, why do you need a PA?'

'I said an *ordinary* business trip. For a while now there's been some unfinished business I've been wanting to deal with. The kind of business that makes your presence essential.'

There was an strange note in his voice, a nuance, the faintest undercurrent of…what?

Menace?

Shivering, she told herself not to be a fool. She was letting her imagination run away with her again.

'I thought it might be a good idea to get to know one another before we start work in earnest, so I decided to combine business with pleasure, and Tuscany is the ideal place to do that.'

'Oh…' she said hollowly.

'I know you share my liking for Abruzzi's landscapes but, other than that, do you know much about the region?'

Making an effort to keep her voice steady, she answered, 'Not a great deal, I'm afraid, and hardly anything about the countryside. Though, from the paintings and photographs I've seen, it appears to be really beautiful.'

He laughed. 'Yes, it is. It's varied and colourful, with vineyards and olive groves and field upon field of golden sunflowers.

'Of course the towns and cities are picturesque and historical, well worth visiting. Florence, Pisa, Lucca, Siena…' Gail was entranced by his words, wanting to know more about all the amazing places he'd been.

'It's around Siena that you'll see the distinctive orangey-red earth that's the origin of the painting pigment burnt sienna, which was used a great deal by the Renaissance painters.

'But away from the big towns and cities it's quiet and peaceful, with villas and farmhouses dotted about, little hamlets and medieval walled towns perched on the hilltops…'

Warmed by his genuine enthusiasm, which somehow made him seem more human, she relaxed a little. 'I hope I'll get a chance to see it.'

'Oh, you will,' he assured her.

'Where exactly are we heading for?'

She was expecting him to say Florence or one of the other major cities, when, his clear dark green eyes fixed on her face, he queried, 'Have you ever heard of Montecino?'

She shook her head.

'It's one of the small medieval hilltop towns I just mentioned…'

Hoping against hope that she had misunderstood, she said, 'You don't mean that's where we'll be staying?'

'Not in the town itself. I have a villa about two miles away as the crow flies. It's a bit off the beaten track, but the scenery is magnificent.'

Her heart sank like a stone.

Had they been staying at a hotel in Florence with plenty of other people around, it would have been bad enough. But there was no way she could cope alone with him in some remote villa.

As she struggled to hide her alarm, Zane added cheerfully, 'Don't worry, it's not completely isolated. The nearest hamlet is only about three quarters of a mile away in the valley.

'Villa Severo stands on a hilltop, with wonderful views over the countryside. The original building—part castle, part house—dates from the mid-seventeenth century and was virtually in ruins when I bought it.

'But it's now been completely rebuilt with all mod cons, including a swimming pool. I think you'll like it,' he added, a note of quiet pride in his voice.

It might have wonderful views, Gail thought bleakly, but if she had had the faintest idea where he was intending to bring her, she would never have come in a million years. How could she spend time so isolated and in such close proximity to Zane Lorenson?

This whole thing had gone disastrously wrong, and when

they reached the airport she would use her credit card and get the first flight back home.

She was about to tell him so when caution made her bite her tongue. It wasn't that she was chicken, she assured herself. But now, while they were still cooped up together, wasn't the time to tell him she was opting out, especially as he'd made it quite clear that he wanted her with him.

Though *why* he needed a PA when presumably in such an out of the way place he would be doing his business by computer, she couldn't begin to imagine.

Made uncomfortable by the possibilities that thought engendered, she pushed it resolutely away and tried to concentrate on how best to explain her change of heart.

After a while she sighed, knowing that however she explained it he wasn't likely to take kindly to the idea. But once she had her luggage and her passport back, if the worst came to the worst she could simply refuse point-blank to go any further.

There was a tap and the steward came in to announce, 'Captain Giardino asked me to say that, unless you want to take the controls yourself, he'll be coming in to land in about ten minutes.'

So Zane was a pilot too, Gail thought. Well, she might have expected it. He was the kind of man who could do anything he set his mind to.

'Thanks, Jarvis. Please tell the Captain to go right ahead.'

When the steward had gone, as casually as possible, Gail asked, 'Are we landing at Florence or Pisa?'

'Neither…'

So presumably they were landing at Bologna.

She was waiting for Zane to confirm that, when he went on calmly, 'We'll be putting down at Voste, a small, privately owned airfield…'

A small private airfield rather than the big airport she had anticipated...

Feeling like some fugitive who, dreaming of escape, had just seen the bars of the cage close round her, she stared at him in complete consternation.

'There's no need to look quite so fraught. It has a more than adequate runway, a well-trained staff and a first class safety record.'

Thankful that he had put her agitation down to being scared of flying, she made a determined effort to pull herself together.

As it seemed she had no alternative but to see this thing through, she must endeavour to keep her cool and make the best of it.

Taking a deep breath, she asked, 'Why did you choose to land there?'

'When I fly to Tuscany we always land at Voste. It's very convenient, just a few miles north of the villa, and Lorenzo da Voste and his wife, Lucia, happen to be very good friends of mine.

'I would have liked you to have met him and his family— he has three young children—but unfortunately they're in Capri at the moment...'

Apparently intent on taking Gail's mind off the landing, Zane talked easily until they had touched down and taxied to a halt in front of a series of hangars and prefabricated buildings.

Several uniformed staff appeared and, while a set of steps was wheeled into place, the steward opened the door of the plane.

Zane pulled on his jacket and picked up his briefcase. 'If you'll excuse me for a moment, I've got a spot of official business to attend to.' Striding down the steps, he disappeared into what looked like an office.

He was back quite quickly, but by that time Gail had collected her belongings and the luggage had been unloaded and transferred to a white open-topped car standing close by.

The late afternoon sky was a cloudless Mediterranean blue, the sun beat down and the oven heat of the tarmac burnt through the thin soles of her court shoes as she was escorted down the steps and to the waiting car.

When she had been settled in the front passenger seat, Zane put her jacket and his briefcase into the back and moved away to have a word with a group of men.

It immediately became clear that he spoke fluent Italian. But then he would, she thought a shade bitterly, while not knowing the language was bound to put her at a disadvantage.

Seeing Captain Giardino join Zane and the little group, she wondered if he would be coming with them and staying at the villa.

She fervently hoped so. It would be a comfort to have another person there, especially someone who could speak English. And where else would he stay?

The airfield was situated on a flat, fertile plain with green, rolling hills on either side. Beyond the white control tower she could see the silvery-green shimmer of an olive grove and away in the distance were stands of what looked like chestnut trees.

To the right, about halfway up the hill, was a large terraced villa with colour-washed walls. It was the only house in sight.

Everywhere was peaceful. Sunshine fell golden as honey on her bare arms and the chirping of cicadas filled the drowsy air. Her worries momentarily fading, Gail lifted her face to the sun and closed her eyes.

The previous night's lack of sleep starting to catch up with her, she was just drifting off when she heard Zane's voice close by.

Her eyes flew open.

He was approaching the car and talking into a mobile phone.

'Sono qui in vacanza… Si… Quando?… Si, si, bene… Ciao, Paolo.'

She was wondering if Paolo was a business acquaintance when, dropping the mobile into his jacket pocket, he said regretfully, 'I'm sorry if I disturbed you. That's the first time today I've seen you looking anything like relaxed.'

'I was just enjoying the sunshine.'

'I think I'll join you.' He took off his jacket and tossed it on to the back seat of the car before removing his tie and dropping it into one of the car's glove pockets.

When he'd unfastened the top few buttons of his shirt and rolled up his sleeves to expose muscular arms, he said with satisfaction, 'Now I *feel* as if I'm on holiday…

'How does your first glimpse of Tuscany strike you?'

'It must be a lovely place to live,' she said, and meant it.

'Lucia and Lorenzo think so; that's why they much prefer to stay here—' he indicated the colour-washed villa '—even though they have big houses in Florence and Rome.

'While Lorenzo is a direct descendent of one of the Grand Dukes of Tuscany, and extremely wealthy, he's very down-to-earth and he and Lucia much prefer to live simply.

'Although they've a house full of servants, Lucia always does her own cooking. Her La Ribollita, one of the most famous of Tuscan soups, is the best I've ever tasted…'

When he slid behind the wheel and started the ignition with a soft roar, Gail glanced around. She could see the airfield staff going about their business, but there was no sign of the pilot.

'Where's Captain Giardino?' she asked quickly.

Zane lifted a dark brow. 'Why do you ask?'

'Well, I… I just wondered where he was staying.'

'He's staying at the villa, as usual.'

Her heart lifted.

As Zane put the car into gear and they moved off, she asked, 'Aren't you going to wait for him?'

She saw the corner of his mouth twitch before, indicating the house on the hillside, he told her, 'I meant *that* villa. Carlo, who is distantly related to Lucia, always stays there whether the family are home or not.'

'Oh…'

Zane gave her a glinting sideiong glance. 'You sound disappointed.'

'Not at all,' she said stiffly.

With smooth mockery, he went on, 'And, before you ask about Jarvis, he's going back to Montecino with one of the mechanics. I hope it won't shock you, but he has a lady friend there.'

Her mouth tight, Gail said nothing.

At the entrance to the airfield the security staff gave Zane a friendly wave, which he returned, and the tall gates in the chain-link fence were swung open for them.

Leaving the airfield, they followed a narrow, winding road along the valley floor. Everywhere was quiet and peaceful. Once they had picked up speed, the balmy breeze of their passing stroked her cheeks like soft fingers and ruffled her hair. Glancing sideways at him, she saw that the tough, hard-headed businessman had gone. With his shirt open at the neck and the breeze flicking a lock of dark hair over his forehead, he looked relaxed and carefree, almost boyish, not the ruthless tycoon she knew him to be.

Seeing him like that made her heart feel as if it were being squeezed in a giant fist, and she sighed for what might have been.

A mile or so along the valley, they passed a small picturesque village before they began to climb the wooded hillside. The scenery was lovely but, apprehensive about what lay ahead, she was unable to relax and enjoy it.

Showing he never missed a thing, Zane asked, 'What's wrong?'

She shook her head. 'Nothing.'

'Don't lie to me,' he said crisply. 'You've been uptight from the word go.'

When she remained silent, he gave her a quick, searching glance and asked, 'Why did you want to work for me?'

The unexpected question jolted her and she stammered, 'I— I needed a job.'

'I'm rather surprised The Manton Group didn't offer you one.'

'There wasn't an opening for a PA.'

'How did you come to hear that *I* needed one?'

After a moment's frantic thought, she said, 'I found out from the agency.'

'And you saw Mrs Rogers.'

It was a statement, not a question, but she answered, 'Yes.'

'When I spoke to Mrs Rogers myself, she told me you were very keen to have the job.'

'Yes, I—I was.'

When she said nothing further, he pursued, 'So you were pleased when you got it?'

'Well…yes.'

'In that case, why have you been like a cat on a hot tin roof ever since?'

Her common sense telling her that it was no use trying to deny it, she said, 'I couldn't help but wonder if I'd made a mistake. If I should have accepted your offer.'

'Why? Because the interview wasn't the standard, polite kind you were expecting?'

'It was partly that… But then everything happened so quickly, and I must admit that having to come away so suddenly, before I'd had time to settle in, threw me somewhat.'

'Well, the die's cast and it's too late for regrets, so I suggest you try and relax a little.'

He was right about the die being cast.

That being the case, the last thing she wanted to do was make him suspicious, so somehow she must try to do as he said and play the part of a normal PA.

In a little while they reached a pair of handsome wrought iron gates set in an old wall. They were standing invitingly open.

The serpentine drive ran between terraced gardens that, with varied trees and shrubs and masses of flowering creepers tumbling over the retaining walls, were a riot of colour.

They had rounded the last bend before the house itself came into view. As Zane stopped the car in a cobbled courtyard, she caught her breath.

It was starkly beautiful, more so than she could ever have imagined. No wonder he was proud of it.

Perhaps because it had been recently rebuilt, and he had referred to it as a villa, she had expected something colour-washed and stuccoed that appeared relatively modern, but this place had an almost medieval air about it.

With a huge arched doorway and arched windows set in high walls built of pale random stone, the place looked more like a small castle than a house.

It appeared to be built on several different levels and boasted a jumble of pantiled roofs at various angles, some with chimneys. At one end, incorporated in the building, was a big round tower with a squat, candle-snuffer roof.

'Like it?' he asked.

'It's absolutely wonderful,' she said sincerely. 'You must have had a brilliant architect to design something like this.'

He shook his head. 'It wasn't designed by my architect. I already knew exactly what I wanted, as I'd been lucky enough to come across a series of old paintings that showed what the original building had looked like before it started to fall into disrepair.

'Where my architect proved his worth was in making detailed plans from the rough sketches I'd had done.'

He restarted the car and turned right through an archway into another courtyard at the rear, where a heavy studded door was standing open.

There were tubs of scarlet and white geraniums and, incongruously, a battered motor scooter with a pillion seat propped against one of the walls.

Zane brought the car to a halt and, as he helped Gail out, a woman appeared in the doorway.

'This is Maria Colasanti,' he told her, 'my caretaker-cum-housekeeper and the lady who manages to organize everything.'

Dark-haired and buxom, dressed in serviceable country clothes, Maria looked more like a farmer's wife than a housekeeper.

As though to confirm that thought, he added, 'Her husband, who worked on a nearby farm, died just as this place was being finished, so she was pleased to take the job. She's turned out to be a treasure.'

'*Buonasera,* Signor Lorenson,' the woman exclaimed, showing strong white teeth as she smiled broadly.

'*Buonasera,* Maria,' he greeted her. '*Comesta?*'

'*Va bene,* Signor Lorenson…'

As Zane introduced the two women, who nodded and smiled at each other, a sturdily built youth appeared and, giving the newcomers a shy smile, began to take the luggage from the car.

The likeness between the young man and the older woman was so marked that Gail presumed they must be closely related.

As though echoing her thoughts once again, Zane said, 'This

is Angelo, Maria's eldest son. Apart from providing necessary transport, he's a big help around the place.'

Retrieving their belongings from the back seat, Zane handed Gail her jacket. His own jacket over his arm and his briefcase in his hand, he left the car where it was and led the way inside, chatting to the housekeeper as they went.

The large hall was light and airy and open-plan, with rustic archways, long windows and an elegant chestnut wood staircase running up the middle.

Turning to Gail, he explained, 'You'll find the three principal rooms are situated in the tower. The library-cum-study is on the ground floor—' he indicated a door to the left of the stairs '—the living room is on the floor above and the master bedroom is on the floor above that.'

Casually, he added, 'Your bedroom is next door to mine. If you follow Maria, she'll show you the way.'

As the housekeeper smiled and nodded, he added, 'When you've had time to unpack and freshen up, make your way down the spiral stairs to the living room and we'll have a drink on the terrace.'

A moment later he disappeared into his study.

Glancing around her curiously, and in spite of everything liking what she saw, Gail accompanied the housekeeper up the staircase, Angelo following behind with her luggage.

At the top of the stairs, the landing was lit by a row of handsome oriel windows which, despite the new woodwork, gave it a much older feel.

They climbed the next flight and, having crossed an identical landing, turned down a wide passageway where Maria showed her into a large room adjacent to the tower.

The windows, curtained in off-white muslin, were open wide, letting in warm air that carried the combined scent of rosemary and lavender.

Glancing out, Gail saw there were magnificent views across the valley, while through the trees she could make out glimpses of the road they had come up by, winding down the hillside.

When Angelo had placed her case carefully on a low chest, Gail said, '*Grazie,*' one of the few words of Italian she knew, and smiled at mother and son.

They returned the smile and departed.

The room, with its *en suite* bathroom, was light and pleasant, with modern furniture and a comfortable-looking double bed. Though Zane had assured her that the villa had 'all mod cons' there was no phone.

Her heart sank.

But surely there would be phones downstairs. If she was careful to chose her moment, she might be able to make a quick call to Paul to let him know where she was and what was happening.

She opened her case and set aside fresh underwear, a silk shift, a pair of strappy sandals and her night things and toiletries, before transferring the rest of her belongings to the chest of drawers and the big walk-in wardrobe.

Then, stripping off her clothes, she placed the chain that held Paul's ring on the dressing table and went into the luxurious bathroom.

A towelling bathrobe had been laid out ready, along with piles of soft towels and a wide array of expensive toiletries. But, after glancing through them, she decided that she preferred her own modest apple blossom, which she had liked and used for years.

Though the shower was refreshing, even enjoyable, the thought of the several hours that she would have to spend alone with Zane before she could go to bed filled her with dismay. But the evening had to be faced and, hopefully, she could plead tiredness and escape early.

She was emerging from the bathroom when a sound like an angry hornet drew her over to the window and she was just in time to catch sight of a motor scooter on the road down to the valley.

It seemed that Angelo was going out for the evening.

But that still left Maria, and though she couldn't communicate with the housekeeper verbally, it was nice to know there was someone else in the house.

When she was dressed, she put on the merest touch of make-up to boost her morale and brushed out her dark, silky hair before taking it up again into a businesslike coil.

Then, after a moment's hesitation, feeling in need of the re-assurance it offered, she dropped the thin gold chain over her head and tucked Paul's ring down the front of her bra.

A quick glance in the cheval mirror convinced her that she looked cool and composed and, determined to stay that way, she set off to face the evening.

A door in the tower gave access to the spiral stairs that Zane had mentioned. Beautifully designed, they were made of the same lovely chestnut wood as the main staircase and had an ornate metal hand rail.

The high heels of her sandals clicking lightly on the steps, she made her way down to an attractive and spacious living room with a huge arched fireplace built of pale random stone and filled with flowers.

Cushioned chairs and couches covered in linen that shaded from oatmeal through to mushroom were grouped in front of the hearth, while the walls were painted a rich, glowing burnt ochre.

Apprised of her coming, Zane was waiting at the bottom of the stairs, his dark, well-shaped head tilted back a little to watch her descent.

He had changed into casual stone-coloured trousers and an

olive-green silk shirt open at the throat. Freshly shaven, his hair still damp from the shower, he looked so devastatingly attractive that her heart began to beat faster.

As she reached the bottom he gave her a little smile and silently held out his hand.

Like someone caught in a dream, someone who had no choice but to play the part allotted to her, she put hers into it.

She instantly regretted it.

A kind of electric shock made her whole body tingle and she snatched her hand away as if it had been burnt.

She regretted that too. The involuntary reaction had been much too revealing.

She heard his soft, amused chuckle as he put a hand at her waist and, walking slightly behind her, began to steer her towards a pair of open French windows.

As they reached them, his hands closed lightly around her upper arms, stopping her dead in her tracks. She felt the warmth of his breath on the side of her neck as, bending forward, his lips almost brushing her ear, he murmured, 'You smell as fresh and delightful as a spring morning. When we met it was one of the first things I noticed about you.

'Once upon a time,' he added softly, 'I knew a girl who wore that same perfume.'

His words made her blood turn to ice in her veins and, standing frozen with horror, she wondered frantically if he knew who she was and, intent on punishing her, had been playing with her like a cat played with a mouse.

Or was she letting her own guilt and awareness undermine her?

Somehow she found her voice and said jerkily, 'That's not surprising. It's very common.'

Without further comment, he released her and together they stepped out on to a semicircular stone terrace with panoramic views across the peaceful countryside that were even more spectacular than the ones from her bedroom window.

The impression that the terrace—with its wrought iron balustrade—was suspended in space was almost overpowering until she saw that it was supported by pillars and that wrought iron steps led down to the courtyard beneath.

On a low table was a tray of drinks and a pair of cushioned loungers issued a mute invitation.

When she was settled in one of them, Zane asked, 'So what's it going to be?'

Her coolness and composure gone, and feeling in need of a bit of Dutch courage, she threw caution to the winds. 'I'd rather like a gin and tonic, please.'

'Ice and lemon?'

She nodded. 'Please.'

As he mixed the drinks, in an effort to steady herself, she looked around her.

Away to the west, the sun was just slipping below the horizon and the *contre-jour* lighting and the long purple shadows made the scenery even more dramatic.

One or two wispy ribbons of cloud had appeared in a sky of aquamarine flecked with palest pink and a balmy evening breeze had sprung up, caressing her forehead and playing with a fine strand of her hair that had escaped.

Had the circumstances been other than they were, she would have looked forward greatly to staying in this lovely isolated spot.

But, as it was, she would have happily swapped all the peace and serenity for the noise and dust and bustling crowds of one of the big towns or cities.

Though surely she would be better able to face the thought of being at the Villa Severo, virtually alone with Zane, when she had managed to talk to Paul and, hopefully, caught up on last night's lost sleep.

CHAPTER SIX

'HERE we are—one gin and tonic.'

Zane's voice broke into her thoughts and she turned to find he was by her side, holding out a glass.

Taking it, she said composedly, 'Thank you.'

'Try it and see if it's to your taste.'

As he spoke, as if determined to destroy any attempt at composure, he brushed the tendril of hair away from her cheek and tucked it behind her ear.

His action turned the intended sip into a gulp and she was forced to cough.

'Not too strong, I trust?' Though his expression was bland, innocent, she thought she could detect an air of satisfaction, almost triumph.

'No… No, it's fine, thank you.'

Telling herself vexedly that she would have to exercise a great deal more self-control, she took refuge once again in staring out over the countryside while she sipped more carefully.

Zane sat down next to her.

Much too close for comfort.

Stretching his long legs indolently, his eyes fixed on the rolling hills, he began to drink his own whisky soda.

Almost as soon as the sun had vanished from view, the sky started to lose its brightness and a purple velvet dusk began to creep stealthily out of hiding.

The cypresses stood out, tall and dark and straight, against the deep blue sky, a myriad stars began to appear and gauzy-winged bats flitted around in the silky air.

'Night falls quickly here,' Zane remarked. Giving her a little intimate smile, he added with evident satisfaction, 'It's taken some planning, but I've been looking forward to this.'

'To what?' she asked sharply. Too sharply.

'To being on holiday.'

Of course. What else could he have meant?

Trying to sound more relaxed, she observed, 'Though it's nearly dark, it's still beautifully warm.'

'Yes, though at Severo, I'm pleased to say, we don't have the kind of intense heat and humidity that Florence can have, the kind that keeps you awake at night unless you have air-conditioning.'

Softly, he added, 'Here you can make love, then lie naked and comfortable in each other's arms…'

Her throat going dry at the intimate picture his words painted, she said the first thing that came into her head. 'I haven't seen the swimming pool you mentioned earlier…'

'It's a couple of levels below us and to the left. You can't see it from here because of the overhang. There's an open-air Jacuzzi too. Ever been in one?'

'No.'

After a drifting silence, he went on, 'It's really something to sit in a Jacuzzi under the stars when the fireflies are out and the moonlit air's still warm and scented with myrtle.'

She saw the gleam of his eyes in the deepening dusk as he added, 'If you've no inhibitions about taking off your clothes, we could try it later…'

Not on your life! she thought.

She had believed Paul when he'd assured her that Zane Lorenson never mixed business with pleasure.

But out here on the dusky terrace, the setting was far too romantic, and feeling the sexual tension that seemed to stretch between them like barbed wire—a tension she had been aware of all along but had refused to acknowledge—she wondered anxiously if Paul could have been wrong.

Though if Zane could have his pick of women, and she was sure he could, why should he have designs on her? Except that, apart from Maria, she was the only woman here, and therefore available.

Though surely if he had wanted a bedmate he could have brought one…?

'Unless, as it's been a somewhat tiring day, you'd prefer to have an early night?' Zane suggested.

Even as she answered hastily, 'Yes, actually I would,' she realized that his voice had sounded light, matter-of-fact, without the slightest hint of any undue intimacy.

But perhaps *she* was the only one to experience that strong sexual awareness? Maybe all the feeling was on her side and sprang from her memories of what had happened that evening so long ago?

All she knew for certain was that it was a great deal more powerful than anything she had yet experienced with the man she loved, and whose wife she was going to be.

But that didn't matter, she told herself firmly. It was just a basic sexual attraction, an animal instinct that had nothing to do with love, nothing to do with the kind of caring relationship that she and Paul shared.

The realization that she had hardly thought about Paul since that morning, when he'd probably spent all day worrying about her, made her feel guilty.

Though *would* he have been worried about her?

Of course he would, she assured herself quickly. He loved her and was going to marry her. He'd bought her a ring.

But if he *really* loved her, would he have pressured her into doing something he knew perfectly well she didn't want to do?

Even this morning, when he must have seen how very unhappy she was, his main concern had been that she should get the job so he could put his plan of revenge into action, rather than for her.

No, she mustn't start accusing Paul of not caring just because she was finding it so difficult to cope. All he knew about her past encounter with Zane was what she had chosen to tell him, so he couldn't be blamed for not realizing just how traumatic this would be for her.

Poor Paul. Feeling ashamed of her disloyal thoughts, she decided that at bedtime, as soon as everywhere was quiet, she would creep downstairs again and call him.

She never normally rang his home phone number. Early in their relationship he'd asked her not to, saying that if by any chance she couldn't get him on his mobile then he didn't want to be disturbed.

But this time, if he didn't answer his mobile, she would. No doubt he'd be eager to know what had happened to her, and just hearing his voice would make her feel more cheerful, more secure…

'Penny for them,' Zane said.

'Sorry?'

'I was offering you a penny for your thoughts.'

'They're worth much more than that.'

'I can well believe it. You were miles away. Would you like another drink?'

'No, I wouldn't, thank you,' she said rather primly.

'So how much for your thoughts?'

'They're not for sale.'

He raised a brow nonchalantly. 'It doesn't really matter. I'm pretty sure I can guess what they were.'

The possibility brought her heart into her mouth.

He smiled as if he knew. Then, taking her empty glass, he set it down and asked, 'Ready to eat?'

She rose with alacrity. The moment dinner was over she would plead tiredness and escape to bed.

They had just reached the French windows when, although there was no sign of the housekeeper, lights flashed on in both the house and on the terrace.

'A time switch,' Zane explained, catching sight of Gail's puzzled expression.

They crossed the living room and went through an archway to a spacious oak-beamed dining room with polished floor-boards and a stone fireplace.

Glancing around anxiously, she could find no sign of a phone, nor had she been able to locate one in the living room.

When she was seated at an elegant refectory table which was set for two, Zane took a seat opposite her and reached to pour the wine.

Waiting on a central hotplate was a selection of covered dishes and a pot of coffee.

It seemed they were to serve themselves.

Unsure of her role, what Zane would expect of his PA, she hesitated, then, indicating the dishes, began, 'Would you like me to…?'

He shook his head. 'As far as I'm concerned, you're a guest. At least until we get…shall I say…better acquainted.'

Unsure how to interpret that, but somewhat reassured by his manner, she allowed herself to be helped to a tasty-looking dish that he told her was Tuscan chicken with polenta.

While they ate, he talked about Tuscany and its culture

before asking lightly, 'If we do a spot of sightseeing tomorrow, which of the towns would you like to see first?'

Breathing a sigh of relief that they were to get out and about, she said, 'I don't really mind. I've always wanted to see Florence and Pisa and, of course, Siena, which I know hardly anything about.'

He smiled at her eagerness. 'It's rated as Italy's most perfect medieval city. And the shell-shaped Campo—where the horse race takes place—is acknowledged to be one of the most beautiful squares in the world.'

'Oh, yes, I've heard of the horse race.'

'It's called the Palio, and each of the city's three districts compete...'

Rather to Gail's surprise, she found that, despite all the stress, her usual healthy appetite was back and, put more or less at ease by the normality of the conversation, she was able to enjoy her meal.

The first course was followed by freshly stewed figs served in a rich golden syrup that tasted of herbs and vanilla and was topped with ricotta.

'That was delicious,' she said as she finished the last spoonful. 'I particularly enjoyed the syrup.'

He leant forward, wiping a drizzle of syrup from her lip. When she blushed and looked away he laughed. 'It's made from Strega, a popular Italian liqueur. Both the main course and the dessert are simple to make but, like a lot of countrywomen, Maria sticks with plain, wholesome food and is an excellent cook.'

As he cleared the dishes and poured coffee for them both, he went on, 'After being used to a farmhouse range, she found the kitchen here a little daunting but she's gradually getting used to it.

'Though when I come to the villa, after the first evening I usually cook for myself.'

Surprised, Gail asked, 'Do you enjoy cooking?'

'After weeks of nothing but business, I find it very relaxing.'

Curiously, she asked, 'Are you any good at it?'

His devilish smile made her heart race. 'I've been told so. But if you'd like to judge for yourself, I'll be happy to give you a demonstration.'

Rather belatedly becoming aware of the ambiguity of the question, she started to blush furiously.

He leaned forward and touched a finger to her hot cheek, making her jump and jerk her head back. 'In order to save your maidenly blushes,' he said mockingly, 'perhaps you should have phrased that query more carefully.'

Once again she could feel the sexual tension tightening, but this time a lick of flame in those heavy-lidded green eyes left her in no doubt whatsoever that the feeling was mutual.

Desperate to find something innocuous to talk about until she could escape to bed, she harked back. 'How long has the villa been here?'

'It was finished about eighteen months ago.'

'When you first decided to build here, did you have any trouble getting water or electricity laid on?'

Though a little smile tugged at his lips, he went along with it. 'No. If I hadn't wanted a pool, at a pinch we could have managed with our own generator and water pumped from the underground spring that rises part way down the hill.

'But luckily both services already passed quite close, so that was no problem and we were able to turn the spring into a cascade.'

Then, with that unnerving ability he seemed to have to know what was in her mind, he went on evenly, 'The one thing we've had any real delay on and the one thing we're still waiting for is to have a landline phone installed.'

Through stiff lips, she queried, 'Then you don't have any phones in the house?'

'No.' He reached to refill both their coffee cups, before adding, 'But these days, with the easy availability of mobiles, a landline is no longer quite so essential.'

'What about the Internet?'

He shrugged. 'As this is primarily a holiday place, I'm quite happy to leave the outside world behind whenever possible. My mobile is all I really need.'

Without meaning to and sounding accusing, she burst out, 'My mobile's disappeared.'

'Really?' He clicked his tongue. 'How annoying for you. But if there are any calls you want to make, you can always use mine.'

While he stood by and listened, no doubt, she thought bitterly.

As though she'd spoken the words aloud, he said quizzically, 'I presume you have nothing to hide?'

Rattled afresh, she decided it would be safer to ignore the question.

After struggling for some degree of equilibrium and finally finding it, she went on, 'You said you knew how you wanted the outside of the villa to look—did you design the inside too? Or was that left in the hands of your architect?'

With a glance that seemed to acknowledge her resilience, he said, 'My architect and I worked as a team. I told him what I wanted, and he told me how I could fit it in.'

She looked around at the spacious surroundings. 'Does that include rooms for the staff?'

He shook his head. 'When I made enquiries and found I could get all the help I needed locally—a housekeeper, an odd-job man, cleaners, gardeners and a couple of men to take care of the pool—I didn't plan for any permanent live-in staff.'

He stretched his legs out in front of him, perfectly at ease. 'You see, when I'm taking a break I don't like to feel con-

strained. The presence of staff—no matter how discreet—is
something I can well do without. I much prefer to have the
house to myself.

'If I want to sunbathe on the terrace or walk about without
any clothes on, I like freedom to do it. I don't want to have to
take into account the feelings of a housekeeper or a maid…'

Going hot all over, her throat dry, Gail asked, 'So Maria and
her son don't actually live at the villa?'

'No. Maria has a house in the village where she lives with
Angelo and her three younger boys.

'As I said earlier, she's turned out to be a treasure. She or-
ganizes the cleaners, the gardeners and the men who take care
of the pool and, when I'm not here, she comes up a couple of
times a week to air the place and keep an eye on things.'

'But she stays when you *are* here?'

He shook his head. 'No. Angelo brings her up each day on
the back of his scooter so she can spend an hour or so tidying
up or doing whatever happens to need doing.'

'Then there's no one else in the house?'

'Not a soul.' As the words rolled off his tongue his eyes held
that devilish glint she was so unnerved by. 'We're quite alone.'
Then, his gaze fixed on her face, he queried, 'Does that bother
you?'

Feeling trapped, her heart starting to beat in slow, heavy
thuds, she denied in a stifled voice, 'No, not at all.'

'You're lying,' he said with a wolfish grin. 'You're scared
out of your wits and you know it.'

Her fighting spirit aroused and determined to refute that
charge of abject fear, she demanded boldly, 'Why on earth
should I be scared?'

He looked as surprised as if a rabbit had turned and
growled at him and, feeling a sense of triumphant satisfaction,
she went on, 'So far as I'm aware, you're not a dangerous

lunatic or an axe-murderer. You're a well-to-do, reputable businessman.'

If she had expected him to appear deflated, she was wrong. Instead, with a little nod of approval, he saluted her courage and agreed, 'You're pretty much right on all three counts.'

She was just congratulating herself when, a half smile hanging on his lips, he asked softly, 'And you've no other concerns? You don't think you might be in any other kind of danger?'

'I don't know what you mean,' she lied.

'It doesn't bother you that we should be here all alone with so much sexual chemistry between us?'

'I don't agree that there *is* any sexual chemistry between us.' She tried hard to sound dismissive.

'Then why do you react the way you do if I so much as touch you?'

'Because, as you're my boss, any undue familiarity makes me feel uncomfortable.'

Though aware that she sounded unbearably prim and proper, she went on, 'I wouldn't have taken the job if I hadn't been assured that you never mix business with pleasure.'

He lifted a dark brow. 'Who told you that?'

Wishing she'd kept quiet, she said hastily, 'I really don't remember.'

'Surely the only person you discussed the job with was Mrs Rogers?'

'Then it must have been her.'

'I very much doubt it.'

A shade desperately, she asked, 'Does it matter who it was?'

'You mean, so long as it's the truth?'

She squirmed under the intensity of his gaze. 'Well...yes.'

'Would it worry you if it wasn't?'

'Yes, it would.'

'Why? With a mouth like that, I can't believe you're cold, and as you told me you no longer love your ex-boyfriend, and you've no current boyfriend to consider, what is there to prevent you from having a little fun?'

'That kind of fun isn't really my style,' she informed him coolly.

'Oh?' He raised a dark brow. 'You told me you'd been on holiday with a male friend.'

Rather than admit she'd lied, she pointed out, 'That was simply a holiday and he wasn't my boss.'

'And that makes a difference?'

'I don't believe in mixing business and pleasure.'

Then, knowing it was high time she got out of there, she added with what firmness she could muster, 'I didn't get a lot of sleep last night so, if you'll excuse me, I'd like to go to bed now.'

'Of course,' he agreed with formal politeness. 'Come along and I'll see you up.'

She hadn't expected him to give in so easily and it was a moment or two before she said with equal politeness, 'Please don't trouble.'

But, following close on her heels, he assured her, 'It's no trouble at all. As a matter of fact I could do with an early night myself.'

She was climbing the spiral stairs, very conscious of how near he was, terrified that he might touch her, when he went on, 'You said you don't believe in mixing business and pleasure. Is that because you disapprove in general or because you feel it might put you in an equivocal position?'

'Both.'

'So you're not the kind of woman who thinks it's a feather in her cap to sleep with the boss?'

'No, I'm not. As far as I'm concerned, I like my working relationships to be exactly that.'

His voice soft and seductive, he said, 'What if I were to tell you that I don't regard this as just a working relationship, that I was hoping it would be a great deal more?'

'You mean you want a holiday companion?'

'You could say that.'

Emboldened by the fact that she had almost reached her room, she retorted crisply, 'In that case I would suggest you go into the nearest town and find yourself one.'

Before she could take evasive action, he had backed her against the wall and put a hand either side of her head, effectively trapping her there.

As she stared up at him, her beautiful grey eyes looking too big for her face, he asked, 'Then you don't find me in the least attractive?'

'No…' Her voice was unsteady and, afraid of what he might read into that, she added for good measure, 'You leave me cold.'

'A brave try,' he congratulated her. 'But I could soon prove the opposite. The sexual tension between us is almost palpable. If I were to kiss you now, you'd go up like dry straw.'

Knowing there was nothing for it but to brazen it out, she swallowed hard and said, 'That's where you're wrong. I'm perfectly capable of controlling *my* sexual urges.'

'You're sure about that?'

'Quite sure.'

His voice as smooth as silk, he said, 'That's a shame—I like any woman I take to bed to be eager or, at the very least, willing.'

'Well, that lets me out as I'm neither.'

He sighed. 'How very disappointing.'

Hardly daring to believe she'd won, she was bracing herself for a further onslaught when, removing his hands and taking a step back, he added, 'Oh, well, in that case, I'll say goodnight.'

Lulled into a false sense of security, she relaxed a little and answered, 'Goodnight.'

As she finished speaking, his hands moved to cup her face and lift it to his and, leaning closer, so that she could feel the sweet warmth of his breath on her lips, he murmured, 'Perhaps just a goodnight kiss to show there's no hard feelings?'

The next instant she was in his arms and his mouth was covering hers.

The shock of it ran through her entire body, tying her stomach in knots, turning her legs to jelly and bringing every nerve-ending zinging into life.

An alarm bell sounding somewhere in her brain told her she should try and stop him, make it clear that she had meant what she'd said.

But she could no more have stopped him than someone dying of thirst in a desert could have refused a life-giving drink of water.

Finding no sign of resistance, he deepened the kiss, within seconds turning her into a quivering mass of longing incapable of coherent thought.

When her slender body grew limp and pliant in his arms his kiss become passionate and coaxing, asking for—*demanding*— a response.

Lost, mindless, unable to help herself, she responded with an ardour that matched and equalled his own.

Feeling that response, he swept her up in his arms like some conqueror and, carrying her into his bedroom, set her on her feet by the four-poster bed and stripped off her dress and sandals.

Then, while she stood in her dainty underwear, he took the pins from her hair and let the dark silky mass tumble round her shoulders, before slipping the ivory satin briefs down over her slender hips and reaching behind her to unfasten her bra.

Oblivious to her surroundings, aware of nothing but him and burning with impatience, she would have helped him but her hands were shaking too much.

When he had released the clip and eased the straps off her shoulders, he tossed the delicate scrap to one side.

As he stood back to admire her beautifully shaped breasts with their dusky pink nipples, he murmured, 'Well, well, well…' Reaching out, he took the gold chain and the ring that nestled in the warm hollow between them and lifted it over her head.

Dangling it between his finger and thumb, he commented, 'A pretty bauble, and one that looks very much like an engagement ring…'

She came down to earth with a bump, every last trace of colour draining from her face to leave it paper-white, before flowing back like a crimson tide.

Oh, dear God, what was she doing? About to let another man take her to bed when she had a fiancé who loved and trusted her.

Suddenly feeling naked and vulnerable and bitterly ashamed, she snatched up the discarded dress and held it in front of her to hide her nakedness.

Swinging the chain gently so that the diamonds in the ring flashed and sparkled in the light, Zane pursued, 'Why aren't you wearing it? No, silly question. You could hardly swear that you have no ties or commitments with that on your finger.

'So who's the lucky man?'

She half shook her head.

'I think you'd better tell me.'

Though the words were softly spoken and could hardly be construed as a threat, the grim look in his green eyes made her shiver.

Her voice a mere croak, she said, 'There's no one.'

'Don't try to tell me that this little trifle came out of a Christmas cracker.'

Gathering herself, she said, 'I wasn't going to.' Then, in desperation, she lied, 'As a matter of fact, Jason gave it to me.'

'The boyfriend you broke up with six months ago?'

'Yes.'

'You didn't mention you'd been engaged.'

'As we were no longer together it didn't seem relevant.'

'Who ended things?'

'I did.'

'Why?'

She had liked Jason but she hadn't loved him and, unwilling to sleep with him, she had grown weary of his persistent attempts to persuade her into bed.

But, reluctant to tell Zane that, she answered evasively, 'It just wasn't working out.'

'But you didn't give him back his ring?' he said, the weight of the ring resting in his palm.

'No.'

'I find that strange. I had you down as the kind of woman who would. You assured me you weren't lovelorn.'

'I'm not.'

'Then why are you still wearing his ring next to your heart?'

Too late she realized that she should have allowed him to believe not only that she was still carrying a torch for Jason, but that there was some hope of them getting back together.

Taking a deep breath, she said raggedly, 'I don't think that has anything to do with you.'

'You mean it's too personal?'

'Yes.'

He laughed mirthlessly. 'I would say we're already about as up close and personal as it's possible for two people to get.

'But, before I make love to you, I would like to know *why* you're still wearing another man's ring.'

'I don't want you to make love to me. It's all been a terrible mistake. I should never have let things go this far.'

'Why did you?' he asked interestedly.

'Because I… I…'

As she floundered, he drawled, 'Don't bother to think up any lies. You "let things go this far" because you couldn't help yourself. You wanted to go to bed with me.'

Backing towards the door, she shook her head. 'I told you, it was a terrible mistake.' Then, in desperation, 'I love P—' her lips were forming the word Paul when she pulled herself up short and hastily substituted '—Jason…'

'You may be wearing *Jason's* ring—' he put the name *Jason* in quotes '—but I doubt very much if you love him. You wanted to go to bed with me.'

Knowing it was useless to keep denying it, she said, 'It would have been just sex.'

'You mean any available man would have done?'

Still backing away, she said through dry lips, 'I was missing Jason…'

Following her, he suggested silkily, 'Well, let's see what kind of substitute I make.'

'No,' she whispered. 'I can't be…'

'Unfaithful to *Jason?*' Once again he put the name in quotes. 'Yes.'

'But you can't call it being unfaithful when it's all over between you and he's been out of your life for six months.'

Trapped, knowing her only option was flight, she tried to open the door but, reaching out a hand, he held it shut.

'I want to leave,' she cried.

'Wouldn't you like this back first?' He held up the ring on its thin gold chain.

Momentarily distracted, she paused, but, instead of giving it back, he slipped the ring into the pocket of his trousers and took her wrist lightly.

'Please, Zane,' she begged shakily, 'let me go.'

'That's the first time you've called me by my Christian name,' he remarked softly.

Ignoring that, she whispered without much conviction in her voice, 'I want to leave.'

He looked down at her. 'I think you want what I want…'

Her wide eyes blinked up at him as his words held her, daring her to hear more. He murmured softly, 'I want to make long, delectable love to you, to explore that beautiful body and drive you wild with pleasure.

'I want to stroke my hands over you—your waist, your hips, your thighs, to find your hidden warmth and sweetness…'

His erotic words made her shudder even before he suited the action to the words.

'I want to bury my face against your breasts and take first one and then the other of those velvety nipples into my mouth…'

The warmth and wetness of his mouth, the slight roughness of his tongue, the delightful sensations his suckling was arousing, drove all thoughts of Paul out of her head and brought the desire she had thought dead surging back to life.

Removing the dress from her nerveless fingers, he tossed it aside. Then, lifting her in his arms, he carried her over to the bed. Held in thrall, she lay mindless, just a quivering mass of sensations, while he brought her to a fever pitch of wanting and skilfully kept her there.

She was making soft little sounds in her throat—inarticulate murmurs—before he left her for a moment to strip off his own clothes.

Naked in his turn, he stretched out beside her and with his hands and mouth resumed the exquisite torment until, unable to stand it a moment longer, she begged hoarsely, 'Oh, please, Zane…'

'Do you want me to make love to you?'

'Yes,' she whispered.

'Quite sure?'

'Yes.'

When he relented and moved over her, she welcomed his weight with pleasure, his masculine scent and warmth, the feel of his flesh against hers, the sheer *maleness* of him.

His first strong thrust caused an explosion of feeling that made her cry out and sent her tumbling and spinning into a vortex of pleasure so strong that all she could do was cling to him as though he was life itself.

Though the craving for him might have been subconscious, she had waited so many long years for this moment.

CHAPTER SEVEN

AFTER her cry, Zane had stayed quite still, his supple body poised over hers, but now he kissed her gently and began to move again, slowly, carefully, re-kindling the spark of desire she had thought, dazed and confused by the intensity of passion she'd felt when he'd entered her, could never reach more incredible heights.

His love-making was controlled and skilful—he knew how to hold back, how to wait, and he was a truly generous lover who put his partner first and gave more than he took.

And this time, though passionate, he was tender, caring, he whispered how beautiful she was, how soft and feminine, how much she delighted him.

Then, in unison, they boarded a sky-rocket to the stars and snatched a moment of supreme pleasure before drifting back to earth.

When their breathing and heart-rate returned to normal, instead of turning away, as she had half expected, he began to use his hands and mouth to take her on yet another sensual journey of pleasure.

Each time she thought she was totally sated and could feel no more, he found new ways to give her fresh delight.

At long last, when she was a limp, quivering mass of sensations, he gathered her close and, settling her so that her head was on his shoulder and his body was half supporting hers, pulled up the thin coverlet.

Almost at once, she was fast asleep.

When she awoke it was to instant and complete remembrance of everything that had happened.

There wasn't a sound apart from Zane's light, even breathing and, afraid of disturbing him, she remained quite still, hardly daring to breathe.

She was lying in the crook of his arm, her head pillowed comfortably on his shoulder. One hand was spread palm down on his bare tanned chest and she could feel the length of one hair-roughened leg against the smoothness of her own.

She couldn't see her watch but, judging by the pale light filtering through the window, it was not long after dawn.

While her entire body was as sleek and sleepily contented as a well-fed cat, her mind was wide awake and seething with a kaleidoscope of emotions.

Although Zane had given her the utmost delight, she felt sad and angry with herself, deeply ashamed of the way she had acted.

Having agreed to marry Paul and accepted his ring, how could she have behaved so wantonly, and with a man who not only didn't love her but who didn't even seem to like her?

The answer was that she had been in thrall, unable to help herself.

To him, she had been simply a woman who was there and available, a woman he scarcely knew, someone who meant less than nothing to him, while he had been part of her life for seven years, lodged in her heart and mind.

In all those long weary years since she had first met and fallen in love with him and experienced sex for the first time, she had never been tempted to sleep with any other man.

It was almost as if he had taken her over, body and soul, making it impossible for her to even consider going to bed with anyone else.

Though she had fallen for Paul, she had been secretly relieved when he had shown no sign of wanting to make love to her. But when he had eventually proposed to her, tired of being alone, wanting a home and a family, she had snatched at the chance of happiness, telling herself stoutly that when the time came everything would be all right.

However, in spite of her attempt to be confident, the doubt had lingered like a dark shadow at the back of her mind.

Until tonight.

Tonight had proved she was far from frigid and for that, at least, she should be thankful. She knew now, beyond a shadow of doubt, that she could make Paul a loving and re-sponsive wife.

That was, if he still wanted her when she told him what had happened.

Just the thought of having to tell him tied her insides in knots, but she couldn't go into marriage with something like this on her conscience, so she would have to.

But how *could* she tell him that she'd gone to bed with Zane Lorenson?

Had it been anyone else, he might have found it in his heart to forgive her, but the mere fact that it was his hated rival would be adding insult to injury.

Though if it *had* been anyone else, she would never have succumbed in the first place. The only man in the world who could have made her react that way was Zane.

Zane, whom she had loved at first sight, with an overwhelm-ing, life-changing love, the kind of love that could move heaven and earth.

Zane whom, in spite of the way he had treated her, she still loved and would continue to love while ever there was breath in her body.

Was it possible to love two men?

But, even as she asked herself the question, she knew with certainty that what she had felt for Paul had been mere infatuation.

She could only thank her lucky stars that her eyes had been opened in time to prevent her from marrying a man she didn't love and—after the callous way he had treated David Randall—she could no longer really like or respect.

She recognized now that the dazzling dream of a home, a family of her own and a happy-ever-after future had blinded her both to his faults and to her true feelings.

But while there was absolutely no chance of a home and a family—any kind of a future—with Zane, she could no more stop loving him than she could voluntarily stop breathing.

Which gave her no choice but to remain solitary. *One is one and all alone and ever more shall be so...*

If only their paths hadn't crossed for a second time it wouldn't have been so hard. But now, having lain with him, having experienced at least the illusion of what it would be like to be loved by him, how could she go on? How could she live the rest of her life without him?

The cold voice of reason pointed out that she had lived without him for the past seven years and, given no choice, could doubtless continue to do so.

What she couldn't—*wouldn't*—do was become his plaything, to be used and discarded as soon as the holiday was over. That would destroy her.

But, if she stayed here, she had about as much chance of holding out against him as she had of winning the lottery without buying a ticket. And while he still wanted her, he wouldn't let her go voluntarily, she was quite sure of that.

Which meant that she had to escape. Now, this minute. Before he awoke.

If only she could locate the keys and borrow the car they had driven up in. That would give her a chance to put some distance between them and it would prevent Zane from following her...

But then what could she do? Where could she go?

After a moment's thought she dismissed the idea of going to the villa where Captain Giardino was staying and asking for his help. It would be too awkward and embarrassing for all concerned.

No, she would be better off heading for the nearest airport. Though she had no euros and only a very small amount of English money, she had her credit card, which would enable her to buy petrol and a plane ticket home.

Her mind made up, she began to edge away from him inch by inch. Sleep had loosened his hold and she was able to ease herself free without disturbing him.

Slipping out of the big four-poster bed, her bare feet silent on the deep pile carpet, she gathered up her clothes and pulled them on.

She had just picked up her sandals when all at once he made a sound like a soft sigh and moved a little, making her throat go desert dry.

Rooted to the spot, she stood quite still, watching his face. The tough, sophisticated man of the world was gone. With his thick hair rumpled, his mocking eyes closed, the long lashes making dark fans on his cheeks, his jaw rough with stubble and his strong mouth relaxed in sleep, he looked boyishly handsome.

She longed to touch him, to kiss his lips one last time, but that would be madness.

Bands of iron seemed to tighten around her heart. How could she bear to leave him when, for the next two weeks at least, she could be with him, getting to know him, watching his face, listening to his voice, spending the nights in his arms…

But at what cost?

No, she *had* to go. That way she could at least keep the remnants of her pride and self-respect.

All she would have to do when she reached London was to contact his office and say she wouldn't be taking the job after all.

He need never know who she really was, or why she had applied for the position; he could get another PA and forget all about her.

Her sandals in one hand, she crossed the room and let herself out. As she closed the door, the loud click of the latch made her wince.

She had taken just a step or two when, with a nasty jolt, she remembered the ring, and Zane slipping it into the right-hand pocket of his trousers.

She couldn't leave without Paul's ring. It was worth a small fortune and, having let him down in every other way, she *had* to return that safely.

Leaving her sandals in the passageway, she crept back into the bedroom and crossed to where Zane's trousers had been tossed casually over a chair.

As she picked them up and slid her hand into the pocket, the rattle of loose change sounded loud in the stillness.

Her heart in her mouth, she glanced at him. His eyes were still closed and he showed no sign of having been disturbed.

Breathing a sigh of relief, she carefully removed the chain and ring and replaced the trousers before quietly leaving the room once more.

Picking up her sandals, she hurried along to her own room. She would have liked to stay to brush her teeth and shower and do something with her hair, but it was too big a risk.

As was packing her clothes.

Already the sun was coming up and Zane might wake at any moment.

Having tossed aside the high-heeled sandals, which would be useless to drive in, she dropped the chain and ring into her handbag, slipped into a pair of flat-heeled shoes and gathered up her jacket.

The only other things she really needed were her passport and the car keys.

Zane had put her passport into his briefcase and the last time she had seen that was when they had first arrived and he had vanished into his study carrying it.

She hadn't a clue what he'd done with the car keys. Hopefully, he would have left them either in the ignition or in his study.

If he hadn't, she would have a problem.

To say the least.

But, as being able to get away depended on having the car, somehow she would *have* to find them.

Taking the main staircase, she hastened down to the hall and opened the door of his study.

It was a big, high-ceilinged room with book-lined walls and a handsome fireplace. To one side was a well-equipped office area and, to her great relief, Zane's briefcase was lying on the desk.

It was unlocked.

Her heart beating nineteen to the dozen, she opened it and, taking out her passport, thrust it quickly into her shoulder bag.

There was no sign of the car keys, so she could only hope that they were still in the ignition.

Everywhere was quiet as she hurried across the hall and let herself out into the rear courtyard. She was attempting to close the heavy door quietly when it slipped from her fingers and shut with a bang that sounded like a thunderclap in the silence and brought her heart into her mouth.

Almost immediately, another shock rocked her. The court-yard was empty. The car was gone.

But Zane had mentioned garages, so no doubt either he or Angelo had put it away.

Making an effort to rally herself, she looked around. At the far end of the cobbled area she could see the wide doors of a pair of garages.

Suppose they were locked?

Though why would they be? No one seemed to bother locking doors in this isolated place.

The first one she reached swung up and over easily at her touch and there was the white car, its top still down.

Hurrying into the garage, which seemed a bit dim after the brightness of the courtyard, she peered into the car.

Her heart plummeted. The ignition was empty.

As she stood wondering what to do for the best, the brush of a footfall and a change in the light made her spin round.

Zane stood in the doorway.

His jaw was still rough with morning stubble and his hair was rumpled. He was wearing casual trousers and a white open-necked shirt only partially buttoned, as though he had dressed in a hurry.

But his manner was easy, laid-back as, holding up the car keys, he drawled, 'Looking for these?'

Her heart thudding against her ribs like a triphammer, she stammered, 'H-how did you…?'

'Know what you were up to?' He smiled slightly. 'I heard the latch click when you closed the bedroom door. I was just about to get up and carry you back to bed when you came back of your own accord and started to go through my trouser pockets.'

His voice caustic, he added, 'I'd always understood that that was a wife's prerogative.'

Flushing hotly, she said, 'Normally I wouldn't have done such a thing, only you'd taken my ring and I wanted it back.'

'There you have a point. And you could hardly leave without it, could you…?'

The way he spoke, almost as if he knew the truth, sent a chill through her, and she had to remind herself that her own guilty conscience was apt to make her imagine things.

'Even though you didn't stop to pack your things,' he went on sardonically, 'as you went to the trouble of retrieving your passport, I presume you *were* intending to leave, not simply to take an early morning drive?'

She made no effort to answer and after a moment he pursued, 'Just as a matter of interest, what exactly were you planning to do?'

When she remained silent, his eyes on her face, he went on, 'I presume that in the cold light of day you regretted what happened last night?'

'Yes, I did.'

'So, at a guess, you were planning to see Carlo—who not only has a chivalrous nature but speaks excellent English—and tell him I'd turned into a Big Bad Wolf—'

Flicked on the raw, she lifted her chin and cried angrily, 'I was going to do no such thing!'

'No?'

'No!'

'Why not?'

'Because it wouldn't have been true. You…' Her voice shook so much she was forced to stop. But after a moment she went on bravely, 'You didn't force yourself on me.'

'Thank you… But you *were* planning to appeal to him for help?'

'I most certainly wasn't! It would have been far too awkward and embarrassing for everyone concerned.'

His glance holding a touch of respect, he asked, 'So what *were* you going to do?'

'I was hoping to drive to the nearest airport and get a plane back to London.'

'Dear me, homesick already?' he mocked. 'And I thought you wanted to come to Tuscany.'

Through gritted teeth, she said, 'I didn't want to come to Tuscany. As a matter of fact, I didn't want to go *anywhere* with you.'

He pounced. 'But you knew perfectly well there was travelling involved before you took the job.'

Having no answer to that, she said defensively, 'I should never have taken it. This whole thing has been a mistake from the start and I want to leave.'

'Why? It can't be the job itself. We haven't even started work yet. And you were honest enough to admit that last night I didn't force myself on you.

'In fact, if you're being *totally* honest, you'll admit that you wanted me just as much as I wanted you…'

She longed to shake his certainty, to swear she hadn't, but no matter how she tried she couldn't bring herself to frame the lie.

'That being so,' he went on, 'I think you should reconsider. After all, we haven't even been here a full day yet. You've given yourself no time to adjust.

'And if you really don't want to share my bed, all you have to do is say *no,* and mean it. When it comes to personal matters, it's your decision.'

She was just assimilating that when he added wickedly, 'Though if I don't agree with that decision, I reserve the right to try a little friendly persuasion.'

The devilish gleam in his eye and the crooked smile that put grooves beside his mouth made him practically irresistible.

She was shaken to the core by the temptation to stay, to have just a few more days in his company. But if she stayed she couldn't trust herself to say no and mean it, so for the sake of her pride she *had* to go.

Though was she making a big mistake in putting her pride first? He was the only man in the world for her and she wanted to be in his bed, in his arms, feel his naked flesh next to hers, enjoy the weight of his body, revel in his maleness.

This would be her only chance to snatch a little, all too brief, happiness.

But could she be happy, knowing that to him it would be just a casual exchange of pleasure, while to her it would be mortgaging her soul?

How could she bear the pain of meaning nothing to him while he meant everything to her? And when this 'holiday' was over and he'd had his fun, she would be left alone and desolate.

'I don't want time to adjust,' she told him sharply. 'I'm going back to London.'

He shook his head. 'I think not. At least not until I'm ready to take you.'

'You can't keep me here against my will.'

'Want to bet?' he asked laconically, and watched her beautiful grey eyes widen.

'Now, can I suggest that we go back inside and act like civilized people?'

'Your behaviour is anything but civilized,' she cried jerkily. 'If you were half civilized you wouldn't be keeping me a prisoner.'

He smiled as if genuinely amused. 'You do have an over-developed sense of the melodramatic.'

'Well, what else would you call it?'

'Hardly "keeping you a prisoner". If you're looking forward to the excitement of being chained up in a dungeon, I'm afraid you're going to be sadly disappointed. I was thinking rather more mundanely of having some coffee and a shower before breakfast.'

Although the thought of a coffee and a shower was extremely tempting, reluctant to give in and go back with him, she hesitated.

But what was the use of continuing to resist? Where would it get her? There was no way she could win. He was so much stronger than she was, both physically and when it came to will-power.

As, with an inward sigh, she gave in and turned to accompany him, she heard his soft laugh and guessed he had been following her train of thought with his usual deadly accuracy.

Swinging the garage door into place, he put a proprietorial arm round her waist.

Angered by his amusement, his ability to walk in and out of her mind, and even more by the casual arrogance of his touch, she made an attempt to pull free but he wouldn't allow it.

Recognizing that he'd thrown down the gauntlet and knowing she was in no position to pick it up, she stared at him stonily.

Looking at her set face, he said, 'On second thoughts, as I hate to disappoint a lady, if you're fancying a spot of melo-drama, here goes…'

He gave a villainous laugh and declaimed, 'Ha ha, me proud beauty, at last I have you in my clutches to do with as I will!'

She was surprised into laughter by his clowning. Laughter that instantly relieved the tension and lightened the mood.

'That's better,' he said with satisfaction. 'Now, shall we go and have that coffee?'

Her resistance temporarily at an end, she allowed him to shepherd her into the house and up the stairs she had crept down only a short time ago.

One flight up, he led her along a wide corridor and through a doorway into an attractively furnished morning room with French windows that opened on to a sunny terrace.

While he switched on the coffee-making machine and produced cups, installed in one of the armchairs, Gail made an effort to order her thoughts. But it was like trying to order motes dancing in the air and she gave up.

As the machine hummed and the appetising smell of coffee began to fill her nostrils, she watched him, letting her thoughts drift.

If the keys had been in the car she would have been gone by now, out of his life, this little episode finished. Over.

But, though it had been traumatic in a lot of ways, part of her hadn't wanted it to end, and that part was treacherously happy to be still here, to be near him, to be able to just watch him.

All his movements had an easy, coordinated grace and he was beautiful, with a wholly masculine beauty. It was a pleasure to be able to sit and feast her eyes on him while he was occupied and totally unaware of her scrutiny.

He glanced up suddenly and, afraid of what he might read in her eyes, she looked hastily away.

Carrying the tray over, he set it down on a small oblong table and handed her a cup before taking his seat opposite her.

While they drank their coffee, which was hot and strong and fragrant, Gail avoided looking at him. But all the time she was aware that he studied her contemplatively as though, having kept her here against her will, he was wondering how to play it.

Though *why* had he kept her here? It wasn't the way any ordinary businessman would treat an employee who insisted on leaving.

But then nothing about their brief association had been ordinary.

And surely it wasn't simply because he wanted her in his bed when, with his looks and charisma—not to mention his money—he would have no trouble finding plenty of willing, not to say eager, women...

He broke into her thoughts to ask politely, 'Would you like any more coffee?'

Shaking her head, she answered with equal politeness, 'No, thank you.'

He rose and, having put their empty cups on the tray, took both her hands and pulled her to her feet, before handing her her bag and jacket. 'Then let's go and have that shower.'

They climbed the spiral staircase up to the next floor without speaking but, when he would have taken her into the master bedroom, she dug her heels in and protested, 'I don't know what you've got in mind, but if you think—'

His voice innocent, he said, 'I thought we'd agreed on a shower?'

'This is *your* room.'

'It's *our* room,' he corrected her.

Our room... Her heart gave a little lurch.

Taking a deep breath and holding tightly to her resolve not to become just a holiday plaything, she said as evenly as possible, 'A short while ago you told me that when it comes to personal matters it's my decision.'

'That's right. So?'

'So I don't want to share your room. Or your bed. I don't want to stay here at all.'

Those clear, dark green eyes smiled into hers. Then, brushing back her long fall of dark hair and nuzzling his bristly face against the side of her neck, he reminded her, 'But I also said that if I don't agree with that decision I reserve the right to try and change your mind.'

'You're wasting your time; I won't change my...' She

faltered to a halt, distracted by the way his mouth was exploring the tender juncture where neck met shoulder.

Ignoring her half formed protest, he suggested, 'Suppose we start by sharing a shower?'

'I don't want to share a shower,' she croaked.

'Why not?' He nibbled his way back to her ear, making shivers run up and down her spine. 'It can be quite exhilarating. We'll soap each other and see who has the most fun.'

Trying to ignore a *frisson* of heated excitement that ran along her nerve-endings, she said severely, 'I didn't come here to have fun. I came to work.'

His lips following the pure line of her jaw, he murmured, 'Why so eager to start work? This is a holiday first and foremost.'

Planting soft baby kisses on her cheeks and temples, her closed eyelids, he coaxed, 'Try letting your hair down. You have no ties, no man in your life…'

Now she had realized that she'd never really loved Paul and had decided to give him back his ring, that was true as far as it went.

But while he *thought* she was his fiancée, *thought* she was still loyal to him, how could she betray him further by deliberately involving herself with a man he hated?

The answer was that she couldn't.

But Zane was going on softly, 'And, beneath that air of unworldly innocence, you're a responsive, passionate woman who's a delight to make love to. A woman who needs a man…'

Clinging to her principles like someone drowning clung to a straw, she said desperately, 'I'm not the kind to have affairs, or to sleep with the boss. I don't want to lose my pride, my self respect…'

'You gave them into my keeping when you slept in my bed last night,' Zane said, dropping a kiss at the corner of her mouth, 'so I can't see you've anything to lose.'

He was right, of course. If she'd valued her pride and self-respect all that much, she wouldn't have acted as she had.

But somehow, the fact that he had said '*you gave them into my keeping*', rather than *you lost them* made all the difference.

He felt the tension, the resistance, drain away and, as he continued with those teasing kisses, he whispered, 'Will it really be such a hardship to stay? To share my room and my bed?'

It would be no hardship at all. Even though he didn't love her, it would mean being as close to heaven as she was ever likely to be while she was still on earth.

But even that thought was lost as he finally claimed her mouth and deepened the kiss.

When he finally lifted his head and led her through to his bathroom she went willingly, anticipation making her heart beat like a drum and turning the blood running through her veins into molten lava.

Turning on the shower, he quickly stripped off first her clothes and then his own and, taking her hand, stepped beneath the flow of water.

Indicating a bottle of shower gel, he said teasingly, 'Your turn first.'

Hoping he would put her rising colour down to the warmth of the water, she squeezed the pine-scented gel into her palms.

His dark hair flattened seal-like to his head, water running down his face and muscular body, he stood there at his ease, giving her no help.

Keeping her eyes firmly fixed on the tanned column of his throat, she began to smooth the gel over his broad, glistening shoulders and chest, his ribcage and his lean waist.

When she came to his flat belly, she hesitated.

She heard his soft laugh before he said mockingly, 'If you feel a maidenly reluctance to go any further, I'll quite understand.'

Blushing furiously now, but at the same time longing to look at him, to touch him, she made an effort to shrug off her inhibitions.

Though their relationship was fated to be just a short one, why allow false modesty to stand in her way? He was her one and only love. The only man she had ever wanted. The only man she *would* ever want.

Lowering her gaze for the first time and glorying in his sheer maleness, she proved that any maidenly reluctance she might have felt had, temporarily at least, vanished.

Her light touch had a powerful effect and after a moment or two he caught her wrists and, holding her hands away from him, told her huskily, 'My turn now.'

Daring, for the first time, to tease him, she said, 'Can't take it, huh?'

Surprised into laugher in his turn, he said, 'Sassy, eh?'

Releasing her hands, he bent to lick drops of water from her pink nipples before soaping her slender body with a thoroughness that made every nerve-ending zing into life and sent her pulses racing madly.

Then, lifting her, his hands cupping her buttocks, he said in her ear, 'Put your arms round my neck and wrap your legs round me…'

CHAPTER EIGHT

WHILE the water cascaded down and the scented steam rose around them, he made long, delectable love to her, leaving her limp and quivering with pleasure.

As soon as their breathing and heart rate had returned to normal he switched off the water and, handing her out, wrapped her in a fluffy bath sheet before rubbing first her dripping hair and then, more cursorily, his own.

When, a towel draped around his lean hips, he had leisurely dried and kissed every inch of her, he helped her into a white towelling bathrobe and tied the belt around her slender waist.

Rather than regretting what she'd done, she was floating on cloud nine, and she could only be glad that she had chosen to ignore her pride and follow her heart.

An ardent and passionate lover, he had treated her as though she was precious to him, making it hard to believe that in reality he didn't care, that she meant less than nothing to him.

In fact his tenderness towards her had given her hope that it was more than just sex, that he might come to care.

They seemed to be on the same wavelength, share a closeness. Several times she had turned to look at him, only to find him turning to look at her at the very same moment.

The robe was one of his and it swamped her, coming down

almost to her ankles, the sleeves hanging over her hands, yet it felt right and she was happy wearing it.

As, her hair in a damp tangle around her shoulders, she began to roll up the sleeves, he smiled and suggested, 'There's plenty of space left in the wardrobe and the drawers, so don't you think it might be a good idea to transfer your belongings?'

She nodded and, the small commitment made, felt a thrill of excited happiness. *Our room...*

Her reward was a kiss and then, as if he couldn't get enough of her, another. 'In that case, if you'd like to go and get organized while I brush my teeth and shave...?'

When she had picked up her discarded clothes and put them in the laundry basket, she reluctantly went.

Loving him as she did, every second in his company, every new thing, was precious to her, and if she hadn't been afraid of what he might read into it, she would have lingered to watch him shave.

Telling herself that she was behaving like some lovesick adolescent rather than a twenty-four-year-old businesswoman, she cleaned her teeth and brushed her hair, before dressing in a summery skirt and top and pulling on a pair of sandals.

Leaving her face innocent of make-up and her dark hair loose around her shoulders, she gathered together her belongings and put them in neat piles on the un-slept-in bed.

When she started to transfer them to the big airy bedroom next door, she found both that and the bathroom were empty. Zane was obviously downstairs preparing breakfast.

As he had said, there was plenty of space in the walk-in wardrobe and the tall chest of drawers and it didn't take long to put everything neatly away. That done, she made her way downstairs to find him.

As she had surmised, he was in the kitchen, which lay

between the dining room and the morning room. Wearing smart casual trousers and a silk open-necked shirt, a tea towel draped around his lean hips, he was turning sizzling bacon in a pan.

Glancing up, he invited, 'Come here.'

She went obediently.

He tilted her face with his free hand and studied her for a moment, before telling her, 'You're the only woman I know who can look even more beautiful and sexy with no make-up and a shiny nose.'

Bending his dark head, he kissed her mouth—a lingering kiss, a lover's kiss, that made her heart lurch drunkenly and opened up a Pandora's box of hopes and dreams.

If only he loved her, if only they were a real couple, sharing a real holiday...

But, recalling what his ex-PA had said about women having no real place in his life, she knew it was useless to hope that he might ever come to care for her.

Yet, even while she admitted that it was like crying for the moon because she wanted it so very much, she couldn't kill that faint hope.

And, no matter what, she had to be thankful that, for the next couple of weeks, she had the chance to be with him, to spend the days in his company and the nights in his arms...

Transferring his attention back to the pan, he said, 'Help yourself to some juice... I trust you like bacon and eggs?'

Taking a glass of freshly squeezed orange juice, she answered lightly, 'Who doesn't? Though at home I usually only have toast and coffee.'

'Well, as this kind of holiday can be...shall we say... strenuous...you might need to keep your strength up.'

Feeling herself start to blush, she looked around the vast farmhouse kitchen while she sipped the cool, tangy juice.

The decor was off-white and burnt ochre and the floor was

made of wide planks of softly glowing wood. Two massive dressers displaying colourful pottery flanked a farmhouse table.

Set between long windows was a wood-burning range and, in front of it, a low sturdy coffee table and a couple of comfortable-looking armchairs stood on a hand-crafted rug.

An electric cooker, a fridge-freezer and all mod cons had been cleverly blended in without detracting from its overall rustic appeal.

'Like it?' he queried.

'Yes, I do. It's attractive and homely. Absolutely perfect for this place.'

'I'm glad you think so. Apart from the fact that it wouldn't have fitted in, I don't really care for the purely-functional-glass-and-chrome-type kitchens.

'If I'm on my own and the weather isn't too good, I often eat in here.'

Taking the dishes of crisp bacon and scrambled eggs, he added, 'But today, as it's so beautiful and sunny, I suggest we eat on the morning room terrace.'

Sitting in the sun, they ate a leisurely breakfast and were at the coffee stage before Zane broke the companionable silence to ask, 'What would you like to do today?'

'I really don't mind. I'm happy to do anything you want to do.'

'What if we have a relaxing hour by the pool, then go to Florence for lunch and spend the rest of the afternoon sight-seeing?'

'If we have an hour by the pool, can we get to Florence in time for lunch?'

'We can if we go by helicopter. I have one at the airfield. It's useful for shorter hops and being able to land almost anywhere makes it ideal.'

Of course. She still hadn't totally caught up with the fact that he was a wealthy man who had the means to order his life exactly how he wanted it.

'So what do you think?'

'It sounds just perfect.'

Smiling at her enthusiasm, he got up and, taking her hands, pulled her to her feet. 'Then let's make a start by having that swim.'

'I'd love to, but I haven't got a costume.'

'That isn't a problem; we can go skinny-dipping. The pool area isn't directly overlooked, so unless someone came down specially…'

Amused by her horrified expression, he added, 'Of course, if you really don't like the idea I'm sure I could dig out a costume for you.'

Breathing a sigh of relief, she said gratefully, 'If you could…'

Hand in hand, they made their way downstairs and across the hall. As they reached the rear courtyard they heard the buzz of a motor scooter approaching and a moment later Angelo appeared with his mother on the pillion seat.

Dismounting nimbly, Maria gave them both a beaming smile. '*Buon giorno,* Signor Lorenson… Signorina…'

Returning the smile, Gail said, '*Buon giorno.*'

'*Buon giorno,*' Zane followed suit and crossed to have a few words with the housekeeper before rejoining Gail and escorting her to a flight of stone steps that curved down the hillside.

When they reached the bottom, she saw that the pool was large, almost Olympic size, and its blue waters looked extremely inviting.

As he had said, the pool area was surrounded by trees and shrubs and was pleasantly secluded. A scattering of sunbeds and loungers were interspersed with umbrella-shaded tables.

At one side, next to a vine-covered arbour, there were two

small white changing cabins which, he told her, had been erected mainly for the convenience of any possible visitors.

He led her into the nearest one, which had a bench running round it, a storage area for clothes, a long cupboard with a mirror and a shower cubicle.

Having rummaged about in the cupboard, which was stacked with towels, towelling robes and various toiletries, he produced a black one-piece swimsuit and a bright yellow bikini.

Putting them on the bench, he said casually, 'Andrea's about your size, so either of these should fit.' Dropping a light kiss on her mouth, he went to get changed.

Andrea... Presumably one of the women he had brought here previously. Gail experienced a swift, painful pang of jealousy.

Though what was the point of being jealous of a woman who presumably belonged in the past? Where, if he ran true to form, in a couple of weeks' time she too would belong.

The depressing thought enveloped her like a dark cloud shutting out the sun.

But if she only had a couple of weeks, what was the point of wasting them being miserable?

As she made an effort to recapture her earlier, more optimistic mood, her old school motto sprang into her mind. *Carpe diem...* Seize the day.

Yes, better by far to try and be happy and enjoy each day to the full than worry about the future.

Running an eye over the costumes Zane had produced, she immediately discarded the minuscule bikini in favour of the more modest black one-piece.

Only when she had it on she discovered that, cut high at the thighs and low at the back and the bust, it wasn't modest at all.

Staring at herself in the mirror, she almost gasped. Though for some years she had regarded her figure as quite reasonable, in the designer swimsuit it was spectacular—the style emphasising her slim waist, the curve of her hips, her generous bust and long slender legs.

Was this how Zane had seen her when he'd described her as beautiful?

Feeling shy, in spite of all that had happened, she ventured forth to find that a couple of towelling robes had been tossed over a chair and he was already in the pool.

Wearing black trunks, he was cleaving the water in a leisurely, graceful crawl without a splash and hardly seeming to breathe.

She stood watching him until, about to make a turn, he spotted her and heaved himself out.

Water streaming from him, he stood and stared at her, then said huskily, 'If by any chance you've changed your mind about having a swim, I can think of something better to do.'

Though very much tempted, she managed to say, 'No, I haven't changed my mind.'

Grinning at her prim tone, he said, 'Pity… Come on, then, I'll race you to the other end and back. The winner can claim a kiss.'

'I'm out of practice.'

'I'll give you a start.'

Very conscious that he was watching, she dived in and, knowing that it had been a good, clean dive, set off at a fast racing crawl.

Though, during her last year at school she had represented her house at all the swimming galas, she hadn't swum for years and knew quite well that, even giving her a start, he could easily beat her.

Still, she was determined to give him a run for his money and was halfway down the pool when he caught up and kept pace with her.

They turned in unison and set off back.

She touched first.

Surfacing by her side, he stood up and shook the water out of his eyes, then gravely offered her his pursed lips.

She was forced to stifle a laugh before saying accusingly, 'You let me win.'

'Does it really matter who kisses who?' he asked.

'Suppose I don't want to claim a kiss?'

Pulling her close, he threatened, 'If you don't collect your winnings I shall be forced to declare the race null and void and insist on a rerun.'

'Oh, well, in that case...'

She stood on tiptoe to kiss him. He had just deepened the kiss when the sharp click of approaching footsteps made them both look up.

Walking towards them was a stunning blonde with a model-girl figure, wearing high heels and a silk designer suit patterned in peacock shades of blue and green and purple.

Judging by her expression, she had seen what had taken place. But, quickly masking the look of jealous anger, she smiled at Zane and called, '*Caio, caro.*'

His face impassive, he answered, '*Caio,* Andrea.'

So this beautiful woman, who reminded her sharply of Rona, was Andrea.

Heaving himself out of the water, Zane turned to offer Gail his hands.

But, feeling a tightness round her heart and a hollow emptiness in the pit of her stomach, she had turned away and was swimming towards the steps.

By the time she reached them, he was waiting to help her out.

As he straightened, the blonde threw her arms around his neck and, pressing herself against him, kissed him full on the lips before bursting into a flood of Italian.

'Careful—' unwinding her arms, he held her away a little '—you'll get saturated…'

Making a little moue, she took a step back and said something, to which Zane answered, 'Not at all,' before holding out one of the towelling robes for Gail to put on and shrugging into his own.

Then, formally, he introduced the two women. 'Gail, this is Signorina Lombardi…'

'How do you do?' Gail murmured, pleased that her voice was steady.

At close quarters, she could see that Andrea was much younger than she had first appeared—at a guess, no more than eighteen or nineteen. But she had a veneer of glamour and sophistication that made her seem considerably older.

'Andrea, I'd like you to meet Miss North.'

'*Piacere,*' Andrea said, her perfectly made-up face cold and set. '*Lei parla Italiano?*'

'No, Gail doesn't speak Italian,' Zane told her, 'so perhaps you'd be kind enough to speak English?'

Her full red lips pouting, she made what was clearly a protest.

Unmoved, Zane retorted, 'You speak excellent English, as I'm quite sure you know.'

'Oh, very well,' she agreed sulkily. 'In order to please you I'll do as you ask.'

'Good girl.'

'Though I still don't find it easy to express myself fully in English.'

He looked about to say, *Rubbish!* Instead he pointed out mildly, 'Then this will be good practice.'

Running a scarlet-tipped finger down the side of his cheek, she accused, 'You're being cruel to me.'

'Not at all.'

Giving up, she observed, 'I presume Miss North is your new PA, no?' Her dark eyes sweeping Gail from head to toe, she added with saccharine sweetness, 'I see my swimsuit fits her.'

As the colour rose in Gail's cheeks, Zane said repressively, 'Miss North had omitted to pack a costume, so *I* suggested she borrow one of yours.'

'I'm sure she thinks it very noble of you to take the blame.'

'Don't be catty, Andrea,' he said, as though she were a child. Then, blandly, 'Don't forget you have a bikini here if you'd like to join us for a swim.'

She shuddered. 'You know perfectly well that I never go in the water, *caro*. As far as I'm concerned, pools are for sitting by.'

'This one was intended for healthy exercise, not just a display of physical charms.'

'You're being cruel again.'

When he said nothing, with a provocative smile, she went on, 'But even if you do enjoy being cruel to me, it's very nice that you're here. I've missed you so much, *caro*…'

Feeling *de trop*, Gail murmured, 'If you'll excuse me,' and began to move away.

His fingers closing round her upper arm, keeping her where she was, Zane drawled, 'There's really no need to rush off.'

'I'd like to go and get changed.'

'Let her go if she wants to,' Andrea said.

'It's what *I* want that counts,' he informed her coolly, 'and I happen to want Miss North to stay.'

Reining in her anger, Andrea shrugged her slim shoulders. 'As you wish. Though I would have much preferred to be able to talk in private, without an *employee* being present.'

As his mouth tightened, she hastily changed the subject. 'You are really very naughty; you didn't say a word about coming to Severo…'

'No,' he agreed calmly and, steering Gail to the nearest lounger, pressed her into it, totally ignoring the pleading look she gave him.

Giving all her attention to Zane and ignoring Gail completely, Andrea chose an umbrella-shaded lounger and, crossing her shapely silk-clad legs, persisted, '*Why* didn't you let me know you were coming?'

'Firstly, it was all rather sudden and, secondly, I understood that you were bored with Montecino and had gone back to Rome and taken Moira with you.'

'Yes, she's staying at my apartment so we can shop together. Rome has all the best shops, and time is getting short.'

Patting the lounger next to hers, she invited, 'Why don't you sit beside me for a while, *caro?*'

He sat down, but in the empty lounger between the two women, rather than the one she had indicated.

For a split second Andrea appeared put out. Then, giving him a little girl look, she asked plaintively, 'You *are* pleased to see me, aren't you?'

His face softening and his tone becoming indulgent, he answered, 'Of course.'

Then, casually, 'How did you know I was here?'

'When I talked to Paolo yesterday he mentioned that you had just flown in, but he warned me that it was to be a working holiday. Still, I couldn't miss the chance to see you, so I decided on a flying visit and caught the evening plane. Paolo loaned me a car so I could come over to see you.

'Unfortunately, I cannot stay long. He wants me to go to Pianosa with him. There is a villa there that he is thinking of buying…

'Though I love my brother dearly, I am not looking forward to the journey. He likes to keep the top down and the sun is bad for my skin. Just driving here it was so hot—'

'Then I'll go and rustle up some refreshments,' Zane broke smoothly into the flow.

As he started to rise, she stopped him. 'There is no need. When your housekeeper said you were by the pool, I told her to bring some cool drinks down…'

At that moment Maria appeared, carrying a tray which she placed on one of the low tables.

'*Grazie,* Maria,' Zane said.

She gave an unsmiling nod and departed, her back ramrod straight.

It appeared that something, or *someone,* had ruffled her composure.

'I don't know how you can stand that surly, arrogant creature,' Andrea complained as Zane helped both women to a tall frosted glass of fruit juice. 'Couldn't you get somebody more…'

'Servile?' he suggested when she hesitated.

'Someone who knows her place,' Andrea finished defiantly. 'She was barely civil to me.'

'Whereas you were perfectly polite to her?'

'Why should I be polite to paid servants?'

Once again Gail found herself thinking how very alike Andrea and Rona were, both in appearance and character. It seemed that Zane attracted, and was attracted by, that type of woman.

Now he was saying, again with that air of indulgence, 'My dear Andrea, when you marry and become the mistress of a house, if you want to keep any staff you'll need to change your attitude.'

'Don't be silly, *caro,*' she retorted airily. 'One can always keep servants so long as there is money to pay their wages…'

With a slight shrug, he let it go.

Brushing back the long, straight fall of gleaming blonde

hair, she complained, 'I've hardly seen you in the past few months, and when I talk to you on the phone you tell me so little. I never really know what you do with yourself when you are alone in London.'

'I work,' he said laconically.

'How boring.'

'While you, I imagine, have been nearly bankrupting your papa.'

'Papa has plenty of money,' she said dismissively, 'and, as I am his only daughter, he wants me to look my best for the wedding.

'Moira and I have been out almost every day, shopping for a trousseau or being fitted for our dresses. Rocco, who has designed all the dresses, says they will look absolutely beautiful, so I hope you will like mine.'

'I'm sure I will.'

She covered his hand with hers. 'Though the wedding is only a month away, it seems a long time before we can be together in church, and I confess I am impatient for the happy day…'

Sitting silently listening, Gail felt as if she had been mortally wounded and was slowly bleeding to death inside.

Zane was going to marry Andrea Lombardi, who was so like Rona. Rona, whom he had once loved.

His ex-PA had said that he had no real place in his life for a woman, but she had been wrong.

No wonder Andrea had been angry and jealous when, with the wedding only a month away, she had seen another woman kissing her future husband.

In the circumstances she had been very restrained. She could well have kicked up a fuss.

But perhaps, as they had been apart and well aware that he was a red-blooded man, she had half-expected him to be having a last fling before the wedding?

Though, knowing he was committed to Andrea, how could he have made love to *her* in the way he had?

The answer was that he couldn't unless he was completely unscrupulous, and she didn't want to believe that.

Even after what had happened that evening more than seven years ago, she had always considered him to be an honourable man.

Yet, thinking about the way he had kept her here against her will, how he had used the chemistry between them to make her want to stay, it seemed he really had no scruples…

Her painful thoughts were interrupted by Andrea getting to her feet and saying wistfully, 'It will be almost a month before I see you again, and I will miss you so much, *caro*…'

'When you get back to Rome you'll be far too busy shopping to give me a thought.'

'How can you say that?'

'Quite easily.'

'You know I am wild about you.' Throwing her arms around his neck, she gave him a lingering kiss, which he appeared rather to endure than return.

A reluctant spectator, Gail found herself wondering how he could be so offhand with his future wife.

Unless he didn't really love her.

But, if he didn't love her, why was he marrying her?

Perhaps he wanted a family, a mother for his children, someone to leave his money to?

Though why Andrea? Admittedly she was beautiful, but then so were a lot of other women. Perhaps he had chosen her simply because she reminded him of Rona—a woman he had wanted and been unable to keep…?

Having freed himself from Andrea's embrace, Zane said crisply, 'You'd better be starting back or Paolo won't have time to get over to Pianosa.'

When she looked crestfallen at his dismissal, he added more kindly, 'Come on, I'll walk back to the car with you and see you off.'

Turning to Gail, he suggested, 'If you'd like to shower and dress, either here or up at the house, I'll be with you shortly.'

Wondering if he intended to go on with their plans as if nothing had happened, she found her voice and queried through stiff lips, 'Are you still thinking of going to Florence?'

Sounding surprised that she should need to ask, he said, 'Of course…'

It was the answer she had hoped for. Going to Florence made it so much easier to put into practice the decision she had just made.

She was turning away when he added, 'I'll give the airfield a ring and ask them to have the chopper standing by.'

Looking anything but pleased, Andrea slipped a hand through his arm and leaned in close.

As the pair disappeared up the steps Gail could hear the other woman talking volubly. She was speaking Italian now but, judging by her tone, she was railing against something or someone.

Probably herself, Gail reflected bitterly.

Though, in all honesty, she couldn't blame her. Had she been in Andrea's place, *she* would have felt anger and resentment.

Who wouldn't?

Quickly she showered and dried herself, while thoughts tumbled through her head like sad clowns.

As she began to pull on her clothes, the question she had already asked herself came back to torment her—when Zane was engaged to be married, how *could* he have acted in the way he had?

But that was a case of the pot calling the kettle black, she realized with shame. When she had gone to bed with him, *she* had been engaged to another man.

So it wasn't all Zane's fault and, though he might have tried to deceive Andrea, she couldn't say he had deceived *her*. He had made no promises, no commitment of any kind, had told her no lies and offered her nothing beyond pleasure and physical gratification.

And, while she had been unable to douse a small glimmer of hope that something more lasting might come of it, she had known and come to terms with the fact that, as far as he was concerned, their relationship was intended to be merely a brief holiday fling.

However, knowing that he belonged to another woman changed everything. She *couldn't* and *wouldn't* come to terms with that.

Though she didn't like Andrea, she couldn't help but feel sorry for her. She knew what it was like to be madly in love with a man who didn't care a jot about her.

Therefore it was imperative that she should go, and as soon as possible. But if she told him to his face that she thought he was acting like a swine and that she intended to go back to London, he might still try to prevent her from leaving.

Supposing he did, even knowing the truth she couldn't trust herself to remain in control of her emotions, and if she let him so much as suspect that she was in love with him it would be handing him a weapon he would certainly use against her.

So, once they were in Florence, she must find an opportunity to slip away. It would mean leaving all her things at the villa, but so long as she had her passport with her she could manage.

All she would need was enough money to take either a bus or a taxi to the airport…

Like most men, Zane carried loose change in his trouser

pockets and almost certainly a notecase in his jacket. All she had to do was borrow what she thought she might need.

Remembering Andrea's passionate embrace, she guessed that the leave-taking would be a protracted affair, so now was probably the best time to do what she had to.

Draping the damp swimming things over a rail, she hastened back to the house and up to the bedroom they had been sharing.

There was no sign of Zane and, having checked that the bathroom was empty, she looked round for the most likely jacket.

Hanging over the back of a chair was the one he had worn at the airport.

She hurried over and, her hands shaking, felt in the inner pocket. Yes! There was a wallet with a sizeable wad of euros.

Peeling off several notes, she thrust them hurriedly into her bag. That should be enough for the taxi fare and any possible airport departure tax.

Her hands still unsteady, she brushed and coiled her hair and applied a touch of make-up. She had just gathered up her bag and jacket when the door opened and Zane came in, showered and dressed, his damp hair neatly combed.

Smiling at her, he observed, 'All ready, I see.'

Common sense told her that if she didn't want him to suspect anything she would have to make an effort to act normally, but her whole face felt stiff and, try as she might, she was unable to return his smile.

He gave her a searching look and a combination of guilt and anger made her heart start to thud so loudly she thought he must surely hear.

But, making no comment, he picked up his jacket and, a hand at her waist, said, 'Let's go.'

CHAPTER NINE

THE drive down the hill and along the valley floor was made without a word being spoken. Gail could think of nothing to say, and Zane seemed to be sunk in thought.

At the airfield the silver helicopter was waiting, its rotor blades whirring gently, its paintwork gleaming in the sun.

A small group of engineers and ground staff were standing by chatting, but there was no sign of Captain Giardino and it soon became apparent that Zane was going to pilot the helicopter himself.

When she was settled in the passenger seat, he slid in alongside and, turning to look at her, asked, 'Your first flight?'

She nodded.

'How do you feel about it?'

'Fine,' she managed.

Clear green eyes looked searchingly into cloudy grey. 'You seem very tense and uptight.'

'I'm quite all right, really I am. How far away is Florence airport?'

'We're not going to the airport. We'll be landing at the Firenze Boscolo Hotel.

'Look, if you're nervous, we can always cancel today's trip and go to Florence another day by road.'

The thought of the possible consequences of having to spend another night under his roof was enough to spur her on.

'I'm not nervous,' she denied quickly, 'and I can't wait to see Florence.' But she was aware that her voice wasn't quite steady and he didn't believe her.

'Well, if you like we could go by road now and stop for a meal en route, but it wouldn't leave much time for sightseeing.'

She might well have chosen that option if she hadn't been so desperate to get to Florence quickly and make her escape. As it was…

'I'm quite happy to fly,' she told him firmly.

'That's good.' He leaned forward to kiss her.

Instinctively she flinched.

Taking her chin, he tilted her face and studied it. 'What's wrong?' he enquired coolly.

'Nothing,' she whispered.

'In that case…' As if making a point, he kissed her with slow deliberation.

When he lifted his head, haunted by the way Andrea had kissed him, she wiped the back of her hand across her mouth.

His jaw tightened as he noticed that telling gesture but he made no comment and, reaching for a set of headphones, gave his full attention to the task in hand.

Their lift-off into the blue sky, though noisy, seemed effortless and soon the airfield was spread beneath them like a scale model.

Fascinated by the novelty of it, she soon found that flying over the sunlit Tuscan countryside was a fascinating experience and one that, had the circumstances been different, she would have thoroughly enjoyed.

Though Zane glanced at her from time to time, he made no effort to talk until, after twenty minutes or so, the countryside began to give way to outlying streets and buildings and Gail found they were approaching a built-up area.

'Won't be long now,' he said above the noise. 'Just coming into view is the River Arno, which runs through Florence…'

She had no trouble locating the broad brown sash of water and as they approached the centre of the city she saw that at this point the river was spanned by several bridges.

'In a moment,' he went on, 'you should get a good view of the Ponte Vecchio.'

In spite of all her woes and anxieties, it was a thrill to see that famous medieval bridge, with its spectacular line of small shops and houses running down either side.

Supported on brackets that overhung the river, they were painted in mellow shades of yellow and, with their wooden shutters, wrought ironwork and awnings, had kept their medieval appearance.

Seen from the air, Florence was absolutely breathtaking, with its imposing squares and magnificent architecture, its tall campaniles and domed churches, its narrow, canyon-like streets and fascinating jumble of rooftops.

By the time they came in to land in the grounds of the Hotel Firenze Boscolo, Gail's earlier sombre mood had changed to one of reckless abandonment.

Zane might have feet of clay, but she would continue to love him while ever there was breath in her body, so she would stop worrying and enjoy to the utmost the short time they would spend together in this wonderful city.

When he had stopped the engine and removed his headset, he turned to her and in the sudden relative quietness queried politely, 'Not too bad an ordeal, I hope?'

She was able to say with truth, 'No, I enjoyed it.'

'That's good.'

She waited for his kiss, but this time he made no attempt to kiss her and she was disappointed.

As the rotor blades stopped whirling and the dust they had

raised began to settle, he jumped out and came round to open her door.

Immediately the heat struck her like a blow from a clenched fist.

He took her hand to help her out.

She wanted him to keep holding it, wanted them to stay hand in hand. But, as soon as she was safely on the ground, he let it go and stepped back like a courteous stranger.

One of the hotel personnel was standing by and the two men exchanged a greeting and a few words in Italian before Zane turned to escort her through the green, leafy garden to the rear of the hotel.

As they climbed the steps to a vine-shaded terrace, where most of the tables were already occupied, a well-dressed elderly man came hurrying to meet them.

'Ah, Zane, how very nice it is to see you.' His English was good, but heavily accented.

'It's nice to see you, Pietro.'

They shook hands with great cordiality.

Then Zane said formally, 'Gail, I'd like you to meet Signor Boscolo, owner of the Firenzi… Pietro, may I present Signorina North.'

Liking the look of this pleasant, silver-haired man, she smiled and murmured a greeting.

Bowled over by that smile, he took her proffered hand and raised it to his lips with Latin gallantry. 'I am delighted to meet you, *signorina*. Zane has told me all about you. This is the first time you have visited our beautiful city?'

'Yes.'

'So after you have eaten lunch you will be going…how do you say…sightseeing?'

'I hope so.'

'Then I must not hold you up too long with talk.'

Turning to Zane, he went on, 'I have set aside for you a table on the terrace, but if you would prefer to eat indoors, you only have to say.'

After an interrogative glance at Gail, Zane answered, 'The terrace, please, Pietro.'

'A good choice on such a lovely day.'

Without further ado they were shown to a table for two in a secluded little arbour at the far end of the stone terrace. Shaded by vines, the perfumed air cooled by hidden fans, it was perfection.

When they were both seated, Pietro said, 'Today my head chef has excelled himself and I can highly recommend his Tonno Fresco alla Marinara, if the *signorina* likes fish.'

'Yes, I do,' Gail answered, and was awarded a beaming smile.

'In that case, may I suggest you start with Antipasto Volente and end with some truly delectable Cassata alla Siciliana?'

Both men waited for her decision.

Though she had little idea what any of the dishes were, she smiled and said, 'It all sounds delicious.'

Nodding to Pietro, Zane agreed pleasantly, 'Then we'll put ourselves in your very capable hands.'

'*Eccellente!* All you need now to complete your meal, which is…as you say…on the house?…is a good bottle of wine.'

They thanked him and he hurried away with yet another beaming smile.

Within seconds a wine waiter appeared with a bottle of perfectly chilled Orvieto and, after a nod from Zane, opened it and poured two glasses.

When the waiter had departed and Zane made no attempt at conversation, Gail took a sip of her wine and, needing something to say, asked, 'How long have you known Signor Boscolo?'

'It must be eight or nine years. He's Andrea and Paolo's uncle.'

'Oh,' she said in a small voice. She had been hoping to forget about Andrea for the next couple of hours. But, biting the bullet, she asked, 'Is that how you met her?'

'No, as a matter of fact it was the other way round. I first met Andrea and Paolo almost ten years ago when their parents took them to live in New York. Andrea was only nine, but Paolo and I were about the same age.

'Though they'd gone to join another branch of the family in a business venture that proved extremely successful, Catrina, their mother, was homesick, and none of them really settled.

'After coming back to Tuscany whenever possible to visit the rest of the family, last year they finally came home for good.'

So Zane had known Andrea since she was nine. That might explain why, that morning, he had from time to time treated her rather like a spoilt child.

At that moment their first course arrived and from then on, apart from an odd comment about the food, they both ate in a somewhat strained silence.

This wasn't how she had hoped it would be and, heavy-hearted, she realized that he'd been distant with her ever since she had rejected his kiss.

Oh, well, perhaps it was better this way. While there was this coldness between them, when the time came it might be easier to run.

The whole meal proved to be first class but, as far as Gail was concerned, she might as well have been eating chaff. It was a relief when coffee was served.

As soon as their cups were empty, they made their way into the hotel to say their thanks and goodbyes to Pietro Boscolo.

'You enjoyed the meal, I hope?' he asked anxiously.

They both assured him that they had, very much.

Obviously delighted, he clapped Zane on the shoulder. 'Not long to the wedding, eh? Will we see you before then?'

'I doubt it. We have a lot of places to visit in the next couple of weeks.'

'Well, if you *can* get over to Florence again, please do. It will be my pleasure to give you lunch.'

The last remark was addressed to Gail, whom he seemed to have taken a liking to.

As she murmured her thanks, he took her hand and added, 'If I don't see you before, we shall meet again at the wedding.'

Alerted by her expression, he asked quickly, 'You *will* be coming to the wedding?'

She said the first thing that came into her head. 'I haven't been invited.'

'Not invited! But you must come! I am sure Zane would want you there, and I know that any friend of his would be more than welcome. I'll mention it to Catrina without delay.'

'Th-thank you, you're very kind,' she stammered. 'But I really don't think—'

'Don't worry, I'll make quite sure she comes,' Zane broke in.

Gail cringed inwardly. Wild horses wouldn't drag her there, but of course he wasn't to know that. He no doubt assumed that their brief relationship was based purely on sex and meant as little to her as it did to him.

Which, in a way, was fair enough. But hadn't he considered his future wife's feelings?

A lot of the time, in spite of his powerful masculinity, he could be caring and sensitive, but when Andrea had been so blatantly angry and jealous of her, how he could be so unfeeling as to invite her to the wedding?

Knowing none of this, however, Pietro nodded and

smiled. 'Then I will look forward greatly to seeing you both on the day. Now, your car is waiting for you, so I will say arrivederci.'

'Grazie...Arrivederci.'

They left by the front entrance and, after the cool dimness of the air-conditioned hotel, the brightness was dazzling. The sun beat down, the air held a furnace heat and Gail could feel the stone slabs burning through the thin soles of her sandals.

A short distance away, a sea-blue open-topped two-seater was waiting, the keys in the ignition.

An elderly doorman, who had clearly been keeping an eye on the car, gave Zane a smart salute and opened the door.

'Grazie tanto.' Some folded notes changed hands.

As soon as Gail was settled in the passenger seat, Zane slid in beside her and a moment later they were pulling out of the forecourt to join the busy stream of traffic.

She hadn't expected them to go by car and she hoped it wouldn't hinder her chances of escaping.

After a while, afraid that if she didn't make some effort at normality Zane might suspect what was in her mind, she asked, 'What exactly are you planning to do?'

'As it's already mid-afternoon,' he said coolly, 'I think it makes more sense to leave the palazzos and museums et cetera for another time and just take a look at the main sights.'

Her heart sinking, she asked, 'You mean by car?'

He shook his head. 'No, bringing the car this far is just to save time. It's really not worth driving around central Florence. There's a one-way system that makes things difficult, and the historical hub of the city is closed to traffic.

'But I know somewhere we can safely park and then do some exploring on foot. Most of the things I was planning to show you are situated in the central traffic-free zone.'

He drove on and a little while later they came to a quiet, privately owned car park where, clearly well known, he was greeted by name and given a space in the shade.

From there they took a narrow *calle* and emerged on to a piazza surrounded by tall shuttered buildings, many with ornate wrought iron balconies.

In the centre of the piazza, almost deserted in the afternoon heat, there was a handsome marble fountain around which pigeons strutted and cooed and drank from water that had over-flowed into a shallow basin.

They crossed the old square, walking a little apart like polite strangers, and a surreptitious glance at Zane's face confirmed that once again his expression was aloof, withdrawn.

Feeling an overwhelming sadness, she longed to slip her arm through his and see him turn and smile at her. Longed to get the feeling of closeness and intimacy back, to make the most of the short time they still had together.

But, reminding herself sternly that he belonged to another woman, she kept walking, staring straight ahead, blinking away the tears that threatened to blind her.

It would be as well if she could slip away as soon as possible. Delaying the moment of leaving him would only bring her more heartbreak.

But she must wait until they reached a spot where a lot of people were milling around. That way, as soon as his attention was elsewhere, it should be relatively easy to disappear into the crowd.

When she had regained control of her emotions and was reasonably sure her voice would be steady, she asked, 'Where-abouts are we starting?'

'At the Duomo,' he answered shortly. 'We'll be there in just a minute or so.'

The Duomo complex, with its cathedral, bell tower and octagonal baptistery, the exteriors of which were banded with green, white and pink Tuscan marble, was absolutely staggering.

'Compared with the outside, the interior of the Duomo is fairly austere,' Zane told her. 'But perhaps the relative bareness helps to make one appreciate the soaring space beneath the Gothic arches and the sheer scale of the place.'

They walked all the way round the cathedral so Gail could truly appreciate its vast proportions, before strolling down the Via dei Calzaiuoli which split the traffic-free area Zane had mentioned earlier.

In a short while they left the busy thoroughfare and branched off to look at some more of the city's glorious architecture.

After a couple of hours they stopped for a cool drink at La Cucina and sat in the open air beneath a gaily striped umbrella.

There was an entrance at either end of the café and a steady stream of waiters and people going in and out like ants.

When Zane called for the bill, seeing her chance, Gail excused herself on the grounds that she needed to wash her hands and freshen up and, heading for the nearest door, disappeared inside.

Making her way to the far door, she waited for a few moments until a small group was ready to exit, then slipped out with them. Only to find Zane had moved from the table and was stationed close by.

'That was quick,' he remarked blandly. Then, 'If you're feeling refreshed, shall we carry on?'

Though it was all quite fascinating, it came as something of a relief when they finally reached Piazza della Signoria, which marked the heart of the old town.

Gail was starting to feel hot and sticky and not a little concerned that, as if guessing her intention, Zane had scarcely taken his eyes off her.

When they had walked around Florence's main square and

admired the surrounding buildings, particularly the grand and austere Palazzo Vecchio and the many wonderful sculptures and statues, Zane asked solicitously, 'Tired?'

Scared that he was going to suggest going straight back to Severo, she said, 'A little, but I'm happy to go on if you are.'

He shook his head. 'I think we've done quite enough in this heat, so I suggest we call it a day and have dinner before going back to the car.'

Then, misinterpreting her anxious glance, 'Don't worry, we've circled round somewhat, so it's a lot closer than you might think.

'Now, is there anywhere special you'd like to go?'

There were many elegant cafés and smart restaurants scattered around the vast square and they all appeared busy. That was an important point, as this would almost certainly be her last chance to make a run for it.

As lightly as possible, she said, 'I don't really mind where we go. I'm happy to leave it to you.'

'In that case, we'll have a meal at Bartolomeo's. It's one of the least pretentious and the food is always excellent.'

If anything, Bartolomeo's was busier than the rest, but Zane was known there and welcomed with enthusiasm. The proprietor came hurrying out and, having shaken his hand, ushered them through a simple foyer and into a pleasant air-conditioned room.

There were no more than half a dozen widely spaced tables, all of which were occupied.

Snapping his fingers, Bartolomeo called an order and, while the two men exchanged a few words, a table for two was speedily set up in a flower-screened alcove by the window.

As Zane had said, the food was excellent and if Gail hadn't been so uptight and jumpy she would have thoroughly enjoyed the leisurely meal of Florentine specialities that followed.

Zane seemed to be waiting for her to speak. Gail, who could think of nothing to say, hoped he would put her silence down to tiredness.

They were sipping some excellent coffee before he roused himself to say, 'Before we venture out tomorrow, I'd like to do a little work on the Rainmaker project…'

It was the first time he'd mentioned work and, taken by surprise, she simply stared at him.

'What do you know about it?'

'W-well nothing really,' she stammered. 'Apart from the name.'

He nodded. 'My Research and Development team, who first came up with the revolutionary idea, named it that. They've been working on it for quite some time. But details of the project have been kept tightly under wraps because of the sheer amount of expertise and money that's already gone into it.

'Tomorrow, before we start work, we'll go through the plans together so you can see what I mean and get a good idea of exactly what's involved.

'However, the overall picture is this…'

Quickly and precisely, he explained what the project aimed to achieve both short-term and long-term.

Gail found it stunning in its scope and ingenuity and, with only Zane's brief account to go on, she could see that if it could be made viable it could bring prosperity to vast regions which at present wouldn't support life because of lack of rainfall.

'What a wonderful project,' Gail breathed.

'Isn't it? Of course there's a long way to go yet, but Rainmaker is the first step on the road.'

He poured them both more coffee.

While Gail sipped hers, she thought about what she'd just learnt. Now she had grasped just a little of what was involved, she knew—even without her change of heart—that she could never have helped Paul try to derail such a worthwhile project.

When their cups were empty, Zane observed, 'You're looking weary. About ready to go?'

She nodded and thought, *It's now or never...*

He called the waiter over and paid the bill before helping her to her feet and putting her light jacket around her shoulders.

They were on their way to the door when a tall, balding man rose from one of the tables and cried, 'Zane! It's good to see you, you old son-of-a-gun. What are you doing in Florence?'

Seizing the chance, Gail murmured, 'Excuse me,' and made her way through to the foyer and into the ladies' cloakroom.

She was hastily drying her hands and wondering if it was safe to make a run for it when the door opened and two elderly women dressed like well-to-do tourists came in chatting in English.

As soon as there was a pause in the conversation, Gail said, 'Excuse me, I know this sounds odd, but did you happen to notice a tall, good-looking man with dark hair waiting in the foyer?'

'I didn't,' the first one said. 'Did you, Isobel?'

'No.' Then, after a glance at Gail's face, 'I take it you're on holiday here and this is someone you're trying to get away from?'

'Yes, that's right,' Gail admitted.

Isobel nodded sagely. 'Some men can be perfect pests. If they buy you dinner they imagine they've bought you.

'Just a minute.' She opened the door and peered out cautiously, before reporting, 'Not a soul. Could he see the main exit from where he was?'

'Yes, I think so.'

'Then, just in case he's keeping an eye open for you, if you turn left when you go out of here, there's a side entrance that leads on to the patio. I know because we came in that way.'

'Thank you,' Gail said gratefully.

'Forgive me for asking, but if you leave alone have you enough money for a taxi back to your hotel?'

'Yes, I have, thanks.'

'Our husbands are waiting out there,' the first woman broke in, 'so if you think you might have a problem, stay with them until we come. Then we can all leave together.'

'I can't thank you both enough, but I'm sure if I can just slip out it'll be all right.'

'Take care now,' they said in a chorus.

Gail smiled and nodded. 'I will.'

The foyer was empty apart from a young couple who were just leaving and she was able to slip out through the side entrance with no trouble.

It was starting to get dusk but the lantern-lit patio was still busy, with waiters scurrying to and fro and new people arriving.

Having hurried across the piazza, she left the pedestrianized area and, hoping to spot a vacant taxi, made her way towards a road which was busy with evening traffic.

The one or two taxis she spotted were already taken and, though she had no idea where she was, afraid to stand still, she kept walking.

After fifteen minutes or so her luck changed. She was just passing what seemed to be a nightclub of some kind when a white taxi with a yellow design drew up by the kerb to drop its previous passengers.

Seeing her hovering, the driver, a bull-necked middle-aged man, leaned over and opened the door.

Thankfully, she climbed in.

Glancing at her, he asked laconically, *'Dove?'*

'I want to go to the airport,' she said, hoping against hope he would understand.

'Inglese, no?'

'Yes. I'm afraid I don't speak Italian.'

'Where you want to go?'

'The airport.'

'*Si, si*...'

Accompanied by hooting horns, colourful gesticulations and a veritable storm of abuse, he did what appeared to be an illegal U-turn and headed back the way she'd just come.

He seemed to speak a word or two of English, so she asked, 'How long will it take?'

She was beginning to think he hadn't understood, when he shrugged and said, 'Twenty minutes, *forse.*'

Not long. She breathed a sigh of relief. The sooner she was on a plane, the happier she would be.

As they headed through fairly heavy traffic, she wondered how Zane had reacted when he'd found she'd slipped away.

Had he just shrugged his shoulders and gone back to the car without her, or had he searched fruitlessly for her?

Given the circumstances, she rather thought it would be the former. A kind of easy come, easy go situation, where one woman meant little and there was always another waiting to fill the gap.

Would things alter when he was married? And if they didn't, would Andrea stand for it?

Gail strongly suspected that she wouldn't. She might turn a blind eye while they were merely engaged, but once she was his wife she would expect, and be entitled to, fidelity...

The journey to the airport was soon over and the driver dropped her outside the smaller of the two terminal buildings.

By the time she had paid him an exorbitant sum and thanked him, a group of four people were waiting to climb in.

When she made her way into the terminal building, she discovered she had been dropped—presumably because she had no luggage—at Arrivals.

The Departure terminal was larger and strangely quiet and

on finding a female member of staff who spoke quite good English, she soon discovered that she was out of luck. The airport handled mainly domestic flights, with only a limited number of daily departures to other European cities.

Nothing could be done tonight, she was told, but tomorrow she would have the choice of either booking on a regular airline or going to Pisa, which was ninety kilometres from Florence and the region's main entry and exit point, especially for budget airlines.

Anxious and dispirited, she tried to decide what to do for the best.

After a moment or two's thought, she dismissed any idea of trying to get to Pisa. For one thing, it would probably cost more money than she'd got.

Which left her with two alternatives. She could take a taxi back to Florence and try to find a small hotel or she could stay where she was.

Feeling hot and sticky and tired out, she longed to shower and clean her teeth and stretch out in a proper bed. But the language barrier and the fact that she had no luggage suggested it would be a great deal easier to simply stay at the airport.

Most of the facilities seemed to be closed, but there was a deserted café-bar still open and, having bought herself a cup of coffee, she sat down at one of the small tables to decide once and for all what to do.

But, tired and dazed by lack of sleep, unable to concentrate, her thoughts kept swimming in and out of focus and, head drooping, all she could think about was Zane. Already she missed him.

Had she been wrong to leave him and run?

But what else could she have done? Cling to him until the very last minute? Make it so that he was forced to push her away? Or, worse, take her for his mistress, his plaything, while another woman reigned as his wife?

No, that would have been soul-destroying. An impossible situation. Tenable neither for herself nor for Andrea, should she ever find out.

Undoubtedly she had done the right thing. The only thing she could have done. Made a clean break.

Now she should be experiencing a feeling of release, a stirring of pride and self-respect that she had been strong enough to do it.

But she wasn't. In spite of everything, she longed for him, ached for him, felt the kind of pain that amputees were said to feel in limbs that were no longer a part of them…

Someone dropped into the vacant chair opposite, interrupting her sombre thoughts.

Her head came up and she found herself looking straight into Zane's glacial green eyes.

CHAPTER TEN

'W-What are you doing here?' Gail asked stupidly.

Zane smiled without mirth. 'Surely you didn't think I'd let you go that easily?'

'But how did you know where to find me?'

'The airport seemed a pretty safe bet, and there are a lot of hotels in the city so it made sense to come here first.'

Smoothly, he added, 'Taxis are very expensive in Florence, but I presume you'd taken enough money to cover the fare?'

A hot flush staining her cheeks, she said, 'I didn't want to have to take it; it made me feel like a thief, but…'

As her words tailed off, he finished, 'But you had only a small amount of English money with you.'

'How do you know that?'

'While we were at your flat and I was waiting for you to finish packing, I went through your bag,' he admitted shamelessly.

'And you stole my phone!'

'I was merely taking care of it.'

'Why?'

'I would have thought that was obvious.'

'It's not obvious to me.'

'Think about it,' he advised sardonically.

Her fighting spirit up now, she said, 'I can't imagine why any normal boss should want to take his employee's phone.'

He smiled grimly. 'But there's nothing *normal* about our relationship, is there? Though you said you wanted the job, right from the start, and in spite of everything that's happened between us, or maybe *because* of it,' he added thoughtfully, 'you've been intent on running out.

'But after we showered together and you agreed to move into my room, I hoped things might have changed.' His gaze never left her for a second.

'It was only when we had our swim and I came back to find you in our bedroom and saw how guilty you looked that I knew they hadn't.

'All it needed was one look at your face to tell me what you'd been up to and what your intentions were.'

'Then I'm surprised you took your eyes off me,' she responded heatedly.

'I wouldn't have done if I'd thought you were still intent on running. But, having dangled the carrot, I fondly imagined you would stay to reap the reward...'

His words were like a kick in the solar plexus. But surely he couldn't have meant what, for one ghastly instant, she had thought he meant...

Pulling herself together, she said jerkily, 'I really don't know what you mean.'

'I'm quite sure you do. Now, if you're ready to go, I have the car waiting outside. We'll leave the chopper where it is and drive back to Severo.'

She shook her head. 'I'm going back to London as soon as I can get a flight.'

His voice cold, he told her, 'I'm afraid there's too much unfinished business between us for me to let you walk away scot-free.'

'U-unfinished business?' she stammered. 'What unfinished business?'

A hint of quiet menace in his voice, he said, 'No man in his right mind enjoys being made a fool of, but even that pales into insignificance compared to being deliberately betrayed.'

'Betrayed?' she whispered. 'But I haven't—'

'I'm quite sure you haven't. But I don't doubt that you would have done, given the opportunity.

'After all, wasn't that why you took the job as my PA—to be in a position to gather, and pass on, secret information?'

'I don't know what you're talking about,' she denied through stiff lips.

'May I suggest you give up on the injured innocent act. It doesn't cut any ice. Now, ready to go?'

Her hands clenched so tightly that she could feel the pain as the oval nails bit into her soft palms, she said hoarsely, 'I've no intention of going back with you.'

'Oh, but I insist. After all, what will your fiancé say if you let him down now after he's gone to so much trouble to set it all up?'

As she stared at him, aghast, he went on, 'Manton *is* your fiancé? It *is* his ring you were wearing round your neck?'

Knowing it was useless to deny it, swamped in cold despair, she asked, 'How long have you known?'

'From the word go.'

'Then why did you hire me?'

He smiled crookedly. 'Why do you think?'

Her tired brain struggled for a moment before the reason became blindingly clear. 'So you could get back at both of us… That's why you seduced me! You were planning to tell him, to gloat, hoping that it would wreck our engagement.'

'No, that wasn't the plan,' Zane said flatly. 'I've no intention of telling him. In fact, as far as I'm concerned, your secret is quite safe.

'Of course, if you don't come up with the goods he may be angry enough to ask for his ring back…'

In a rush, she said, 'I have every intention of giving it back to him.'

'May I ask why?'

Biting her lip, she refused to answer.

Watching her face, he hazarded, 'A guilty conscience, perhaps, because you were a willing partner in this "seduction"?'

When she remained silent, he said, 'You'd be a fool to let it worry you. Manton is no saint.'

Infuriated by his careless dismissal of something that she still felt ashamed of, she hit back, '*You* might be totally without scruples when it comes to personal relationships, but that doesn't mean everyone is.'

His eyes narrowed. 'Perhaps you'd like to explain that remark?'

'I wouldn't have thought it needed explaining.' Then, in a rush, 'I can only feel sorry for Andrea.'

His eyebrows shot up. 'May I ask why?'

'She's obviously madly in love with you, and it must have been awful for her to find the man she's going to marry in a month's time playing around with another woman.'

After a moment he agreed solemnly, 'Awful indeed.'

'How *can* you be so callous, so uncaring?' she raged at him. 'Paul may be no saint, but he's twice the man you are.'

'In what way?'

'I'm quite aware that there have been women in the past, but he would never treat me like you're treating Andrea.'

'You think because he's given you a ring he's been faithful to you?'

She lifted her chin defiantly. 'I'm sure he has.'

Zane laughed. 'I don't like to burst your pretty bubble, but you're quite wrong.'

'Of course you would say that,' she cried, her voice full of contempt.

With a glance at his watch, Zane remarked, 'If he's not staying out too late I'd gamble pretty well everything I own that at this very moment he's in bed with another woman.'

As she opened her mouth to defend Paul, Zane went on, 'You don't have to take my word for it. Try ringing him and see what happens. You should be able to tell from his reaction whether or not you've caught him out.'

'You took my phone.'

Reaching into his pocket, he brought out his mobile and offered it to her. 'You can use mine.'

When she hesitated, he asked, 'What's the matter? Scared I might be proved right?'

'No, I'm not. But the whole thing seems…I don't know… wrong, distasteful.'

He shrugged. 'Well, of course I could have been misinformed, but you'll never be sure if you don't give it a go.'

Seeing her waver, he suggested, 'Tell me the number and I'll get it for you.'

She gave him Paul's home number and watched him key it in.

'If it bothers you,' Zane went on, 'don't think of it as possibly catching him out. Just tell him what kind of mess you're in and see what he says.

'Perhaps he'll saddle his white steed and come charging to the rescue.'

Angered by his mockery, she took the phone and listened to the number ringing.

She was just about to give up when the receiver was lifted and a sleepy female voice mumbled, 'Hello?'

Without conscious volition, Gail found herself asking, 'Is Paul there?'

'He's asleep. Can't it wait until morning…? Oh, very well… Paul… Paul… Wake up… Some woman wants to speak to you…'

Feeling curiously numb, uncaring, Gail pushed the *end call* button and handed back the phone. After a moment, she asked dully, 'What made you so sure?'

'My detective told me Manton had a woman living with him and has had for some time. I thought at first it was you, but then he showed me a photograph he'd taken of them leaving the apartment together early one morning.

'Though it was only taken with a phone, it was good and clear. It seems Manton's taste runs to tall, curvaceous blondes…'

Then he wasn't on his own, Gail thought bitterly.

Watching her face, Zane said with a hint of genuine sympathy in his voice, 'I'm sorry if it's come as a shock to you, but I couldn't see the point of letting you live in a fool's paradise.'

He was right, of course, but knowing made her feel both hurt and angry. Hurt that Paul had just tried to use her, and angry that she had allowed him to.

But she recognized that it was her pride that was hurt rather than her heart. And the fact that the engagement had been merely a ploy made her feel a lot less guilty about her own actions.

So she had escaped lightly.

Or had she?

There was still Zane to answer to and he wasn't the kind of man who would easily forgive what he clearly regarded as treachery.

But what could he possibly do to her if she stayed where she was and refused to leave the airport?

Nothing, surely?

Though she still felt scared, even her fear seemed less sharp, blunted by tiredness.

Pressing her fingertips to her throbbing temples, she wished fervently that he would just go and leave her in peace.

Exhausted, both by the heat and the roller coaster of emotions she'd ridden all day, the only thing she wanted at that moment was to be left alone. She longed to fold her arms on the table, lay her head on them and simply close her eyes.

Watching her face, he said, 'It's been a long day and you look shattered. You should be on your way home to bed.'

'I'm staying here.'

'That's where you're wrong.' Taking her elbows, he lifted her to her feet.

'I won't go back,' she insisted, trying in vain to free herself. 'If you don't let me go, I'll scream blue murder.'

When he made no attempt to release her she took a deep breath, but before she could carry out her threat he pulled her into his arms so that she was off balance and his mouth came down on hers, stifling any attempt to cry out.

Holding her tightly, he kissed her until she was dazed and breathless, then asked softly, 'Ready to admit defeat?'

'You can't make me leave,' she said huskily when she'd managed to regain her balance. 'Someone is bound to realize that something's wrong.'

'Don't bet on it. Italians tend to be hot-blooded, romantic, and to an outsider this will appear to be just a lover's tiff.'

'I'll tell them I'm being kidnapped.'

He laughed. 'How do you plan to do that when you don't speak the language?'

'There's someone here who understands English.'

'Where?'

Gail looked around but there was no sign of the woman she had spoken to earlier and, apart from a sleepy-looking youth who was in the process of closing down the bar, a couple of female cleaners and, in the distance, a security guard, the terminal appeared to be deserted.

'Please, Zane,' she begged jerkily. 'Don't make me go back.'

Just for an instant his expression softened. Then it hardened again and he said grimly, 'Manton may have put you up to this in the first place but, to put it bluntly, you're the one on the spot and I want…' He paused.

White to the lips, she whispered, 'Revenge?'

'Let's call it recompense.'

Handing her her bag, he urged her towards the exit.

Though she strongly suspected that he could well be both cruel and ruthless, beaten, defeated, bone weary, she allowed herself to be shepherded out of the building.

Outside, it was a lovely moonlit night. There wasn't a soul in sight and everywhere seemed to be quiet as the grave. The car, its top closed now, was waiting nearby in the pick-up area.

As soon as she was seated, he slid in beside her and fastened both their seat belts. A second or so later, with a muted roar, they were underway.

Almost before they had left the airport environs, she was sound asleep.

She had no recollection whatsoever of the journey. The first thing she knew was fingers stroking her cheek and Zane's voice saying, 'We're home.'

She opened her eyes and, trying to fight off the relentless waves of sleep that threatened to engulf her, struggled out of the car.

He helped her across the courtyard and into the house, but her legs were like a rag doll's and already her leaden eyelids were starting to close.

She felt herself lifted in strong arms and, her head pillowed comfortably against his shoulder, she gave up the fight and let herself sink back into the blessed oblivion of sleep.

When she opened her eyes it was broad daylight and she was alone in the big bed. Still partially entangled in the golden cobwebs of sleep, her mind was blurred, hazy, anything but clear.

Yet she felt a foreboding, a sense of anxiety and loss she couldn't immediately account for.

Then memory opened the curtains a crack.

Zane was planning to get married and, because she couldn't bear to stay, she had managed to give him the slip and run.

But if she had run away, what was she doing here in his bed?

Almost immediately the curtains were swept aside.

Zane had caught up with her at the airport. He knew that she had been intending to spy for Paul and, intent on punishing her, he had made her come back with him.

She could recall nothing of the journey and had only the vaguest recollection of arriving back and being carried upstairs to bed.

But she was naked, so he must have undressed her, and the dent in the other pillow confirmed that during the night he had slept beside her.

Now it was day and quite soon, no doubt, she would have to face him and answer for what she'd done.

Not that she had actually *done* anything. But Zane would no doubt say that the intention had been there. And perhaps it had, just briefly.

Though she knew now that even if Zane had been ignorant of her role as a spy, and the opportunity had arisen to pass on the information Paul had wanted, she couldn't have gone through with it.

But she would never be able to convince Zane of that in a million years.

Though it was warm and the room was filled with sunshine, she began to shiver.

A glance at the bedside clock showed it was nearly midday.

She had slept for almost twelve hours, and she felt unrefreshed and apprehensive.

What she needed was to brush her teeth and shower.

Emerging from the bathroom some fifteen minutes later, physically refreshed but even more apprehensive about what lay ahead, she pulled on clean underwear and a light cotton dress before brushing out her long seal-dark hair.

Leaving it loose and still slightly damp, she gritted her teeth and made her way downstairs, telling herself that it was better to face him than have him come looking for her.

Dressed in casual trousers and a short-sleeved olive-green shirt, he was just emerging from the morning room.

As always, her heart turned over in her breast at the sight of him.

Considering that he'd had a great deal less sleep than she'd had, he appeared to be the picture of health and vitality. His clear green eyes were brilliant, his lean tanned face looked alert and dangerously attractive.

'Good timing,' he greeted her mildly. 'I was just coming to see if you were still asleep. Lunch is waiting on the terrace. You must be hungry.'

Trying for normality, she agreed, 'I am, rather.'

'I'm afraid you'll have to put up with my cooking again,' he went on smoothly. 'I gave Maria the day off so we could have a little…privacy.'

'You're trying to scare me,' she accused.

Hearing the quaver in her voice, he observed with satisfaction, 'I appear to be succeeding.

'But there's no need to look like a frightened rabbit.'

Anything but reassured, she preceded him on to the sunny terrace and sank down in the chair he pulled out for her.

As he sat down opposite her and reached to pour her a

coffee, wanting to get the whole thing over with, she took a deep breath and began, 'Zane, I'm sorry I—'

'May I suggest we eat lunch first,' he broke in coolly, 'and leave any apologies and explanations until later.'

They ate chicken, fresh bread and crispy salad without speaking. A tense silence hung in the air.

Gail refused the fruit and cheese that followed, but accepted another cup of coffee.

'It's getting very hot in the sun,' Zane remarked. 'Shall we move into the shade to drink our coffee?'

They moved to chairs where the wisteria above them cast shadows on to their bare arms, making strange tattoos of flowers and leaves.

Her coffee finished, Gail put her cup on the low table and, realizing that Zane was waiting for her to speak, deliberately remained silent.

After a little while he smiled that wolfish smile. 'But a rabbit with attitude, I see… Now, if I remember rightly, you were about to apologize.'

Wanting to say, *Apologize be damned,* but knowing it would be useless to fight him, she said simply. 'Yes, I was.'

'And you'd like me to forgive you?'

'I'd like you to believe that if I'd been given all the information Paul wanted, I would never have passed it on.'

'I do believe it.'

She made a little sound, almost like a sob of relief. Then she said passionately, 'I never wanted to get involved in the first place, and when I was offered an interview I was…'

'Hoping you wouldn't get the job,' he finished for her. 'That was fairly obvious. You couldn't hide your relief when you thought you hadn't.

'But at the same time you didn't want to let Manton down

so, when I finally offered you the post, you felt forced to take it. Though you clearly weren't a happy bunny.

'I got the distinct impression that you were planning to tell Manton what a swine I'd been to you, in the hope that he'd let you off the hook…'

So that was why he'd taken her phone.

'But it would have been a complete waste of time. He wasn't likely to relent, having set everything up so carefully.'

'When did you find out?' she asked breathlessly.

'Some time ago, Moira, my ex-PA, suspected what was afoot and warned me.

'She and a woman named Julie, who went to the same gym, had become friendly. But Moira's no fool and it didn't take her long to realize that whenever my name was mentioned, Julie was pumping her for information.

'Then she discovered that her new friend was Manton's sister, and told me about it.

'Manton had already managed to plant one spy but, because we'd rumbled her, she must have proved to be virtually useless.

'When I checked things out it soon became obvious that he was planning to try again with someone closer to the action.' He paused to sip his coffee, then went on.

'I hired a good detective to keep an eye on his comings and goings and who he was associating with. As soon as I had all the gen, and knew who he was hoping to set up as my new PA, I decided to facilitate matters.'

'Facilitate matters…?'

'I told Mrs Rogers that when Manton approached her, she was to agree to send Miss North for an interview straight away.'

'So you knew who was coming before I got there?'

'Oh, yes.'

'When you knew the whole thing was a set-up, I don't understand why you chose to see me, let alone offer me the job…'

'I thought you'd decided it was so I could get my own back by breaking up your engagement?'

'But if you knew Paul had another woman and didn't care a jot about me, that theory doesn't make sense.'

Brushing that quibble aside, Zane said, 'Tell me, how did he manage to pressure you into doing something you clearly didn't want to do?'

When she didn't immediately answer, he said, 'I presume he made it a test of your devotion?'

'Yes,' she admitted wearily.

'You must have loved him very much.'

'At the time I thought I did.'

For what seemed an eternity, Zane sat without moving a muscle.

Then he took a deep breath and asked carefully, 'What about now?'

'I realized I'd been mistaken about my feelings.'

'Presumably that was last night when you found he'd only been using you?'

'No, I knew before then that not only had I never loved him, but I'd never really liked him. It was just a kind of infatuation.'

'Then why do you look so lovelorn?'

Startled, she said, 'I don't…' Then, more positively, 'I'm not.'

'Pity. I was rather hoping…'

Letting the words tail off, he remarked, 'You don't seem to have much luck with the men in your life.'

Pulling herself together, she protested, 'You make it sound as if there've been dozens.'

'I know about Jason and Manton. How many others have there been?'

She hesitated, then, not wanting him to know just how lonely and barren her adult life had been, said, 'A few…'

'Lovers?'

'Just casual friends.'

'The sort of casual friends you go to bed with?'

'No, I don't make a habit of going to bed with my men friends.'

'Presumably you went to bed with Jason?'

She shook her head.

'You're not telling me he didn't try?'

'No. He tried too hard. I was fond of him, but I didn't love him and I didn't want to go to bed with him. That's why we broke up.'

'So you'd only go to bed with someone you loved?'

Realizing she'd walked into his trap—if it *was* a trap—she froze.

But he merely said, 'So that just leaves Manton.'

'Apart from a few kisses, he never as much as touched me.' Her little smile held a tinge of bitterness. 'I wasn't aware he had a woman living with him, so I stupidly put it down to him having good old-fashioned principles.'

'The kind you were brought up with?'

Suspecting derision, she said coldly, 'I know it's unfashionable, laughable even, but I—'

He held up a restraining hand. 'Believe me, I'm not knocking it. I'd like the woman I marry to have those kind of principles.'

'I'm sure she has,' Gail said stiffly.

His handsome green eyes brilliant, he studied her heart-shaped face with its high cheekbones, neat nose, generous mouth and beautiful almond eyes beneath dark silky brows, before saying reflectively, 'There's something I'm curious about.'

'What's that?'

'You indicated just now that you would only go to bed with someone you loved…'

Seeing where that was leading, she said hastily, 'Or someone I was very strongly attracted to.'

'So you were very strongly attracted to me?'

'W-well, yes.'

'On your own admission, I seem to have been the only man you've been "very strongly attracted to", so how do you explain the fact that, though you were evidently inexperienced, you weren't a virgin?'

Her face scarlet, she took refuge in anger. 'I don't have to explain. It's none of your business.'

'Oh, but I rather think it is…

'Let me tell you a story. Seven years ago, when I was young and foolish, I fancied myself in love with a glamorous blonde whose name was Rona…'

Watching the colour drain from Gail's face, leaving it petal-pale, he went on, 'She and her family—her American father, English stepmother and young stepsister—lived in New York.

'As well as being glamorous, she was smart, sexy, uninhibited and fun in bed. Yet I always thought that, like a spoilt child, she had a certain vulnerability.

'She seemed to be what I was looking for and I was all ready to propose when I discovered that I'd been just a stopgap while she tried to find a man with more money.

'You've heard the expression, Don't shoot the messenger? Well, in my case I did. That is to say I took my anger and disappointment out on an innocent young girl who, fancying she was in love with me, attempted to console me.

'I've never forgiven myself for that.

'Later the same evening, I went round to the apartment block where she lived. I had intended to tell her how sorry I was for being such a brute and beg her forgiveness.

'However, circumstances gave her a chance to get a little of her own back, and I spent most of the evening trying to convince the police that I wasn't some kind of criminal.

'Do I need to go on?'

'No,' she whispered. Then, hoarsely, 'I'm sorry. I shouldn'
have done it, but I was hurt and angry—'

'And you had every right to be. Though just then I was too
furious to take that into account.

'Then next day when I'd cooled down, I made anothe
attempt to see you, only to be told that both you and you
mother had packed your bags and gone.

'Rona's father said he'd no idea where you'd gone or wh
you'd left. I had a nasty feeling it was because of me, and I fel
even worse.'

Gail shook her head. 'Though I was only too glad to leave
New York, it wasn't because of you. My mother wanted to ge
away…'

Briefly she explained where they'd gone and what had
happened to make her mother finally decide to end the
marriage.

'I'd no idea things were so bad,' Zane said soberly, 'and a
no one was sure whether you'd gone for good, for severa
weeks I kept calling, hoping you might have returned.

'When she discovered I knew the truth, Rona admitted tha
the weekend on Chator's yacht had proved to be a disaster.
gather she had unexpected competition—three in a bed.

'She said she was sorry she'd lied to me, and swore she sti
loved me. She wanted things to carry on as if nothing had
happened…'

'And did they?'

He shook his head. 'There's a lot to be said for being totally
disillusioned. It removes the rose-coloured spectacles, make
one able to walk away. I realized I had a lot to thank you for.'

She looked up at him with wide, innocent eyes. 'Then you're
not still mad at me?'

'No. But I'm still sorry for the way I treated you. It coul
have put you off men for life…

'Perhaps it did... Have you really loved any man?'

Only one.

When she said nothing, he pressed, 'Have you?'

She shook her head silently. Then, needing to change the subject, she asked, 'When did you realize who I was?'

'When my detective showed me a photograph of you. I could hardly believe my eyes. I'd been trying to find you for seven years.'

'I'm surprised you still recognized me.'

'Though you've grown up and matured, and the colour of your hair has changed, I could never forget those eyes. They're the most beautiful eyes I've ever seen on a woman, and they've haunted me.'

Some impulse at self-flagellation made her say, 'Andrea has beautiful eyes, don't you think? In fact, she's a beautiful woman altogether.'

'I totally agree. With that perfect oval face, the long blonde hair and big brown eyes, she's grown up to be a stunner. It's just a pity she's not my type.'

'Not your type!' Gail sat up, shocked.

'No, I much prefer a woman who has a heart-shaped face, hair like black silk, clear, dark grey almond eyes, with an even darker ring round the irises, and a wide, passionate mouth.'

Trembling all over, she demanded, 'Then why are you marrying Andrea?'

He laughed softly. 'I'm not.'

'But she talked about having a dress made for her, about you and she being together in church...'

'That's right, but the dress that's being made for her is a bridesmaid's dress, and we'll be in church together because I'm the best man.'

'Then who's getting married?'

'Moira, my ex-PA, and Paolo. They first met a couple of

years ago in New York and became friends. Then friendship
blossomed into romance, and in a month's time they'll be man
and wife.

'Andrea was highly delighted when the pair got engaged
and offered to help them with the wedding plans. She was even
more pleased when Paolo asked me to be his best man.

'Though there's a big age gap, she fancied she was in love
with me and, in spite of getting no encouragement, I think
she's been cherishing hopes that one wedding might lead to
another.'

'Poor thing,' Gail murmured, feeling sorry for the other girl.

'Don't worry, it won't last long,' he said confidently. 'In a
few months' time she'll have transferred her affections to, hopefully, a more grateful recipient.'

He leaned across and, taking her hands, pulled her out of her
chair and on to his lap, cradling her to him.

His lips against her temple, he murmured, 'You see, unlike
you, my constant nymph, she's always been a butterfly child.

'You once said you loved me. It's my hope and belief that
you love me still, and I want to hear you say it…'

He hadn't said he loved her and, while she would have given
everything she owned to hear him say those three words, what
he had said would have to do.

Turning her head to look into his face, she told him, 'I loved
you then and I love you now. I've never stopped loving you.'

'That's good, because if you didn't love me I don't know
what I'd do.

'For seven long years I've tried to find you and for all that
time you've haunted me. I couldn't get you out of my mind or
my heart.

'Then, when I finally found you again and I thought you
loved Manton, I nearly went mad with jealousy.'

His face pressed against her throat, he whispered, 'You'

never know how much I've longed to hold you in my arms. To kiss your lips and wipe out the past. To tell you how very much I love you, and to ask you to be my wife.'

When, too full to speak, she sat in a blissful silence, he said anxiously, 'You will, won't you?'

Making up her mind to tease him a little, she queried, 'Will what?'

'Be my wife?'

'I'll have to think about it.'

'*Think* about it?' he echoed in mock outrage.

'I'll need to know just what kind of husband you'll make before I say yes.'

'What if I promise to be sober and upright…?'

'Well, that's a start.'

'Generous, caring and faithful?'

'Even more important…' Then, softly, she asked, '*Will* you be faithful?'

'Do you doubt it?'

'No.'

'Good.' He kissed her. 'Now, where was I? Oh, yes, I promise to always stay by your side, to love and cherish you and keep you happy in every way…?'

'Can you promise things like that?'

'Why not? Loving and cherishing go hand in hand, and I could no more stop loving you than I could stop breathing. And, as for the rest, I know of at least one way I can keep you happy…'

'Oh, what's that?'

'In bed.'

'I see,' she said demurely.

'So what do you think?'

'I'm starting to think that marrying you might not be a bad idea. Though, before I finally say yes, you might need to refresh my memory on that last score.'

Standing up with her cradled in his arms, he kissed her and said, 'My love, I would say "the pleasure's all mine" except that I prefer that kind of pleasure to be shared.'

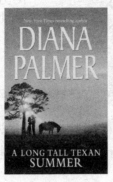
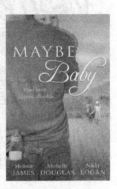

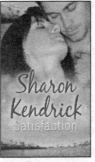
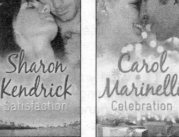